ALL THE WORLD DROWNING

All the World Drowning

Benjamin Preston

Book design by Elissa Weber Preston. Cover design by Lisa Grillos. Cover image: *Wisconsin No.48*, published 1857 by J. H. Colton & Co., courtesy of David Rumsey Map Collection. www.davidrumsey.com

Publisher's Cataloging-in-Publication Data:
    Preston, Benjamin
    All the World Drowning / Benjamin Preston.—1st ed.
    p. cm.
    1. Wisconsin—Fiction.   2. Young Men—Fiction.   3. Cults—Fiction.   4. Schizophrenia—Fiction.   I. Title

PCN#2015946335
PS3551.P747 2016
ISBN 978-0-9964652-0-5
ISBN 978-0-9964652-1-2 (e-book)

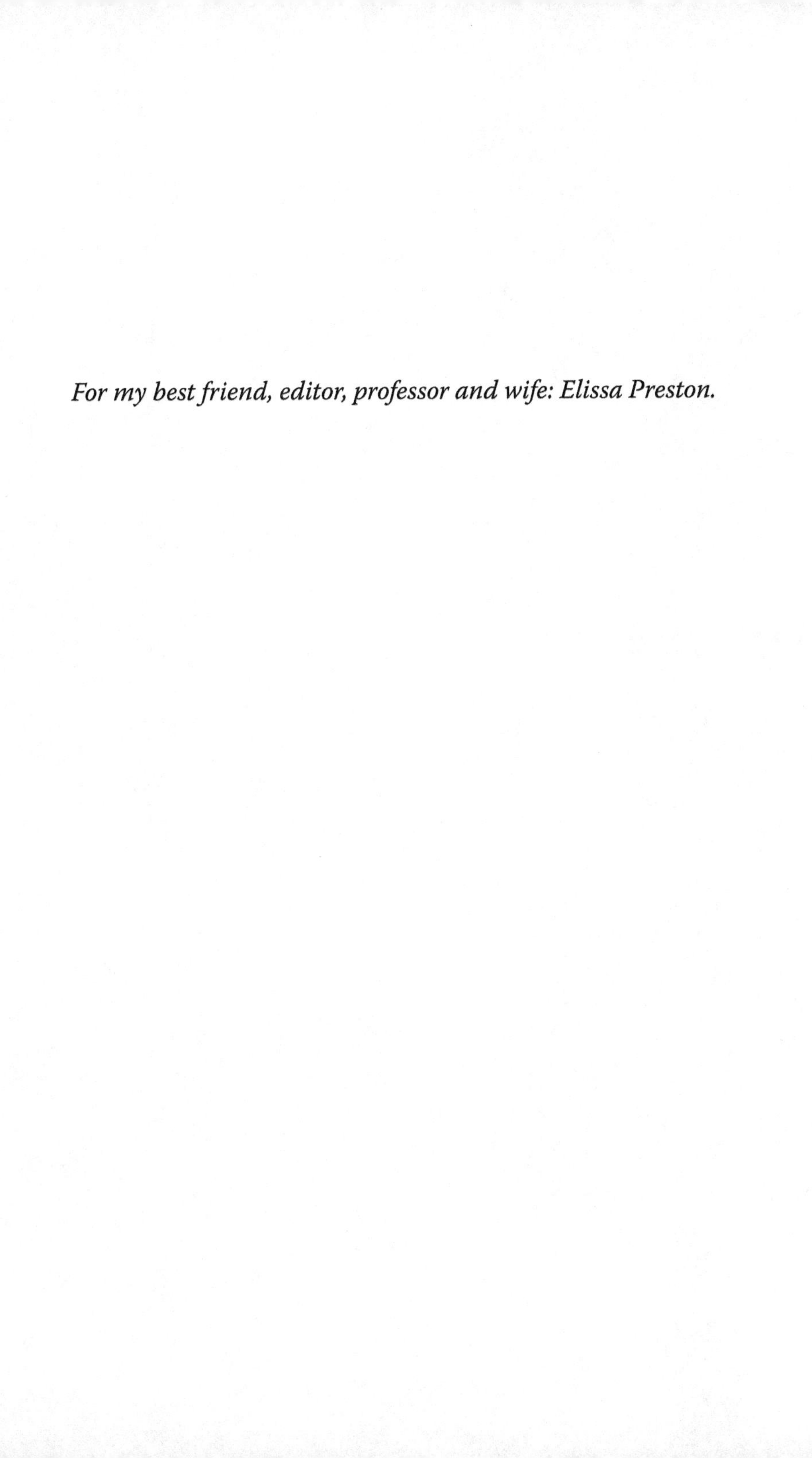

For my best friend, editor, professor and wife: Elissa Preston.

ALL THE WORLD DROWNING

Prologue

We have razed the good trees. We have razed the coulees. We have razed those sandstone bluffs of the driftless zone, that enigmatic pocket of land that the receding glaciers never scoured. We, in place of the sheets of ice, have razed them, and in our wake have sprung the fields and the wealth of generations. We have done this, we strange prophets of family Godwin, drifting in the sediment land. We were men with overcoats and handlebar mustaches, eyes like hollows of madness, shouting out rampant visions to the miners and the farmers, Norsemen, Amish, and German, who settled these valleys of western Wisconsin like windblown snow.

Nothing is known of Regnus Kazimir Godwin's origins. He arrived, discalced, in a settlement of pioneers outside of Venus, Illinois territory, a town recently ravaged by savages. The wreckage of homes was strewn like carcasses of bison upon the flatlands that the settlers had righteously claimed from the native inhabitants a generation before. Amidst the smoldering carnage, a lone white church remained, reaching out of the earth like a gloved hand.

The preacher dead, it was left to Regnus to gather the remaining townspeople. Shaking with fear, they followed him as he bent in prayer for guidance. The evening light of spring illuminated the clerestory. As he called upon the Lord amidst the dire remnant of the congregation, a small boy called out, "An angel!"

Regnus Godwin looked up. "Behold! The face of the angel became the warm peace of the light of God. The light itself became a javelin, and pierced me through the heart...." So he wrote.

His body lurched. It seemed to him the church itself grew virescent with primal forest, and through the forest he saw a pool of silver light which bent like clay to an anguilliform river; and at its center, an island the shape of a tear. "Thus it was revealed to me, the true location of the garden of Eden."

On the fervor of Regnus's vision, the entire community soon set out to return to the womb of the world. They traveled the wagon routes north to Madison and the labyrinth of logging roads and miner's routes west, until Regnus looked down one day upon a coulee and saw the Kickapoo River in an ignifluous stream of sunset. He went down to the winding, twisting river, cast off his clothing, and entered like a babe into its current. Others followed and were taken aback to see his body begin to glow with an ethereal light. As it died he came ashore, holding a tablet of silver scrolls.

He declared the place to be the terrain of his vision and led the people of his congregation in the creation of this new Eden. Cabins were built, pesky old-growth forests cleared, fields plowed and planted by men and women content to sweat in the humid summer air.

Regnus married a girl of seventeen named Clara Shoemaker. Sundays he preached, and other days he worked tirelessly side by side with Clara and the townsfolk. Under the tending of Regnus, the men and women quickened from the ashes of their past. Clara gave birth to two sons. For three years harvests poured in of wheat and corn, and dairy cows' bounty. New Eden flourished—until the last maple leaves were swept too early to effulgent graves and the fall winds howled and the snows of the fourth winter began in October.

A garden of Eden indeed, at negative thirty degrees and eighteen feet of snow! Whatever winters had they known previously, they were not prepared for the severity of 1833. What fateful apple from what tree had they plucked to call down such wrath? Twenty of the sixty-three in New Eden died by January.

In the throes of the freeze, the starvation, and the death, whatever had tethered Regnus to this world seems to have come unraveled. His visions returned, but now darker; he raved of floods and death. He began to wander.

He appeared, half-starved, in neighbors' fields. Once he was found with his head resting on the frozen cumulus of a dead cow, blue from head to foot. Brought in and set by a fire, he shot upright, reanimated, springing back out the door and into the woods. He was said to have materialized in various communities across the coulees, stumbling out of the cold in frothing madness. In the spring, he burst into a church in Viroqua, where the men of the village subdued him. They tied him in the pastor's quarters to quieten and continued their service. When they returned, all that remained was a frayed rope and a single boot.

Regnus was finally found among the snow and the woods a few miles from the family's land, the spring buds of a large maple coming to life above him on half-frozen branches. Several men from New Eden made their way back into the woods to recover dear Regnus's body: frozen, barefoot, toenails blue and splintered, his torso already eaten half-away beneath a tattered shirt. They wrapped him in canvas and dragged him back through the still-thick snow. After the thaw, they buried him on the hill behind the house.

Clara raised Amos and Jeremiah here rather than move into town. They lived, and we live, in Regnus' snowy wake. We live with the hauntings and the visions—his ghosts.

—from Coulee: a History of the Family Godwin
by Kazimir Jonah Godwin

Chapter One

I WAKE UP AND FROST IS AT THE EDGE OF MY WINDOW, a pale light. There is snow falling. I wake up and sunlight streams onto my bed sheets. I am warm in my Underoos. I wake up and I am four, I am five, I am six. I am a small boy playing in the snow along the banks of the Kickapoo. I am chasing Grandma's chickens around the yard. I am running with Eliza in the labyrinth of cornfields.

These are memories like relics hidden in the land, fragments buried far below the furrows and then finally reborn, arrowheads turned up by a plough or bones churned from an effigy mound. Pieces of a lost time revealed to the sun again, entered into the cycles of knowledge and rebirth. The earliest fragments come back to me from the years before the visions and the madness, the drugs, the prophecies; before Silas had come home; before Leanna had left; before my family began to fall apart.

The summer of my sixth year began in a slow heat, and I was left to play with Eliza in the fields surrounding my family's land. We crawled among the gravestones, a past I could palpate. The cold limestone tombstones were wet with the melted snow, the names, once marked in lapidary precision, now faded. Lichen and moss grew over the dates of their deaths or disappearances, the births of their children. The ever-present scent of decaying leaf lay under the spring thaw.

I whispered the stories of my ancestors to myself. I walked the newly-churned earth in search of arrowheads.

My father was not home that June. In the evenings, Grandma, Leanna, and I took dinner on Grandma's porch. Sometimes Leanna was too sad to come out of the the trailer, so it would just be Grandma and me.

Afterward, we would sit on the porch swing. Fireflies danced in the fields, first in ones and twos, and then in armadas of light.

"Tell me a story," I'd say. Gray hairs mixed with brown were damp against Grandma's forehead.

You come from a long line of vagabonds, murderers, prophets and madmen, she would begin, in her voice that sounded of sad crickets and smelled of pie and Jack Daniels. She drew her stories from diaries kept in the old steamer trunk in the attic—lives embalmed in overstuffed journals amidst Union hats, faded photographs, and moth-eaten dresses. Inscribed in the faded D'nealian of my ancestors were the stories of my forebear Regnus Kazimir Godwin, of his sons Amos and Jeremiah, of Amos's sons on down to my father: mythic figures to the young boy I was. The tales were heroic epics when told by my father, cautionary tales when told by my grandmother. These were the evenings of my summers in those years when all was bathed in light.

In early July, the air grew heavy with moisture and burst on us nearly every afternoon with a thunderstorm. Tornados touched down a few hours east of us. The weather cooled then for a day or two, as if the tornadoes had sucked up all the water and heat in the air and spit it into the heavens. But with each sunrise the heat increased and soon I was sweating in my bed again before the day had even begun, waiting for the sun to come over the horizon so that I could wake Leanna.

Morning light filtered through pale yellow sheets hung with clothespins over the windows. They billowed out as the fan passed, casting quick shadows over her room. Outside, wind chimes rang.

I climbed into bed next to her, hoping she would notice. Her lips expelled tiny puffs of air, and her dark curls lifted in limp salute with each pass of the fan. A wiry arm ran over her chest. Her eyes opened as I touched her shoulder. "You can't sleep again?" she asked.

I nodded. "When are you gonna get up?"

She gave a clipped laugh and stretched. "What for? We got nothing to do."

"We could help Grandma in the garden."

"Oh boy, what fun." She stood up, the back of her hair wet with sweat. "Seven-thirty and we're already swimming in the air." She pulled back the yellow sheet and bent to look out the window, then fell backward onto the bed and closed her eyes again. "What am I doing here?" she whispered to herself.

"I had a prophecy dream like the kind Dad was telling me about," I told her.

She rolled her eyes. "Well, if that God guy comes again with more prophecies, ask him what the hell he thinks he's doing to me. I'd like to know."

"Okay."

She turned away from me, pulling the bed sheet over her head. "I'm gonna sleep a little longer. Go to Grandma's and get some milk if you want breakfast. We won't be getting any more until your damn dad gets back with some money. You can tell me all about your dream later. Okay?"

I went down to the pond where Grandma's yard touched County Road NN. Behind me the yellow sheets swayed in the window of the double-wide. The trailer slouched in front of the dilapidated red barn surrounded by high grass, but Grandma's old farmhouse, with its screened-in porch, sat in a penumbra of groomed lawn that stretched behind the barn to the vegetable garden in the back and down to the willow and the pond in front. Eliza jumped down from a willow limb and joined me in shredding cattails into airborne puffs.

A bow and arrow materialized in her hands. "Enough cattailin'. Let's go up to the ridge and shoot us some buffalo."

We crossed the Kickapoo at the bridge just down from our house and climbed up the hill till we came to a clearing at the top where lacy maple seedlings sprouted. Eliza and I stood on a large sandstone boulder and looked down at the river. The hill dropped two hundred feet through elm, ash, white pine, black and red oak. As far east as the eye could gather, the Kickapoo caught the morning light and glistened as it turned through the bluffs toward the Wisconsin river. Square patches of farmland spread like watercolors from the river's edge, green, yellow, and brown. Hills rose up between plots of farmland and obscured the river, but it always reappeared, all the way to the horizon. If you turned and looked west, upstream, you could make out the first tiny houses of the town of New Eden and the steeple of the church.

The sun glinted off the top of a vehicle crossing the bridge. I put my hand to my eyes as Eliza crept on her belly among the grassy seedlings toward another buffalo. A warm breeze blew. The vehicle came into focus: a blue and white Dodge van.

I hopped down from the rock. "It's the Whale! Let's go, Eliza, Dad's back!" I shouted.

I was out at the bridge when he rolled into the driveway. I ran. The Whale spewed black exhaust from its misplaced blowhole, and out from it my father resurfaced—long wild hair, unkempt beard, huge limping frame.

In one motion he turned and saw me, picked me up and spun me around. "There's my boy!" His beard was rough on my cheek.

Leanna was at the doorway in a peasant dress, her arms folded. He picked her up too, swung her around. She laughed despite herself. He carried us in a jog toward the pond.

"Put me down!" Leanna shouted.

"It's a good day for a swim!" my father said, picking up speed.

She beat her little fists on his shoulder. "Don't you do it!"

He dove with us into the pond. We staggered to our feet, laughing. Leanna jumped on Dad's back and pulled him back underwater. We emerged soaked to the bone and waded to shore through the muck. Grandma stood under the willow, a straw sun hat shading her face.

"Hey-hey, Mom! Come on in—the water's fine!" Dad shouted and staggered over to her with arms open for a hug. Strands of algae clung to his hirsute frame.

"Oh no you don't, not like that!" She started to turn. "Damn but you're a mess. Don't touch me!" He lifted her up in a bear hug. "Put me down, Aeneas! Aeneas! Put me down!" she shouted through laughter.

"Glad to see ya, Mom!" he called out and capsized her. She spit a mouthful of water on him as she tried to stand and fell backward. He grabbed her arm and helped her to the shore. Leanna and I lay in the shade of the willow, and they joined us.

"Where'd you go this time, Dad?"

"You know, kiddo, I was all over—Texas, New Mexico." He unbuttoned his flannel and tossed it onto the grass. The bone handle of his survival knife stuck out at his hip. "Doing the work of the Creator."

"Hope the Creator paid you this time," Leanna said.

He smiled. "Yeah, I got some money."

"Good," Grandma said. "You owe for groceries."

He and Leanna went to town to buy steaks and whiskey. Grandma glowed as we gathered peas for the evening's feast. Dad was home, and the whole property felt a sudden surge of energy. Robins sang their songs, the air crackled with impending storms, and the crickets raised their volume a notch. Even as a boy, Grandma told me, he animated every room he entered: good china always fell from the shelves, animals were somehow provoked at his mere entrance into a domicile, and other boys would immediately conspire to beat him up.

"When we moved back here after the Korean War, the other kids wouldn't leave him alone. His name caused him a lot of grief."

"Who is he named after?" I crawled among the pea vines to find the pods she couldn't reach. The humid air lay over my face like a sweaty pillow. Tornado air.

"Your grandpa loved ancient history, epic poems. *Aeneas* was the name of a warrior and wanderer."

I thought about my name. "I'm named after my great-great-great-great-great Grandpa."

She nodded. "You sure you got the number of 'greats' right?"

"I'm gonna be just like him."

She shook her head. "I hope for your sake you're not."

That evening Uncle Roald and Cousin Jethro came for dinner. We took a picture on Grandma's porch: Leanna and I kneel in front of what appears to be a clan of giants from a Brother's Grimm illustration. Grandma, six feet tall in her jeans and flower print tank top, holds her whiskey-Coke. My father, at six foot seven, grins out from a beard half as long as me. Great Uncle Roald was six foot ten, fingers as thick as carrots, eyes all the better to see you with. He had a scar on his left cheek where a bullet had entered, and a scar on his right cheek where it had decided it wasn't his time to die. He would massage his index finger in the exit wound while he mulled over bridge hands. The crew cut he also got in Korea and had kept since. Not a bristle ever moved or even turned gray; only the top wore thin from overuse.

To his right is Dad's cousin Jethro. At birth, Jethro was over fifteen pounds; Aunt Rosa died of hemorrhage that afternoon. Roald never took another wife and raised Jethro himself. You could fit a dozen of me into Cousin Jethro's blue-jean overalls, and it seemed he never wore anything else. By the time of the picture, at seven feet tall, he was already well over three hundred pounds. Later on, when everything was coming to a head, he must have been four hundred or more.

At dinner Jethro sucked down six ears of corn from the bowl, kernel casualties strewn about the table like the massacre at Bad Ax and dangling from his beard like yellow flies. My seat was next to him, and I lost my appetite somewhere in the folds of his greasy overalls, next to a glob of gravy. For my entertainment he'd pluck a few kernels from his beard and drop them into his mouth. "I love leftovers," he'd say and bust out laughing, mouth agape.

"I swear, you're your own Johnny Carson," my dad said. "Dammit Jethro, can't we have just one meal here without watching the corn drip off your teeth?" Dad dropped his fork to his plate. Jethro laughed even harder.

"Enough, boys," Grandma said. "Aeneas, don't swear at the dinner table."

Dad shook his head and picked his fork back up. "So Roald, how's the farming business?"

Roald and his crew cut sized up my dad. "Makes a living. Better than running around like some gypsy in a van."

"Ooh. Harsh, don't you think? I didn't say nothing about farmers," my father said between bites of steak. "It's good work, taking your living from the land. All the better when this whole da—darn country of greedy hypocrites comes crashing down."

Uncle Roald grunted and took a long drink of milk. Uncle Roald didn't like the family's hippy streak, namely my father, and looked down on him for persisting to live. Roald had fought and lost friends in Korea so we could be free and by God the hippies ought to get that through their long hair into their thick skulls. He had a rifle, a tractor, and a farm up in Sparta, and that was about all a man needed. Once, I surprised him while he was digging in the yard and he swung around ready to punch me in the face. "Dammit, Kazimir, don't spring up on me like that—you're likely to get killed!" he said with his usual joviality and went back to his shoveling.

After dinner, Leanna, Jethro, Dad and I went down to the trailer. "We'll leave the grumpy old bastard to Grandma," my dad said.

Leanna mixed a drink. I sat on my father's lap, toying with the rummy runs splayed on the Formica of our kitchen table. Cans of Pabst accumulated on the floor between my father and Jethro as they recited the lore of their school days together, louder with every beer. "Old *Anus* Godwin!" Cousin Jethro barked.

"Sons of bitches," my dad muttered over his can. "Aeneas. Damn. I might as well have been named Sue." He laughed.

Boys from New Eden were not partial to references to antiquity, even the epics. Had Grandpa not considered the tessellations of the name, obvious even to the mind of a child?

To add injury to insult, my father had a damaged leg from a run-in with a stray dog when he was a toddler and thereafter limped in perpetual three-four time. By the time his parents had moved him back to the family land, he was already bigger than all the other third graders in his class. So it was up to the fifth and sixth grade rogues to put this limping Godwin jerk in his place.

"Joe Brody, Kaz." He picked a card up, laid down a set of jacks, and discarded the four of clubs. "Know any kids named Brody, Kaz?"

"I don't know any kids but Eliza."

"Well, Joe Brody was two years older and used to beat the snot out of me and Silas and just about every other kid younger than him. The teachers knew too, Kaz, and did nothing." He picked up a card from the deck, stared at its back, turned it over and nodded.

"What's a teacher?"

Jethro jumped in. "So we all show up for the first day of school— Silas in second, your dad and me in fourth. Your old man had to stay in the first ten minutes of recess for throwing food at lunch, so Silas and me went out by the swings. We were minding our own when out comes Joe Brody. 'Godwin, you're in my swing,' he calls out to Silas. Silas keeps swinging and humming like he didn't hear him. Back and forth, back and forth. Brody didn't like his attitude, so when Silas gets all the way back on his swing, Brody grabs him by his hair and yanks him clean off."

"Silas swears he never heard him," my dad added.

"Yeah anyways, Brody gets on the swing, and when he pushes off, Silas just stands directly in front of him, blocking his path. Brody sends a flying foot into Silas's chest, knocking him out of the swing area, over the cement curb and onto the grass. As Brody swings back, Silas stumbles up and stands again. Brody swings forward and hits him with both feet. Knocks him down again. Silas stands up again, this time staggering around, Brody swings a few times, laughing at him.

"I could see your dad coming down the steps. Brody starts on his backswing and Silas sways into his way again, when I see Aeneas rearing back behind him, and then—"

"Right in the back of the neck, Kaz!" said my dad. "Sprained my wrist with that punch. Hurt for a month. Brody slumped right over, and when he swung forward he flopped onto the ground like a sack of potatoes." He fell silent. His arm muscles were tensed up.

"Mrs. Lovejoy comes running over, screaming and screaming," Jethro continued, taking a sip of his beer. "Your dad gets suspended for three days."

"She stood right there the whole time, as Brody beat up Silas. The moment I do something about it, she sees everything." He leaned back.

"The way he slumped out of the swing and was just laying there, I thought you killed him," Jethro said. "Silas had a branch in his hand and started poking Joe with it like a dead bird. He never wanted to hurt anything. Wouldn't even shoot birds with our b.b. guns. I don't think he liked what your dad did to Brody."

"You don't mess around in a fight, Kaz. The one willing to go to extremes is the one who walks away. Brody was willing to beat on someone, but I was ready to kill."

"What happened to Brody?" I asked.

"He didn't bother us anymore," my father said. "You know, Kaz, a little violence created a lot of peace for us."

"Aeneas was always the brawler, Kaz," said Jethro, "but the ladies, the ladies loved Silas." He winked at me. "He was never interested. My guess is he was probably queer."

"Silas ain't queer, he just wasn't any lover. I'm the lover *and* the fighter in this family," my dad said. "Ain't that right, baby?" he called to Leanna.

"Whatever you say, Aeneas. Whatever you say."

"Tell me about Uncle Silas," I asked my Grandma the next day. Dad and Leanna had kicked me out of the trailer for a few hours, and I was helping Grandma hang laundry.

The summer wind rippled undershirts on the line. "Well, what do you want to know?"

I shrugged.

"I haven't seen him since before you guys moved in to the trailer. He had always been restless and one day he just took off. That would have been, what? Four years ago. How old are you now?"

"I don't know."

"You were maybe two. I don't know either because you weren't living here, just going around with your dad and Leanna and the band. " She sighed. "Four years is a long time not to see your son."

"Is he like dad?"

"No, he's just—really gentle." She kept thinking. "Never did well in school. Great with his hands. Loves nature. Kind of like you."

"I want to be like dad."

She sighed again and hung up a pair of blue jeans. "Silas was a miracle at catching fireflies. You ever done that?"

"I keep trying but I can't."

"I saw him do it once when he was fixing a car at the station. It was early evening, about this time of year. He took a cigarette break and was leaning against the wall. I was inside chatting with the cashier. The sun set and the fireflies were floating over by the ditch. He squats down and flicks his lighter on and off, on and off, and there comes a firefly straight at him. He put out his index finger, and I'll be damned if it didn't perch right there. He brought it over for me to take a look. It had an unusual color to its light, more silver or purplish than the usual green. Anyway, it lifted off and I thought it would be gone, but no, it flew right to his shoulder.

"I was gonna give him a ride back here. He was still living upstairs. Not that he ever stayed there—he mostly slept under the willow with his mutt Skeeter. But he decided to walk. He set out whistling a sweet tune to calm the firefly. He used to see how quiet he could keep his heart or how evenly he could walk. Those little games with himself were the only competition he ever took part in. When he got back, the firefly was still blinking away on his shoulder. We ate dinner on the porch and it was still there. I don't know what ever happened to it. A week later Silas and Skeeter, they took off. I haven't seen him since."

"You miss him?" I asked.

"Oh yes, I miss him all the time. So does your father, I bet. They were best of friends."

"That's like what I keep seeing in my dream—a man in a field of fireflies," I told her. "I bet it's a prophecy and he's coming back."

She shook her head. "Well, I don't know about that stuff." She finished putting the laundry on the line and picked up the basket. "I wish sometimes you all would come and stay in the house. It gets lonely at night." We went up onto the porch where the ice cubes in her whiskey-Coke had disintegrated. She took a sip anyway. Her hand shook a little, and the caramel-colored liquid dripped down her blouse.

My father's beaded necklace danced in the hairs of his chest as he shouted over the engine's hum. "Regnus Kazimir Godwin, founder of the family. That's where I got your name, Kaz," he told me. I remember the deep growl of his voice. I remember sitting in the passenger seat of the Whale on a clear night north of Eau Claire. Trees, houses, and fields slipped past. "It's because we have his blood, because we are in the line of a prophet, that Ephraim found me. We can be free of the illusions mankind is slave to. When the Revolution comes, it is men like us, men of true sight, who will remake the earth."

I did things with my eyes to make the landscape around me slow. I stared at telephone poles, elder trees. I'd relax my eyes and watch it flow by in a blur. After a while, I looked up into night sky. "Dad, what's the story of the stars?"

He stuck his head out the window. His long hair and beard flailed in the wind. "They're gifts from the Creator, Kaz, our precious gifts. That one up there is called Orion. He's a hunter."

"Why's he up in the sky?"

"The gods put him up there because they were pleased."

"Grandma said there's just one God."

"There is—not in the way Grandma says, but, yes, just one God. One creative source. But a long time ago people thought there were lots of gods. There was a god who lived in the sea, one of the wind who had big cheeks, and one called Zeus who was their king. He wore a toga and threw thunderbolts at people when they were bad." He laughed, making his beads rattle. His bare belly heaved over his belt buckle.

"Does the real God wear a toga?"

"Well, no. God doesn't really have a body. The Creator is everywhere. He's kind of like a ball of light, or like nothingness. You could say he looks like nothing."

In the picture book of Bible stories Grandma had given me I'd seen pictures of God, and from these I knew certain things about him. I knew, for instance, that he had a beard.

"How can something look like nothing?"

He laughed. "You will know, someday, Kaz. You will see and know the will of the Creator, the way Regnus did, the way Ephraim has taught me. Leanna said you had a prophetic dream. Maybe you have the power too."

I told him about my dream. I told him I thought it was Uncle Silas on account of the fireflies.

"You have the sight, I think."

"What does that mean?"

"You can see into the spiritual world. You can see a spiritual future."

"Like ghosts and stuff?"

"Kind of. Do you see ghosts?"

I shook my head.

"The sight is a gift that runs in this family. You—you may be the one we're waiting for."

We pulled over and camped, later, in plaid flannel bags on the unfolded rear seat. My father leaned over and pulled the sleeping bag up to my shoulders. The smell of his sweat in the dark, the crickets courting through the summer air.

"When are you going away again?" I asked.

"Pretty soon. I have some important work to do. We're doing it right now, too, but mostly my jobs are not in Wisconsin."

"How are we doing it right now?"

"Well, we're picking up some furniture in Chetek for me to re-upholster. That's part of the work I do for Ephraim."

"Leanna wants us to go too, when you leave."

"I know. I think it would be better for you to be here for now. It's important for you to know where you come from."

"Tell me a story," I said.

"There once was a man. He lived and he died."

"No dad, a real story! About my ancestors."

He laughed. His beard drifted over my face like a cloud.

Amos and Jeremiah Godwin were the sons of Clara and Regnus. Amos was a difficult child, but he redeemed himself and decided to become a preacher at the same time Jeremiah began to take his dive. Jeremiah drank and gambled in binges that lasted weeks. Leaving the farm, he made his way up to the lumber camps of the north around Trempealeau. When they cut, they would fill the Mississippi a mile across with logs, and he and the others would stand on them all the way down to LaCrosse—even sleeping—where they'd unload at the mill and hustle up to the bars that overlooked the river. In July of 1864, Clara received news of Jeremiah in jail. He had beaten his foreman to near death in a drunken brawl. Clara pleaded with him in jail but, she wrote, "He is half-crazed, shouting about the end of days. One can scarce tell if it were the drink, or that a terrible spirit has inhabited him. Speaking to the air, he argues with something that none but he can perceive."

When he was released, she took him back to the farm, where for a time he seemed to recover. But within a few months he began to complain of ghosts whispering to him. He would blurt out random accusations to members of the family over the dinner table. Ashamed, and claiming he had no control over his outbursts, he took to eating alone. Soon he disappeared, but mysteriously reappeared wading out of the Kickapoo and into the front yard. Then one day Amos found him leaning against the side of the barn covered in blood. He had cut out his own tongue to stop the voices.

As soon as it healed he ran away again. He rambled in and out of towns, disheveled and dirty. Clara writes that Amos left to hunt him down, in hopes of bringing him back to the farm and performing some sort of exorcism. But Jeremiah was impossible to track. He seemed to be able to cover unbelievable spans of distance. He would be seen in

Spring Green one day, and a day later on the outskirts of Prairie du Chien, a hundred or more miles away. Amos had no way of finding him.

Things came to their crux in Farewell, Vernon County, March of 1865, when he stabbed a man to death. He wrote in his statement that God had told him to "wash his blood in the wings of angels." The killing made headlines all across the four states.

"He made no defense," claimed my father. "He believed the apocalypse would come before he would be subject to the judgments of man. It did."

"How?"

He smiled. "Ask Grandma. She'll tell you." He kissed me on the forehead and rolled over onto his back.

"How come we don't live in the house with Grandma?" I asked to keep him from falling asleep.

He closed his eyes. "Ghosts, Kaz, there's ghosts there."

Grandma shucked peas. I'd helped her harvest them in paper bags, and now I let the dirt flow down the drain as I sprayed them in the sink. "What happened to Jeremiah Godwin?" I asked.

On June 29, 1865, while he was still waiting for his trial, the deadliest tornado in state history hit the town. Every house destroyed, all but the courthouse relieved of its roof. Cows in trees, Mrs. Weeden's silk dress found in Juneau County, eighty miles away. Amos rushed to the aid of the town and with his congregation picked through the rubble of the damaged jail. Not a sign or a sliver of Jeremiah. It was as if he had been picked like a plum by the hand of God and swallowed whole. From then on rumors spread of his haunting the land. Jeremiah Godwin became the boogey man of southwest Wisconsin.

"What do you think of Jeremiah's story?" Grandma asked.

"God told him to do all that stuff, so it's okay."

"That's what I was worried about," she said. "How did he know it was God?"

Dad banged through the screen door and grabbed a handful of

peas from the colander.

"Aeneas! Leave some for dinner."

He grinned at her and popped the handful into his mouth. "You heard the end? So what's the moral of the story?" he asked.

"Don't go crazy," I said.

"No. Obedience. Jeremiah was taken up by God because he did what God told him to do—or what he thought God had told him to do."

"How can you know it's God?"

"You can't. You do it anyway. Just do it and God will sort it out." The screen door banged again as he bounded away.

Grandma had said nothing, but had stopped shelling peas and was now staring after him with an expression I'd never seen on her.

I slipped up beside her and put my head on her belly. "Grandma, can you really see ghosts in your house?"

She wrapped her large arm around me. "Did your father tell you that?" She stroked my hair. "I can't see them, but I can hear them."

"What do they sound like?"

"Eustace, who lost his left leg in the Indian wars—he stamps his peg leg on the wooden hall. Amos, he was a preacher, whistles low and sweet too, old hymns. Sometimes it's hard to tell if it's the wind howling or Amos whistling."

"Did you ever see Jeremiah?"

Suddenly she laughed. "Kaz, you know what ghosts are made of?"

"What?"

"Buuulllshit." She chuckled. "Just like your father. Sorry—he's my son, but he's full of it."

But in the creak of the halls of the old farmhouse I searched for those phantoms anyway. I spent days with Eliza in search of them. We'd wait in the dark corner on the stairs hoping for a shadowy glimpse, and once just about gave Uncle Roald a coronary when he came upon us unsuspecting. We dug through the old steamer, found the union hat of Ennis Godwin. There was a faded picture of my grandfather and beneath it a Navy sweater. I pulled it out and held it to a shaft of air made substantive by light and dust. "Put it on, I want to see what you look like in it," said Eliza. I draped it over my shoulders, and the heavy wool trapped the heat of the attic to my skin. My fingers dangled inside the sleeves.

"He was a cook in the navy during the Korean war." Grandma was leaning in the attic doorway. "After the war we got married and moved back here. Roald ran the farm and Herbert—Grandpa—joined the merchant marines as a cook. When your father was six, Herbert left for a stint on the Great Lakes. One evening he was chopping carrots and serving stew somewhere on Lake Superior. Come morning, he did not report for duty. No one ever saw him or any sign of him."

When the ship docked in Grand Marais, the captain sent word of his disappearance. An anonymous pair of hands gathered his things together. The steamer trunk arrived in New Eden a month later.

"I didn't want to believe it. I refused to even look through his old steamer at first. I still thought he'd come home. He was just missing and would come back, or he was off rambling like all the other Godwin men he had told me about. He might not have drowned, even if he went overboard … miracles happen to Godwins. But finally I knew he wasn't coming back." In the trunk had been old papers, journals, news clippings, two soiled uniforms, a small hand-carved chess set, toothbrush, shaving strop and razor, cream. His red and brown hairs brindle the shaving case to this day.

"He was a great father, a perfect husband," she told me. She sniffled. "I thought about moving us back to my family in Chicago. The boys liked the countryside though, and I knew how important it was to your grandpa that his sons would know their land. Godwins had lived here for a hundred and thirty years by that time. So I just stayed on and raised your dad and Silas here. I did it in memory of Herbert, I guess, but now it's home to me."

She was quiet a moment. The old house creaked. "Your grandpa was a gentle and steady man. How I ever got your father and Silas out of that, I'll never know."

Neither of us moved for a while. The wind whistled in the elms, the big willow. What is the whistle of wind and what the whistle of ghosts? How does a boy discern the steps of a specter from the creak of a house? I took the jacket off and handed it to her. I was wet with sweat. She smiled and folded it carefully, then set it back in the trunk. She bent over; the shaft of light caught her glasses. Discs of gold.

My father and Leanna argued that night. Leanna's voice woke me when the moon was halfway across the sky. "Enough of this shit, Aeneas!" she yelled. The hall lights turned on. "I want out of here."

"You got to stay a little longer, Leanna. I'll get things set up. We'll be in Arizona by winter." Their shadows slipped by the crack in my doorway. They went down the hall, out the door and into the yard. I heard them speak in angry whispers. I closed my window quietly and felt the air press in around me. I imagined myself trapped in a web; the air became strands caught in my lungs and I could barely breathe. I wanted to beg Dad and Leanna to come back in and help me, but I was too afraid.

Dad woke me the next morning. "I gotta go tomorrow, kiddo. Ephraim needs me out west."

"When will you come back?"

"Soon, I think, maybe a month."

Cousin Jethro came for a last dinner. We ate a heap of barbecued burgers on Grandma's porch. My dad strummed his guitar intermittently.

"You should have heard his band, Kaz" Jethro told me. "Your dad and the boys, they really could play. Levi, this Amish kid we knew in high school, was the singer. They'd tear it up on stage, get wasted, and beat the trash out of someone nearly every night. Fantastic entertainment all around."

"Grandma says the Amish are passi—paffis—"

"Pacifists? Well, Levi obviously wasn't, was he?" Jethro mowed down his burger.

Dad chuckled. "The name of the band was the Militant Amish,

Kaz. I think you get the picture."

They had a hit song, "Hippies Arm Yourselves," that went all the way up to forty-four on the country charts back in seventy-one. I had seen the map of the U.S. on the wall in my father's bedroom. A pin stuck in every town they'd played in. Geographic acupuncture. The pin heads made a rainbow in concentric spirals broadcast like radio signals across the heart of America.

"The Militant Amish had broad appeal, Kaz," my father said, chukling. "The rednecks thought we were anti-hippy and the hippies thought we were anti-redneck. One time I got slapped by a peacenik girl after she heard the song. I think she was the only one I ever met who knew what it meant."

"What did you do when she slapped you?" I asked.

"I had a kid with her." He grinned at me. "That's you, kiddo."

"What was my mom's name?"

My father shrugged. "She called herself Rainbow. After you were born she took off with some other hippies. Guess she wasn't ready for a kid. I took you with us on the road and would take care of you. First two years of your life you spent in bars and concert halls."

Leanna leaned forward from the porch swing. "So that's how I met your dad," she told me. "He's lying on the grass with you asleep on his chest in a park in Prescott, Arizona, outside the college. I had seen his band the night before and so I went over to talk to him."

"I was asleep at the time, too," Dad added. "I was busting my butt raising you and still traveling with the band. We played all night and often we just slept in the Whale or out in some park. She comes up to me all pretty and such and wakes me up."

"I had got a job as a waitress at a truck stop, but I really didn't want it. I wanted to travel, you know? It was the seventies. So I asked your dad if I could hitch along with the band, not realizing what I was getting into."

"And I said sure. I was drinking and staying out and Leanna would help watch you. It was a fun time, but not a good one, you know? I already knew Ephraim, I'd even had my vision, but I hadn't let it change me. But its force was at work within me. And one morning I woke up and I knew things had come to a head. I needed to clean up. I wanted to live a spiritual life—I wanted to pursue my music as a conduit into the spiritual world. I decided to give up the band and I went to see Ephraim again. He took me up to a sacred lake high in the Rockies and healed me. It was a magical place, Kaz. A portal between the world of the living and the world of the dead."

"So anyway…" Leanna took a sip of her wine. "Then he didn't want you to have to grow up that way—running around and everything. He wanted to move back here and raise you right. He wanted to help Ephraim spread his work or whatever. I said, 'Yeah sure, Wisconsin—sounds great.' What did I know? I was just a hippy. All I knew about the place was cows and cheese. 'It's all natural and stuff,' he tells me. 'The pastoral lifestyle,' he says. It's freakin' negative thirty here most of the year, ya know? So here I am, raising his kid in a trailer while your dad runs around with that damn cult."

We were all quiet. My father closed his eyes and exhaled loudly as if hissing. "It's not a cult, Leanna. It's not a cult."

"Well, whatever it is, you're running around doing whatever he asks."

"This is my life. This is what I've been called to do. It is the most important work anyone could conceive of. I'm preparing this nation for the coming of the Revolution."

"Spare me the diatribe, I've heard it already," she said and finished another glass of wine.

My father's face flushed with color. I picked at my burger. He stood and began to descend the steps heavily.

"Where are you going?" I asked him.

He looked me over as if deciding how to answer. "I'm going down to the river to get some peace. C'mon with me."

We walked in bare feet over the grass. He continued his hiss-breathing the whole way. The sun was just setting and swallows darted back and forth above us in the purple-red light. "Let's go out there in the river, and be still and become one with it." He took off his shoes and waded part way into the river, and then he reached for my hand. I took off my shoes, held his hand and waded in behind him.

"You don't listen to naysayers," my father said. "Trust me that there is a spiritual world to be experienced beyond the physical. Trust me that there is a war going on for the spiritual life of the human race, and one day mankind will revolt against the Beast. The work I do with Ephraim is preparing us to survive in a future where few will. We are preparing to make a better world right here on this earth, not just on some cloud in the sky. It'll be in your time. You will have to be ready."

"What should I do?"

"You don't have to do anything. I will teach you all you need to know. Just promise to trust me."

"I promise."

The river swelled and spun around my legs. The current was strong and were it not for my father's strength, I wouldn't have been able to stand this deep in it. He dipped his hand into the river. "Remember, Kaz: there's more to this world than just what we can touch."

His hand cupped water from the Kickapoo and he poured it over my head. It dripped down my forehead, down between my eyes.

I still see him in my mind's eye: he stares into the curve of the river. Swallows dart over the evening water, the sound of their wings like a benediction. He looks beyond where they fly. He smiles.

Chapter Two

A HEAVINESS DESCENDED AFTER MY FATHER LEFT. Peas drooped on the vines; clouds filled the sky all day long. Leanna hibernated, staying in bed most of the days, coming out to make spaghetti or macaroni and cheese and to smoke cigarettes on the porch.

I drew pictures in crayon. She watched the rain from across the table. I looked up. She caught my eye, sighed, and stood, fishing in her pocket for her lighter.

"When your dad comes back we're going with him. We gotta get out of this place before I kill myself, I die and I become a ghost, kiddo. I become just another ghost like your father says he's always seeing." She lit her cigarette. She looked out the window again. "Crazy bastard," she mumbled under her breath. I went back to drawing. If she became a ghost, would she be made of bullshit?

Long, humid August days, I was left to fend for myself. I would fish with Eliza, wander around the woods, or help harvest the vegetables in Grandma's garden.

One morning, I was eating my cereal Leanna came whistling down the hall. She walked past me, rubbing my head; her hips swayed as she searched the fridge. She grabbed the milk and took a seat across from me at the table. Her curly brown hair fell down over her chest. She smiled at me. I smiled back. "I'm sorry, kiddo. I've been a real mess." She poured cereal into her bowl. "But I've decided on some things and I'm feeling better now." She took her first bite of cereal. "I'm not gonna let circumstances get me down. There's still life to live and enjoying to do. You follow me?"

I nodded hesitantly.

"And I've decided no matter what, I'm not gonna be in this state come November. That's a promise."

"It's cold in the winter."

"Yeah, the cold isn't so bad," she said, smiling. "It's the loneliness."

I suppose she told me these things because she had no one else to tell. I thought then that I could try to be her friend. Then maybe she wouldn't be lonely. Then maybe she'd stay with me and Dad.

"So, let's do something today, kiddo. What do you want to do?"

I considered my options. "Maybe let's play hide-and-go-seek."

"Where, outside?"

"In the barn."

It was full with the frames of couches and chairs, fabrics, and my father's tools lined up on an old table in the middle. I was not allowed to go there on my own. Leanna counted to a hundred while I ran and hid, mingling myself into the cotton belly of a half-stuffed chair. Dad did peculiar styles of upholstery, a small niche, and people would send their stuff to him from Florida, Kansas, California. He had explained that to me—only that. Even later, when he and I were on the road together, that was all I knew of what he was doing.

"Ninety-eight, ninety-nine, a hundred … ready or not, here I come." She found me and chased me to goal. Then I counted and she hid.

I climbed into the lofts when it was my time to hide again. She counted slowly, and I climbed in silence. Rat droppings were mixed with a film of dust and dead flies on the floor; moths danced in the light of the hayloft. Boxes of fabric, big crates of chairs, had come from afar to rest here like flotsam. From a box that held a chair carcass, standing gently on the springs so they would not squeak, I watched Leanna search for me. She crawled under the work table and peered into couches. Light through the slats in the barn illuminated her hair. A breeze blew in from the door. Her peasant dress swayed.

A figure of a man stood in the doorway.

Almost at the same moment Leanna turned and saw him too. She looked at him, squinting. "Are you looking for Aeneas?"

"Kind of," he said, as if stumbling on the words.

"He's not here. I'm his—girlfriend. Leanna."

"My name's Silas."

She walked toward him. He was backlit by the light in the doorway. "You're his brother?"

I stood, revealing my place. "I told you, Leanna! I told you he was coming home!"

"Who's that?" Silas looked up at me.

"I'm Kazimir. I'm my dad's son," I called down.

"Is your dad named Aeneas?"

"Yep."

"Nice to meet you, Kazimir. I'm your Uncle Silas."

"Kaz isn't mine," said Leanna. "I've been taking care of him with Aeneas."

I didn't understand why she said that and it made me mad. I got down from the rafters and ran over to them. Silas leaned in the doorway, thin, maybe taller than my dad even but half the weight or less. A short-sleeved flannel shirt drooped off his body, a small rift in the thread visible on his left chest. His long curls hung in greasy streaks down to his shoulders past a short, trim beard. "You look like Jesus," I told him.

"Kazimir!" said Leanna. "That's not nice."

"Well, he does."

Silas smiled and shook my hand. "Go in peace, young Kazimir," he said in his best Jesus impression, giving me the sign of the cross. I laughed. "Is Mom home?" he asked us.

"She's inside," Leanna responded.

"I think I'll go see her."

I wanted to follow Silas in, but Leanna touched my shoulder. "We'll keep playing," she said. "Let him and Grandma have some time alone."

That night we had dinner with Silas and Grandma. Grandma cried into the blackberry pie as she made it and kept asking where he'd been. "Oh, all over," he said.

She pried for specifics. "Where's Skeeter?"

"Had to put him down."

"Why?" asked Leanna.

"Snakebite."

"How'd you do it?" Grandma asked.

He looked at the table. "Just put him down," he said. He took a bite of his roast beef.

"I remember," said Leanna, "coming home one day from school and seeing my favorite calf lying kicking and moaning from a rattle-snake bite. My dad said we had to put her out of her misery. So he went into the barn and took out his rifle. And he loaded it up and put its barrel right between the eyes of the poor thing. I started crying and crying and he put the gun down and tried to explain why he had to do it. After I calmed down and I said goodbye, he took the gun and put it to her head again. Killed her right there. I was so sad."

"Your father was a good man?" Silas asked.

She laughed. "That was the about the only decent thing he ever did. Worst thing about it is that we had beef for two weeks after that. I never made the connection until it dawned on me years later."

"Where'd you grow up?"

"Arizona. On a ranch there." She smiled. "Been out there before?"

"Nice in Arizona," he nodded, glanced at us. "I saw Aeneas's band once. In Nebraska."

"That had to have been years ago," Leanna said. "Why didn't you say hi to him?"

"I don't know. Just couldn't." He ate his green beans, looking at Grandma and then me and then Leanna. "Saw you too. You were there."

"What town was that?"

"Oleana."

"I remember. I had just met him then," she said. "What were you doing there?"

"Just passing through. Trying to get out to the Rockies to live for a while."

When the morning came, I found Silas silently drinking coffee in our kitchen. He smiled at me. He had slept under the willow in his bedroll. When Leanna awoke, we had eggs and then Silas took us to the river and taught me to bait a fishhook and cast properly. Leanna spread a blanket under a maple and read her book. We walked downstream together, careful not to make a sound or to cast our shadow over the water. Then he rolled his flannel trousers and waded into the current. He was quiet; he had the ability to cast and reel without vibrating the water about him. A crane stood downstream, and over time, we made our way catching brookies until we were parallel with it. I waded along the far shore from it. Silas stood in the water within ten feet of the crane and it never moved.

We caught thin brook trout and attached them to a blue line that I dragged with me as we went. We came back with a week's worth of catch. I held it up for Leanna to see.

"That looks well past your legal limit."

"What's legal supposed to mean? I live off what I catch," Silas said, smiling at her.

"Well, you'll be living high off the hog then."

He laid them on the river bank. "Let's grill 'em up," he said. He sent me to find wood while he gutted the brookies with a filet knife. He began to twirl a shoestring-and-maple bow.

"What'cha doing, Silas?" I asked him.

"You never made a fire like this?" I shook my head. "How about you?" he asked Leanna.

She gave him a long look, then shook her head. "I tried it a few times when I was a kid, but could never get it started."

"Come here, I'll show you how. It's not hard if you use the right woods."

She put her book down and scooted over to the edge of the blanket. He showed her how to bow and explained the spindle board. She began to make long even strokes and it was not long before a whisper of smoke began to rise. "That's it," he told her. Then a tiny red eye dropped onto a waiting leaf. Silas lifted it between her face and his. "Blow on it, get underneath it." She put the bow down and blew hard, then again and again. More smoke poured from the leaf. Silas blew too, and all of a sudden the dry leaf erupted into fire. He set it under the tipi of sticks I had made and they both blew more. Soon the fire was glowing.

Leanna fell back, laughed and clapped her hands. "I can't believe I did it. I can't believe it!"

Silas took from his pocket some rosemary and foil that he kept there for chance encounters with food. He wrapped the fish with the rosemary and threw it onto the fire.

"How did you learn all this?" Leanna asked.

"Just from traveling around. Had to learn to get by on my own."

"That's a nice way to live. Just moving around, living off the land. You seen a lot of the country since you left here?"

"Yeah, been pretty much everywhere but Hawaii. Been down to Mexico, Guatemala too."

"Must have been fun."

He leaned back on his elbows next to her and surveyed the river. "It's nice to be back, though."

Uncle Silas was washing our dishes, whistling. I stood next to his legs, which were similar in height and girth to young birch trees. "I dreamed that you would come home. My dad says it was a prophecy."

"Well, I don't know nothing about prophecies." He began to whistle a little, then stopped. "Your dad's still doing stuff with Ephraim then?"

"Yeah, they're preparing the Revolution. I'm gonna be part of it."

He took the last plate, rinsed it and set it on the drying rack. "Well, all that prophecy stuff goes pretty far back in our family, I guess." He let the water out of the wash tub. He whistled a little more.

"You're just like some of them old Godwins," I said, "walking all over."

"Well, some of them were just crazy," was all he said.

Silas moved in under the willow and got his old job at the station back. He embedded himself in our lives like an arrowhead in the fields. He was around to buy us groceries, to play in the barn, to take me fishing. With his old pocketknife, Silas and Leanna and I would carve sticks into spears and try to spear trout in the Kickapoo. Her dress hiked up, she held Silas's shoulder for balance. Her laughing, him smiling. Silas incarnate in my life now. Nothing would ever be the same.

When the coarse noise of wheels on the gravel brought Dad home again a few weeks later, we were weeding the garden with Grandma. Tomato plants were taller than me, sunflowers on the verge of stardom. I ran to him; he picked me up.

"Look who's here!" I pointed at Silas, standing there with Grandma and Leanna amidst the peas and peppers.

"Oh shit, it's a miracle," he whispered, "just like you dreamed." He laughed, put me over his shoulder and ran to Silas, tears in his beard.

Beginning that night, after doing dinner dishes, Dad, Silas and I would go fishing. We'd head out to the river and cast lines, pull out brook trout. Leanna would protest that I shouldn't be up so late, but Dad would say it was part of my education. "When the Revolution comes, Leanna, Kaz is gonna need to know how to catch his own food," he'd tell her, and she'd roll her eyes.

Silas and my dad always drank beers as they fished. After a few casts Eliza would be standing there, the water purling around her calves.

"Catchin' anything?" she would ask. Then I would follow her into the woods, and there we would play until I heard my dad calling. Sometimes through the trees I'd glimpse them standing side by side on the river bank, Silas with a cigarette in his mouth, grinning at whatever story my dad told.

"We're gonna have a big old party, kiddo, to celebrate your birthday and Uncle Silas coming back."

"When?"

"Soon, before the corn's over." My father was pulling staples from a chair. "We'll have big old barbecues going and all the hippies will come down from Viroqua."

"When's my birthday?"

"It doesn't matter what the date is, Kaz, it's the spirit that counts. And you, you're advanced for your age." He took a swig from his beer. "You know who's gonna be there?"

"The hippies?"

"Ephraim. He's coming from Montana. He's bringing a bunch of his people."

"Do I have to meet him?"

"It's an honor to meet him. He's not like other people—you'll see what I mean. He vibrates at a different energy level. Some people can't even see him."

"Is he a ghost?"

"No, a being of pure spirit."

"Bullshit?"

He looked surprised. "What did you say?"

"Is he made of bullshit?"

"*No*, he's not made of *bullshit*, the farthest thing from it. Ephraim's as close to pure truth as anyone in this profane world. And he wants to meet you."

"Why me?"

"He knows how special you are. How you were born on the sacred lake. How you had a dream of Silas's return." He paused, as if weighing whether to continue. "I had a vision of your role in the end times. I have to raise you to be prepared."

"How are you doing that?"

"Teaching you things. Especially now that Silas's here—he knows all kinds of stuff about survival. He knows fishing and tracking and how to make fires and how to pick through dumpsters. All the stuff you'll need to know someday." He beamed over the dusty barn. "The universe led him back to us. It was meant to be, kiddo."

In late August we had the big party: my father's friends stumbled out of smoky vans and buses, drums throbbed, patchouli mingled with the smell of corn and grilled ribs. Waldorfers from Viroqua brought their drums of ceramic and leather, their gongs, tambourines, and maracas, their beat-up guitars, their laughter and cheers, their urchins in hand-sewn tunics. The hippies had a grand time talking up the farmers on the porch with their buzz cuts and overalls. There was rummy and whiskey-on-the-rocks with Grandma's church friends and Uncle Roald's farm hands.

"Which one is Ephraim?" I asked my father as he strummed his guitar.

"He hasn't come yet," he told me, never losing the beat of the djembes. "He'll be here in the evening, I think. Be patient."

The fireflies flashed their love songs as the evening came on. Mosquitoes gathered and we clung to the bonfire behind Grandma's garden. The sun went down at eight or so, and the older crowd diminished. Leanna put pajamas on me and set the fan on my bed. I opened up the window next to my pillow, pressed my face to the screen and felt the summer wind. Among the drums and guitar music I could make out my father's deep voice on occasion. I knew he was playing his guitar, too, his fingers bending notes which rose into the atmosphere like the fireflies and the rhythms of grasshoppers.

Leanna set herself down with a story book, but I squirmed.

"Where are the other kids sleeping?" I asked.

"They sleep in their van," she told me.

"Is Ephraim coming?"

"I hope not." She looked off out the window. "What's your dad said about him?"

"That he's important and he wants to meet me."

"Hmmm."

"I want Dad to put me to bed." So she went out and I could hear the whole trailer creak with her steps. After a short time another silhouette emerged from the barn side. You could always know him by his silhouette: a tall pear. You could always know him by the way he walked, his right leg dragging ball and chain.

"Dad!"

"Hey there Kaz, you need a shh-story?" The slur of his half-drunk speech. He grinned at me from the other side of the window screen, beer on his breath.

"Is that your band?"

"The Militant Amish? No. They're not around anymore."

"Is Ephraim here yet?"

"Nope, Ephraim's not here yet."

"Is he still coming?"

"Probably not tonight."

A great weight lifted from my shoulders. "Can you tell me a story?"

He listed in through the front door, shaking the whole trailer, and appeared at my bedside. His fulgurate hair waved from head and chin as he knelt to give me a kiss and rub my curls.

"Well, son, there once was a man. He lived and he died."

"No Dad, a long story."

"There once was a man. He lived, he got old, and he died."

"Dad, you know what I mean, a real story. Like the Three Little Pigs."

I lay back and listened as he began. "Cimarron Godwin, they say …." Somewhere in there I fell asleep. My father made his way out of the house, his footsteps the rhythm of my dreams.

The pulse of drums woke me, the standing waves of their beat. I listened to the party out by the bonfire; there was no way I was going back to bed, no way of keeping a boy from that sort of thing. I pushed in the plastic latches of the window screen, knocked the screen onto the grass, and jumped out. I made my way through the shadows to the garden, then crawled through the rows of peas. Above the music was the voice of Leanna laughing. I crept through the carrots, where a stray cat watched me, and then into the tomato plants by the scarecrow in the back.

In the flickering murk of shadow and firelight, I could see, or thought I could see, my father in a vinyl chair playing guitar, half in light, half imagined. Around him were the drummers, in front of them were dancers. Barefoot feet with toe rings passed near my head.

Shadows moved in and out; I saw Leanna weaving among the face-less figures. Then Uncle Silas came to her, holding her hand while she danced about him in circles and her face shone.

As my eyes adjusted, I realized there were new people who had not been there before I went to bed—a half-dozen bearded men and long-haired women. Little children danced as well, many younger than me and less dressed. At the far edges of the fire I could see a large, round tent had been set up. I knew that it had to be Ephraim's, and these must be his people.

"Is that Kaz?" Cousin Jethro's massive shadow fell suddenly on me. "C'mon out here." I crawled out from the plants.

"I couldn't sleep."

"No doubt, with all the noise we're making. Come looking for your old man?"

"Yeah." He led me around the fire.

"Couldn't sleep, big guy?" My dad grinned, still strumming.

" I wanted to hear you play guitar."

"C'mon over here, Kaz." I sat in the grass by his leather boots and socks; his feet were bare.

"Dad, is Ephraim here now?"

"Yeah, he showed up a few hours ago along with his friends in a big school bus all the way from Montana."

"Should I meet him?" I tried to focus on feeling honored and sup-press my pounding heart.

He smiled at me. "I was gonna bring you to meet him in the morning, but all right, since you're already up. We're gonna play a little more and then we'll go meet him."

"What song are you playing?"

"The song of the universe, my boy." He passed me a small drum. "Just play whatever your soul hears. It's true communication with the Source."

And there I sat, wrapped in sound and smoke, trying my hardest to add what I could, trying to turn on my soul and listen. I played and played, banged and banged on skin of the drum.

After a while, my father stopped strumming and just sat and listened. He closed his eyes and clutched the ends of the lawn chair as if bracing himself for lift off. I heard Leanna sing over everything, like a fairy tale, a lullaby. My father opened his eyes and smiled.

"Let's go see Ephraim."

He stood and took me by the hand, and we made our way around the outskirts of the fire. I could see Leanna watching us as she sang. We reached the front of the round tent, and my father lifted open the flap.

Inside, a circle of candles radiated a mercurial central light through the smoke of several incense sticks competing for olfactory dominance. I hid behind my father's leg as we neared the candles, and my heart thudded, matched by the slightly muffled pounding of drums outside.

We stopped at the edge of the circle of candles, opposite a hookah and a deck of cards. I looked up at my father as he lowered his head and prayed softly.

I gave a shout and jumped back. A man was standing across from us, appearing abruptly, as if by magic. Candlelight flickered on his drooping white pants. A satchel at his hips was held by a thin leather strap that ran across his wiry muscular chest. He was older than my father, with a thin red beard covering his chin, large doey eyes, and a head that looked like it would float away if not tethered to his chest by his neck.

"You're Kazimir," he said.

"How do you know?" I asked.

He laughed. "Your father told me." He knelt down Japanese-style, lit the hookah, and inhaled.

My father crossed over with me in tow and took a pull off it as well. They both exhaled, and the perfumed smoke danced among the candles. Then my father passed me the hookah.

"Take only a little bit, kiddo. It will help you to see through the veil."

I sucked on the tube and immediately coughed into the candles.

I was on my hands and knees, feeling as if I was going to be sick, and then the next thing I knew I was fine. I sat next to my father and watched the engraved dragons dance on the hookah. My fear dissolved into curiosity.

"A long time ago," Ephraim began. He took the pipe back from my father and set it next to him. I followed it in the candlelight. "Kazimir, look at me."

I looked up. "Sorry."

"A long time ago, the great prophets used this sacred pipe to see the spirit world. They inhaled it and their sight was cleared of the obstacles of the physical world. Sadly, in many religions today, this important aspect of the ritual of prophecy no longer exists. They do not see with the eyes of their eyes. They only see with their eyes." He looked piercingly at me, and I busied myself with being looked at. I tried to sit very still so that my father would be proud.

"I want you to see past the physical, so you can feel the truth of what I speak to you. Do you understand?"

"Okay."

He paused for effect. "We need true prophets to lead us when the Revolution comes. We need men strong and bold, directed by the many voices of God, to lead us out of the great destruction."

"Okay."

"I think you may have the potential to be such a man, Kazimir." He pulled a card from the middle of the deck and held it up to me so I couldn't see the front. "I am going to play a guessing game with you, Kazimir. I want you to guess the card. See this card not through the eye of your head and your brain, but through the eye of your eye."

I stared at it, trying to see out through my eyes. I imagined my eyes were merely a window to look upon the world.

"Eight of hearts," I said.

He looked at the card and smiled, then slipped into the deck.

He nodded at us. "You must keep to the training your father has set forward for you. Work with your uncle in preparing for the physical Revolution. He knows the things of the hand. Work also with your father to learn to see beyond your hands."

"All right."

"I see it now, young Kazimir. We will meet again one day. Your father will lead you to us when it is time. You will stay with us, the people of my community."

My father stood. "Thank you, Ephraim."

We left. Outside the tent my father picked me up and put me on his shoulder. The party had mellowed a little now. More people were sitting around the fire, but music was still being played.

"Did I do good, Dad?"

"You did great, Kaz." He took me over to a blanket and set me down. A pretty woman handed him a beer, and he lay next to me, staring off into the fire as I watched the world spin around me. My spirit was soaring with images of the things Ephraim foretold. I would be ready.

Later, I remember only the arms of my father like branches of a tree I lay cradled in, and the gentle shift of weight from leg to leg as he carried me away from the firelight. Drifting, I felt us step up into the trailer, shuffle onto the carpet. Drifting, I stirred enough to hear my door creak open, the fan blowing in the room.

"Dad"—my voice fading—"tell me a story."

"There once was a man...."

But I never heard the full sentence. I was asleep before he finished. He disappeared behind the door I never saw him close, and somewhere in my dreams his footsteps sighed.

CHAPTER THREE

FOR THE NEXT WEEK, I CLUNG TO MY FATHER'S SIDE, crawled around the barn and squirmed through odd tunnels of wood stripped from old furniture as he worked. Once, I saw something move in the rafters, and I stood still to catch it again. My dad looked up from sanding the arm of a chair.

"What are you doing, Kaz?"

"I thought I saw something. Maybe a ghost."

"What did it want?"

"I don't know."

"Why don't you follow it and see?"

"I don't know, Leanna says all the ghost stuff is weird."

Dad continued sanding the armchair. "Weird. Weird, Kaz, comes from the old English, w-y-r-d. It means fate, or destiny. Our fates are always weird, it seems."

"Yeah, I know what you mean."

"You do, don't ya kiddo? Hey, I'm going away again for a month or so. Gotta deliver some of this stuff. You watch after Leanna while I'm gone, got it?"

"Okay." I looked down at the ground. "I miss you when you're gone."

"Don't get all sentimental, kiddo. I gotta do this work; I know it takes me away a lot, but it's gotta be done. For the sake of the world."

Silas slept by the willow, though Dad had offered our living room floor. He said he would come in the trailer when the weather changed, but the long heat continued. Silas didn't like to sleep in the house with Grandma because he always rose early and didn't want to wake her with the old house's plaintive creaks.

"Kaz, wake up." Silas would touch me on the shoulder before the sun had risen. I'd rub my eyes and crawl out of bed, walk quietly past Leanna sleeping in her room, out to the living room where Silas's sleeping bag, tarp, and pillow would be neatly rolled in the corner behind the couch. It got so that I'd always be awake before he came in, I was so used to it. But I liked to let him rouse me anyway.

We'd go down to the river and cast our lines. He was a magician when fishing; trout materialized on his line nearly every place he cast. He fished to eat and would never sit in on our meals unless invited.

Occasionally in those early mornings we'd just explore. Maybe it was why he could fish so well; he spent half his time observing. Silas would walk down the bank of the Kickapoo, head bent, and look through the mud.

"There's deer track." He would point to two swipes in the mud. "How big you think it was?"

"Pretty big, probably a buck."

"Probably." He nodded his head in thought. "Used to get hungry. Back when I was living in the mountains out west. Mid-winter, I'd drive around until I hit a deer with my truck. Then I'd eat for weeks." He grinned.

"You're not supposed to do that?" I asked.

"Illegal. The government only lets you shoot deer at certain times; they don't care when you need to eat. But the deer gives you its life just the same in deer season or in the middle of winter.

"Shhhh." He squatted down and looked across the river. I did the same. The grass moved and swayed. The head of a coyote appeared; then her whole body slipped between the grasses and she came down to the river where it banked and slowed. She looked around briefly and began lapping up water. She finished her drink, sniffed the ground, and disappeared again into the grass. Silas turned to me and grinned. "Magic."

This was the magic Silas brought me to. This was the spell of mystery he saw in the world. He needed no interceding prophet, nor special breath, nor occult vision to read the cipher of God.

And in those times, he would give me the lessons that my father had asked him to. Silas knew animals; he had followed deer and elk and all sorts of things through the woods since youth. "Tracks are like stories," he said. "Mud is a book. You can read the story of the summer on the banks of this river."

We'd see the tracks of a beaver, then find its lodge in a tributary to the Kickapoo. We'd stop at a spot where fur and bones covered the ground. Silas helped me reconstruct the scene of the coyote's kill, checking branches and earth, making guesses and imagining what it was like. I imagined the throes as the coyote pounced.

"I watched a deer get taken down by wolves, once. Big old buck, a black wolf hung from its head and wouldn't let go. The other three dragged at its sides and back end until it went down. That was in the Boundary Waters. Used to spend a lot of time up there. Your dad will take you someday."

"Where is it?"

"Up north, Minnesota and Ontario, in a place where people can't build houses or even drive cars. It's as close to wild as this country will allow."

"Did you used to go together?"

He sighed. "With Aeneas? Oh, used to, yeah. I lived up there actually, for seven months. He came and visited a lot."

"Does my dad like it?"

"Well, he had his big revelation up there, so I guess he likes it for that."

"Was Ephraim there too?"

He looked at me. "You met that guy, huh?"

I nodded.

He rubbed my head and we looked out at the river together. "Life is gonna be pretty wild with your dad and all. Just remember to come out here. The river, the silence."

After dinner I took my bow and went outside. Eliza and I tracked a bobcat down past the barn, through the field, and around Grandma's house, and caught up with it by the big elm. There I knelt and drew an arrow. I hit it square in the hind and it tried to run off. I chased it down to the pond when suddenly it turned and sprang back at me. I wrestled it to the ground and drew my imaginary knife and stabbed it to death. I watched it die, and I was suddenly sad. I felt I had killed a real thing.

Eliza shook her head and then took my hand and led me to a clearing. The sun was setting and the first flashes of fireflies began to singe the air.

Over by a protruding piece of limestone she pointed for me to go forward. Thin spider webs brushed my face. I looked up, and in the fading light I made out the geometrical tracings of a web spun from the branch of an oak tree, anchored to the rock.

"Watch," urged Eliza.

I looked up and saw it: the flash of a lightning bug. Then as its ember faded I saw the little fella fly right into the web. From the center a dark ball began to spring toward it. I reached up to pull the firefly out.

"Don't touch it, Kaz."

I looked at her.

"You do and you're choosin' its life over the spider's—just because it's pretty, just because you like it. Life is bigger than a single livin' thing."

I wasn't used to her speaking like that. I put my hand down and we watched the spider work on its meal, the fireflies' lights diminishing around us as the sun set. I tried to steel myself to what I saw. I breathed and prayed for its soul.

I made my way back to the trailer in the dark. Silas and Leanna were by the sink doing dishes. "Hey Kaz, you catch anything?" Leanna continued to dry a plate.

"Big bobcat."

"Great, probably saved our lives," she said, and smiled. "Time to get ready for bed now, big guy. Get your PJ's on."

Pajama'd, tooth-brushed, I returned to ask Silas to put me to bed tonight. "Do you know any Godwin stories?"

"Well, now, let's see. I guess I know all those same ones as your dad, but I'm no good at telling them."

"Tell me about something you and my dad did when you were kids."

"There was the time I cut your dad's ear off."

There's a picture of that day in a scrapbook, and I had seen it. *Aeneas can you hear Silas behind you?* is the caption on the back. The black-and-white, eight-year-old Aeneas kneels front of a tinseled Christmas tree. I had traced my finger down the cowboy hat and plaid shirt, gun holster slung to his hip, cap gun drawn and pointed menacingly. Beneath the cowboy hat were two whole ears like anybody else's.

"He knelt down to reload the old six-shooter in case he needed it to fend off bandits or Injuns, I guess. And I snuck up behind him with a pair of scissors and snipped the tip of his ear off. He didn't even know what happened," Silas told me. "I really didn't either, but I saw the blood running down his neck, and I started wailing. I became convinced that I had to find the missing piece, and I got on my hands and knees and was tossing wrapping paper and bows left and right trying to come up with it," Silas said. "When I found it, I put it in a Dixie cup and held it all the way to the hospital."

"Why'd you do it?"

"I don't remember, Kaz. I was so young—but I remember that little bit of ear all gummy with dirt and hair from the carpet when I found it. Made me sick."

"Did you love my dad?"

"He was about my only friend when I was growing up."

"Me and Leanna are your friends now."

"And I love all you guys." He kissed my hair and left me to sleep. I could hear his and Leanna's voices from the kitchen of the trailer, but I couldn't make out words.

The weather was hot and dry in mid-September, and the edges of maple and oak leaves began to go crisply golden. It was a Sunday. I fished with Silas in the morning but felt too sick to go on with Grandma to church. I spent the rest of the day trying to sleep under the willow and drawing pictures with crayon of the Beast and the Revolution. I tried to put myself in, fighting the Beast, but it looked like the Beast was merely stepping on me. My own pictures filled me with dread. I sat in the embrace of the willow's roots, under its shaded dome of spiraling limb and leaf, almost afraid to leave.

As the evening came, the first firefly rose from the grass. I had a small obsession with them, and every night was mesmerized anew by their lyrical lights. With the insect's fire, my mind was put to ease. It lit again, farther away. I crawled from beneath the willow's hair and stalked it down the driveway, into the shade of the barn. I tried to catch it in my cupped hands, but it seemed to fade away at each clap of my palms as if it were no insect, but a ghost of fireflies past. I became aware of someone watching me. I turned to see Silas and Leanna standing over by the trailer.

"That's not the way to catch 'em," Silas told me. "You gotta use a flashlight and a Mason jar."

"Maybe after dinner we can go out and try to catch you some," Leanna said. "Supper's on. Come eat."

Excited now, I followed them over to Grandma's porch and scarfed down beans, corn, and trout. The sun set low to a full moon rising and Venus shone bright on the horizon. When we were done with dinner I helped clear the table with Grandma, and came out to find Silas and Leanna had assembled all the necessary tools.

We stalked the fireflies in the endless labyrinth of chest-high corn behind our house.

"Two flashes with your light, then wait, flash twice again," said Silas. "Then, when it's near enough, you raise the jar till it surrounds the firefly, and screw the lid back on."

Within a minute Silas had caught several in one jar. He gave them to Leanna. "Living lantern."

"Great! Now I can read in bed."

He grinned. She took it and held it up to his face. "You look like a ghost!" she said. "I feel like the queen of fireflies. You should make me a crown of fireflies. And daisies."

"Yes, my lady; maybe we could add a tomato from Mom's garden," he suggested.

She laughed. "And a trout head from you-and-Kaz's fishing expeditions."

Then he went about catching them with cupped hands, as I had tried earlier, and adding them to Leanna's jar. Though I followed Silas's instructions exactly, I could never screw the lid on my jar quickly enough. Leanna heard me grunt in frustration after yet another failed attempt and glanced at her watch. "Bedtime," she said and marched me back to the trailer. She set the Mason jar and flashlight on my nightstand.

"We can try again tomorrow." She turned the fan on, and looked at her watch, glanced at the door. I asked her to tell me a story.

"I don't know too many of them Godwin stories," she told me.

"Then give me a your-family story," I begged.

"Well, there aren't too many good bedtime stories from the Florsheim lineage, Kaz. It's mostly been pretty sad."

"So are the Godwin stories."

She cocked her head at me. "Godwin stories are just weird. You can deal with weird. Florsheim stories are sad, Kaz. They'll give you nightmares. They are nightmares." She pulled out a picture book from my shelf. "It's Mike Mulligan or nothing."

After she left I lay in bed, played with a loose tooth. Maybe the house was too quiet. I had the sense that ghosts were about but couldn't tell why. "Leanna?" I called out, but there was no answer. She must be outside still. I saw my flashlight and Mason jar on my nightstand, so I decided to get up and try to catch a firefly again.

I popped my screen out and climbed down onto the grass. The moon was diffuse in a veil of cloud. I wandered to the cornfield. "Leanna?" I called. I made my way deeper into the field and then I saw a firefly flash just below my right knee. I flashed it back with my light, and it flashed nearer its battery-powered paramour. It was right by my chest. I eased the jar around it and this time managed to screw the lid into place. It blinked again, and its light reflected off its translucent prison. I put my eye to one of the air holes in the lid and watched its dark shape bump up against the glass and self-immolate. It bumped again against the glass and I suddenly realized it was flashing at its own reflection. Then I heard what sounded like a coyote yelp.

"Leanna?" I called out. There was no response but the crickets. "Silas?" Only the same. I made my way toward the sound I had heard. I had my flashlight, but I didn't use it. I wasn't sure anymore that I wanted Leanna to see me.

I moved between the corn rows, deeper and deeper into the field, until I came to the hill of gravestones like an island in a sea of corn. Then the moon cleared itself from the clouds. And I saw Leanna—her naked form, her hair hanging down past her shoulders. She was seated on top of Silas, who lay on the slope of the hill. I was too young: aliens might as well have landed right there, a nuclear bomb detonated, and I would have understood such events as much. But it made me sick in my stomach, sick like some winged animal was trying to get out of me.

My firefly lit its jar, bumped against the glass. Crickets chattered; a soft wind blew. I stepped backward into the shelter of the cornfield. I made my way as quietly as I could away from them. Then I ran.

CHAPTER FOUR

"LEANNA?" I YELLED OUT. MY DOOR OPENED and she stood in my doorway backlit by the hall light. Dad was still gone.

"Nightmare again?" she asked. The rain came down outside.

"Yeah."

"You wanna tell me about it?"

"I was on a park bench with Ephraim. There was a tornado coming."

"Ephraim?"

"Yeah."

"Go on, sweetie."

"Ephraim said it was up to me to stop it. And then I got sucked up, and everything got sucked up. And then the trees and the houses were all spinning like a washing machine. And then I woke up."

"You been watching TV again at Grandma's?"

I nodded.

"Saturday morning cartoons? The Tasmanian devil, Kaz?"

"Uh-huh."

"Well, I think your imagination is getting the best of you. You're dreaming about those cartoons, big guy, that's all. Don't worry too much." She ran her hand through my hair and rested it near my ear. After I shut my eyes she got up and made her way to the door.

"Leanna?"

"Yeah?"

"Remember that night we made the firefly lanterns?"

"Yeah?"

"What were you and Silas doing?"

She turned to look at me. "What're you talking about?"

"I came out later to catch fireflies. I saw you guys naked."

"What were you doing out there?" she asked.

"I went out to capture a firefly."

Outside the wind beat against the loose screen on my window. I could hear a distant car pass.

"I don't know what you're talking about. I just went to bed after I put you to sleep," she said in a quiet voice.

"But I went around looking for you."

She fumbled for a pack of cigarettes in her jeans but didn't find them. "I went over to Grandma's to borrow some sugar. Look, hon', you didn't see anything out there, okay? At least you didn't see us. Maybe it was some teenagers from down the road or something. Maybe Silas has got a girlfriend. I don't know." She found her cigarettes in her jacket pocket. "If you start yapping away before you know what you're talking about, you could really hurt people. You understand—sweetie?"

"Sorry."

"It's all right." She lit up a cigarette. "Just get some sleep, huh?" She kissed my head, took a drag, and exhaled in the hallway.

"She's a liar," said Eliza, lying next to me.

I rolled over and held hands with her. "How do you know?"

"I was there. I saw it, too. That was her and she was with Silas, humpin' away."

"What's humpin'?"

"It's not something she should be doing with your dad's brother is what humpin' is." She sighed. "Don't blame her. Silas treats her right. If I was Leanna, I'd rather hump him, too."

I let go her hand. "You're gross, Eliza. Shut up."

I lay awake thinking about it more. I couldn't talk to Leanna or Silas. I didn't think Grandma would want to know. I had to wait for Dad.

I said less and watched more for the next month. I noticed Silas's long glances at Leanna. I noticed their walks together every evening when he came home. Silas was my only real friend. I wanted him here so I could learn to ice-fish and build tipis and track animals in the snow, but now the pleasure I used to take in our adventures was corrupted. There was a place of black dread deep inside me if I thought too much about Silas, or Leanna, or even my father.

A cold wet wind had blown us closer to November and most of the leaves had fallen and were heaped into piles in the yard. Silas and Leanna jumped into the piles. She covered him in doubled-over masking tape and then immersed him in leaves. They laughed. I watched them from a low branch in the willow. Grandma sipped a hot toddy. Leanna pointed at me. "Go get that little boy, Leaf Man!" He marched toward me zombie-style. I climbed higher into the tree so that he could not reach me, and I would not come down.

"Don't you want to play in the leaves before they go into the compost, Kaz?" Grandma asked.

I shook my head.

I had nightmares. Nightmares of fireflies and the hill. Fireflies dead on the ground like tinsel. I couldn't sleep anymore. I was sick to my stomach. Grandma worried and gave me medicine to take, but Leanna wouldn't let me. She didn't believe in medicine.

Eliza tapped her bare foot on the other side of the river as I made my way across the stones. "It's gettin' away."

I pulled an arrow out and notched it when I reached the other side, and Eliza ran up the wooded hillside, her tattered white dress muddy and soggy from the steady drizzle. I would have followed her anywhere. My first love, an imaginary figment. A wood sprite.

In a clearing we knelt as we sighted the buck. She fired intuitively and struck the buck in the hind leg. She was more cavalier than me with her arrows, their being imaginary and not as prone to breaking. I was still aiming when the buck leapt into the air and came running straight toward us. I fired just in time and hit it in the chest. It staggered, slid, and fell dead just inches from us. Eliza let out a shout and danced around its still-warm body. I fell back, breathing heavily. Could I really have been run over by an imaginary stag?

"I don't want to do this anymore," I told her in a near panic. "This isn't even real. It's all stupid and you almost killed me."

"Buck up, Mr. Prophet-Boy. You gotta be ready for the Revolution."

That night I watched her freckles in the firelight as she dug into the meat, grease smeared around her lips. She stared into the firelight; the feral glow of her green eyes bewildered me. I wanted to kiss her.

"You're so brave," I told her.

"Cut the sweet talk. I just do what I gotta do to live."

I was sick to my stomach at the thought of seeing Dad. When he did drive up, in the cold early November drizzle, I ran and hid in his bedroom until Grandma came and got me.

I wanted him to know. I wanted him to help me make sense of things. Maybe it was a vision, a prophecy. Maybe Eliza was wrong and it meant nothing.

We had dinner with everybody at Grandma's and I could hardly eat. Afterward, my father, Leanna, Silas, and I went back to the trailer. Dad got out his guitar and brow-beat Silas into bringing out his fiddle.

"You never play it anymore."

"I wasn't never any good is why."

"You're good enough to play in my living room for an audience of three. It'd be good to hear it again."

Silas rosined his bow. After a few false starts—"I always get real nervous when I play"—he began to fiddle Old Joe Clark. Dad taught him the melodies of a few Militant Amish songs, and he picked them up right away. Leanna sang their old songs and smiled. She glanced at Silas. He looked down at his hands. My father hadn't noticed.

I listened to them, paged through books, lay on the floor covered in beer cans, stared at the ceiling. My stomach gnawed at me until I went and lay on my bed. Their songs and laughter drifted down the hall.

Eventually, the uneven tempo of my father's footsteps creaked toward me. A stumble and a shuffle, a knock on my door, then he entered.

"What's happening, big guy? You still awake?"

"Hey, Dad?"

"What's up?"

I didn't answer.

"What is it, kiddo? Go ahead, tell me what the matter is. I'll fix it up for you."

"I don't want you to leave anymore."

"I don't always like being away so much." He tousled my hair. "Maybe I'll take you along this winter. Maybe you and Leanna can come with me—a family road trip. We'll live in the van until the weather gets better. Would you like that?"

I nodded. "What about Grandma?"

"Oh, I don't think she'd be too into it. But maybe Silas could come."

I shrugged. "I don't want him to come, though."

"But you guys are best buddies," he said.

I whimpered. Tears beaded in my eyes.

"What's going on, kiddo?"

Then I told him what I had seen. He emitted a windy sigh, hugged me tight and stared over my head as I wet his flannel shirt with my snot. "You gotta stop that now, Kaz, quit it now," he said pulling his shirt away. "You're gonna have to be strong. I'll fix it up. It was probably nothing—just like Leanna said. It'll be fine."

I rested my hand in his hair till my fingers fell to the shelf on his ear where they rested like little mice, and I fell asleep.

A loud crash and my eyes sprung open.

"Son of a bitch!" my father roared. I ran down the hall, heard Leanna shouting as I stepped over my father's guitar.

"Aeneas," whispered Silas as he tried to get up from the broken mess of the kitchen table. "I'm sorry. I'm sorry, but we love each other." His voice cracked.

Dad bull-rushed him, knocking him through the screen door. It busted off with them. The rail of our little porch went, too. They fell to the ground.

A hand came to my shoulder. I pulled away from it. Ran to where the door once stood. My dad straddled Silas, wailed and screamed obscenities, beat his fists into Silas's face.

I felt something brush past me. Leanna leapt from our porch onto my dad's back. A jerk of his body sent her flying into the wall of the trailer.

"Oh fuck, fuck you, you fucking son of a bitch," he screamed, and hit Silas some more.

Leanna leapt back on top of him, and this time he bowed and she flipped over his back and landed on Silas.

He hit her. Hit her again. Then she rolled away and got to her knees. She held her face and screamed and screamed. "Stop it!" she screamed. "Stop it, goddammit, Aeneas! He didn't do it. It was me. I love him."

Silas tried to keep his arms over his head. Dad yanked his wrists with one hand and hit him with the other until the swinging of his fist slowed and finally he fell over, panting, beside Silas.

Sounds. Silas moaning. Crying. My father's panting.

"Oh god, oh god, oh god—" Grandma in her nightgown running toward us. Sirens. A fire truck. An ambulance. The red and blue flickering, flickering on the willow, the trailer, me.

"C'mon Kazimir—" A blanket around my shoulders in the light mist. Grandma led me away, led me to her house. My father, on his knees, cried out. Eliza watched for me from the porch. I turned and saw Leanna, her hands on her face, and a man kneeling over Silas. Then the police car, the hirsute mass of my father draped and hunched, looming over the officers. His hands cuffed behind him. His flannel shirt ripped and dirty with dead leaves, blood, and the still-wet stain of my tears.

CHAPTER FIVE

"Come here, Kaz."

I put down my rake and sat down next to Grandma by the chicken coop. She handed me a Thermos lid of warm Kool-Aid. I drank it down and she chuckled. "You look like a clown with those red lips." She lay back and I lay next to her and we watched the clouds.

"I got a call from Silas. Says his face is pretty badly broken. He's heading up north to stay with some friends. Leanna's gone west for now."

"What about Dad?"

"He's—gotta be away for a few days still. I'm sure he'll be home soon." She sat up, wiped her hands on her sweatshirt and looked me over. I kept my eyes fixed on the clouds, pretending not to see her watching me. "Roald is coming over in a couple hours. We can play horseshoes or maybe he can take you fishing."

"I don't want to fish with him. He doesn't like us hippies."

"Well, we can play horseshoes," she said to me. "We should do something together, get our minds off things."

Pines rustled in the evening breeze and all of us wore winter jackets. Roald sipped whiskey and they talked in low tones about what had happened. We threw horseshoes at the damp sand pit. Roald didn't think too well of Silas, Leanna, or my dad. "Silas is a bum. He's nothing more than a bum. And that Leanna's a whore."

"There's no need for that kind of talk," Grandma said, and threw her horseshoe. It clanked against the bar. "It's not as if Aeneas is wholly innocent. He's left Leanna and Kaz here alone for long stretches, and we've always known he has this violent streak."

"Damn right. If you ask me, you should be raising Kazimir right here. Leave that guy outta the picture. He's a nutcase. Absolute damn lunatic."

I glared at him. "Don't talk about my dad like that."

Grandma threw her second horseshoe and it, too, ringed the bar.

He glared back at me. "Someone's too big for his britches."

"Roald, shut up," said Grandma. "*You're* too big for youfr damn britches—talking about my son like that. Kaz has been through a lot and he doesn't need you wisecracking about the family. If you're gonna act like this, go home."

Roald and I avoided speaking for the rest of the evening, though we ate dinner together and he gave us a formal goodbye from the porch steps. I missed Leanna. I missed Silas. I missed my father. I didn't know if any of them were going to come back, ever. And it had been my fault. I should never have said a thing.

Two more days passed. I helped Grandma in the garden. We nailed boards over a hole in the floor of her chicken coop. I went to fish in the river and caught a trout, which she broiled. She read me books out on the porch. She spent time on the phone talking to grown-ups about grown-up things that I couldn't quite make sense of. I knew she was talking about me and my family.

I could hear her up in the night. The creak of the fridge opening, a spoon scraping on a bowl. The downstairs bathroom would flush a half-dozen times. A shower would start at three a.m. She had breakfast ready for me by six, then in mid-morning would collapse in her bed and sleep for several hours.

One morning she was having her nap and I lay drawing on the living room floor when all of a sudden the screen door closed and I felt the cadence of my father's footsteps rock the house. I ran out to the porch.

"Dad!"

He scooped me up and gave me a long hug. He wore a new flannel shirt, but the same old jeans, and he smelled like a bar of Irish Spring. "Where's Grandma?" he asked.

"Sleeping."

"Go on upstairs and pack. We're going on a journey, kiddo."

"What about Grandma?"

"We can call her later. Right now, God wants me to get you and go, so we should go."

"Where are we going?"

"All over, Kaz, we've got important stuff to do."

I brought my things out to the Whale.

"You heard from Silas and Leanna?" he asked me as he backed out of the driveway.

"Silas got out of the hospital," I told him.

"Where'd they go?" Dad asked.

"I don't know."

He thought on that a moment. "Anyway kiddo, we're going on an adventure. You ready?"

"I guess so."

"You're gonna have to be brave. Sometimes you're gonna have to be alone. You ready for this?"

"Yes," I told him, though I had my doubts. I had never been on an adventure before, unless you counted those with Eliza.

The week after that blurred into one long car ride. The sky dimmed and the sun set, but the clouds on the horizon never seemed to get any closer no matter how many days we traveled.

We headed to the desert southwest. Every few days we'd pull off the main highways and park on dirt roads at the edge of nowhere. Dad would string a tarp out from the top of the van and we'd sit in its shade and wait. He read my story books to me until I knew them so well I could read them myself.

Sometimes Dad took out his guitar and sat in his lawn chair. I understood the guitar was a sacred thing. His guitar was prayer and he needed to be left alone when he played. So I'd brush warm sand away and lie on the cool layer below. I'd page through the books. The wind blew sand into the pages and into my hair. I shielded my eyes with my hand until it passed, and then I continued.

I daydreamed of the Kickapoo, of my feet in a current of water. I turned a page and read about a man and his steam shovel. I wondered if we would see a volcano. I wondered if Leanna was from near here and why she liked it better than Wisconsin. Back home there would be snow now, and Grandma would be alone.

The dry air thinned the guitar chords. The wind took the notes and cast them into the distant mountains.

Time after time, hippies materialized from the deserts, dusty, gaunt, smiling. Sometimes they held in their hands the reins of ponies or horses. Frequently the buzz of ATVs and a billowing worm of dust announced their arrival minutes ahead of them. I don't know how my father had communicated our presence there. They seemed to just know. They'd greet my father with long hugs followed by hookah sessions under the shade of the tarp. Jade necklaces clacked around their necks, canvas or straw hats shaded their eyes, intricately carved walking sticks bore their weight into the sand. I handled these as our visitors smoked from the hookah. My little fingers traced the faeries, the bears, the goats on mountain peaks. I was too shy ever to say anything to the strangers, and rarely did any of them speak to me.

They'd unstrap crates from ATVs and work the contents into the couches and chairs that we kept in the Whale. It never occurred to me how odd that was, for people who lived deep in a trackless desert to stuff furniture. Even after all of what happened later on, I have only the slimmest idea of how it worked.

Back in the Whale, we climbed into the dry mountains of the southwest. Beyond the peaks and hills we saw the glimmer of Albuquerque, Santa Fe, Prescott, Flagstaff. Their lights looked like the legs of spiders spreading from the city centers. We'd enter through slits in their bellies, navigate the intestinal tracts of pavement, deliver furniture to warehouses, to dusty, cramped shops filled with jade and Indian relics. Then we'd slip through their arachnoid clutches and head into the vast expanses of the darkness.

Dad held up a card from the deck as he steered. "What is it?"

I tried to burn a hole in the card. I tried to close my eyes and peer through my forehead like a periscope.

"C'mon, stop looking at it and *see*."

I blurted out the first thing that came to mind.

He shook his head. "Focus, dammit. Why can't you focus?"

He had me close my eyes. "Focus on your breath, every time you inhale and exhale. Count one, then two, three, etcetera, etcetera. Get it, Kaz? You focus the mind until it dissolves into the universe. Then you will see and hear truly."

I practiced special breathing techniques for hours, my eyes half-open in the passenger seat. Thoughts of my family drifted through my head. Silas, Leanna, Grandma, Jethro, Roald were branded on my retinas. And Ephraim's face was superimposed upon them all.

Wind rattled through the crack in the window. It spoke in tongues I would never understand, its whisper drowned by my father's voice.

"You know, Kaz, you don't need people. You don't really even need family. Look around you, listen, all you need is the earth. Earth is the sole companion of man, the only true gift of God. Friends, family, they will change, but the earth has everything you need, has a bond for you greater than any mere human. Human relationships are tiny, fragile things. You must first love the earth."

That made me wonder about Grandma. "When are we gonna go home again?"

He was quiet for a while. "Kaz, you *are* home. Wherever you lay your head is home."

"What about Grandma?"

"Grandma lives in Grandma's house. That's not our home. I figured it out. Our home is everywhere—it's here, it's all places."

"Including Grandma's?"

"Yes—but not right now. I wish it didn't have to be this way, Kaz. But it does. *Deus vult*. God wills it."

We rode south on a long straight stretch of New Mexico's highway. The wind boiled up through the rusted floorboard. As the shadows tumbled out of the sky, he pulled off the highway, down dirt roads and onto national forest land. "Free living on the forest land, kiddo. Only place left in this country a man can live without paying for it. Know what I mean?"

"Yeah."

He handed me a peanut butter and jelly sandwich and looked out at the sun. "The Beast is destroying this place. It's raping the hills and the mountains to feed its empty soul."

"What's the Beast?" I asked.

"You know the lights when we go into towns?"

"Yeah."

"That's it right there. That's what it is. But it's more—it's like a dark angel and it rises over the whole land. Its breath is the black exhaust of modern man. Electricity is its poison, cement tar and oil the fluids of its body, its claws are skyscrapers. That is the Beast."

The mountains were little more than hills here, dotted with pines and low creosote bushes. The rock was rust-colored, intensified in the late-day sun. We camped by a large tree, and I spread out our sleeping bags as my dad got dinner ready.

"It's a beautiful country, beautiful, beautiful land. And we're burning it all, raping it." He looked at me. "A few years from now, everything you know is gonna come crashing down. You ain't gonna be *able* to see the country anymore. Think of it, kiddo: no roads and no way to get gasoline; no trains, no airplanes; no institutions or schools or colleges. No jobs, or factories, or televisions." He made an exploding sound. "If the Russians don't get us first, we'll do it to ourselves."

"Who are the Russians?"

"A bunch of assholes just like in this country, only they speak a different language. They want to take over the world and so do we and we can't both do it so we're gonna have to kill each other. That's why we're going on this trip; to see this land before you can't. There's no future in this world."

"That's why you sell furniture?"

He laughed. "Yeah, okay, that's why we sell furniture. It's all for you." He took a bite of his tuna sandwich. "So you have sixteenth-century French marquetry to show your children after the Revolution. No, my work is more than bringing chairs to people. I saw it, Kaz, saw it in a vision, the whole wide earth being swallowed by the Beast. My work is as a messenger-warrior, fighting the Beast, spreading the news, waking people from their dream of enslavement."

I looked behind me at the Whale. Inside it was an antique couch and coffee table that we were driving to someone in Phoenix.

When the stars came out, we walked up to the top of the hill and lay on our backs. He showed me Hercules, Cetus, the Big and Little Dipper, Polaris. Then, after being quiet a while, he placed a small rock on my chest.

"This is you, Kazimir."

"I'm a rock?"

"Not quite, well, yes, well … Kaz, you're bigger than just your body. Part of you is in that rock, in those hills over there, in the stars. Part of you is beyond anything you can see or touch or feel."

"What part of me is that?"

"The biggest, most important part. The part you always have to have. You stop breathing, you still have a few minutes to live in your body. But you ever disconnect from that part of you, and you are dead."

"How do you know it's there?"

"Someday you'll hear it. You'll hear the voices of yourself in everything." He looked me over and looked away. "I don't know, maybe not—maybe it's not you. Right now you just have to practice and believe. Practice listening for it. Believe you hear it until you do."

I stayed up as long as I could keep my eyes open, doing the breathing, and when I could not focus anymore, I lay down and tried to listen to God in the wind again. Chills ran up my spine as I did, and I could not shake the overwhelming feeling that something was watching me.

Eliza lay next to me. "What're you so worried about?"

"The Beast."

"Haven't I taught you how to defend yourself? Your bow and arrow, don't you got them in your dreams? Just kill the dang thing."

She wiggled her toes in the starlight.

I dreamed it like she said, taking her bow and firing arrows at the Beast as it crept toward me, but my arrows were impotent and it came and devoured me. I woke then and lay awake. I thought about my breath. I concentrated on keeping it going. In, out, don't forget. I knew that I breathed while I slept, but feared that while awake, if I lost concentration, my breaths would disappear.

I spent months like that, half-dreaming, half-waking, until the whole world seemed a dream and I would nod off at a moment's notice.

I remember we were at a truck stop in Colorado Junction. Trucks lumbered by in the rain as Dad called Grandma. I could hear them arguing.

"He doesn't need any damn school, Mom. He's attending the university of life," he said and hung up. We got back on the highway.

"Did Grandma say anything about Silas or Leanna?" I asked.

"They split. They went off together after he got out of the hospital."

"Are we gonna see them?"

"We can't trust them. It's best if you just forget them, kiddo. Block them from your mind."

I breathed and my body seemed to melt into the seat, to expand to the size of the Whale, then the highway.

As we went north, following the thaw, the mountains began to rise out of the ground like the spine of a dragon. Up in Montana we entered into them, chugging along a labyrinth of muddy roads that climbed higher and higher up their flanks, until my dad stopped at a clear spot on a little hill overlooking a creek. We set up our tent, cooler, and sleeping bags under a pine and started warming some food over the fire pit.

"I have a special meeting tomorrow high up there." He pointed to a distant ridge of mountains. "It's a meeting of sacred ones in the Crystal Mountains. I took that—that *Leanna* up there, you know? The sacred mountains called to me to let her come. I played her my music there. You can't just take anyone up there."

His face was red, his eyes watery. I thought he might cry, or explode. I didn't know what to say.

"And you can't go, Kaz, not yet. When the time is right, the mountain will call you. But I hear no voice now. You'll have to stay here."

"By myself?"

"Yeah, I think so. You're gonna have to be brave, but you got cereal and sandwiches in the cooler, fishing poles, and there's a stream right over there." He gave me a solemn nod. "Besides, I want you to have the chance to fend for yourself. So you're gonna have to be brave and careful, got it? Just make sure you can always see the tent."

He left the next day at sunrise, trailed by the Whale's plume of exhaust. I watched him go and then went back and opened the cooler to get out the milk and cereal. The sun turned the sky to orange. There was a slight breeze blowing off the creek. I grabbed the deck of cards from beside the fire pit and started to guess the cards.

"What're you eatin' that junk for?" asked Eliza as she sat on the ground next to me. She was wearing a coon-skin cap and gnawing on jerky.

"This is all the breakfast stuff in the cooler."

"Well, you got fishin' poles, don't you? Why don't we catch some fish?"

I stuffed the cards in my pocket.

The creek bed was filled with smooth red, brown, silver, and blue pebbles unlike any I'd seen. I picked through them and tried to skip the smoothest of them across the water. The water ran only two feet deep as it wound between the banks. It had been wider once; we stood in an old river bed as we fished. I took my shoes off and let the edge of the creek trickle over my toes. Within ten minutes I had landed a little brookie and kept it on my blue string in the river, attached to a rock so it wouldn't get away.

"This is great. Old Silas would be proud," said Eliza.

"I'm not supposed to think about him," I told her. A shiver ran down my spine. "Something's here," I said.

"Like what?" Eliza asked.

"Something's watching me."

"C'mon, Kaz, there's nothin' around, I'd sense it myself. I've got ears like a jackrabbit, a nose like a marmot."

"I guess you're right," I said. Her words relieved my anxiety a little; I could always trust Eliza. I threw my line back in.

The air heated up to pleasantly warm by mid-morning, and we had caught no more fish. "They're hidin' out from the heat," Eliza told me. I reeled in. I sat down with my back to the sticky trunk of a pine and did my breathing exercises, trying to get that feeling like I was melting into the world again. Instead I just fell asleep, waking up to move as the shade shifted. It was a pleasant and soothing sleep, Eliza beside me resting as well, and I would have probably slept the entire day had I not been woken by a crashing sound.

I sat up. From where I was I could not see the campsite, but the sound had come from that direction. Eliza was already standing, and motioned for me to join her. She slung her bow and notched an arrow and we crept toward the campsite.

Another crash. Something up by the tent. We let the water muffle our footsteps. When we came to the base of the hill, we got on our bellies and crawled over the dead grass, over the marmot holes and ant hills, until we were within sight of the tree and tent. Something moved in the tent. It emerged. My breath stuck to my lungs.

A cub: a shaggy blond bear cub with rounded ears like a teddy bear emerged from the tent and disappeared from our view behind a boulder as it trundled toward the fire pit. We slid farther, then stopped when it stopped. When it resumed we crawled forward again, finally reaching high enough to see the fire pit.

The contents of our cooler were spread all over the ground like the entrails of a slain moose, and the cooler itself was lying on its side like the carcass. The little cub sat munching a container of peanut butter, oblivious to us. I started to stand up, hoping to scare it off, when Eliza grabbed my arm and yanked me back down. She pointed.

The boulder began to stand, and oddly enough, it had four legs and a large furry butt. It trundled to the cub and rooted about the piles of food.

I felt a warm trickle of urine run down my right leg. Every muscle in my body seemed locked away from the commands of my brain. Eliza re-notched her arrow, and motioned for us to go back down the hill. I couldn't move. *Breathe*, I thought. *Keep breathing, merge with the hill, and it will never find you. Breathe and unlock your body.*

I inhaled, and when I exhaled, I prayed for my fingers, unlocking them, then my arms, my head, my shoulders. I breathed and prayed until my body came back to me, all the time watching the grizzly and her cub merrily consume my lunch and dinner. When I was free, we crept backward down the hill.

It must have taken us ten minutes to get back to the creek. Then we high-tailed it to the pine tree we'd napped under.

"Climb up," Eliza told me, and I scooted up its sappy trunk until I was twenty feet off the ground. She followed.

"Why don't you shoot it with your bow?" I asked her.

"Are you kiddin'? It would just make her madder. We'll stay up here until they're all full and good and gone, then we'll get down."

"I knew something was there. I felt something watching me."

"Nothing was watchin' us. If it was watchin' us it would have et us—at least you, I don't think I can get et by grizzlies."

I choked back some tears. My dad had told me to be brave. I looked down and saw the urine stain on my pant leg. I tried to spread out so it would dry before my dad saw it. Then I pulled out the deck of cards and tried to see through them to pass the time.

"What is that you keep doin' with them cards?" Eliza asked.

"I am trying to use my true eye and see through them."

She just shook her head.

After a time I put away the cards and tried to breathe. I half-closed my eyes and concentrated on my nostrils until I began to feel that weird sense that my whole body was expanding again. Then a new sensation: the world seeming to be sucked into me.

Eliza touched my arm. I opened my eyes to see the bear and her cub coming down the hill toward us.

"I called them," I said out loud, amazed at my own power, the hair on my arms standing again. I had summoned my own funeral. "Oh God, don't take me now," I prayed, and immediately I was ashamed. I should do what God wanted of me—even if it was to die. But I knew I wasn't strong enough to follow that will, and now all these special powers Ephraim and my father had given me had back-fired.

The bears began to follow the creek; I held my breath, tried not to make a sound. I imagined spitting out all the world I'd sucked into me, spitting it back into its place. Maybe then the bears would leave me alone.

They stopped at a green pocket where the water pooled. Mama and cub dipped their heads to drink. Mama's head came up, and she cocked it inquisitively; but instead of coming toward me, she waded a little farther out into the creek and submerged her head again, this time coming up with my trout, the blue line still through its gill. She laid it out, and she and her cub devoured it.

When they finished they left the remains on a boulder and sauntered right underneath us. I could see the individual hairs of the mother's back, the muscles rippling under her fur. The cub played as it went, investigating tiny flowers, chasing a fly. They followed the little creek into the denser trees and disappeared from sight.

"We're lucky—"

"SHHH!" I told her.

Eliza giggled. "We're lucky we were downwind of the campsite, or they would've smelled the piss on your leg and chomped you up."

"Shut up!" I hissed. She laughed more.

"Let's get down," she said.

"No way. I'm waiting till Dad comes back."

"Oh, come on, all the food's et. They're long gone."

"My special powers though—"

"Your which?" she asked as she hopped to the ground.

"My special breathing powers attracted them. I sucked them to us."

"Right, your special powers, Mr. Prophet. They came down here cuz there was food."

"But then they came down the creek, right to where we were."

"They needed a drink after the big meal. Plus the fish. She ate your fish."

"No, they came because I called them. If I come down they might come back."

"Okay, fine. That doesn't make any sense, but you can stay up there all night if you want. I'm going explorin'."

She went off in the opposite direction of the bears, and with no one to talk to I was lonely and bored. I couldn't even do my breathing or the cards because I feared they might attract the bears.

Bats began to dart over the river as a full moon came out in the east, and in the last dim glow of twilight I saw a spray of headlights on the landscape. Crickets chirped. Soon the Whale came chugging to the top of the hill and rolled to a stop at the campsite. I heard the engine shut off and the door slam.

"KAZ?" my dad shouted out.

"DAD!"

"Where are you?"

"Down by the creek, in a pine tree."

Soon I saw the beam of a flashlight on the hill and I called again.

"What happened?" he asked as he drew near.

"A bear and a cub came and ate everything." I told him all about it as he helped me down.

"Damn, you're awful sticky," he said as he helped me out of the last branch. "But you did the right thing getting up there and staying till I came back."

We elected not to camp there another night.

I felt ashamed and weak and stupid as we packed up our stuff, but at the same time relieved that my father was there.

"Can we go back to Grandma's now?" I asked as we pulled away in the dark.

"Not yet. I got more stuff to deliver out west," he told me.

"But I miss her."

"Meditate and pray on her, try to fuse yourself with the world, and you'll feel her presence."

"I don't want to do that stuff, grizzly bears might come."

"Were you meditating when the bears came?"

"I was sleeping. But then when I hid in the tree, I meditated and I felt them get sucked into me."

"I've never heard about that power—well, maybe something like that. The mere power of your spirit would protect you, though. Nothing could hurt you."

"Really?"

"Yes. If you truly believe, it will be like a shield."

I thought about that, but I knew my faith was too weak to be a shield—or to make me think being eaten by a grizzly was a good way to go, even if God wanted it. Instead I wanted to cry. I wanted to go home. I wanted Grandma or Leanna to hold me. Or just Grandma—I had to block Leanna from my mind.

We met more hippies outside of Boulder. Delivered some chairs in Denver, then we went south, meeting some of Ephraim's people in Towaoc, where we loaded two antique sofas and delivered them in Phoenix. Then we went and camped for what must have been several months in the mountains of northern Arizona.

Along the way Dad had picked up some survival books, and he worked through them steadily with me. "The Revolution's coming," he'd say. "You gotta know this stuff."

"Isn't Silas supposed to teach me?" I asked once.

He grabbed my chin and made me look at him. "Listen carefully, Kazimir—I was wrong about Silas. He's part of the Beast. Get him out of your head."

It was fall in the Rockies. The leaves were turning and rivers of yellow aspen wound up the mountain sides. Parked on an old logging road, we made a shelter of sticks, aspen leaves, and pine needles. It took two days, but in the end it was large enough for both of us and pretty warm. We stayed in it for a week, setting a couple traps and catching a rabbit in one. My father used the book to teach us how to skin it. He showed me how to start a fire with a piece of flint we had found. We shredded some cotton from an undershirt into a fluffy pile and nicked the flint with a knife until a spark fell on the wadding.

I held it up to my face and blew and all at once it ignited into a fireball. I screamed and dropped it on the ground. My dad laughed and laughed. "You look like an old man!" he hollered, and showed me my face in the rear view mirror. I wiped the mirror clean with my sleeve. Where my eyebrows had been were streaks of white, my bangs white and black curls. I thought I was staring at my own ghost.

They had not altogether grown back when we finally returned to Grandma's.

<h1>Chapter Six</h1>

The trailer lay on her land like a stain that wouldn't go away. The porch and screen door were still broken and lying next to the old flower beds.

A frigid blast of air knocked me sideways when I got out of the Whale. I had forgotten how cold it could be in Wisconsin, had become accustomed to the relative balminess of the west. At one degree the cold penetrates everything, chilling your body even when you race across the yard, up the steps and into the warmth of Grandma's living room. It stays with you even through the hugs and kisses and the fretting over singed eyebrows.

"Dammit, Aeneas, try feeding him once in a while," she told him as she sipped whiskey. "He looks like he's lost ten pounds."

My dad lit a cigarette. "We're going feral, Mom, getting ready for the future."

"There's not much future in starving to death." She looked him up and down. "You look like crap, too."

He exhaled. "Kaz and I are people of the soul. Food is a thing of the flesh."

"Oh, bullshit! You don't have any use for your soul if you don't have a body. Now feed your kid, or leave him here so I can." She looked over my face. "What the hell happened to his eyebrows?"

"I was starting a campfire," I told her.

"Oh for crying out loud," she said and led me into the kitchen to cook dinner.

Uncle Roald and Cousin Jethro came over for pork chops. I ate till I couldn't fit any more in and then finished off with some ice cream, which melted nicely into the spaces around the chops in my belly. Roald asked me tersely about the trip and I told them about catching the rabbit, building the shelter, and how I was nearly eaten by a bear, omitting my special powers and the fact that I peed my pants. Then when I was stuffed sick, I went to lie down in my dad's old room upstairs.

I could hear the grown-ups talking and then I heard Roald and Jethro departing. I felt the door to the house close again. I knelt on the bed and looked out window. The headlights on the Whale lit up the falling snow as he drove away. I lay down huddled under the quilt. After a while, Grandma came to check on me.

"Your dad went out to visit some old friends," she said as she sat on my bed and stroked my hair. "I missed you, Kazimir. I was worried sick for you."

"I missed you, too. It's all right, though, it was mostly fun. We were up in the mountains."

"How were the mountains?"

"They're like a new home."

"I bet." She petted my head. "Silas and Leanna came by when you guys were gone."

I didn't say anything.

"They miss you. They'd like to see you."

"Dad says I can't see them anymore."

"Well, your Dad doesn't need to know, does he?"

"Why'd they do all that, Grandma?"

"People make mistakes. They just fell in love. Someday I hope you'll understand. You know, your dad was leaving you and Leanna alone a lot. He shoulda seen it coming, I guess. I'm not saying I don't understand why he got so angry, but sooner or later he's gotta come around. Silas's his brother."

I shrugged.

"I was wondering, Kazimir, how would you like it if you stayed here with me?"

"What about Dad?"

"Well, we'd have to see. He might come and go, like before. I guess you'd go with him sometimes." She paused. "I worry about him, you know, and maybe raising you isn't what he's cut out to do. He's got some funny ideas. Leaving you alone like he did when that grizzly came—that's just not right. You could stay here with me and we could get you to school, maybe make some friends. You gotta be a little lonely while traveling, eh?"

"Yeah, a little. I have Eliza."

"Of course you have her. But you got to have real friends. I know Silas was a friend, wasn't he? You gotta miss them, huh? You miss Leanna?"

"I don't know," I said. "When are they coming back?"

She shrugged in the dark. "We have to wait and see."

My father didn't come home for three days. I woke up every morning, did my breathing, and practiced seeing through a deck of cards I kept in my shirt pocket. I spent the rest of my time stuffed into snowsuit and mittens while Eliza and I played in the yard. On that third afternoon, while we were making an igloo, the Whale rumbled up. It turned into the driveway, followed by a Skylark. A man I didn't know got out of the driver's seat, waved as he walked around the Whale, and pulled open the passenger side door. My father slumped over in it. The man pulled my dad out of the seat and slid him to rest in the snow. Then he walked over to the waiting Skylark and hopped in. The driver honked as they peeled off.

"Is he dead?" Eliza asked me.

I went over to my dad. Exhaust fumed out of the tailpipe of the Whale. "Dad?" He stunk of alcohol and sweat, and his right eye was bruised. He mumbled something and then rolled onto his stomach.

"He's drunk," Eliza said. "Freakin' loser."

"I think he's sick," I told her.

I climbed in the passenger seat and reached over to turn off the engine. The Whale died with a shudder, and in the silence I climbed back out to check on my dad.

"I should get Grandma."

"What's she gonna do? She can't carry him and you can't either. He's the size of a small bar."

"A what?" I asked.

"A bar—a big furry animal—claws, teeth. Like what we saw up in Montana."

"A bear?"

"Yeah, a bar." She rolled a snowball and whipped it against the willow tree.

Then she kicked him several times. "Wake up!"

With her help, I rolled him over and wiped the snow from his face. He winced when I touched his eye. "Dad?"

After a couple seconds he opened his eyes and adjusted to the sight of me leaning over him.

"How's things, kiddo?"

"You sick?"

"Just fine." He sat up and looked around. Then his stare just seemed to fix into the distance. "Let's go sledding."

That evening, after the sledding, Grandma worked on her knitting, and Dad and I sipped hot chocolate on the couch. He pulled out a deck of cards from his pocket and started to shuffle them.

"Cards, Kazimir." I had the feeling he was speaking to Grandma. "Cards to play di-vert-ise-ments, to pass the time. But do you know where they come from?"

Grandma looked up. "From the kitchen drawer."

I giggled.

"Ha, ha, Mom, very witty. It so happens that *cards*, Kaz, come from *Tarot* cards. You know what Tarot cards were for?"

"For Tarot?"

"Exactly, kiddo. Tarot—to tell of fates and to divine the future." He held one up, the red rinceaux like a tiny wall. "What is it?"

I closed my eyes.

"Show Grandma what you can do, kiddo. Focus."

I shot laser beams hard into the corner of the card, where I knew the number would be. Grandma shook her head. Somewhere down the hall Eliza snorted. "Hearts."

My father's eyes widened. "What card?"

"Seven."

He flipped it over: the jack of hearts.

"You got the suit right!"

"Come on, Aeneas," said Grandma, "there's a one in four chance of getting the suit right."

"Well, he's just starting to understand his inner eye."

"A little math education will develop that eye right up, you know."

"This is his education. *I'm* his teacher."

"Really? What math does he know?"

"Are you kidding? Boy can already do complicated geometry and algebra far beyond the college level."

"Where does he learn this?"

My dad made a casting motion. "Think you don't learn physics and math when you fish? Physics, music, art, too. His mind does extraordinary amounts of math instantaneously just so he can place his lure exactly where he wants it to go. He figures this better than any engineer or rocket scientist could predict on paper."

She shook her head. My dad continued. "He can navigate with the stars. He can track animals, knows their homes and habits better than any book on any teacher's desk. He can draw. He's learned philosophy—lots of ontology and metaphysics, epistemology, musicology. He's learning about his soul, his spirituality. He's a regular Renaissance man. And now he's learning to use parts of his brain that most of us only guess at."

"Guessing is about the right word for what he's doing." She got up and poured some whiskey into her hot chocolate. "You wanna see an inner eye, Kaz?"

I nodded.

"Here, give me half that deck." My dad counted off twenty six cards and handed them to her. She paged through them briefly and set them aside. "Now hold up one of the cards you have left."

My dad did.

"You tell me the suit and I'll tell you the card." she told him. "What percentage do I have to get right for you to consider me a prophet?"

My dad thought. "How 'bout forty percent."

"Well I have a one in thirteen chance, right? So raw luck would get me something like seven-and-a-half percent correct."

"You only got half the deck, so fifteen percent."

She snickered. "So better than fifteen percent and I'm a novice prophet. Forty percent and I'm a regular Elijah. What's the first one?"

"Spades."

She looked at me. "Nine." She got it right.

My dad held up the next one. "Clubs."

"Queen," she said immediately.

"Nope. It's a four."

She got only three out of the first ten, but then nailed fifteen out of the last sixteen.

"Eighteen out of twenty six." She looked at me. "What's my percentage, Kaz? Better than fifty percent?"

"Yeah, I think so."

She got up and tousled my hair as she walked past us. "That's almost seventy percent, Aeneas. Am I a prophet or what?"

He leaned back and paged through the cards. "You've played bridge your whole life."

"That's right. I count cards. I figure percentages. You want magic, you want to predict things, that's what you do. People can't see through cards. There's no such thing as an inner eye."

"That's just what this modern world has taught us to believe. There's stuff going on in this world bigger than what we can touch and feel. Bigger than math. But the Beast doesn't want us to feel that. *It* wants us to ignore our spiritual selves so we don't notice it sucking our souls right out of us. I won't have my son learning to be that way. I want him to be in contact with his true self. I have to show him the way."

"What's the way? Starvation? Irresponsibility? A three-day drinking binge?"

"Oh, dammit!" He threw the cards across the room and stormed out of the house.

The Whale started up and drove off.

I got off the couch and started to pick up the cards.

"Don't bother, Kazimir, I'll take care of it later."

I didn't say anything, just continued to pick them up. When I got them all in a pile I went out to the kitchen table and one by one, I tried to see through them. She came in and sat next to me, then held me in her arms as I tried to singe a hole right through those cards to see the other side.

It was a Saturday, a week later, and Grandma had gone into town for groceries. I came down the stairs to see him making himself some coffee. He smelled like vomit and Folgers.

"Hey there, kiddo." His hair ran thin and willy-nilly around his head, over his eyes.

"Where did you go?"

"You know how things are. When you get work you gotta do it."

I nodded knowingly.

He got the skis from the barn and took me out along the Kickapoo. The snow had melted and refrozen along the river. He broke trail in front of me, bursting far ahead and then waiting, his breath forming nebulae in the air as I neared.

"You know what I was saying about work?"

"You gotta do it when you gotta do it?"

"Yeah. Ephraim's got more work for me. Stuff like you and I were doing—you know, going around, delivering things."

"When're we going?"

"Yeah—that's just the thing. I was thinking that I don't know how to do any of this stuff, secular living. You understand? Maybe we should go out and live with Ephraim...." He was having trouble putting thoughts together. "God has told me different, or I would. He tells me you gotta be here. I don't understand it but I guess this is the place for you to become what you will, not on the road with me. So with that in mind, I think Grandma's right, you should go to school."

"I can read already."

"I know you can, you can read real well. Just maybe it would be better if you stayed here for a few months. You can come with me when school gets out."

"When is that?"

"I don't know, June sometime. I can't remember."

"You went to school, right?"

"When I was a kid? Yeah, yeah, it was a blast—all kinds of kids to play with, lots of coloring stuff to do. You get to have homework."

"What's homework?"

"Real important stuff you do when you get home. Helps you learn. I learned all kinds of stuff in school, kiddo. It's where I learned some of the stuff I teach you."

"If you know it all then why do I have to go? You can just teach me it."

"I was off in the woods there the other day. I was playing my guitar and after while I felt someone next to me, singing. At first I was afraid to look, but then I worked up enough courage and I looked. It was an angel. I played and she sang and what she sang was that I needed to go off now and that it was best if you stayed here. So that's what we should do. Understand?"

"Okay."

"I can't pretend to know why—you know how it is, God calls and I must follow." He squeezed my arm. "Anyway, I gotta go—I can't stay around here all the time. I got important work to do all over the place. Real important."

"What makes your work important?"

"Can't get more important than an angel telling you to do something, can it? I'm doing more than moving furniture, Kaz. I'm fighting the Beast. I'm saving souls."

That night I dreamed the house was burning down. Shingles flew off with the smoke, and amidst the flames a great bear hunted me. It snorted behind me as I ran down the hall. I came to the stairs; the smoke was pouring up from below and I couldn't see. I started cautiously down the stairs, placing my hand on the rail, warm to the touch. I felt my foot sink into something soft that I could not see. It was a human arm.

Then I was down. I felt my way along the hallway and as I passed by Grandma's bedroom, I saw a large human eye slowly burning there. It gazed at me, the streaming smoke reflecting like a river in its iris.

Then I stood in Grandma's garden as the house burned down. The eye looked out through the window as the flames consumed it. Shingles tumbled down around me as the house crashed. Everyone I knew was in there.

When I woke I spent a good hour convincing myself that I didn't smell smoke. Then, just when I was calming down, I heard something move outside my window. Shivers ran up my spine.

"C'mon Eliza," I said, pulling the sheets from the mattress. "I think it would be safer if we slept under here." She sighed and followed, passing out as soon as we were settled underneath the bed.

I had just nodded off and it was still dark when my father knocked on the door.

"Kaz?" He turned on the reading lamp and got on his hands and knees. "What're you doing down there?"

"I heard something snooping around the house."

"Well, you can come out. It's safe."

He slid me out by the armpits and helped me to settle on the bed again. Then he sat down next to me, the bed depressing enough to make me slide toward him. He put his hands on his knees.

"I gotta head out now," he told me.

"When are you gonna be back?"

He shook his head. "Depends on what Ephraim needs me to do." He looked out the window. "I want you to keep up with your praying and breathing. It'll help you through anything. Develop that inner eye."

"I will," I said and bit my lip.

"Don't miss me kiddo, don't miss me when I'm gone. Rely on yourself, not on anyone else, even me. Trust only in God."

"I will, I'll pray every day. I'll pray for you, too."

"You know what I want you to pray?'

"What?"

"*Deus vult.* That's all. That means 'God wills it.' Don't pray for people or for things or for life to change. It's useless. You understand?"

"No."

"Pray only that you can accept what God wills. Develop your faculty to see what this truly means."

"*Deus vult,*" I said.

"Take care, kiddo," he said, and kissed me on the forehead. His rough beard enveloped my face.

His warmth lingered after he left the room. It stuck with me as I heard him start the Whale in the freezing cold of morning, stayed as I heard him back out of the driveway and head out onto the road, until the sound of the Whale no longer carried through the air. I didn't watch him go. I hid under the covers, trying to stop my jaw from shaking.

At first I prayed so that I wouldn't cry. I didn't want to cry. And then I realized I was being foolish. *Deus vult,* I whispered, and focused on my breathing until the urge was shuttered, and a stillness came and settled deep into my bones.

"TODAY YOU'RE JUST GONNA SEE THE CLASSROOM," Grandma told me as we got out of the car. The school itself looked like a Communist-era nuclear bunker. Fencing surrounded the building and the snowy asphalt yard, barren except for one distant tree that grew by the northern enclosure of the fence.

Grandma registered us at the front desk. "You scared, Kaz?" she asked in a whisper as we followed the short, high-heeled principal down an empty hallway. "You can tell me; it's okay if you are."

"No," I lied.

She nodded and reached her hand out for mine. I took it.

"Well, I'm a little nervous. Nervous for you, too. This is gonna be different. I hope you like it."

The principal opened a door and led us to a little table where a caged guinea pig munched on food pellets. Bad artwork and math pages with little red numbers scored on them provided decor to a room otherwise made entirely of cement and painted the color of kidneys to suggest, I suppose, a brick schoolhouse. Two windows behind the teacher's desk afforded a panoramic view of blacktop. Kids my age sat in desk rows.

At the little bustle of noise we made by sitting, faces turned back to stare at us. They looked me over for weakness, for coolness, probed me to see where my shields were down. I focused on my breathing and tried to put lasers into their foreheads with my eyes so they would turn around.

The teacher cleared her throat and raised her voice, self-conscious now. Kids sat in rows and some listened to her, mostly the girls. Boys stared out the window or threw things at each other or looked back at me.

Eventually a bell rang and everybody filed past me as they went out to put their coats on. A few seconds later I saw them through the window running out onto the blacktop. The teacher approached us, smiling.

"What do you think?"

I shrugged.

"He hasn't ever seen a school," Grandma explained.

"Well," the teacher affected her caring teacher voice. "This is a place children come. It's a place for learning things."

"I know what a school is. But why do we gotta learn *here*?"

"So we can grow up and go to college and get jobs."

"My dad says soon there aren't going to be any jobs or colleges or anything."

The teacher glanced at Grandma.

"His dad's got a lot of unusual ideas," Grandma explained. She chuckled and patted me on the head. I moved my head away.

"Why aren't there going to be any of those things?" the teacher asked me.

"Dad says the Beast will destroy it all, if the Russians don't get to us first."

She looked at me. "Pentecostal, eh? We got a few other Pentecostal kids in the class. Maybe you'll get along."

"What the hell is a Pentecostal?"

Grandma slapped me on the back of the head.

When we were walking away, I asked Grandma, "What do I need to go to this school for?"

"For learning things, to teach you how to be when you're older."

"Why does there have to be a building for that? Aren't we already doing it?"

"It's just the way we do things in this country, Kazzy. It's not so bad."

"Don't call me Kazzy. I don't like that."

"All right," she said. "An education is good for you, Kaz. It'll help you sort out the poo from the pizza in this world."

"What's that mean?"

"It means sorting out fact and fiction. I made it up myself just now. Anyway, if you don't go to school, they'll take you away from me. I don't want that. The government comes and takes you and puts you in a home for wayward children. I'd rather you go to school."

That scared me into going.

A few days later she dropped me off again. The principal led me in again and sat me at one of those desks. I didn't have any pens or pencils or paper. Everyone stared. Voices blurred into each other as I watched a plastic bag dance in the wind outside the window. The seat was hard and uncomfortable and I fidgeted until finally I took off my sweater and made a cushion of it. I sat in my row and tried to make sense of what was going on. I tried to listen to what the teacher said. At one point she read a story. We all sat on a carpet and listened. I liked that well enough. When we were done I decided to go to the bathroom.

"Where do you think you're going?"

It was the teacher's voice. I stopped at the door, taken aback. "I gotta take a dump."

Snickers and giggles filled the classroom.

"In a classroom, Kazimir, you have to ask if you can go to the bathroom."

"But I already know I can go to the bathroom."

More snickers.

"What I'm saying is you need my permission."

"Just to take a dump?" Laughter.

"Yes, even for that. And please, that's not appropriate language for the classroom."

"What isn't?"

"What you said. That thing you said."

"That I know I can go to the bathroom?"

Everyone laughed loudly. She shook her head. "Just go, but remember next time to ask."

I came from a place where we picked our food from the garden, tried to catch it with traps, or caught it fishing; where we used Mason jars for just about everything and hadn't heard of Tupperware; where there was no TV and little radio. The old house creaked and groaned, and our ancestors were buried out back in a place you could walk to through the snow to touch their limestone graves. I was raised wild. And from the perspective of the wild thing I was, what school had to offer seemed poo, not pizza.

These kids had come from all over, many not even born in New Eden. Their world was a place of neat tidy containers. They ate applesauce out of little plastic containers and drank from juice boxes. They carried lunch boxes with photos of country boys and their orange Charger, cowboys, some guy with a sword made of light and a dog-man behind him. I began to feel the cords of my stomach twist and knot.

There was too much about these people that I didn't comprehend. I didn't understand them, and I hated them. I hated the stupid desks and the people in them, the drawings on the walls and the walls themselves. I hated the blacktop waiting for me. I hated the whole "learning" thing.

"How come your jacket's all dirty?" a kid asked me when we went out to recess.

"Dirt got on it," I told him. He went away.

"You wanna play kickball with us?" two boys asked.

"What's kickball?"

They laughed.

"I don't like kickball," I said, trying to cover up my ignorance.

I watched the boys play as I made my way past the jungle gyms, and out to the only tree, bare against the gray sky. I watched them just so I would know what kickball was next time someone asked. I was watching them when a voice came from the other side of the tree.

"You don't have any idea what they're playing, do you?"

I didn't recognize his face as much as I recognized the glasses jutting out from underneath a mop of hair. He sat behind me in class. He had a goofy grin on his face.

"In fact, judging from your behavior, you don't have the slightest idea what *any* of this is."

"Are you real?" I asked. I'd begun to suspect the only kids who wouldn't laugh at me were imaginary.

He nodded his head. "I think so." He looked me over. "Are you from a different country or something?"

"I don't think so."

"If you were, I guess you'd know. Are you a ghost?"

"No."

"You can't be then. Ghosts have to say if they are."

"Kind of like pigs. My dad says if someone's a pig they have to say if you ask them."

He squinted. "I don't know much about pigs. I wonder if pigs can say they're ghosts."

"My dad says pigs will lie about everything except if they're a pig or not."

He looked up at the sky. "You sure act like you're from a different country. My cousin's a missionary and he brought some people back from Africa and they were looking around like you are."

"What's a missionary?"

"A person who goes and saves people's souls."

"My dad does that."

"What's his name?"

"Aeneas Godwin," I told him.

"What's your name?" he asked.

"Kazimir. What's yours?"

"Micah. Your name sounds biblical, too."

"I don't know what that's supposed to mean."

"I bet my dad knows your dad. He knows everybody," he said.

"So does mine. He's the baddest son of a bitch in four counties."

That day I went home and told Grandma I had made a real friend.

"Good," she said and nodded. "What about your imaginary friend? You still see her?"

"Eliza? Yes."

"You're seven now. I think that's too old to have imaginary friends. Don't you think?"

"How should *I* know?"

"Point taken, Kazzo. Well, I think you're too old. It's time we stop babying you. It's time we make an imaginary funeral for your imaginary friend."

"Eliza's not going to like that."

"I imagine not, but I'm just trying to help you out. Other kids will make fun of you, and besides, you need to start getting adjusted to the modern world a little."

"Are we gonna get a TV then? All the kids do is talk about TV."

"We don't get stations out here, and we can't afford a satellite dish. You'll just have to do without it, Kazzo." She gave me a head rub.

"I don't care, TV's boring anyways. I don't like being called Kazzo," I added, moving my head away. "Don't call me that."

Micah's dad did know of my dad. "He says he went to high school with your dad, and he's bad news. He says your dad beats people up and went to jail."

"Yeah. They deserved it."

"Plus your dad used to sing mean and ungodly songs. I told him your dad does missionary work."

"What did he say then?"

"He said, 'You don't have your facts straight.' I told him you seemed like you needed Jesus, and Jesus tells me to help you. That's what I tell them when I want to do something. I tell them Jesus said so."

"My grandma already gave me a Jesus. He's on my wall."

"That's good. Then he's nearby so it'll be easy to meet him. Jesus told me to guide you to him."

"Does that make me your friend?"

He smiled and gave me a hug. "Yes."

Grandma sewed me a new quilt for my bed. It had patches with robins, little boys fishing in straw hats, mountains, and a boy and a bear cub playing. "That's to keep the scary dreams out," she told me. At night I sat down on top of the quilt and I did as my father told me. Every night I set my alarm, then sat still and counted my breaths for ten minutes. After a time, when I felt calm, I would take the deck of cards from my nightstand, shuffle them, and try to guess the suit and number. Sometimes it went well, other times it didn't. Most times it was in between. No matter how often I did it, though, I never seemed to get any better.

I would try that for a good half hour every night, and sometimes afterward, I would lie in bed unable to sleep. I would pray and pray. I would try to pray just *"Deus vult"* as Dad had told me to, but I couldn't. "Why can't I *see*?" I would ask God. And there would be no answer. Loneliness for my father or Silas or Leanna would come and I would beat it down.

"Maybe your fake eye burned out," suggested Eliza.

"What are you talking about?"

"Some people are blind with their real eyes—maybe your fake eye is blind."

"It's not fake. It's my dang inner eye."

"Either way, maybe it's blind. You need to compensate with your other senses like blind people do."

"Maybe. Ephraim did say I should listen with my sacred ear."

"My guess is you're deaf, too. Maybe you have an inner nose. Maybe you can sniff out the future."

"Shut up, Eliza."

She laughed. All the same I tried. Nothing but the musty stench of the upstairs. The smell of my father's old music books, the antiques mildewing in old steamer trunks, Silas's childhood toys.

"Silas called," Grandma told me. She was playing cards with Uncle Roald and Jethro on a Saturday night. Jethro had just moved out of the house in Sparta and was working as an accountant outside of Madison. He had come up to visit Roald, and they both decided to call on Grandma.

"Where's he at?" I asked.

"Somewhere up north," said Roald. "You know him, he moves around like all the hippies in the family."

"He's coming here?" I asked.

"He said maybe in the spring, when Aeneas comes home. He wants to time it so that he can talk to your dad," said Grandma.

"I don't think Dad wants to talk to him."

"It's his brother," said Jethro. "Look, they gotta make up. They've been friends their whole lives. Us three used to be inseparable."

"They're both on the move all the time," said Grandma. "He's gotta talk to him sometime soon or the years are going to get between them."

Eliza and I wandered up the ridges and looked down at the Kickapoo. In the snow, Eliza wore bearskin boots and a matching coat. Her hair was matted on one side, with twigs in it. That was the side she slept on, she explained to me. Near the top of the ridge, a family of white-tailed deer grazed on bark. We snuck up to them on our bellies. Then, when the time was right, we fired our arrows, making the kill.

As we gutted the big one, I took a good long look at Eliza. Her whole body existed like a fog. I tried to get my imagination to bring more truth to her skin, the quaver of the bear fur, the tiny freckles of her face. I needed to know each freckle's shape, each mole over her whole body. The more I imagined her, the more real she would be.

That was when I realized I wanted to marry her. "I love you."

She sat up from inside the deer carcass, blood streaks on her face. "Here we are guttin' a deer and you start talkin' all namby-pamby. What is this?"

"I love you. I want to marry you someday."

"Well, I love you too, Kaz, but I can't even begin to tell you all the things wrong with the situation."

"I mean, I *really* love you. I don't even *like* too many people. But I *love* you."

She smirked. "Don't think I didn't hear what you and Grandma were sayin' about me just the other day. You're gonna have a funeral for me soon, and here you are sayin' you wanna marry me."

"I didn't say I wanted a funeral for you. My grandma said I should."

"Well, she's a smart lady. Maybe she's right."

"No, I don't think I ever want to be away from you—ever."

"That's sweet but maybe she's right. You're pretty old for an imaginary friend." She raised an eyebrow. "It's kinda weird."

"Why would you say something like that?"

"Silas and Leanna thought so. The kids at your school will too if you ever talk to me there."

"That's not true. None of it."

"Fine, it's not. But my advice is don't test the idea," she said.

"Why are you saying all this?"

"You started it."

"I didn't start nothing. I just told you I love you."

She laughed. "Maybe. Maybe I love you, too. Maybe my inner nose likes your smell. Maybe that's why I stuck around for so long. But it's never gonna happen. I'm *imaginary*. You can't marry your imaginary girlfriend. Someday I'm gonna get out of your head. Someday I'm gonna head back up to the mountains and just billy-goat around like I used to and leave you alone."

"You were a billy goat?"

"Yep." She went back to gutting the deer. I was dumbstruck, and for the first time, I didn't understand whom I was talking to. How could my own imagination argue with itself? And as quickly as I knew I loved her, I knew it had to end. I stood up and turned my back.

"Fine. This is the end then," I said out loud. I waited for her to respond but she didn't.

"This is your funeral. Don't you have anything to say?"

Still no response.

"Fine, *you are dead. You are gone.*" I waited for some action on her part, some protest. When I turned around there was nothing there. I panicked, tried to summon her back. Nothing worked. I knelt in the snow and cried.

CHAPTER EIGHT

SUMMER VACATION SMELLED LIKE RAIN. I was barely able to move in the humidity. As I pulled weeds in the garden, mosquitoes bit at me, and I slapped at them in return. Grandma gathered lettuce leaves for our dinner. I put any worms I found in a Mason jar for use in fishing later. I was taking a break in the shade of the barn, counting my worms, when Silas's old Civic came rolling into the driveway.

Grandma stood and laughed as she wiped her hands on her shirt. Silas got out of the car awkwardly and gave her a big hug. "Oh good Lord, it's good to see you," she said, laughing and crying. She went in and mixed some lemonade, spiking hers and Silas's with whiskey, and brought it back to the porch swing.

Grandma suggested Silas and I take a canoe down the river together. I knew Dad wouldn't want me to be so chummy with him, but Dad wasn't there, so I went along to make Grandma happy. I helped him pull off his canoe from the top of his rusty Civic and we plopped it into the Kickapoo from the bridge.

"Your father ever come home?"

"No."

We paddled a long time in silence.

"How's school?"

"Stupid."

"Yeah, school is."

"Where'd you go?" I asked.

"Oh, up north."

"Where up north?"

"Boundary Waters. Took care of this fella's cabin on Crane Lake."

"Is it real cold?"

"Yeah, pretty cold. Chopped wood, ran some trap lines on a dogsled."

"Sounds fun."

"It's good."

We paddled in more silence. A blue dragonfly hovered around my paddle.

"I could take you up there sometime," he suggested.

"No thanks."

"I'm sorry, Kaz."

"What?"

"I'm sorry. I screwed up."

"Where's Leanna?"

"She went back out to Arizona for a few weeks." He steered the canoe around a corner. "Then came to stay in the cabin with me."

"Why didn't she come here?"

"She just felt awkward. Do you miss her?"

"No," I lied again.

We turned another corner. The Kickapoo takes almost ninety degree turns every fifty yards or so.

"My dad says you're full of shit."

"I messed up bad." Silas sighed. "But your dad never loved her. I love her, Kaz, and she loves me. And we both still want to see you and Mom. I want to try and make it up to Aeneas."

I focused on my breath. "He doesn't like you anymore."

"But we're brothers."

We floated for another hour. He showed me how to paddle upstream and how to prevent capsizing. I tried not to enjoy myself, but I couldn't help it.

The next day he left, saying we should call him when my father came home. He said he'd come back and bring Leanna to see me.

But as time went on and no one visited, I learned not to think about the people I missed—the people who'd loved me, raised me, and disappeared.

In the fall, when school began again, Micah and I sat under the big oak reading books while other kids played kickball. Snow came and we sat in cubicles in the library. Winter marched into spring. Micah and I played chess and checkers and talked about Jesus. The yellow-green buds of spring thrust out above us. Micah told me that being saved and bringing Jesus into my heart would change everything. His parents wanted me to go to church with them, but Grandma wouldn't let me.

"We've got our own religion."

"Micah says when Catholics eat bread, they're really eating Jesus' guts."

"Anybody who says there's something wrong with Catholicism hasn't closely examined their own shit. How old is Micah anyway?"

"Same as me."

"So what the hell does he know? How is someone your age supposed to know anything?" she said. "His church has a lot of hate in it. Not to say everything's all perfect with Catholics, but you don't need that. You don't need it any."

She took me to mass. I would stand and sit with the rest. I mumbled out the songs to the top of the steeple, listened to them echo back to my ears with nothing changed, nothing added.

I secretly believed everyone was full of crap. It had been my experience that grown-ups and children alike didn't know anything at all. I wanted Grandma not to leave me, so I went to church and said not a word against it. I wanted Micah to be my friend so I listened and spat it all back. And when I was alone, I would take a deck of cards from the kitchen drawer and practice. Sometimes, when things were good, I would hit five, ten in a row. I could feel it, I could see it in a different place in my head. But more often I would get five or ten in a row wrong. I couldn't understand what was different when I saw and when I didn't. But still late at night, I would sit and breathe, sit and pray. *Deus vult.* The only response: the empty creak of the house.

The March day my father came home, I knew right away he had changed. He didn't seem to look at anyone. He bent down and hugged me and told me that he missed me.

"You all right, Dad?" I asked.

"Tired from the drive."

"I've been keeping up with my seeing."

"That's good, that's a good thing."

He talked to Grandma while she made lunch and he ate with us, then went out with his guitar to take a walk by himself. "I'll take you fishing later, kiddo."

I heard the screen door close and watched him from the kitchen window as he crossed the front yard and made his way down to the river. Grandma smiled at me.

"You gonna call Silas?" I asked her.

She got up and went to the phone. "I hope Aeneas sticks around long enough to see him."

I went outside and made my way along the fields, then down into the woods by the Kickapoo. The sky was overcast and there was one of those winds that cut through whatever you wear. The radio said to expect eight inches of snow that night.

Through the bare trees I could see where my father was sitting on the far side of the river, the guitar in his lap. He was playing but the sound was drowned out by the river. The Kickapoo had thawed two weeks earlier and was running high.

He took off his mittens and continued to play. After a time he pulled out a pipe from his backpack and took several puffs from it. He leaned his head back against the tree and played again. His body moved furiously with the mute music he made. He seemed to be working himself up into a rage. His hair flailed. His legs kicked mud and leaves; his head butted against the tree; he writhed as if each note was being wrung out of him. Then he fell back and slumped against the tree. He looked then like he had been wrung dry, as if the spirit that animated his hand had sapped all.

I felt a chill of fear—not for him, but for myself.

When my father came in, he went into his old room and fell asleep. He didn't get out of bed for two days. I took soup and bread to him a few times at Grandma's behest. He was always asleep, or pretending to sleep.

The snow cometh. Eight inches fell in the dark, and another seven the next day. The telephone lines went down with the snow. Electricity went out and we had to light our way around with candles. School was cancelled and the wind blew the icy snow sideways so it was no fun to go out. I found my dad's guitar and tried to pick songs that I'd heard.

"He's never taught you to play, has he?" Grandma asked as she knitted.

"No."

"He should. He's pretty good with the thing."

"I'm not musical, really."

"That's like saying you're not walk-able. Everybody's musical. If your dad would ever stick around you could learn." She sighed. "I wish I could afford some lessons for you, Kaz. I just can't. I wish I could."

"It's okay, Grandma," I told her.

She looked at me with sad eyes. "It's not much fun around here for a boy, is it? There's no one to play with."

"I got you and Micah."

We smiled at each other. "Maybe Silas and your dad will make up. Then they'll both come around more."

A few hours later, Silas's white Civic plowed through the snow drifts in the driveway. His canoe was strapped to the top and hovered over his windshield like a thundercloud.

"You carried that thing all the way down in a windstorm?" Grandma asked as he came in.

"Thought I'd store it in the barn. I'm gonna head down south for a while." He looked at me. "You can use it if you like."

"Thanks."

"Blew off up near Eau Claire. Had to drag it back through the blizzard and tie it back on. Got a dent in the side now, so it'll paddle kind of funny."

"Why didn't you bring your sled dogs down here, too?" I asked. "We could have used them today."

He grinned. "Not my sled dogs."

He went out to untie the canoe. We watched him go. "Guess I better go tell Aeneas." Grandma squeezed my shoulder.

She disappeared upstairs while I sat and tried to read. Soon, Grandma came back down and set some coffee brewing. The screen door creaked open and the whole house shook as Silas stomped the snow off his boots.

We waited. I couldn't read. Snow pelted the window in gusts.

It was a full hour before I heard the ceiling begin to creak with my father's steps. I heard the muffled thump as he descended the stairs. I tried not to watch him as he came down. The kitchen was quiet.

My father came into the living room, thickly bundled for the out-of-doors, and stared out the window for a few moments before throwing open the door and barging toward the barn. He stomped back a few minutes later with some skis, stopping to sit on the porch steps and strap them on.

Silas appeared silently behind me and touched me on the shoulder. I stepped aside. The door shut only part way behind him.

"Hey," I heard him say.

"Hey yourself."

"Been a while."

"Not long enough."

"Where're you going?"

My dad laughed. "Nice spring day like this, thought I'd go out for a little ski trip. Why don't you come along?"

"I don't think that's a good idea."

"Why not?"

"Storm's still blowing around. It's supposed to snow some more. It's late."

"You drove through it. Obviously with the canoe that must have been pretty risky. Why not ski?"

"I just think it's a bad idea."

"Something being a bad idea never stopped you before."

"I'm sorry, Aeneas."

"Sorry? What's that supposed to mean?"

"I …" Silas paused. "I don't know what else to say. You won't want hear it."

He laughed again. "You were my *brother*. I don't want to see you, I don't want to hear about you. Nothing. Don't ever try to get ahold of me, don't ever try to talk to me again, or I'll kill you."

My father stood on the skis and pushed off. Moments later he was obscured by the billowing snow. God knows where he went.

When Silas came in, Grandma hugged him, and as she did his eyes settled on me. "I'm sorry," I mouthed to him. But it was no use. Within a couple hours, he got in his little Civic and headed out. He was never good at staying still.

I lay under the quilt that night. The trees scratched at the roof. Grandma kept the porch light on for Dad, and outside my window the snow swirled in pocket tornadoes, gales, waves. I waited and waited for my father to return. Below me I could hear the house creak with Grandma's movements as she waited, too. I prayed with my eyes closed, prayed *Deus vult* over and over in my head, a thousand times, ten thousand times. Sometime in the night I was overwhelmed by the silence of the house and a cold shiver ran down my spine. A great pressure sat on my chest and squeezed the air from me. I tried to let out a scream but it came out dulled and muffled. I panicked, tried to wrest myself from bed, writhed my arms and my legs to escape, but could not move, could not get free. My limbs were so heavy, exhausted. I gave up panic and surrendered under the burden of the invisible weight. My mind collapsed inward into darkness.

In the morning, I awoke to find myself able to get out of bed but dull and weighed down. I ate a bowl of cereal. I was watching the snow pelt the kitchen window when I heard the porch door close, felt my father's steps in the floorboards. I watched him come in, sniffle, make his coffee.

"Mornin', kiddo."

I looked at him. "What happened?" I asked. "Where did you go?"

He wiped his nose. "I gotta get out of this place, Kaz. All kinds of bad memories."

I nodded, blinking back tears. "I wanna come along."

"Not right now. I got all kinds of stuff going on. I got responsibilities, you know; big stuff is going on."

"For the Revolution?"

"Yeah. Other stuff, too. I'm doing special training that will help me channel my powers." He poured himself a cup of coffee. "How you doing here?"

"It's all right. I made a friend."

"That's good." He sipped his coffee. "So it looks like I'm not going to be able to come around much anymore. I got some real important work to do, and it's going to keep me busy for a long time."

"All right." I had sucked my tears back into my eyes and I focused on keeping them there.

"I'll miss you, but you know, Kaz, when the Lord says go, you go. When you're ready, I'll take you up to the Boundary Waters, Kaz. Everything will change after that. You'll understand then what I'm doing. You'll know."

"Sounds nice."

He gulped down his coffee. "Yeah—nice. So I gotta go then. Say good bye to Grandma for me. Remember to pray."

Chapter Nine

Through great drifts of snow, Micah and I roamed the fields and forests. Nestled into blankets, we read books and wrote stories. We talked into the night.

Years passed by.

Grandma and I lived off the pension she received from the Merchant Marines and from the money she got for renting out the farmlands. It wasn't much. We expanded the garden so that it took up more than half the yard. I tended the fruit trees. In the summer we had so many vegetables we would trade them to some of Grandma's bridge partners in return for venison. In the fall, we spent whole weekends canning apples and cherries. We ate them all winter. We got by. Other than the chores necessitated by growing our own food, I was given free rein to wander the forests and fields, house and barn. I fished all day sometimes. I lay for hours on the little hill of tombstones and spent entire afternoons in the attic. Grandma had raised two boys before me and had none of the paranoia younger parents have.

Roald would come by a few times a month and play cards with Grandma. He didn't approve of how she let me run about. I needed structure, discipline. I needed a pair of shoes. Did she want me to end up like Silas or Aeneas? She should get me on Roald's farm so I could learn the value of hard work.

She never did. She just drank her whiskey, made fun of his haircut, and beat him at cards.

Jethro, too, would stop in from time to time, bringing a cooler full of steaks to grill. His manner was gentler. He saw a lot of Aeneas and Silas in me. He'd tell us that we should sell the old place and move in with Roald. Grandma determined that's what Roald wanted but wouldn't say, so he sent Jethro to say it instead. She wouldn't be budged. "I'm gonna die in this old house," she simply repeated.

Micah played bass. He jammed with the older guys in his church group. "Jammin' for Jesus," he'd say. They liked him, and some of them were rough kids at the high school, which translated into a sudden respect in middle school. We attained and smoked cigarettes. We smoked until we were sick, hanging out in the tipi that Silas had helped me build ages ago.

"I don't know if Jesus loves you when you smoke cigarettes," I told him.

He pondered that in his Micah way. "There's a difference in Jesus' love and my parents' approval."

"Doesn't Jesus want you to obey your parents?"

"What does it matter what Jesus wants for me if he loves me no matter what?"

"I don't know."

"My dad wants me to be a preacher—fine. But I'll do it my way."

Maybe he was the prophet and not me. It would be a great relief if it were true. I could be normal. I was doing all right in school. I had a friend. My grandmother was still around, and with my father and Silas out of my life I was keeping a straight head, keeping average.

Then one day in the summer after seventh grade, I took Micah up to the hill above the Kickapoo where Eliza and I used to hunt.

"Hey!" He bent down, inspecting a lawn of ferny growth. "You know what these are?"

"Maple seedlings?"

"That's mari—jo—wanna."

"What?"

"Bud. Mary Jane. Cannabis. Pot."

"Really?" I knelt to look at it. "How do you know? I always thought they were just baby maple trees."

"I've seen pictures. That's definitely pot." He looked around. "Look at this; it's all pot. This whole clearing is someone's marijuana operation. How come you never took me up here before?"

"I didn't know at all about the pot."

"I wonder who ...." He thought a moment. "This has gotta be your dad's."

"My dad's?"

"Who else would come up here? No one lives within five miles of this place."

"He hasn't been home in years. How do you propose he takes care of this?"

"I bet he used to grow it back in the seventies, and it's just gone to seed and gone feral and it's still growing here."

"So can we smoke this?"

"Well, not right now—we gotta wait till the fall. I don't really know how to harvest it, but I bet we could find out."

"Then we can smoke it?"

"Man, if we harvest this, we can smoke some and make a fortune out of the rest."

"You think so?"

By that fall we had discovered several other fields of marijuana growing in the forests along the Kickapoo.

Micah did some research with the high school kids in his youth group, a mean and sordid bunch of chain-smoking talking mullets, and we went back out in early October and harvested a small selection of the crop.

We spent every hour we could collecting the buds; and using his connections from church, we made a boatload of money, which we hid in the forest in a metal box.

And we kept a little for ourselves, enough to last the winter. On Halloween weekend, we camped in the tipi by the river and smoked it for the first time. My mind loosened from its earthly tethers, bumping against the invisible walls of its confinement. I realized that this was what they—my father, Ephraim—wanted of me. It was no coincidence that I'd found my father's plants. He may have been gone, but I felt their eyes watching me.

A few days after the end of my eighth-grade year, I woke up to the unmistakable sound of my father's guitar. I got out of bed and went downstairs expecting him to be in the kitchen or on the porch. Nothing. A spray of water misted through the porch screen. Grandma smiled at me from outside. In the already-warm morning air she watered our vegetables.

I felt sick in my stomach and sat down on the porch swing. The feeling of my father's nearness made me remember old times. My hand brushed my lip. I was fourteen and proud of the little blonde-and-red peach-fuzz mustache. Grandma noticed but didn't say anything. Micah thought I should keep clean for the ladies. Roald had said I looked like the dirtballs that worked on his farm. Jethro didn't seem to care either way. My father or Silas would care; they would've noticed and been proud. They would've welcomed me into the land of the bearded. But I hadn't seen either of them in years.

That afternoon, as Grandma was watering the garden, I took a walk around the property. I half-expected to find him at work in the barn among the leftovers of his upholstery. Nothing. I went into the old trailer—dilapidated, the broken door set inside. The linoleum gave way on my third step. I extracted my leg and continued. The place smelled like a woodchuck den. My bed was still there, the blankets and sheets filled with debris and shredded. A hole in the mattress looked like the entrance to some animal's lair.

I sat on the end of it and felt something push back against the cushion under my rump. I sat upright and did my breathing, and after a time, when the thoughts of my life had disappeared, I began to recite my father's prayer. I felt myself expand, the room bending and then curling as it expanded with me. And as its walls moved into the space of the yard, the sound of my grandmother's hose running in the garden filled the world. I heard waves of water begin to lap at the edges of the trailer. Water rushed into the windows. The trailer creaked and groaned and soon was moving.

I saw myself float out of the trailer, tumble in the waves. Tomato plants, cucumbers floated past me. A lawn chair. A squawk, and Bertha the hen went by. We were swept past the willow, then I tumbled under the water as I was washed down the hill. Soon the current of the river had me, was dragging me down. I surfaced for air to see above me a blood red moon. "What are you doing with yourself?" the moon whispered to me. "I am being pulled under," I told it. "So then drown, as all things do," it said, and the tides rose again, and the cold brown water filled my nostrils, filled my mouth. Our toaster oven sank below the surface, fireflies lit the banks, and then Grandma's body began to drift past me. He hair floated in the water like fishing nets and her head turned to face me. She spouted a stream of water from her mouth; it arced through the night air into a mist that showered onto my head like lead weights and pushed me below the surface. The heave and pull of the current finished me.

I came to myself still in the trailer, a cold sweat over me. The room rocked and I braced against the wall until the dizzy spell passed.

Grandma was standing at the doorway with a whiskey-and-Coke in her hand when I came out.

"What you doing in there?" she asked.

"Just looking around," I said.

She took a sip, taking an ice cube into her mouth and then spitting it back. The ice clinked against the glass. "You miss your dad, huh?"

"I don't know. A little I guess." My voice squeaked; I was at that age. "I used to think about him more. I used to do all the breathing and stuff he wanted me to do, expecting him to come home and take me with him again. I don't really do it anymore."

"That's probably good, Kaz. He hasn't been much of a father." She shook her head. "Neither of my sons—dammit—they never come around."

"I'm here, Grandma."

She smiled. "I know, and I love you for it." She waved her hand at the trailer. "I ought to get that thing hauled away, but I can't afford it."

"You could sell it," I said.

She laughed. "To whom?" she asked. "A family of badgers?" She put down her drink and gave me a sweaty old-lady hug. I put up with it until she'd had her hug fix. Then she set me free, picked up her whiskey-and-Coke, and went back out to the garden. Her sweat had stained my shirt. The smell of her flower perfume stayed with me all day.

It wasn't a week later that my father actually did come home.

I was out at the tombstone hill reading when I saw the Whale pulling into the driveway. My heart raced but I didn't budge. I wanted to run out and see him like I did when I was young, but I thought that would be foolish. He was just going to leave again.

Grandma's greetings carried through the thick air. I could see her give my father a hug. They went into the house for a time. I just stayed and read. After a half hour the screen door closed and he made his way through the garden and the young corn out to me.

"How's my boy?" he said.

"I'm fine."

"Grandma says you're a good student, and a big help here." He was dirty and disheveled, his hair long and stringy.

"We get along well," I said and shut my book.

He came over and gave me a hug, lifting me off the ground. "Bless you my son, it's good to see you." He looked around the place, his hands on his hips, and smiled. "Looks to me like you're still learning for the end times. Here you are, growing all your own vegetables, taking care of the chickens. You're learning to provide for yourself outside the clutches of the Beast."

"I guess you could call it that," I said. "Others call it poverty."

"You know, Kaz, poverty's best anyway," he said. "Anyway—I have a special trip planned. I'm going to teach you how to survive in the world of the future. We can leave in a couple days, head up to the Boundary Waters."

"Can I bring Micah?"

"Who's Micah?" he asked.

"My friend. He'd love camping."

"This isn't exactly camping, Kaz. I'm taking you up to teach you physical and spiritual survival in preparation for the Revolution."

"Well, Micah likes the outdoors and he's real spiritual."

"Kazimir, you have special gifts passed down to you from your ancestors, and one day I will take you on a vision quest, and what is revealed then will tell you how to bring about a better world. This trip is a preparation for your future vision quest as well as for the Revolution. I want you to take it seriously. Having him along may impede you."

I sighed and squinted at him. His body was eclipsing the sun. "I won't go without him."

When I told Micah, he doubted his parents would share his enthusiasm.

Thomas and Nelly Petty were saved and were sure of it because their hearts were with *Jee–suss*, and they were sure of Micah's too, although he did his best to take the wide and easy road to hell when they weren't watching. What Nelly and Thomas were not so sure of was that they wanted their oldest son, who was bound to be a preacher some day, corrupted by Aeneas and Kazimir Godwin for an entire week.

"The way I see it the problem is three-fold," said Micah. "A kind of trinity in its own right. The first—we'll call it the Father for reference—is that your old man and his friends are well known rabble-rousers, backsliders: they're not straight with the Lord." He broke into an imitation of his mother's voice. *'Micah, I am afraid for your everlasting soul. I have heard rumors about Aeneas Godwin.'*

I finished rolling a joint and handed it to him, then leaned back in the lawn chair. I grinned and listened to the river rush past as Micah lit it and inhaled, coughed a couple times, and passed it back to me. As I smoked, I kept a steady eye on my bobber.

"Second—we'll call this problem the Son—*'Secondly, young man, you have not been doing your work around this house. The dishes, the trash, the lawn. And your room is a pigsty. I feel in recent weeks you are out of integrity with the commitments you have to this family.'*"

"That's rough," I told him.

"Third, the problem of the Holy Spirit. *'Micah, you need to pray and consider with Jee-suss the path of the Lord and seek Him for answers concerning this friend you have made and this trip you intend to take. Seek first the kingdom, Micah, and His righteousness, Micah, and all else will be provided for you... do you understand me, young man?'"*

I gave him a round of applause.

"We never get to go anywhere," Micah told me. "Not with seven kids. When it was just me and Jen and Philip, when I was maybe five, we went to Branson, Missouri. We went to Wisconsin Dells once, and that's it, man. You're so lucky that your dad took you all those places when you were young."

"You're lucky you've got parents who are home."

Micah had promised her that he would spend several days searching his heart and praying earnestly . Meanwhile, he earnestly set about appeasing his mother and father.

To solve the problem of the Son, he saw to it that the backlog of chores was soon done and his brothers and sisters neatly tucked into their beds each night with prayers and Bible stories.

To mollify the Holy Spirit, he explained to his mother that Jesus had told him in a dream that Aeneas Godwin, though a soul adrift, had come from a long line of ministers and was a man of visions and spiritual insight deliberately clouded by the devil. The Lord needed good, God-fearing folk to enter into Aeneas' life and set his sails straight. He assured her that he was of such faith and fortitude to do the job and sensed it was his calling to be a witness to both me and my dad.

"You believe that?" I asked him.

He was quiet for a moment. "Somewhere in me, maybe. I mean, I've been witnessing to you since the day I met you."

"Really?"

"Why else would I hang out with an anti-social like you?"

"Point taken," I said.

Finally, there was the matter of the Father. He explained to his parents that Aeneas Godwin was a big believer in the End Times and an ardent survivalist who planned to teach us prerequisite skills for a successful Armageddon.

"This sat well with my father, who believes the End Times are right around the corner. Of course, it fails in logic. I mean if I am one of the saved, taken in the rapture, then I don't need survival skills, right?"

"I guess so," I said.

"You on the other hand, Kazimir, better get real good at skinning rabbits, you sinning, backsliding rabble-rouser," he grinned. *"For the end is nigh..."*

I could hardly stop laughing. "Micah, when the end comes, your pot-smoking false-prophet ass is gonna be right there with me."

And so when June eighteenth came around, the nine members of the Petty family watched our '68 Dodge van rumble into their driveway. Micah was kissed and hugged and was sent with the Lord into the great Whale that had been prepared for him. And the doors parted and closed about him and there was a great gnashing of gears, and we were on our way.

CHAPTER
TEN

A FALLING STAR STREAKED ACROSS THE SKY; the yellow stripes on
the road pointed to where it had fallen. My hand was out the window,
and I felt the wind whip it like a fly in a hurricane as we rattled down
the highway at seventy miles an hour.

"A good sign, fellas—it went right across the highway out there."
My father pointed to where it fell, where Hercules knelt and aimed
his arrows.

With Micah sprawled in the backseat, we drove all night. At first,
cornfields spread on each side of us, interrupted only by gas stations
and adult-toy stores. Northward, fields gave way to corridors of trees
and a thin strip of stars overhead. Conversation was hard over the
hum of the Whale's engine, but Micah looked contented, dangling
his hand as I did out the window and letting it flap in the breeze.
By three in the morning I had dozed off, and some time later I was
awakened by the bumps in the road. We had slowed and were jolting
down an old lumber road somewhere on the northeastern finger of
Minnesota that juts over Lake Superior. The air smelled of pine and
mist; the sky was of a blue just before sunrise. Finally my dad turned
the motor off.

"Let's get some shut-eye," he said, dragged out our sleeping bags
from the back of the Whale, and collapsed into a coma. I crawled out
of the front seat and dropped off next to him.

"How long you been up?" I asked Micah when I joined the land of
the living the next morning.

"I don't know, maybe an hour. What's for breakfast?"

I lay my head back on the sweater I had balled up for a pillow.
"Whatever we catch, man. We didn't bring anything but the bare essentials, and the bare essential didn't include any food. It's a survival
trip, after all."

He looked at me to see if I was serious. "But the bare essentials do include six bottles of Wild Turkey and an eight-hundred–dollar guitar?"

I nodded.

"Cool. Well, we can go try to catch some trout, eh?"

We slipped two poles and a tackle box from the Whale, made our way down to a little river maybe fifteen feet wide, and worked our way along its banks. Before our first cast, Micah pulled his one-hitter from his pocket and we had our pre-fishing smoke. "One hit each—I only brought the bare essentials."

I exhaled and silken veils of vibration covered the water as it rippled by. A jay's song deconstructed in my brain, each note becoming a separate reality. Tiny trout worked against the current and split upon a rock. And the swirls of their flow became locks of hair and the solemn face of the rock took shape before me. The shadowed impression at its base became a mouth that curved in an O. I listened for its words but they were muffled below the susurrus of the river. Then the face was gone again and I entered into the world of sound and vibration, becoming one with the river in my quest for food. I smiled, and I understood. This was what the rock had come to show me.

Six trout on our line, we made our way through the underbrush and into a haze of campfire smoke. My dad sat in lotus and gazed at the jumping flames. He smiled when he saw us coming. "I see you've begun your survival training, providing for yourselves from the universe's abundance. A noble way to take breakfast."

"Looks like you already had yours, Mr. Godwin," Micah said.

My dad stared at Micah and then raised his half-drunk bottle of Wild Turkey in salute, took a sip, and stared into the fire. "Part of my meditations," he offered.

I held up the trout. "Should I filet them up, Dad?" He nodded.

After breakfast our Revolution training began. We put together a large lean-to of pine branches, sticks, and a big downed trunk. It was a nice day to work, partly cloudy and maybe eighty degrees, the humidity of late summer having not yet set in. "Why can't we just sleep under the stars?" asked Micah.

"You notice how the smoke stayed low to the ground this morning instead of rising to the sky?" my dad answered. "That means it's a low pressure front—the weather is going to change and rain is coming."

"Wouldn't that be high pressure?" Micah said.

"Whatever you call it, we're probably going to see rain in the next twenty-four hours, so keep working on that roof. Cover it with dead leaves. It's gotta be an arm's length in thickness. Then we'll be nice and dry inside."

My dad went off to set some traps, and Micah and I worked the rest of the morning stuffing our lean-to with pine needles and grass.

"Where's he get all this survival stuff?" Micah asked.

"He's been learning all this for years. Books and friends, I guess. We did some when we traveled together, too. Up in the mountains. He says it's preparation for the coming Revolution."

"Does he really believe in the End Times? I mean a Revelation-of-John-style End Times?"

"I don't know. Don't you Pentecostals believe in that stuff?"

"People in my church do. They think it's about to happen with the Russians. But people have been expecting it since Jesus died. Two thousand years now and no End Times."

"End Times is different from the Revolution, I think. The Revolution is my dad and Ephraim's idea. You have to ask him if you want to know more," I told Micah, tired of the religious talk.

"Well, maybe I'll just do that, then."

When we finished we crawled into our lean-to shelter and smoked a little and waited for Dad with our stomachs growling.

My father had set several different types of traps, and we spent hours walking about as he explained each one. Most consisted of heavy rocks propped up by precarious sticks and occasionally some rope.

"So when the End Times come, where do we get the rope?" asked Micah.

"From a hardware store. Or your garage, or your shoes, or your neighbor's garage."

"Okay, but if that's true, couldn't I just get some Bisquick from any of those places too and forego the figure-four deadfall trap?"

My dad chuckled. "I like you, Micah, you're a sharp kid—lazy, but sharp. You know, what you said is all true, kid, and it's good to think about how to use the refuse of mankind; that will be especially helpful in the beginning. But that stuff will run out too, and you'll need know how to catch your own meat—as well as make your own rope, eventually. We can make cordage sometime, but we just got a week here. So keep the hypothetical situations to a minimum and do your best with what I'm teaching; got it?"

"Yes, sir."

After that Dad taught us how to make the snares. One we set on what appeared to be a rabbit path, and we set another outside a rabbit hole. We then spent a few hours trying to whittle old men's faces onto sticks. Now starving, we checked the traps, but nothing had been caught.

"You'll just have to learn to go without, boys," my dad said, leaning against the wheel of the Whale and picking up his guitar. We grabbed our poles and made our way out to the river.

"You guys set those traps out when you traveled?" Micah asked me.

"Yeah, a few times. Silas was more of the trapper. He and I used to set a few behind the house when I was young. It takes time to get them right, though. At first, they never fall when they're supposed to. But Silas could do it, and eventually I could, too."

"Well, it seems to me that the fishing pole is the most efficient survival method yet."

"Sure, but you get those traps set up and you don't even have to be there. That's what makes them so nice. You wait, man, I bet we catch something yet."

Micah pulled out his box. "You want a hit?"

"Not right now. It'll just make me hungry. Let's catch some dinner first."

We landed more trout that evening, including one longer than my forearm. We fried them over a campfire that Micah started with one of dad's bow-and-spindle sets. The night was overcast and smoke filled the woods around us once again. My dad sat back and finished off the rest of his whiskey while we picked the burned trout flesh from our plates.

"So Mr. Godwin—"

"It's Aeneas. You don't need to call me mister anything."

"Oh okay. Sorry. So Aeneas, I was thinking about all this stuff we're getting ready for. We call it the 'End Times,' my family and the church. You call it the 'Revolution,' right? Is there any difference?"

"The Beast is destroying our fields, is enslaving us by the yoke of our economy, is cutting down all the trees and heating up the earth like a can of soup in an oven. It's oppressing our souls and turning us into mechanical workmen unable to feel the glory of existence. It's bent on separating us from our true selves and exploiting our Earth for its malicious ends—"

"The devil, then. This Beast is the devil?"

My dad grew quiet like a bellows empty of wind. "That's what I saw, yeah."

"So who's the Antichrist?"

Dad got up and made his way through the haze to get his guitar. He came back and threw a couple branches on the fire before seating himself.

"You gotta understand something about the book of Revelations, Micah, something your parents may or may not get, but probably not, probably they don't get it. Revelations was a vision. A vision is not a physical truth, it is a different reality than the physical world. Think of the word 'sense,' kid. Make *sense*? Our five *senses*? We are evolutionarily geared only to make sense of what can be *sensed*, that is, what we perceive in the physical world. When we are touched by messages from somewhere else our brains can only perceive them as objects and actions that they know."

"What about like people flying around and stuff in our dreams?"

I asked.

My dad sat down. "Our brains can put any combination of things in this world together no matter how ridiculous. What they cannot do is make up something truly original—it can only make fresh combinations. You understand what I am saying? I can't say much more because we don't have the words. We don't have the words because we don't have the objects or the experience to say what is not sense-ible. But the universe could have any number of things going on that we cannot gauge or control or test with our sciences."

My dad finished off the rest of the bottle and took a seat next to the pile of firewood.

"So you're saying Revelation is like that?" asked Micah.

"I am saying that somewhere in us—maybe just in some of us, I don't know—we might have a different sense. It might have a place in the brain, even."

"So, you're saying that all this about rapture and the Antichrist is just us interpreting religious communication into images that make some kind of sense?"

"Yeah, you got it now. Rapture? Get yourself some guns and some survival skills, you ain't going anywhere. The Antichrist? The paradigm of the world is the Antichrist. And you know what? Your Bible-thumpers and fundamentalists with their clean-shaven faces and their covert prejudice and their Ronald Reagan trickle-down crap are the Antichrist's little cronies. You wanna do God's work, Micah, wake them people up when you get older."

My dad got up and tossed more logs onto the fire and walked off. We watched him fade into the smoke.

"Where's he going?" Micah asked.

"For a walk, I guess."

The fire licked at the edges of the pit. Micah threw another log in and soon it was too hot to sit near. My stomach made a wheezing sound like a coyote yapping, which set Micah laughing. He reached into his pocket and produced his weed. "Your dad's a lunatic." He inhaled, held it, and released. "Or maybe a prophet."

"Or some mixture of the two."

We nodded off by the fire and woke to big drops of rain on our faces. We crawled into the lean-to and slept to the rhythm of raindrops on the handmade roof.

"The rodent skewer, my boys. Ingenious in its efficiency like no other hunting tool ever devised by man or ape."

The early afternoon sun beat down on us, and a sticky heat rose up from a field composed of grass, wild violets, and small hills of loose dirt.

"What about a rock?" Micah asked.

"You have to aim with a rock. With the rodent skewer, you just lay down and wait for a gopher to pop his head out."

"You can miss."

"Aha, Micah, that's where you're wrong. The little fella sees you, and scoots back into his hole. However, as unnatural selection would have it, they almost always scoot six inches down or so, and then they wait for you to go away. And then, boys, is when you strike. You simply jab the stick into the hole—like this—and skewer yourself a gopher or a marmot or whatever."

"Right on," Micah said. "Let's try it. Got to work better than those traps."

It was day four and we had subsisted entirely by the lines of our fishing poles and some unripe raspberries we found along the river. We were hungry and tired and ready for something new. So we lay on our stomachs in that little field, letting the sun soak in, each of us watching a different hole.

"Hey, what lives in these holes anyways?" whispered Micah.

I shrugged and kept my eyes on my hole.

"Hope it isn't a badger," he snorted. I ignored him.

I stilled my breath and tried to concentrate on the sun's heat on my back or the humid grass on my belly. I focused and waited, staring at the hole in the grass, ready to take some furry critter's life to nourish mine. Somewhere a creature used this patch of blackness in the earth to sustain itself. I imagined myself as such a creature. What would be my world if I could crawl into that hole, like Alice, just crawl in and never see daylight again, never see trees or birds or sky, never see Micah, Grandma, or my dad?

The sound of snoring pulled me back to the present moment. I looked over to see my dad's body heaving with the weighted respiration of sleep, his face lying directly in the hole he was supposed to be watching. Micah snickered.

"Master survivalist, Aeneas Godwin," Micah whispered to me and laughed even harder, rolling in the grass.

"Micah, shut up, you're gonna scare off the gopher," I hissed, which only made him convulse further. I shook my head and watched him make a fool of himself. I was so distracted by the two of them I nearly missed it when, out of the corner of my eye, I saw a brief blaze of fur pop from the hole.

I and the gopher exchanged knowing glances, and it ducked back into the hole. For a lone second, I thought I had lost my dinner. Then adrenaline hooked my blood and I rammed my skewer down the tunnel.

A high pitched squeak resounded in the cavern and I felt the gopher jerk back from the stick. The weight of its body resisted against the barbs as I tried to pull it out.

"Oh man, you got one! You got one!" Micah came running over and did a little jig. The noise must have woken my dad because I heard him shouting something, too. I yanked at the gopher, its resistance less now as its life drained from it. I eased the little body out of the earth till I could see his nose, then his ears, and finally his limp sack of a body come into the light.

The skewer had punctured his face above the left eye and protruded out his back. We watched him twitch and spasm into a final stillness, and then my father picked him up by the skewer and turned it in the air.

"You've taken it, Kaz: your first kill of the survival trip. Let's go back and dress him and grill him up for dinner." He handed the stick to me, and I held the gopher in front of myself like a quivering foot-long marshmallow.

"Shouldn't we try to catch a few more?" asked Micah.

"No, gophers are solitary. There aren't any others in this field."

Micah gaped. "You've got to be kidding." He scanned the field full of pockets and tunnels, then turned a disgusted face toward me. "Not to take away the glory of the accomplishment or anything, but that thing won't even feed one of us. Which might work out because I don't know if I even want to eat it."

"It's an experience, Micah," Dad said. "You're learning how to survive in the End Times. Be glad we caught anything."

"Well, can't Kaz and you take your bows and go shoot us some rabbits or deer or something?"

"You need a license and it's gotta be in season," I told him, "and I guess you don't need any of that to hunt gopher."

I looked at the furry little perisher dangling from the stick, two front teeth jutting out.

Micah shook his head. "That's all right, you two dig right in. I'm gonna go catch some more fish and pick some raspberries. And when I do, you're plenty welcome to share in the bounty once again, I don't mind—I've been providing all week." My dad and I stood in the little field next to each other and watched Micah walk back toward camp.

My father's hairy gut protruded well past his belt; threadbare jeans, relics of the seventies, soaked up to his knees and maculated with dirt. His beard hung down to his belly button, its gray and white streaks like cirrus clouds enveloping a mountain.

He grunted as he watched Micah fade from view. "Why the attitude?"

"I don't know. I think he's hungry. We've hardly eaten all week."

"He's been ornery the whole time."

"He's been hungry the whole time."

"Well, I'm hungry too," my dad said. "What do you say we head back and grill this big boy up?" He flicked the gopher in the head with his finger.

"I can't eat that. It reminds me of Sammy."

"Who's Sammy?" Dad asked.

"He was our class pet in first grade."

"You killed this thing with your own hands, Kaz. You take a life like that, you gotta make its sacrifice worth something. By eating it you sustain its energy; you enter into the cycle of life and complete its role in the ecosystem. If you don't eat it, you're destroying that bond that you created when you killed it."

I rolled my eyes.

He shook his head. "Dammit Kaz, sometimes I can't believe you're my son. Don't you understand anything? We kill to sustain our lives and honor the cycles of life and death. By hunting you enter into a pact, a treaty with your prey. You cannot violate that pact."

I looked at the gopher again, tried to imagine eating it, and couldn't get the image of Sammy out of my head. I could still imagine his warm cuddly body nestled up against my stomach. "There's no damn way I'm eating that."

"My God, when did you get so sissy?" he bellowed. "The Beast and his pre-packaged crap is all you want now?"

Then his forearm rammed the side of my head. I went down.

"Now look at what you made me do. Dammit Kaz, get up."

I tried to stand but my head spun. Stars sparkled all around me and some sound rattled in my head like a bag of cockroaches as I raised myself on all fours.

"Get up, dammit!"

I did as I was told. I staggered up and looked him in the eye.

His eyes softened with shame. He looked away, but then back. "What are you looking at? You're my son, and I'll hit you when I see fit. You've gone your whole life with one whack to the head, that ain't much."

We stared at each other.

"Dammit all, it's your kill, you skin it and dress it. I'll eat the whole damn thing myself, but I'm not gonna let it go to waste." He tossed his hunting knife at my feet. I took it.

I went back with him to the campsite and skinned the gopher as best I could while he got a fire going and worked on the fifth bottle of Wild Turkey. I left it in the pan when I was finished and stood up.

"I'm going for a walk."

"Suit yourself," he said and sat down, closed his eyes, took a meditative breath, and took up his guitar.

The side of my head swelled and throbbed. I tried to shrug off what had happened. He had hit me once, that was all. I couldn't get too mad at him.

I wandered a long time through the birch and maple, up a hill, until I came to the little river where we had been fishing. I sat down and listened to its sounds. After a while I started following the river downstream. It was hard going through the bushes, and finally I decided to wade in. The current chilled me to my upper legs, but it wasn't strong. I let the river lift my feet from the gravel and let it float me downstream. Gray clouds in a blue sky went by me as the back of my head dipped into the water. The coolness calmed my aching head.

I shut my eyes, and when I opened them again, her bare feet dangled off the bank above me. Her white dress smeared with dirt and grass stains, those dark curls falling down past her shoulders—she turned and looked at me.

"Eliza! What are you doing here?"

"So not even a 'hello' or 'it's been a long time?' I haven't talked to you in like six years." She laughed and swung her feet back onto the rock. "You disappeared me, remember."

"And now you're back?"

"You called me back."

"No I didn't."

"Yes, you did, or I couldn't have come."

She was more beautiful than I'd remembered.

"You look older," I said.

"I guess I stay the same age as you."

"I guess so."

She stood and spun around. "Still want to get married?"

"You said that was impossible." I felt myself turning red.

"Maybe it is, but I have a feeling you're not going to find anyone else to put up with your sulking."

I couldn't hold back a smile. "How does all this work, Eliza? How do you get to return to me?"

She shrugged. "I'm just a pawn in your little spiritual chess games."

"I've got to be the only fourteen-year-old in Wisconsin with an imaginary friend who won't go away."

She frowned. "If you don't want me around, then let me go, jerk-face. I've got plenty of other things to do with my time."

"Like what?"

"Wouldn't you like to know." She climbed off the bank and waded out to me. "Is this any fun?"

"Better than nothing."

"Can I join you then?"

"If you promise not to bother me if we see Micah or my dad. It's embarrassing. It's like sucking my thumb or something."

She rolled her eyes. "You've become kind-of a jerk."

"Just promise and you can come."

She put her hand over her chest. "Scout's honor—this time. Someday you're going to have to own up to the fact that I'm around, though. I don't want to hide our love forever." And we tilted our heads back onto the water and drifted silently down stream.

After a time, I gazed along the river bank and saw Micah reeling in his line. I tapped Eliza and she did as she promised. I made my way to his side of the stream, stood and slid out of the water dripping wet.

"Where've you been?" he asked.

"Took a walk up the river some and let the current take me back down. Catch anything?"

He held up a rope with five trout strung to it, most of them undersized. "Lots of them in there, but I think we fished out the big ones already. You eat the gopher?"

I shook my head.

He laughed and cast his line back out into the water. "What was your dad thinking not bringing any food along?"

"Won't the Good Lord provide? Isn't there some Bible verse?"

"Very Christian of you, Kaz. *'So do not worry, saying, "What shall we eat?" or "What shall we drink?" For pagans run after all of these things, and your heavenly father knows you need them all. So seek first the kingdom and his righteousness and all else will be provided unto you.'* Is that what you're talking about?"

"Maybe. Seems relevant, doesn't it?" I said.

"Yeah, but he also said to be fishers of men, and I'm not about to eat anybody. At least not yet," said Micah.

"Ha, ha. Let's get back, I'm freakin' cold and hungry," I told him, feeling myself start to shiver. My headache was almost unbearable.

"You wanna smoke a little before we go?"

"Hell, yeah."

A huge fire roared. Dad sat cross-legged playing his guitar as we came back to camp. The sun was about to set, and it was getting a little cooler. I stood near the flames to try to dry.

"Catch anything, Micah?" Dad asked.

"Five little ones," he answered as he bent over and began filleting them on a tree stump. My dad glanced at me and laughed.

"Did Micah catch you in there, too?"

Instead of replying I continued to shiver.

"Kaz, you know getting your clothes soaked is about the worst thing you can do in a survival situation. You get wet and they don't dry this time of day, then you get your sleeping bag wet and you freeze all night and it never gets better. People die like that."

I nodded and kept shivering.

"So you finish off all that gopher in one sitting, Mr. Godwin?" asked Micah.

"Damn good stuff, Micah. Keeps a man's constitution up."

I tried to tune out their banter and I closed my eyes. I was really cold, colder than I should have been considering the fire and how nice it was out still, even with the sun going down. I shut my eyes and concentrated on stopping my body from shivering, concentrated on the warmth of the fire on my back as I turned. My dad started into a fingerstyle song of his that was fast and beautiful. The sound trickled into the fire, rising like steam into the night air. After a time I looked up at the smoke lifting into the sky. A full moon was just breaking over the horizon and one or two stars began to glimmer. I listened to the song and it seemed to transport me to a time long ago, some ancient memory, my fingers reaching out for a forgotten face. I was struck by a flood of homesickness—for Grandma's place, for the trailer, for my family to be together once more, for none of those things that happened ever to have happened. Then I shut it out. I didn't need them. I didn't need any of them.

Micah dropped the fish into the skillet and they began to crackle. "Gopher fat's good for frying," I heard him say.

"Good for eating too," said Dad, putting down his guitar and taking a drink of Wild Turkey.

No matter how hungry and cold, I couldn't handle the smell of the fish frying in gopher fat. I got up and staggered away from the fire.

"You want us to save you some?" Dad called. I shook my head.

I undressed outside the lean-to and crawled into my sleeping bag and lay there listening to them eat the trout. Micah said something I couldn't hear and my dad laughed. Then he started to play his guitar again. After a little while the music stopped and my dad's uneven footsteps came toward the lean-to.

"You all right in there?" he asked, crouching by the entrance.

"No."

"You wanna tell me what's the matter?"

I hesitated for a moment. "Sick."

"You're sick? From not eating, or from thinking about the gopher?"

"No."

He thought a moment. "How's your head?"

"It hurts. Dad, this isn't the Revolution. We're just in some national forest. I don't want to be here."

"That's not your decision to make."

"Well, I'm used to making my own decisions. Grandma's been raising me. You can't come home and expect me to follow your every wish, to do everything you want me to do just because you're my dad."

"When I say 'That's not your decision to make,' Kazimir, I'm not talking about the normal father-son struggles of adolescence. Of course you don't want me telling you what to do. But what I'm talking about here is bigger than me and bigger than you."

"Look, we can hop in the van at any moment and in two hours be eating at a restaurant and sleeping in a motel."

Outside I could hear the crickets now, and Dad slapped at a mosquito. "There's only three days to go. That's nothing."

"What's going on?" Micah called from the fire.

"Maybe you can help me, Micah. Kazimir's spirit is down. He wants to quit. He wants to pack up and drive into town and get some food and a shower. Help me talk him out of this rut."

"Shit, you gotta be kidding, Aeneas, I—"

"Did you just swear?" I asked him, shocked. Micah was a bad apple sometimes, yes, but in the seven years I'd known him I'd never heard him swear.

He seemed surprised himself. "I believe I did. I believe I said 'shit.' Well, how about that—the perfect term to describe this trip. I've had enough of this too. I'd love to get out of here."

My dad started pacing. He looked up at the night sky. "I guess that's my answer, then."

Finally he agreed to sleep in the van, sobering up enough to drive while we packed. After an hour and a half of gathering things and stuffing them into the back of the Whale, disassembling the lean-to, and dispersing the fire—I did this all in the nude, much to Micah's amusement—we were ready to hit the road.

We woke my dad, and soon we were euphoric in the jolt of the wheels over the potholes. In an hour, when we turned onto the highway, the susurrus of pavement soothed and lulled me; and many hours later, when we exited into Duluth, my stomach and I were reawakened by the epicurean neon glow of roadside diners. I looked back at Micah to share the excitement, but he was dreaming soundly on a pile of sleeping bags.

I looked back out the window down the strip of food establishments, trying to ascertain if any were still open. "What time is it?" I whispered to my dad.

"Two-thirty."

"Are we gonna stop for some food?"

"Yep."

"Where?"

"You'll see."

Denny's was the only place along the road that was lit inside, and we passed right by it. The sinking feeling in my stomach was now only partly hunger.

Down the road from the Denny's was a burned-out neon sign signaling Andy's Supermarket and Bait and Tackle Store. The Whale slowed here and my dad flipped off the lights as we turned into the parking lot.

"Can't we get some food before we pull off for the night, dad?"

"Yeah, what about that Denny's back there?" said Micah, now awake.

My father didn't acknowledge his question. "What were you saying a couple of days ago, Micah? This isn't 10,000 B.C. anymore, is it? Primitive isn't necessarily what you guys are gonna need to know when the Revolution comes. You will be living on the rotting carcass of the Beast and his systems—his paradigms. You'll graft plastic and cordage from hardware stores, and you'll be sacking boxes of Bisquick from the charred remains of our temple to industrial agriculture, the supermarket."

He was excited now, which annoyed me.

"We're gonna break into Andy's Supermarket and Bait and Tackle Store?" asked Micah, his voice cracking.

My dad gave his wiseman smile. "We're not breaking in anywhere. We're continuing your survival training." He pointed to three large green dumpsters resting against the back of the store. "Refuse, boys, refuse—the way of the future. Inside those sleeping metal stomachs is the bounty of the modern age. Add up all the good food Americans dump into those things across the country in a day and it would be enough to feed all of humanity."

"Aren't Americans part of humanity?" Micah whispered, nudging me. I shushed him. The last thing I wanted was to delay our meal, such as it might be, to hear my father's answer to that ostensibly rhetorical question. But he was already swinging back a metal lid and working his way over the side.

I got out and followed him into the dumpster, making Micah boost my foot. He stood on a milk crate and watched us for a minute. Soon he tipped back the cover on the dumpster next to us and crawled in himself.

It's difficult to describe the excitement that accompanied our supermarket smorgasbord, but I imagine it's much the same feeling that accompanies the discovery of sunken treasure. Red apples with bruises, oranges with a touch of mold, brown bananas, six bags of Wonder Bread merely a day over their sell-by date, perfectly good mayonnaise to put on it.

Micah found a half-dozen sub sandwiches wrapped in cellophane and tossed them out to me like pop flies, laughing hysterically. I peered over the lip of one dumpster to find my dad already inside, shoveling two-day-old bear claws into his mouth. Moving along, I found four unopened boxes of Cocoa Puffs, and along with them several packages of Bisquick, which I ceremoniously handed over to Micah.

"Hey, Mr. Godwin—I mean Aeneas—look what the Beast left us here!" shouted Micah. Dad's head popped up and he beamed at us.

When we had emptied all the culinary loose change from the dumpsters, we loaded what we needed for the next day and drove off. By that time it was four-thirty in the morning. Dad found an old shipyard along Lake Superior and parked the Whale in a line of run-down vehicles at its gate. We blended right in. One by one we dropped off to sleep as the sun rose and hit the waters of Lake Superior.

The cry of seagulls greeted me when I woke. Micah still slept in the backseat, but the driver's seat was vacant. The backing lights of a forklift came from behind the rusty fence.

I walked out to the lake and took the pathway that ran along the water's edge. It ended at a large pier stretched over the water. Ratty little tourist shanties crowded the pier's edges where it cast itself into the cold blue of Lake Superior. Seagulls cried. A small boat was tied to the piling behind one of the shanties, and it creaked against the pier as the water dipped. An oil tanker diminished far off.

Near the end of the pier were some tourist displays, including a display of various shipwrecks that had occurred on the Lakes. On a big gray map of Superior and Michigan, an X marking the spot of each disaster was accompanied by the name of the boat, the date, and the number drowned. I traced my hand down it and tried to imagine dying like that. I made my way around the displays. There on a bench sat my father.

I could have mistaken him for a statue but for the strands of gray hair blowing in the breeze. A bald patch was beginning to take root on the top of his head, yet the hair around it was as long and curly as ever and hung down past the shoulders of his flannel shirt.

For the first time, I noticed a sadness that seemed to leak out of him. He was a man half-beaten by life and was, at that time, only thirty-seven. Being so young, I thought him old; but what I saw in him wasn't age. It was emptiness.

I touched the welt on the side of my head as I watched him. My whole life to that point I had seen my father as a hero, invincible, a mover of mountains and knower of the secret sums of the world. Now, for the first time, my father no longer seemed to me capable of stepping off the edge of that pier and walking plainly across the water to the oil tanker at the horizon.

He didn't notice the weight of my hand when I placed it on his shoulder, but just stared off into the distance, rhythmically nodding his head. I waited for him, not wanting to wake him from whatever daydream or vision had taken him. On his lap lay his guitar, but his hands rested flat and still over the muted strings. Finally, after a time, he turned and looked up at me without familiarity. Our eyes locked for a moment; he snorted and looked back out to the water.

"I'm sorry," he said.

"It's all right. It doesn't hurt."

He grunted. "I'm sorry because I haven't been around." He wiped his nose. "I—I don't know what's going on sometimes. Honestly, I don't even know where I've been all these six years—there's just big gaps."

"I wondered where you were, too. Grandma and I both did. I guess I thought you had things to do with Ephraim that were more important than us."

"Some dads spend all their time working to provide. They think it's for the best. But the best thing I can do for you all is to try to save the spiritual life of this country. And for this end God just takes me up sometimes, uses me, and leaves me someplace."

"How can you tell it's God, Dad?"

"When it happens—I know. When I get control of myself again, it's different. It's like now. I can talk, I can have conversations. Then— it's like I'm a puppet."

"Is that what it's like to talk to God?"

He pinched his forehead between his thumb and index finger. "Yes."

"I still breathe and meditate and pray every night like you told me to," I lied. "I just don't hear God like you do."

He didn't look at me, just gazed over the water. But I could feel his resolve change, his moment of doubt pass.

He sighed and stood up. "We'll have to watch you, see how you grow. You need to continue with your studies even when I'm not there."

"I'll try," I told him, though I knew I wouldn't.

He gave me a long look. "Let's go," he said.

CHAPTER ELEVEN

For weeks he stayed with us, working on the Whale or running errands for Grandma in the day and leaving every night to visit people he knew in the area. I slept all day the first day back from up north, and in order to avoid him, I continued the habit. I woke in the evenings, floated about the house when he had gone out for the night.

"What happened between you two?" Grandma asked me one night. She mended a pair of my shorts as she sat on the porch. Her forehead creased in the light of her sewing lamp.

"Nothing really. I'm just a little tired of him, you know?"

"Haven't seen him much until recently. Now he's around all the time, eh?"

"Yeah."

She nodded. "He's pretty intense."

"That's about right."

When I did see my father he seemed increasingly agitated. He paced about the house in the evening as he waited to go out. He played his guitar on the porch as the sun went down. It was a time he didn't want to be disturbed. When he was done, he'd wander down to the river and back. As much as his presence made me uneasy, I also felt a need to be seen by him, a need for him to be here.

Dinners were small talk and lots of silence. On Sundays Roald and Jethro came over to play horseshoes and cards. Dad enjoyed seeing Jethro again. But when they were gone he continued to pace and wander about by himself.

One evening, I woke as the sun was hitting the horizon. Out the window I could see my father at the back of the Whale putting boxes in. A white van was parked behind him. A dark figure sat in the driver's seat.

The low rattle of the Whale idling filled the air outside as I opened the screen porch.

"What are you up to?" I asked as I neared him. He stood up from where he was stuffing another crate into the back.

"Hey, Kaz." He half-smiled. "Hey, I decided I better get going again."

A cardinal sang in the willow. "What? Were you just going to leave without saying goodbye?"

"No, no, I was going to come up and say goodbye when I had this stuff packed." He shifted his weight and put his hands in his pockets. "Grandma went into town. I told her I was going a few nights ago, and I said goodbye just before. I would've told you earlier, but you haven't been around much."

"When are you going to be back?"

"Oh, not for a while I think. Not for a long time," he said looking up at the sky. "I've got important things and well, I just don't feel comfortable settling here, I guess. I'd take you but you got to go to high school."

"That's all right, I wouldn't want to go anyways."

"I see." He closed the back door to the Whale and waved at the guy in the white van. The fellow backed out of the driveway and took off. "I've got to go where the Spirit leads me, you know."

"I guess. Or maybe you don't like staying in one place."

"It's like I was saying, sometimes I don't even know where I go or how I get there. I'm feeling that now. Going to do some work for Ephraim, and then just get out there wherever the universe leads me."

He walked over to me, held out his arms. "Well, I gotta go now. I'm not real good at goodbyes." He gave me a hug. His body seemed thinner, even though it was covered in a wool flannel that was completely out of season.

"High school this fall, huh?" he said as he got into the Whale. "Boys start getting to be real assholes around this time. I got into a lot of fights in high school—it was before I got religious."

"Right."

He shut the door, which swung open again so he slammed it several times until it stuck. "Well, don't take any shit from anyone," he added out the window. "You can be peaceful later on. If you get into a fight, don't mess around. Fights aren't boxing matches—you fight to kill and you'll win without needing to kill. Rips his nuts off."

"I'll be sure to do that."

"Take care, son. Say bye to Micah, take care of Grandma."

Then he pulled out of the driveway. A cardinal lifted from the willow and followed the Whale down the road. I felt empty. Anxious. I went to the tipi and smoked.

It would be years before I saw him again.

I went to the public high school. Micah went to a small Christian school. We talked on the phone and got together every weekend. I made no more friends. I skied in the winters and studied, read philosophy and nineteenth-century classics. I canoed up and down the Kickapoo fishing, camping, and getting high. I read Thoreau and Whitman. I ignored girls and they ignored me. I drifted through high school an unknown, using all my sick days to cut out. At times, I dreamed of getting out of Wisconsin—following the universe's call, or whatever, back to the dry stretches of the southwest or the spine of the Rockies. But then I'd sit up in the hills and watch the fawns tottering about, or I'd scour the land after a rainfall and follow the tracks of a bobcat, and I'd feel complete again, right here in this dinky little place.

In the falls Grandma and I harvested our vegetables and our apples and pickled, canned, mashed, and sauced for weeks. Micah came to help. Jethro came to help. Roald came every Sunday for horseshoes and whiskeys-and-Coke. The sun went up and down. The leaves fell off trees. Micah and I harvested the marijuana in the forest. We sold it to his friends. I hid my money in the forest, hoping to save it for college, hoping to use it to get away. Micah continued to smoke and play music his parents didn't like.

All in all, I was becoming the average angst-driven, maladjusted, introverted youth. I had chosen to be content to drift through school toward college and some inoffensive job. Maybe I thought that in this way I could escape, that I would manage to slip off the hook of God or Ephraim or whatever had caught my father for its own uses. Maybe I thought I could cut the line that bound me to my family history.

School let out in June's haze and I drifted into the summer before my senior year. I spent three months up on Roald's farm, saving cash and generally busting my ass in the dirt and hay. Roald drove me hard, doing his best to whip the slacker-hippy tendencies right out of me. He was determined to show me how great a farmer's life was. I kept a stash in the barn and smoked every evening to escape.

Micah worked as a counselor for most of the summer at a Christian boot camp up north, so I hadn't seen him much. But near the end of August I finished working for Roald, and Micah and I took Greg's canoe out of the shed, headed down the Kickapoo to Wildcat Mountain, and settled into an illegal campsite far away from the tourist population. There the sun lit our bodies as we laughed, fished, and smoked till our brains were good and fried. I had shot up to the height of my father, and was lean and strong from the summer's work. It felt good to ease my spinners into the river again with my old friend.

"All we've done here is fish and smoke," Micah said as I handed him back the pipe.

"Paradise," I told him and cast my line again.

"You're an addict, you know," he said.

"I know."

"Hey—what's the difference between drugs and food?" Micah asked.

"What?"

"Nothing. *Nothing* is the difference. Food tips the chemical teeter-totters in your body. So do drugs. There's no real difference. Drugs are just stronger, heavier—like fat kids who plop down and shoot you up to the sky." His glasses magnified constellations, galaxies, nebulas of pimples and freckles. Three years into high school and he still didn't shave.

"I'm not in your Future Ministers of America fraternity, my friend.

So who are you trying to convince?"

"The whole world is a drug. God has us swimming in drugs, chemical cocktails of food and drink."

"Is that what they're teaching you at your Christo-Nazi high school?"

"You know they don't even believe in chemicals—the word isn't mentioned in the Bible. I gotta learn science in my spare time."

"That's science? Sounds like opinion," I told him. I felt the tug on my line. "Got one."

We had a regular genocide going on along the river bank, brookies waiting on blue strings for their imminent deaths. Micah lit his pipe again as I reeled in a trout the size of a hammer handle. He sucked in and held the smoke in his mouth, squatted down and unhooked the brookie from my line. He spread its gills with his thumb, and holding his lips to their pink flesh, exhaled into it. It stopped fighting, settled as if trying to pay attention to something new. It glanced at me. "Groovy," the fish said. I chuckled. Then Micah let it down to the water and swayed it gently until it found its bearing. Micah's hand relaxed its paternal grip. The fish shivered and slid away. We watched it opalesce in the light of the sun and merge into the shadows of the river, back behind the fallen tree where I had caught it.

"*Deus vult,*" I whispered.

We were two little gods of the river. We had caught our limit, so from then on we blew smoke into every catch as we released it to the water. Is it an epiphany? I wondered. A piscine satori? Will life ever be the same to them now that they've seen the sun and the land? And at base, aren't our impulses or goals, emotions and thoughts just nerve and flesh too? How can we know God any more than these fish can?

"Breathing," I said that evening as we lay along the banks, our faces pressed up against the sunset. "It's a drug; monks control it to get religious experience. Every breath exchanges oxygen and carbon dioxide."

"It's all drugs: seeing, hearing, touching, tasting, breathing. We want dope or coke or whatever so we can see *past* the chemicals, to see behind things. Every drug is just a cry for God." We listened to the geese passing. The smoke from our cook-fire filled the air. The water dappled by sunlight looked like a tattered party dress.

My mind slipped back to my father: his absence worried me. I hadn't seen him since the survival trip, yet I knew he watched me. He followed me. Or someone from Ephraim's group did. They watched me and I had not yet figured when they did it, or where, or how.

"I was thinking…" started Micah. "You remember Oldenburg from my old church group?"

I nodded.

"I ran into him on Tuesday, we caught up a little."

I looked him over. If I were an astrologer, what portentous signs would I find in his pimple galaxies? His moppy blond hair was almost pink in the evening sun. I leaned over and poked at the fish that fried on the fire.

Micah stood and went over to where the canoe was stashed in the rocks, pulled it a little farther onto shore. "Well, he's got a nice place, redone '65 Mustang, this killer stereo. I asked him what he was doing with himself, you know? Not like there's a lot of work in Viroqua. 'A little of this, a little of that,' he tells me. I told him I was working as a camp counselor up north, maybe looking for something that pays better. So he says, 'Hey man, you should work for me,' and I say, 'What do you mean?' He grins at me and says, 'You *know* what I do,' and I nod because right then, I figure it out."

"Where's this going, Micah? What are we talking about here?"

"Hold on, man. 'How much can I make?' I ask him. 'As much as you want.' He gives me his number and says if I need work to give him a call."

I pulled my fishing hat over my eyes and watched water lap up on the little island where we were camped. Micah took a fork and pulled some flesh off the fish. "They're done," he told me. We ate in silence.

"So, what's this involve?"

"Delivery service."

"That's why you need me? Cause I can get my Grandma's car?"

"I'd want you in anyway. This could be big money, man. More than we make piddling about with our little crops. You want to go to Madison, I want to go to seminary, and we need the money."

"And if we get caught—great. Future priest—"

"Minister. Catholics have priests."

"Whatever. Future minister caught with local anti-social running drugs? Sounds like a great headline."

"Oh come on, half the pot supply in the four state area is grown in our little corner. This stuff goes on everyday and no one gets caught."

"You trying to get kicked out of your little nutball school?"

"Maybe. My parents can't really afford it anyway. I either finish with a flurry or go out with a bang."

"My Grandma would be so pissed. She doesn't want me to end up like my dad."

"Were talking about transporting drugs—drugs that should probably be legal anyway. You aren't touring the country beating the pulp out of people and joining cults."

"I don't wanna get caught, Micah. I get into Madison and get the hell out of here. No more living at Grandma's, no more ghosts."

"Kaz, this money's your ticket out. Besides, it's a little hypocritical of you to smoke like you do but refuse to accommodate those who don't have their own supply."

I thought some more as I packed our little pipe for an after-dinner smoke. The sun went down on our paradisiacal canoe trip. Tomorrow we'd be back in civilization, a place where I didn't have many allies.

We lay out and finished the pipe. Stars popped into the sky above.

"Let me think about it."

A symphony of frogs began with a few bold calls that lengthened and twisted in my mind as I went deep into their world of sound. Micah's inhalations and exhalations joined in counterpoint. The frogs' calls transformed into the calls of sparrows, then into human voices. "Hello," they said. And the trees replied, "Good evening." I recognized their voices but could not place them. I lay awake, so stoned and tired

I could not wrest control of my head. Drumming and chanting filled my ears, and I felt a dark presence that I could not see. Then I felt it in my back. Reaching under my sleeping bag, I unearthed a fish hook.

Soon I was drifting in and out of dreams, waking each time to a swirl of stars and meteorites, the rush of river voices. Was it God speaking?

I drifted off and woke one more time in the night to feel the gaze of eyes pinning me to the sand. Someone wanted to speak, but nothing came, only a mute blackness I could make no sense of. A fish jumped. I could feel breath in my hair, the voice of some secret that I did not have the ears to hear. Father? I wondered.

And then I realized: Jeremiah. He was next to me, his mute voice upon me, and yet I was watched from across the river. I crawled out of my sleeping bag and walked down the bank, checking to see if the eyes followed.

Wandering along the damp sand, remembering the story of Jeremiah that my father had told me, I could still sense the eyes watching me, and I knew whose they were. In whatever way they could, I knew they watched me.

Chapter Twelve

When we got home from the camping trip, I went to the trunks of old memories to see what they would hold. I breathed in the way my father had taught me. I couldn't help it if it was part of my father's ridiculous religious rigmarole, it settled my mind. What sounded like distant talk radio crackled in and out of the air. Grandma was below me in the kitchen. I pulled the pipe out of my pocket and took a hit, letting it go out the attic window. Now I was calm, and I sat back down.

I lifted the top of one trunk and began to sift through the papers and clothing and old trinkets, pulling out everything that pertained to Jeremiah. There wasn't much: an old newspaper clipping about the tornado, a wool slouch hat with his initials embroidered into the band. Downstairs, the phone rang. I sifted through other items in the trunk: a Civil War hat, journals, a lacy dress, a pocket knife. At the bottom, rocks. I pulled them out. They were smooth and sharp. Not rocks—arrowheads; they had spilled from a cigar box. I opened the box to put them back in with the others, letting them slip between my fingers. The last one was not right. I clenched my fist quickly, before it could escape, and slowly reopened my fingers, exposing a fish hook made of aged bone. Gingerly, I held it up to the fading sunlight, and it seemed to whisper to me. I held it to my ear. "Tell me what you've come to tell me, Jeremiah." But it said nothing more.

"Kaz! Micah's on the phone," Grandma called up the stairs. I put the hook into my pocket and went down.

"What's up?" he greeted me.

"Just looking through some old family stuff."

"Great. Good for a man to know his roots. So, any thoughts on my idea?"

I paused first. "Let's do it." My heart beat fast even as I said it. As much as the idea scared me, the money enticed me. My whole life had been an economic millstone around Grandma's neck, and she had no money for college. What I had in the coffee can in the forest and the money I had from my summer work at Roald's amounted to a little over three thousand dollars. I would need more.

"Fine. So it'll go something like this. On Saturday, whomever—whomever will probably just be Oldenburg but could be somebody else—will call your Grandma's, give us a whenever to meet the whoever and put the whatever into our car. Whomever will tell us to go wherever. Then whoever passes us a bag with our cash in it, and we go deliver."

"How much?"

"Don't know yet."

"Right, so you sleep over Saturday, I get the station wagon Sunday?"

"That's what I'm thinking."

"Fine. And Micah?"

"Yeah?"

"You better look up how to use objective cases, man. I don't think you've got them right."

We hung up. I took the little hook out of my pocket and placed it to my ear. I couldn't hear a thing. I shook it. Still nothing.

"What the hell are you doing, Kazimir?" Grandma asked. She'd been watching me.

I held out the hook. "You seen this before?"

Grandma glanced at it. "Looks like an Indian fishing hook."

"I just found it up in Grandpa's old arrowhead box." Then I pulled out the arrowhead that I had found the night before. "And I found this beneath me last night."

She took it and looked at it. "Another arrowhead."

"Yeah, weird huh—that the hook was in the arrowhead box and the arrowhead was by the river."

"I guess." She seemed to eye me suspiciously. I took it back from her.

That Saturday I picked up Micah and we had dinner with Grandma. After a game of rummy, we hauled out our sleeping bags and headed up into the forest along the river and down to the tipi Dad had been so glad to see me build. *You gotta know how to do this stuff, Kaz, when the Revolution comes you'll be living in style.* An angry hippy, that's all my old man was—a hippy gone sour.

"Where's the old man nowadays?" asked Micah as we set up.

I laughed. "Shit, I don't know. He's all over, living off berries and gophers, healing people with his guitar or whatever."

"Preparing for the Revolution?"

"Yeah. Lots of traveling preachers, prophets in my line."

"I'm familiar with that type; I just can't figure out how you turned out Catholic. Your people ought to be in my church."

"Some of them probably were. But Grandma's a German Catholic. It was all the rage around here a hundred years ago," I told him.

After falling silent a moment Micah asked, "Have you seen anything yourself? Any visions?"

I paused, tried to pitch my voice to be casual. "Nah. My dad swears there are ghosts here, though."

"He is crazy, but he might be right about that. Cause I've seen some pretty crazy stuff at church, man: speaking in tongues, possession, stuff that you wouldn't believe." He grinned, then was serious. "You should come sometime. God speaks there."

"Always the missionary. You're probably right, I wouldn't believe it. God apparently speaks in LSD, too. Anyway, how do I know it's the voice of God and not just me thinking it is? Or maybe it's just the devil doing his God impression to convince me of something, huh?"

"You ask—or you cast him out." He thought about this more. "But maybe those are just rules we make up to give credence to our own ideas. I mean, people do all sorts of crazy shit saying God told them to do it: Charles Manson, Jonestown."

I'd almost told him about the voices that I had been hearing, the native relics that I had been finding. But after the Jonestown reference I thought I'd let it lie. "You know as well as I do it's not necessarily the spiritual seeking that causes all that, Micah. It can cause just as much good. And people do a hell of a lot of bad stuff without God being involved at all. People do a lot of bad stuff, period. Hitler was no Christian. Genghis Khan, Pol Pot, Napoleon."

"Well what's the difference then, whether you hear God or not?" Micah asked. "What's the difference between all that spiritual insight and hallucination?"

That floored me for a moment. "Nothing, I guess. We do this drug run and all it is maybe is selling tickets to an amusement park of God, that's all. But some of us want more than an amusement park ride. Some of us want more than to live in a constant spectacle."

"Like you? Like me? Do we want more than that?" He said it with his usual ardor, but there was a weakness, a coloring of gloom, to the content. I didn't want him to become melancholy—not Micah. "Anyways, let's hotbox this tipi," he said.

We smoked until we could hardly remember our names and lay still in the ether of darkness. My head floated after the calls of barred owls to distant places. Only worry, the worry of who watched and how and what would come tomorrow, tethered me to this world.

In the night I awoke to something probing around my sleeping bag. I froze in fright as it searched over me. I breathed, I controlled my breath to keep my mind still. It touched my leg, my stomach, my chest. Then it was gone.

"Come here," whispered a voice I recognized but could not name. I crawled out of my sleeping bag and walked down to the river. "Come here," it whispered again. I thought it was coming from the bank, maybe from another arrowhead or hook, and I dug around on my hands and knees to see what I could find on that moonless night.

"Come here."

And this time I realized the voice was the river itself. The current rippled and swung and grew into a chorus of whispers.

A hand touched my shoulder and I jumped. It was Eliza.

"Dammit, Eliza, don't scare me like that." I settled myself down. "What do you think it wants from me?" I asked her.

"What does *what* want?"

"Whatever's whispering that."

"What's whispering *what*?"

"That."

"Huh?"

"Oh, go away," I told her and she did.

I sat down by the bank, and took the hook from my pocket. I rubbed it and listened. But nothing again was said. Nothing but the Kickapoo winding its long way to the ocean.

I didn't sleep. By morning my head felt like a bucket of pancake mix. I hit the pipe a little more to take the edge off. At first light I staggered through the fog to the house. I decided to cook up some waffles for the three of us.

"Mornin' Kaz. Micah up yet?" Enter Grandma in her bathrobe.

"Still."

"Still ... what?"

"Still sleeping."

"What are your plans?"

"I don't know."

She nudged the phone. "You told me you were going fishing with the Oldenburg boy. You should give him a call. I want to go to church this morning, so you need to drive me."

"I'm not calling him. I don't know him. He's Micah's ... friend."

"Oh, it'll be fine. He's a nice boy. I used to babysit him, you know."

She did? What weird world was this? "No, I can't call him. He'll call soon enough, I'm sure."

"You gotta learn to reach out a little, Kaz."

I escaped to the bathroom, splashed warm water over my face, and brushed my teeth. I looked at myself and didn't recognize me. The border between my hair and the air seemed to dissolve. I needed to sleep. I filled the sink and washed my face again. The sound of Grandma talking came through the door.

"Hello, Kevin, this is Mary Godwin. Did I wake you, dear? ... Good. We're trying to work out plans for the day. What time did you want to meet Kaz and Micah ? Oh, all right. I'll tell them. Okay, bye-bye."

I was out in the kitchen to hear her hang up. "What the hell are you doing?" I asked.

"I called Kevin for you. He's such a nice boy; I'm sure you'll get along with him.

"Did he cancel?" I asked.

She shook her head. "Kaz, you'll get along with him, don't be so worried. He said to meet him at three."

"Where?"

"At his place in Viroqua. That'll work fine. You can drive me in, drop Micah at his place for church, and pick me up. Then you can have the wagon the rest of the afternoon."

I walked into the church as they were taking communion. Long rows of Catholics swayed in the aisle like cattle to a slaughter. I crossed and genuflected and took a seat next to no one in particular. I closed my eyes but couldn't sleep there, feeling like a fish out of water. I relived my younger days, when Grandma would take me to church. When did I stop coming along? I couldn't remember.

Remarks were made and the closing hymn was mumbled off by the congregation like children caught cheating on a test. I felt the priest and his entourage drift past me. *From out of the depths, I cry out to you, O Lord.* Someone whispered to me, someone brushed my shoulder. I opened my eyes and followed behind with the rest of the congregation.

"You look sick," Grandma said as I drove her home. "Are you all right?"

"Micah and I were up all night talking. I'm pretty tired."

"Maybe you shouldn't go."

"No, I'd like to meet Kevin. He sounds nice."

"Well that's awful social of you."

"What's that supposed to mean?"

"It means you've lived here your whole life and made one friend. I'm happy you're looking forward to meeting Kevin. It's nice is all."

"Why do you go to church?" I asked her. "I mean, is it just a social thing to you, or do you find some happiness or what?"

"Oh, I don't know, lots of reasons."

"Do you pray and stuff?"

"Yeah, I pray. I think it's important to pray."

"But you swear like a sailor and you drink and stuff. That's not very Jesus-y."

"What are you talking about? He turned all that water into wine. And he had a temper worse than a little swearing. It was just righteous anger."

"How come you stopped making me go to church?"

"Oh, what's the use? You'll come to whatever religion you come to."

"Like my father?" It came out harsh, harsher than I'd intended. Grandma sighed.

"What do you know about Ephraim?" I asked her.

"Nothing. Absolutely nothing. When your dad started coming around with that prophet crap, I told him to stuff it. I don't want to know anything about it. I don't want to know anything your father does out west."

"Was Silas into it? Or Leanna?"

"Silas would listen. He always listened to Aeneas, but religion was never his cup of tea. Leanna—I doubt it. Her and her beads and her incense and her hippy streak. She didn't like all your Dad's talk about a God. She preferred words like 'Universal Spirit' or 'Creator.' Like it makes a difference what you call something we can't name anyway." We were quiet for a while. "You know what I pray for you, Kazimir?"

"I didn't know you prayed for me."

"I do. I do all the time. This is what I pray—a variation of an old Catholic prayer—*Lord, he believes, help him in his unbelief.*"

"I do believe, Grandma. I just don't know what it is I believe in."

"Careful with that," she told me.

I dropped Grandma off at twelve-thirty. I put my fishing pole and tackle box in the back of the station wagon to keep up the illusion that we were going fishing. I stopped for gas and wound my way down back roads to Micah's place. It was one-thirty.

Micah's little brothers and sisters were chasing him, hanging on his shirt and legs. They pulled him to the ground and piled on top of him. When he saw me he waved and extricated himself to go into the house and clean up.

"Why, hello there, Kazimir."

I jumped at the sound of the voice and spun around. Micah's dad grinned at me like the Cheshire cat in a polo shirt.

"Hello, Mr. Petty. How are you doing?"

"Oh fine, fine. Glorious day the Lord has given us, isn't it?"

"Yep, yep, sure is," I replied into his vacuous smile.

"What are you two up to?"

I drew a blank. "Oh, you know, a little of this, a little of that."

"Oh fine." He glanced into the car. "Fishing, I suppose?"

"Yep, yep, sure, there'll be some fishing."

"Fine, fine."

"Yep … yep."

He continued his smile. "Nice and fine."

"Yep."

We would've continued our witty banter indefinitely had not Micah emerged at that point.

Mr. Petty gave him a peck on the cheek. We got into the car, and as we drove away, he reminded Micah that Jesus did indeed love him.

"He loves you too, Kazimir."

"Well, tell him thanks for me, Mr. Petty," I called out the window.

"Pull out over there," Micah said as I turned out of the driveway. I pulled onto a side road and we smoked our pipe.

"You're an addict," he told me.

"Tell me about it." I restarted the engine.

Now the handful of hooks and arrowheads in my pocket felt heavy and I pulled them out. I was surprised to see that they had morphed into human eyes. This is what they were. Eyes, and they were the ones who'd been watching me.

I cracked open the window and let them slip into the running air.

"What are you doing?" Micah asked.

"Throwing something away."

He looked back, and then shook his head. "It's a hundred and fifty dollar fine for littering."

"I'll risk it."

We found Oldenburg's place right around three o'clock. A cherry-red '65 Mustang was parked out front, and there was Oldenburg washing it down. He was shirtless with a pair of black jeans vacuumed sealed to his legs. He was thin in all places but his mullet, which stuck out from the back of his head like a game of pick-up sticks. A narrow, chiseled face was half-covered by a pair of aviator glasses, and the reflection of the station wagon flashed in them as he watched us pull up.

"Hey, hey, hey, what's happening, fellas?" Water trickled from his hose and he looked over the top of his sunglasses at me. "You Kazimir?"

I nodded.

He laughed. "Woooah, dude, you look just like your old man. You know your Grandma used to babysit me?"

"Yeah, she mentioned it the other day."

"Oh man! I barely remember that, I was like three or four, you know. You weren't even born."

Micah leaned out his window and motioned Kevin over. "Kevin, you got the—the—you know?"

He looked down at Micah. "Wooaah, little man, hold your fookin' horses." He leaned in and lowered his voice. "Let's go on upstairs, make it look like a visit, you know. My landlord is home."

Oldenburg lived in an apartment above a detached garage, decorated with all the accoutrements one would expect from a twenty-year-old with no child support to pay yet. We came up the stairs and through the kitchen that reeked of stale beer and took a seat on the zebra skin couch. Kevin slouched in the leopard print chair. A red fur rug spilled like a pool of shaggy blood toward a glass coffee table. Displayed on this table were the requisite lava lamp, a two-foot-long bong, and a pair of Roman sword replicas. Along the far wall were a huge stereo system, a thirty-inch TV, and a BETA video-cassette player that blinked 12:00. An electric guitar in the shape of a red V further displayed his virility. Shelves lined every wall, and from these an array of hard liquor bottles and empty beer cans—Blatz, Wild Turkey, Old Style, Jim Beam—stared down at us like spectators in the coliseum.

Kevin reached back and pulled a few cans of Blatz from a mini-fridge obscured by his easy chair and tossed them to us. "Wow, Kazimir fookin' Godwin. What brings you here?" He cracked his beer open and took a sip.

"Oh, you know, interested in making a little extra money."

He shook his head. "I never thought I'd be working with Aeneas's son. Wow. The world works in funny ways, man."

"You know my dad?"

"Oh hell yeah, he's a legend, man. Apparently one crazy S.O.B. when he was younger."

"Yeah, I guess so."

"Used to do shit like this too, you know. Like father like son."

"Sure, like father like son."

"So didn't he, you know, start losing it?"

"Piss off, man. We came here to do some work, not for twenty questions about my dad."

Kevin put up his hands. "Wooaah, back off pit bull, I'm just making conversation."

Micah cut in. "Hey, Kevin, can we just get to it?"

Oldenburg looked over at him a second, then laughed and leaned back in his chair. "Man, you guys are way on edge. Hold your fookin' horses, you know, you don't have to be there till eight and it's only a forty-five minute drive, okay? It's an easy little run I'm setting you up with; there's nothing to it." He sucked down about half his beer, and leaned over the coffee table. "Look here man." He held out his hand

and a pile of mushrooms magically appeared in it. "We'll have these for lunch and it'll be like we're old friends again for the very first time. I'll get your delivery and tell you where to go, and you can be on your merry way. Stop and go fishing or something, you got the time."

He looked at us and we nodded at him, took the mushrooms. I leaned back into the couch and closed my eyes. I could hear him moving things around, the swords sliding across the glass and Hot Rod magazines, but even with my eyes closed the whole world spun like I was out at sea. I sank deeper into the couch and heard Micah's voice as he made conversation with Kevin.

I fingered the bone hook in my pocket, trying to make it whisper. "What is that thing you're always touching?" came Eliza's voice from behind me. I hadn't asked her to come.

"It's just a fucking fish hook!" I yelled out loud. I opened my eyes and Micah and Kevin were looking at me. Micah smiled. "So it is."

I closed my eyes again. Eliza was gone, but now someone else had come in, come across the linoleum and into the living room. Kevin talked to this person, and I could feel them looking at me, but I couldn't make out what they were saying. Not kind, whatever it was. No one ever had anything kind to say.

I heard Micah take a pull off the bong and cough. Things grew quiet, and I sank into the couch like a bowling ball in a black hole. I felt this new person's stare: angry, tight, hostile. He would kill me if I slept. He was that kind of person.

"Kaz." Micah nudged me. I opened my eyes. "You fall asleep?"

I shook my head and looked around. Kevin was staring at me over the top of his beer; Micah held out the bong and I took it. He lit it and I sucked the whole thing down; my lungs felt like two trees in a forest fire, and I went into a paroxysm.

A short man wearing a vest and a wool slouch hat stood in the kitchen. He opened a dark, cavernous mouth and spoke wordlessly, then leaned against the fridge with his arms crossed and stared at me. I looked away.

The world spun again and I heard Micah laugh at something

Kevin said. His laughter shot off into the distance, through windows, grazing trees, over hills. The man in the kitchen kept staring.

I closed my eyes again. I began to feel a great weight on my chest, and I gaped at the air with my mouth. Then what felt like a hook sank into my esophagus, as if I had swallowed something sharp and cold. I screamed and sat up, thinking the man had shoved one of the swords down my throat while I slept.

Micah stood. "We're going." He held up a plastic grocery bag. "Kevin gave me directions."

I got up and followed him out the door. "Where's Kevin?"

"He's talking on the phone with somebody."

The man was gone from the kitchen. Good thing: I would've strangled him right there.

"You all right to drive?" he asked as we went down the stairs.

"Fine."

Out in the car, Micah gave me directions to the parking lot in La-Crosse where we were to be at eight sharp. He put the package inside my tackle box for good measure, and we were off.

"You know him from church?" I asked.

He thumbed through an envelope of bills. "Man, there's two hundred bucks in here. He said we would get the other half when we get back. The other half? That's two hundred apiece."

"The next time we do this, I don't want that crazy bastard around."

"Who? Kevin?" He thumbed through the bills.

"No, that whack-job in the kitchen."

"I don't know who you're talking about."

"He came in for a while and was just staring at me."

"Maybe it was his landlord."

I tried to focus on my driving but kept slowing down and speeding up. I saw people by the side of the road in bonnets, men with wide mustaches. The sun was getting near the western horizon; shadows launched themselves from the tops of trees onto the road. My head spun and ached.

"Do you think those mushrooms were laced?" I asked.

"Could've been. Kevin's pretty wacky. But I didn't feel—"

"Kind of funny that Kevin knows my dad," I cut in.

"Small world. Two hundred when we get back, man. We could do this a few times a week, man that's good money...." Micah kept talking. Birds flew across the road and turned and flew back. They're practicing, they're practicing, I thought to myself. Practicing for the journey east or west or whatever direction they're going—south, probably south. Going to slip the winter like slipping a punch. A mother and daughter walked on the side of the road, dressed like they were from the old West.

We could go fishing. We had time, we had all the time in the world. They turned to look at me as I drove by. Were they real or was I hallucinating? Were the birds real? Then the short man was there beside us again. The fish hook bit into my leg.

"KAZ, BUGGY!"

I jerked the wheel. Ran the brake to the ground. The orange triangle on the back of a buggy was inches from my bumper. The smell of brake fluid, the shake of the wheel on the gravel shoulder. Don't hit it don't hit it, don't let it be real.

Hallucinations don't go *thump.*

We smashed into it at thirty miles an hour. Its rear end slid up the hood of the station wagon until it lodged firmly against the window. The big orange triangle covered my view. As I slowed, I felt it shift forward, so I had the good sense to speed up just fast enough to keep up with the horses that pulled the thing. The horse-driver eased us all onto the shoulder, steadily slowing, until we came to a stop.

I killed the engine and we both sat there a second. The whole world was filled with brake smoke. From around the buggy came a large bearded man in overalls and a fishing hat.

"You okay?" I asked.

"Yes, we are fine." He looked at me closely. "Art thou mad?"

The Amish. This is Amish country, and I had hit an Amish buggy. It was no hallucination. I turned around to see if the people walking along the road were there: nothing. I turned back and the man was still staring me down.

The man's daughter climbed down and ran to hide behind his leg.

I could've killed them. Could've killed them both. The little girl holding onto her dad's pant leg and biting her finger, the man in the straw hat. He looked twenty-three, maybe twenty-four, that was all. Just going about his farm work on an August evening, let his daughter come along for the ride, and I'd almost killed them.

Hay flitted about the air like strands of hair. The whole thing was full of hay. Some had poured out onto the front windshield, down onto the ground, right to my feet.

"Oh God, I'm sorry, I'm so sorry," I franticized, pacing about.

The safety triangle was bent, but the buggy had escaped any real damage. I suggested I could back out and let the buggy fall to the ground and be on my way. He didn't like my idea, instead wanted us to hold up the back end while he rolled the axle back in place. The wood that held it in was split, but he figured he could make it the quarter mile to his brother's farm. We were agreeable to anything. Micah and I went to each side of the buggy and lifted. The Amish guy rolled the car back in neutral and then went to roll the axle. His little girl had moved off to the ditch and watched me as I supported the weight of the thing on my hips. I winked at her. She just stared at me. Then she turned to look down the road. I followed her gaze to see a cop car pull in behind us.

He flashed his lights briefly just to make us nervous. Micah and I exchanged glances through the hay piled on the hood of the car.

"Looks like you fellas had a little fender bender, eh?"

"Yep, sure does look like that, doesn't it, sir?" Micah replied.

"You mind telling me what happened?"

"Can you hold on till I'm done supporting this horse buggy?" The officer's radio went off, some code, some police shorthand. The Amish man rolled the axle back into place. I noticed the sun had gone down. "Set it back down, carefully," he said.

Micah and I eased it into place as the cop made his way around our car. I watched him out of the corner of my eye as he made some notes near the trunk, flashed his flashlight through the back window onto the tackle box that held our contraband. Watched him as he continued to look around the passenger side. We fitted the axle onto the buggy and stood up.

The cop kept the flashlight in my eyes. "Whose car is this?"

"My grandma's, sir."

"Where you boys headed?"

"Into LaCrosse, visit some friends—sir."

"Uh-huh, you mind telling me what went on here?"

I explained how I saw a squirrel and swerved to miss it; not exactly original. He didn't sound like he believed me, wondered about what speed I was going, and I said probably too fast. On and on. He asked Micah some questions, and then our victim, who was efficiently pinioning his axle.

He said he needed us to fill out accident reports and sent us to the back of the cop car to do so. We saw him outside talking to the Amish man, standing all the while right next to our back window. Cars slowed and gawked. Micah and I had time to fit our stories together quietly. It went on and on, Micah's account five pages, mine seven. We would've still been writing had not the policeman tapped on the window with his flashlight.

"You writing a novel in there?" he asked.

"No sir, just the facts, I'll be done in a second." Micah got out and handed him his report. "No novel sir, that would be perjury, wouldn't it?"

"What's that?"

"Perjury, right sir? Novels are fiction, so it would be perjury."

He sneered, "It's all fiction, son, everybody sees it different."

"Right sir, everybody but God."

"God don't write no accident reports, son." He paged through Micah's pages as if they were a four-year-old's drawings. "Spell everything correctly?"

"Yes, sir."

I got out and gave him mine also, to which he gave the same

illiterate look-over. "Well, the buggy's broke. Bartholomew and his daughter walked down the road to his brother's farm. He said the damage is easily fixed and there's no need to pay anything. No injuries, not yet. We'll see how he feels tomorrow. You know, you boys...." He then launched into one of the standard state patrol lectures given to teenage boys, fingering his belt and scratching his ass as he spoke. We both made sure to look him in the eye the whole time so he knew we were listening.

I vowed never again to allow for a lull in my vigilance. He handed me a ticket for inattentive driving and we parted ways. Micah and I got back in the car and pulled onto the highway. I watched him in my mirror as he followed us another mile or two and then turned around. I kept driving in silence.

"What time is it?" I asked.

Micah looked at his watch. "Oh, man. Eight forty-five."

I sped.

We got to LaCrosse at nine o'clock. Drove up and down and to the outskirts of town until we found the vacant parking lot. We pulled in against the gate of a factory. No one was there.

"Nine-fourteen."

"What happens now?" My heart tried to claw its way out of my chest. I imagined being beaten by thugs in a black van and left in an alleyway, being shot, being dumped in the Mississippi, the station wagon found parked on some gravel road miles away, blood stains on the interior, inattentive driving ticket positively ID-ing the vehicle of the murdered youth.

"Find a pay phone."

"And what?"

He shook his head. "Call Kevin, I guess, and call my parents and tell them I'll be late."

"You seem awful calm for someone who's probably gonna get beaten to death because of this."

"There's nothing we can do about it now. We're late, that's it. We call Kevin and tell him what happened. There's a Kwik Trip right down the road."

I got out of the car and paced around the parking lot, looked up at the stars, smelled the yeast from the brewery in the air. Micah got out too. He talked in a calm voice. "Hey Kaz, you go call, I'll stay here and wait to see if anyone comes." His voice was calm but I could see the stress on his face. He smiled at me. "You look like a beast, man. Have you taken a look in the mirror lately?"

I didn't care to. I knew he'd be right. I hadn't combed my hair or brushed my teeth or showered in two days. I hadn't slept all weekend, had been high as a kite for thirty straight hours. I had driven for over four hours today, been to church, nearly killed a family in a horse buggy, run a load of drugs and been late, had hallucinations or whatever they were for days straight—not all necessarily in that order. Order wasn't important. I couldn't make or keep order at that point; time wound about my life here like time in some Indian myth. Except the nine-seventeen the nine-twenty-two, whatever ticked on Micah's watch; that remained linear. Now we were going to pay for it.

Micah gave me the change in his pocket and a twenty from the envelope. "Go make the calls, get us some burritos or hotdogs and a few sodas—we haven't eaten all day. I'll wait here. We'll figure it out, don't worry. It's in God's hands now. I promise you, you'll be fine."

I didn't know how good a promise that was. I sighed and nodded and for the first time all day, I smiled. I made my way across the parking lot, suddenly aware of how incredibly thirsty I was, and imagined getting to that Kwik Trip and buying a ten-pound water-sugar-sludge drink. My throat ached and burned. All that smoking, all that drama.

"What are you going to do with those drugs if you can't deliver them?" asked Eliza. She strutted alongside me.

"Give them back I guess. Or just whatever Kevin tells us to do."

"The whole idea was half-baked if you ask me."

"I didn't ask you. Now go away."

"You're always telling me that. Who the hell made you the boss?"

"It's my damn head, just leave me alone."

She sighed. "This is the last time you tell me what to do." Then she was gone.

My head throbbed from the dehydration. I had just hopped to the other side of the fence when a black van went by me, turned into the lot, and made its way straight for Micah.

I jumped back over the fence and went into a jog as three large guys got out of the van. They surrounded Micah, and I could hear them saying something, but I couldn't make out the words over the sound of my own steps. I closed in. All three wore black. One guy was heavily tattooed on his forearms, another was bald and had a long goatee. The third I couldn't see as well because he stood behind Micah.

The one with the tattoos faced me. "Who the hell are you?" His fist balled up.

"He's just my friend. He has nothing to do with this," Micah told him.

"Shut up," suggested Goatee.

I slowed to a square stance and faced the Tattooed Man. I was at all limits and no longer cared. Right then and there I decided they might kill us, but I was gonna mess them up as best I could while they did it. And when I figured that, things got real easy. The fear went mostly away, or was simply choked by my newfound swagger.

"Who the hell are you?" I asked back, balling my own fists. I felt my jaw tighten and willed myself to relax it. I would keep him at bay with my long arms, long jabs and footwork, not let him get under me, not let him grab or hold me. *DON'T mess around when it's life or death, Kaz. It ain't a boxing match—there are no rules, no referees. Rip his nuts off, gouge his eyes out.*

"I'm here for a deal," growled Mr. Tattoo. "A deal that was supposed to go on an hour ago. Now who the hell are you?"

"I'm Kazimir Godwin."

His fists relaxed. He was shorter than me by a good six inches but thick and ripped with muscle, a barrel chest, huge forearms, and a deadly stare. "Aeneas' kid?"

I knew right then I had them. They were aware of Ephraim's cult.

They were part of it all and they knew my place in things. They could never touch me.

I nodded. "We got in a car accident, that's all. Your stuff's here, it's just late."

"An hour late. That ain't right. You owe."

"Your shit's here. I don't owe anything. Micah, get their stuff," I said, not taking my eyes off him.

I could barely make out his tattoos in the dark. They were spiders. All those eyes. He was the one. He was the one who'd been watching me all this time. I'll kill him, I thought. I'll kill him.

The car door buzzed when Micah opened it, and as the dome light illuminated the tattoos, they morphed into the devil on a throne surrounded by succubi. I couldn't figure out how he made them do it, but it was probably part of Ephraim's powers. He thought I hadn't noticed.

The door shut. Micah handed Mr. Goatee the tackle box. He opened the latch, rifled through the garbage bag and closed the box. "It's good."

Tattoo stared at me, a vacant, empty, Vietnam-vet stare. People were always staring at me. I hated it. I would've beat the tar out of him if it came to that. I would maybe die, but I'd take those eyes out with me. I'd hold them in my palms so tight, they'd find me still with them when my body washed ashore. He could do whatever he wanted to me and Micah, but I'd take those eyes. I was furious now, almost shaking. I couldn't wait till they made a move, just so I could do it. Just to feel those eyes squish in my palm. I was thinking so hard about it I grinned from ear to ear.

But I was cocky, stoned, tripping on mushrooms, and before I knew it somebody hit me in the back of the head and I hit the gravel like a sack of wet cement. Tattoo gave me a couple sharp kicks to the stomach with his steel-toed boots. I curled into a ball and he kicked me in the small of the back for good measure. "Tell fucking Olden-burg we're done with you," he said, then took a step back. "Get out of here." The other two stepped off as well.

"You first," I told him.

He kicked me twice more, then backed off. They left in a cloud of exhaust.

"Can you drive?" I asked Micah.

"Yeah, sure."

I handed him the keys.

The eyes haunted me. The eyes of the little girl, the cop, Kevin's grinning eyes, and cold tattoo eyes. That vacant stare that made my heart jump with anger whenever I saw it. They would be there in my dreams and in my waking. They would follow me wherever I went; they would lead me wherever they wanted me to go.

"Man, I thought you were gonna kill that guy," Micah told me.

The eyes followed me.

"I gave him your tackle box, Kaz. Your tackle box is gone. Sorry. We'll use the money to buy you some new stuff, man. I bet four hundred can go a long way...."

"Micah?"

"What?"

"Micah, you know those people you see when you smoke weed? Where do they come from?"

"What are you talking about?"

"The people, the voices, all that crap. What's it all come from? Are they ghosts? Do you see them in your church?"

"Maybe that's the 'shrooms."

"Stop messing around. Like what you were talking about before. Chemicals and brains, and fish. What if it's God's voice that whispers to you when you smoke?"

"I don't hear voices, Kaz. There are no voices in the weed."

What hooked me from the jaw at Kevin's suddenly lurched me forward, slamming my head against the dashboard. *Be still.*

"Woah, Kaz, what's going on?"

"Pull over."

He pulled off the road. I tried to get out but was pulled out instead.

Be still. Until what moves all else moves you, it whispered. The hook lurched and caught in my stomach, making me vomit. All the people watched.

"Oh man, Kaz, what's going on?"

Ephraim and his Revolution. My father wandering around the countryside somewhere, homeless. Screaming at people about the End Times. *The Revolution Kaz, the Revolution! The universe will tell you when to go. You'll know when to act, my boy. It will be like God acts through you.*

Micah got me back in the car and got me home. I don't remember how.

We didn't talk to each other for weeks. I hardly slept the whole time, barely ate. I wandered around the house, sifted through my ancestors' things in the attic. Their journals whispered to me, their pictures bulged as if they held back a flood.

I rubbed the hook in my pocket as my bruises and cuts healed. A relic. An Indian relic. This was the cause of the voices. I wandered the fields, found arrowheads, stones, beads. *Follow us.* I could feel a cadre of walkers behind as I went.

Finally, I took the box of my grandfather's relics and the others I had found and went down to the water's edge and threw them in. I dreamed in the night I was a fish drowning in air. Woke in cold sweat. Woke to the silence and then the creak of Grandma's house. Ghosts, ghosts that I could not see, whispering things I did not have ears to hear. Oh dear God, I thought in my lucid moments, just unhook me from these nightmares, just let me back in the water. No more puffs of smoke in my lungs to make me see the world anew. Give me the old world. Oh dear God, don't let me drown here on dry land.

Chapter Thirteen

SOMETHING HAD GONE WRONG IN ME THAT DAY: the wires in my head got crossed, the machinery got jostled and never quite worked right again. I knew it had happened; I felt awry but couldn't altogether control myself. I wondered whether this sense of something askew was exactly the shift in paradigm my father had wanted for me.

There were SAT tests and college applications and senior projects, things I forced myself through for the sake of escaping the eyes. Micah played nearly every day with his Christian punk band. We hardly saw each other.

"I'm thinking of doing this after I graduate," Micah told me on the phone in the late fall of our senior year.

"What kind of work is there for a bass player in a Christian punk band?"

"More than you'd think. It's taking off. Christian rock is the wave of the future."

"The next epidemic," I snickered. "Punk music went out in 1983, Micah, you're five years too late."

"Well, apparently the Pentecostal youth of America are five years behind, 'cause we got gigs offered all up and down the southeastern seaboard. I think if we really push we could go pro. Forget ministry."

"What do your parents think of that?"

"Haven't really told them."

"When are we gonna get together again?" I asked. "Like old times— smoke, go skiing, stare at frozen birds."

"I don't know, I've been so busy with school and playing in the band. Soon I hope. You doing all right?"

"Yeah, I don't know. The same."

As the snow came down and the wind blew and the ghosts creaked through the house all winter long, I found more arrowheads, more hooks. I realized that they were for me, somehow; they were intended for me. I took them and kept them in a Mason jar by my bed. *Follow us,* they whispered, and I hid my head under the pillow. I wrapped them in duct tape, in a towel, and then more duct tape, and this seemed to shut them up well enough. I smoked marijuana in my room. I studied and I immersed myself in books of philosophy; it was all that could keep me focused. I found it harder and harder to read, but the clear, precise thoughts of philosophers were an antidote for the chaos in the world: specific words to drown out the rumbling voices. I would close my eyes and breathe. Try to clear my mind with my breath, blow away the heavy webs that burdened my life, burdened all living. I willed to the world to speak to me, to burst through the mesh of my disbelief.

In mid-February I sat down to dinner with Grandma. I started into my food and felt her stare.

"Not eating, Grandma?" I asked.

"Haven't been feeling hungry lately," she said. I nodded and went back to shoveling in my green beans. She continued to watch me. "Are you okay?" she asked me finally.

"What?"

"You've been acting funny. You've always been unique, Kaz, but… well, you've been spending an awful lot of time in your room."

"Busy studying."

"Haven't seen Micah in a while. You've just been doing nothing all winter."

"I ski."

"Yeah, you ski. That's it. You don't even shower anymore."

I sniffed my armpit. "I don't smell anything."

"Well I do. It's not healthy. Why don't you call Micah, have him come out this weekend."

"Micah's busy. He's got his new band, and he's studying hard."

"He's the only friend you've ever made. Friends are important."

"The earth is important, Grandma. Friends come and go."

"Well, people are part of this earth, too."

"I've just been thinking a lot; big changes, you know. Going off to UW Madison next fall, leaving here and everything. Just been thinking."

"Don't think too much. You're part flesh, too. Don't get stuck up in your imagination. I didn't spend eleven years of my life raising you here so you can go wacko like your dad or your great-great-grandfather."

"Who says my dad's nuts? Maybe he's just religious."

She laughed. "Oh, bullshit. You know as well as I do there's a thin line between the two."

"Remember when I asked you to marry me?"

Eliza smiled. I sat on my bed and packed my bong. She sat on the chair, on top of a pile of clothes. "You boys, always falling for the wrong kind of woman."

I finished off a hit from the bong and lay back. "By that you mean intangible?"

She laughed. "Yes, tangibility, that's one thing that's wrong with our relationship."

"What else?"

"How about the fact that you don't shave, shower, or comb your hair? And you stink."

"How the hell would you know? You're a figment of my imagination."

"I don't pretend to know how, but I know. Besides, I can see you, too, and it's not attractive. If your beard was all manly, I'd like it, but all you get is those patches of curly shrubbery over your face. You look diseased. Get ahold of yourself, Kaz, you look like you're homeless." She shook her head and disappeared.

I lay on the bed and let my mind drift. I wouldn't let her faze me. What did she know about coping with the exigencies of reality? I was picking behind my ear when something pricked the back of my head. I pulled the pillow out of the case, then slit it open with my pocketknife and began to dig around. Inside the batting was another carved hook. I reached into my bed-stand and extracted my Mason jar from its swaddling, adding this latest curve of bone. The jar was now two-thirds full.

I sat up in bed and tightened the lid, swathed the jar in towels, and re-wrapped the whole thing in duct tape. Whatever they were, they couldn't get through the duct tape.

I found more and more, in my desk, my locker, my bedroom, on the porch. I attended to studies, smoked pot, read, watched the snow fall thrice weekly, twice weekly, by the hour. I felt like I was waiting but didn't know what for. As the snows receded I found a scattering of arrowheads in the matted yellow grass of the front yard.

I graduated in the spring, a rainy day that stuck me one last time in the sweat-stink of gym with a hundred other petulant graduates. No one from my family watched me walk; Grandma was sick in bed that whole week. Later, a card came from Silas and Leanna with twenty-five dollars in it.

I had graduated with honors and had been accepted to Madison, but I started to lag on the paperwork to enter in the fall. I thought I might travel first. I might go somewhere, see some things—any things that presented themselves outside the sterile walls of classrooms. I wandered the fields all month, not wanting to work with Roald, not wanting to see anyone but Grandma. I played cards with her, made dinner, gardened, fed the chickens. Then in late June, out in the tipi, Eliza and I made our travel plans. She sat beside me tending the fire. My feet were cold and I took my shoes off and held my toes to the flame.

"We should get out of here, forget school," said Eliza abruptly. "We should canoe down the Kickapoo, out to the Wisconsin. Or maybe take a long, long walk. It's the only thing that will keep your head on straight." She held a twig into the fire, then put it out.

"I'm not crazy," I said, rolling another joint.

"I didn't say you were."

"I don't want to be part of all that human stuff anymore," I said and lit my joint.

"That's as sane as anything anyone can say."

We lay and listened to the rain pattering on the tipi. The whole place smelled like campfire and mildew. Mildew like the old trunks in the attic.

I told Grandma of my plans to travel and she sighed. "Why not college?"

"The inside of classrooms feels like all I know."

"You've been more places and done more things than most kids."

"All before I was seven."

She rubbed her eyes. "You got a full scholarship to a good school. Why don't you just travel in the summers?"

"I want to see what's out there. I don't want to be trapped."

She stared at me. Dark circles under eyes welling up with tears. She looked thinner, frailer than I remembered, sitting in her nightgown before a jigger of whiskey and a hand of cards. "How much time you think I have in this world, Kazimir?"

I had never considered this before. "It's just for a little while, Grandma, maybe a year or something. I'm not gonna leave forever. I'll come back."

She still stared at me. I looked away, then back at her. "I promise I'm coming back. I'll go to college. I'll visit you on the weekends, and stay in the summers."

She wiped her eyes and sighed. "Just go do what you want to do, Kazzy. I can't make you do anything, you know. You gotta live your life just like everybody else."

"I'm coming back, Grandma, I promise."

"What's your plan?"

"I thought I'd canoe down the Kickapoo, out to the Mississippi and then take it all the way down to New Orleans. Then maybe hike west."

"A regular John Muir. Oh, my boys."

I found Silas's moldy external frame backpack in the attic. Grandma patched my sleeping bag and bought me new paddles for the canoe. Eliza and I went on test runs down the Kickapoo. When I paddled, the world became still; my thoughts cleared. Travel was what I needed. To get away from my ancestors, the arrowheads, the cryptic whisper of ghosts.

In August, I turned into the driveway, back from buying dried goods for my trip, and there he was, looking over the trailer.

"There's my boy!" my father said, dropping a hammer and coming toward me. "How are you?"

"Hey. Where you been, Dad?" I stopped short of hugging him and he stood in front of me.

"Oh man, just traveling, you know. Been real busy. You don't have to call me *Dad* anymore; *Aeneas* will do."

"Traveling for two years without stopping?"

"The path of energy is long."

"What the hell is that supposed to mean?" I heard a buzzing in my ear.

I walked toward the screen door of the trailer, my dad following. "What are you fixing up the trailer for—Aeneas?"

"I'm fixing it up so we can move back into it," he replied.

I looked him over.

My dad went to his cooler and extracted a couple beers. "You want one, kiddo?"

"You don't have to call me *kiddo* anymore. *Kaz* will do." I walked around the trailer. Weeds had grown high around it, one corner had fallen off the blocks, the kitchen window was broken, and the inside reeked of mildew.

"I came back, Kazimir, because I remembered that you graduated."

"Wow. You remembered. So *I* should congratulate *you*."

"It's time for your vision quest."

"For my which?"

"Your vision quest."

I held up the grocery bags. "I'm already taking a trip of my own."

I told him about my plans.

He nodded. "I understand your desire to strike off. But you need to come with me first. I'll take you to the Boundary Waters, Kaz. It's time you came to know your prophetic powers."

"My prophetic powers? What the hell do you know about my prophetic powers?"

He walked away from me about ten steps, turned and came back. His eyes were watery and he put his hand on my shoulder. I wanted to knock it off but didn't.

"Trust me, Kaz. Trust me."

I stayed out in the tipi that night, ignoring dinner. I packed my pipe and smoked and tried to keep my mind bounded by the chapters on Hume and Spinoza, to stay tethered to their logos.

"What's your old man want?" Eliza asked.

"He says it's time I go on a vision quest with him," I told her.

"You going to do it?"

"I don't know. We got our own trip."

She lay down next to me and watched the stars. "Not many chances to do something with your dad."

"Not my fault."

"Still. Maybe there's still time to make peace with him. We could go on our trip after."

"Kaz."

My dad's voice woke from my sleep. I rolled over to see him crouching in the doorway. "C'mon, let's go fishing."

I dressed and met him out in the barn, where he was looking around for our poles.

We bought some worms at the gas station and headed up to Bear Creek.

"Been out in the wilderness at all?"

"Since you left two years ago? Yeah."

"Good, commune with nature. You have to connect with land and creatures. Your meditations?"

"Haven't been keeping current on it, to tell the truth. Found some things to take its place."

"There's no substitute."

"Reading philosophy and smoking pot seem to work just fine." I watched for his reaction.

"You should start again. How's Micah doing?"

"Shitty, never been worse." I stared out the window. "Actually I don't see him too much anymore. He's real busy getting ready for college, taking care of his siblings, playing in his band."

We drove in silence.

"Grandma talk to you at all?" I asked finally.

"About what?"

"About Silas."

"What does she have to say about him?"

"That you should make up with him."

"He's still with Leanna, eh?"

"Yeah, they live up north."

"And what did you do last night?" He changed the subject.

"Communing with the wild. Not that it's any of your business."

We reached North Bear Creek and he pulled the Whale to the side of the road. We got out. A nice day again, the leaves making a verdant patchwork along the creek. I dropped a worm and bobber into the river and pulled out *Of Superstition and Religion*. I couldn't focus enough to read it, and kept checking my bobber and watching Aeneas cast along the edge of the river.

"So, last year I met some friends of yours," I called to him. "Kevin Oldenburg, for one."

"Oh yeah, old Kevin, Grandma used to babysit him. Wild kid."

"Now he's a wild adult. Says he works with you."

"Sure. He helps me and Ephraim out sometimes." He cast back out.

"Says he does more than upholstery with you guys."

My dad glanced at me and glanced back out at the river. I jammed my pole between a few rocks and walked over to him. "You mean he runs drugs?" he asked me.

"You run drugs?"

"I run drugs."

"Aeneas the drug runner."

"Aeneas the drug runner. How'd you meet Oldenburg?"

"Through Micah. We did a run for him."

He did some Darth Vader breathing. "Kaz, I am your father."

"Is that what we were doing when I was young and we were traveling all over?"

He shrugged. "Sure. Some of it."

"You've told me my whole damn life how important the things you do are, how it's all part of some cause, and that I fit into it somehow. It was all bullshit. You've been running around ruining people's lives."

A dark ridge formed and bore down over his eyes. "You have no idea what's bullshit and what's not. I do it for reasons, not for money." Strands of hair tossed about his forehead like composted hay. "You ever seen mass-farmed chickens, Kaz? Stuck in a cage, packed ass to ass and fed their own ancestors in the form of pellets by tubes down their throats. Fed so much their legs crack under them and they just sit till their throats are cut. Even when you open a gate, none of the chickens leave, so conditioned are they to the world they know. Learned helplessness. We live in those same cages and don't know it. Drugs give us a glimpse through the door. Most people don't even know there's a door out there."

I said nothing, just bent and took a rock and skipped it across the river. I waited for the inevitable diatribe against the Beast. His weight shifted on the pebbles as he cast again.

"The Beast is a keen predator. It has taken drugs and twisted them, corrupted us by them. We party like idiots—I used to be one, I know. It has sucked out the vital spirituality of drugs and fed us the carcass with marketing, television shows, money-grubbing gurus. It twists their use to allow us to avoid the question of our own enslavement. But drugs are still one of the few ways to see through things, this illusion of reality that isn't remotely all of reality. And even in the nonsense of pop culture, there's potential in drugs to let us see reality. They are some of the few weapons we have." His eyes became glossy and he gazed over the river.

I laughed. "Basically, your little cult supports itself by running drugs, and then it turns philosophical to justify itself. And I'm supposed to be a part of that?"

"You have to be, Kaz. You talk skeptically, but I believe you have the gift of prophecy. It has been passed down from our ancestors to you."

"And you've got some plan for me and my prophetic powers?"

He smiled beatifically at me. "It was about your age I had my first visions."

"So?"

"Have you?"

I ignored his question. "What's your big plan for me?"

The smile remained on his face. "And the voices. You've heard the voices. I heard them, too. What can you do with them but drink them away, medicate them away? We have no place for such things in normal society. No essays by Hume or Nietzsche will help you. Ephraim gave me a positive place for my powers. A place where they are honored and developed."

"And that's what this vision quest is?"

"Exactly."

I looked out at the river. My bobber had sunk beneath the surface, so I crossed to it and began to reel it in. "How long."

"Just a week. I have the knowledge to help you," he said, coming to my side to take the trout off the line. "Come with me," he whispered.

Bob Dylan blared from the tape deck.

"The only thing to listen to when you're going to the North Country, kiddo," he yelled as I paged through a magazine. His spirits were up again. As long as he was moving he was happy.

The van leaned around a foggy curve. Pine trees loomed in the mist.

"Breathe it in, man! Stick your head out the window and breathe—it—in."

I leaned out the window, closed my eyes, and let the smell of the pine and the fog slip over me like a veil of silk. He was right; it was wonderful, invigorating.

"That's the smell of freedom, Kaz." He let out a barbaric yawp. I laughed at him, my head in the same wind of the same joy.

By mid-afternoon we had arrived at our destination, just north of Ely. We parked the Whale along the side of a dirt road and got our equipment together.

I unstrapped Silas's beaten canoe from the top of the Whale and carried it out to the water. "So is this vision quest anything like a survival trip?"

"It's totally different. There's no backing out like you did before, I'll tell you that. We go out there and you stay."

"What am I supposed to do?"

"The same thing people have done on their quests for millennia. You sit there and let the universe reveal what it will."

In the late afternoon, we set off in the canoe. Its glide on the surface of the water, the loons dipping into the depths of the lake, calmed me. I paddled the front, my father the back, with a heap of things between us in garbage bags: a blue tarp, a bag of rice and some apples, cooking utensils, garlic salt, pepper, thirty feet of rope, two fishing poles with tackle.

In addition, I had brought with me about half an eighth-bag, which is a sixteenth if you're keeping score; enough, I felt, to deal with my father for the trip.

We trolled off the back of the canoe, catching several bass and pike as we went. Dad was a floating ecology textbook. He identified the birds by their calls and described the history of the rocks. Even if he made some of it up, it sounded good.

A little past eight o'clock, we glided onto shore. We strung the tarp up between two pine trees. "Just as insurance. We can probably sleep under the stars tonight."

I gathered firewood and smoked a joint while my father cleaned the fish. He grilled them to the forlorn calls of a loon in search of its mate. He leaned against a log and ate the fish. I sat cross-legged, eating the rice absently, paying more attention to the loon.

"You know, Kaz, you should eat up, you got a long couple days ahead of you. You're gonna need everything you can get for the vision quest."

We boiled water and made a pine-needle tea that tasted vaguely of laundry water. "Lots of nutrients in that, you know. Used by the Ojibwa and the Voyageurs as a kind of medicine." He pulled his hip flask from the pocket of his camouflage cargo pants and poured some of its contents into his tea.

"Another fine medicine. Want some?"

The whiskey loosened my tongue. I told him about the drug run gone wrong and the Amish buggy. He seemed to think it was all pretty funny. "Oh man, I remember those days. So you screwed up a little, no big deal."

"I almost killed two people," I said.

"Just people, Kaz, there's four billion more where they come from."

The horizon glowed green and yellow and lit the sky. In the swirl of the northern lights, stars appeared like ships far offshore. I went to relieve myself in the woods and smoked a little more, returned, and sat, listening to the quiet, trying to merge with the lights in the sky. We sat in silence, watching the ever-changing patterns, until they began to fade, little by little, into black.

The smell of pike cooking over the campfire met me in my dreams. I had barely slept and was still cold in the shade of the trees.

"Make sure you get some fish with your rice. It's the last thing you'll be eating for the next few days." He sat before the fire, the pan over the flames sizzling and a pot of water working up to a boil.

I ate myself full.

"You ready for this?" he asked.

"I don't even know what *this* is. How can I be ready?"

"In life we never know what will come. We still have to be ready."

I shrugged. "I guess I'm not, then."

He looked me over. "You're ready. It's time. It's the time I foresaw."

We paddled across the lake and portaged a thin sliver of land that led to a larger lake. The wind was strong and we canoed into steady waves that I feared would capsize us. Finally we reached the marshy shallows and paddled through a maze of waterways till we came to land. We portaged from there again, the canoe over my head, the tarp full of goods in his arms. "No one comes this way because of the portage—mile and a half," he told me.

"I get that," I grunted.

The land finally opened to a stretch of water long as it was wide, dotted with large cliff-like islands. He pointed to the largest of the islands, and laughed. "There, there it is. That's where we're going. Oh man, it's been so long! I don't even remember what year it was."

We put the canoe into the water and set off. "It must have been seventy or seventy-one when I met Ephraim. He said I had the gift, and sent me to a guide named Fishermoon who lived near Grand Marais. Silas and me came up to drop peyote with him. One time with peyote was all I needed. Since then, I have been able to see. We found this place, that island right out there. Dropped our buttons and away we flew."

The sheer cliff of the island loomed nearer and nearer. "That's when I saw it all, my boy. I jumped out of the canoe and swam to the cliff right in front of us. Scaled it, bare-naked. Silas shouting for me to come down—can you imagine Silas shouting, the only time I ever heard him raise his voice—and Ephraim's laughter reverberating off the wall. He wasn't even here in body, but his laughter was every-where. I got up and sat up there and watched Silas and his shadow. I watched them try to figure out how to get up where I was."

"I don't have to climb up there naked, do I? Because I don't want to do that."

"No, you don't."

"That's not part of a vision quest?"

"Well, it kinda is—if you're on peyote. But you're not."

"Is Ephraim meeting us?" I asked, suddenly suspicious.

My dad gave me a toothy grin. "He's already here."

We skirted the fifty-or-so-foot wall of granite and made our way to the back side of the island, which was studded with rocks and a few pine trees and nearly level with the water. We climbed from there, picking our way up the rocks, using scrub pines as handholds, until we reached the top. A large crack in the granite led to the cliff's edge. I hesitated, but he beckoned me to come. After a long moment, I got on my belly and crawled over. He hopped into the crack, which came up to his waist and was about as long as his body. "Look down in here, Kaz." He pointed to the inside wall.

Petroglyphs: a man with a bow, a bird, an arrow, a spiral above them. "The Ojibwa came here, too. For thousands of years they left their sacred markings on this rock. They came to seek visions of a greater world. Now they are nearly all gone, destroyed by our greed and hatred, the Beast we created in our own image."

"Those are really beautiful, Dad—Aeneas—but I still don't understand what you're expecting from me on this vision quest. I'm no prophet. I see things, yeah. But I do a lot of drugs, you know."

He pulled out a playing card from his shirt pocket.

"No, I don't want to guess your card, Christ."

"You already know what card it is—you guessed it years ago. Ephraim saw it in you. I see it too. I think deep down, you know something great is going on inside you. You will need to be strong to deal with the powers you have." He grinned a reassuring, quasi-fatherly smile. Had I been shorter, I thought, he would have tousled my hair. "Have some faith in yourself."

"Thanks for the pep talk, but I don't think there's anything to have faith in, Aeneas. Let's just go down and camp out, go fishing and stuff."

He shook his head. "You're letting the fear of your own destiny overcome you. You and I—our lives are not our own. You don't understand, Kazimir, what this all means. You don't understand. I can't let you *not* do this."

"But—"

"ENOUGH!" It echoed over the lake. He breathed two long breaths. "I'll see you in three days, Kaz. That's it. It has to be this way. *Deus vult.*"

He leapt off the cliff with a shout and plummeted into the water. The bastard knew I would not jump.

I stood and rushed down the back side as quickly as I could, trying to beat him to the canoe. "Aeneas!" I shouted as I ducked past pine branches and slid on the fallen needles. He was pulling the canoe into the water next to him and stepping into it from a rock. "DAD!" I screamed. The paddle was in his hands. Halfway down, I stopped. I couldn't catch him. I climbed back up and out as near as I dared to the cliff's edge. I saw him already far off. "Three days, Kaz," he called out to me.

I shouted obscenities until he became a tiny silver dot on the far shore and then disappeared into the wilderness. I was alone.

Chapter Fourteen

This is what the youngest prophet of the lineage of Godwin will do with himself on the rock, I said to myself; this is what he will do in his time in the wilderness. He shall get as high as possible on the sixteenth-ounce the Lord hath given unto him. He shall build a shelter from the pine tree down there. Maybe swim to the shore if he can. He shall not stray too close to the edge of the cliff. He shall try his damnedest to have no vision whatsoever, not to participate in the dream state of his father's world.

I rolled a shaky joint, smoked it, and let my mind wander into the layers of wave and harmony in the water. I stared into the water below. My body detached from my sight, and I floated in the rhythm of the water on the shore, in the sound of my own breath: that wave of air breaking in the cavernous body. I drifted in and out of sleep, waking to dragonflies gathering around me like dust, glinting in the light. I woke again and watched a little yellow butterfly kiss its shadow on the rock. It seemed to stick for a moment, a hesitation in its rhythms, then flung itself back over the surface of the water.

On the rock it had kissed, I made out the glistening of a spider web. My mind drifted. He had missed the little butterfly; the strands still vibrated in the breeze. Butterfly lives and spider dies, butterfly dies and spider lives. Nothing ever turned out just good. Some evil was always present. The whole world was weighed down by darkness. Ecosystem? No system really, it never held, it always broke under the weight of living. And one animal's greed, overpopulation: starvation, death. Not a system—torture. Ecotorture? What is the root of *ecos*? My father would know.

A low row of thunderclouds gathered on the horizon. I built an impromptu shelter underneath the pines. Hunger reared its head and I pressed it back down; there was nothing to eat. I sat down, suddenly tired, and closed my eyes. The weight of the air seemed to press down on me, constricting my breath into tight spasms. It would crush me. I could die here. I could die if I did not slip from its oppressive weight. Eagles would pick at my liver, beetles gnaw my eyes. I would die here, maybe, tangled in a great net, tangled and caught like some sea mammal, trapped below the surface, drowning.

When the rain broke and the clouds parted, I climbed the back of the cliff and edged out to a location comfortably far from the sheer face. Tufts of purple clouds migrated into the light of the setting sun like a herd of psychotropic buffalo. I imagined strolling to the edge like my father had and leaping into the reflections of buffalo on the water. The thought made me weak.

My father had leapt from it. He could leap and I could only crawl on my belly. He could trust and I could not. *Trust, Kaz, comes from truss, to tie or bind something together.* He was a fish caught on the line. He could feel it tug him, and he knew no other way of going. A fisher of men. Whatever Micah and the Pentecostals thought of Jesus, whatever was written, it was in my father. My father was caught on a line. He was led over the edge of sanity or over the edge into the spirit realm, half-dragged, half-leaping to his fate.

I could not feel the tug. But I could sense the ominous presence of something fishing for me. A looming shadow over the surface of the water, the echo of a voice in the current calling to me.

That's what you must do, I suddenly thought, if you want him to cease controlling you. He had power over me because he was brave and I was cowardly. I would not sit here and wait for him and Ephraim to send a crazy vision to me. I would not let them yank me into their world. I would jump, I would be a man, I would show them that there was nothing to be afraid of.

I could do it. If I could not jump, I could just fall off, which amounted to the same. I sat and eased my legs into the crack. Gripping the sides, I inched my toes closer and closer to the edge. My heart raced. My palms sweated, the world shifted. Then my knees wobbled and I would have collapsed but I held myself up by my arms. I stepped back, collapsed against the wall of rock, and breathed as if I had just sprinted.

Eliza stood over me and shook her head. "It's sad to see how wussy you've become. What's a little jump in a lake?" She looked into my eyes and smiled, the freckles on her nose wrinkling. "Here, I'll show you."

I reached for her shoulder, but was too late. She leapt, her white dress fluttering like a flag of truce. She hit the surface, making hardly a sound or a ripple, and slipped deep into the lake like a stone. Seconds later she reemerged, spitting out water and laughing. "It's safe," she told me. "You have to jump out a bit from the cliff and you're fine." Then she dissipated into the water.

Clouds gathered again and rain came down in fits and starts that night. My lighter was too wet to spark. I was cold, wet, hungry, tired, stiff, and angry. Before dawn I crawled out of my little cave. *You see, Kaz, you see, Kaz.* Those stupid survival skills he'd taught me since the day I could stumble across the grass toward him. This was the culmination of his plan eighteen years in the making.

I looked out on the water. The sun managed to sneak a few rays through the clouds. A scattered rain still fell; a family of loons slipped through the mist.

One loon dove, disappearing from the surface. The world went silent as I watched for her, as if someone had pressed the mute button—as if it, like me, were holding its breath while waiting for her return. She surfaced, splitting the water near the shore where I stood. Some of the clouds slid open and sunlight hit the water and meandered toward a few rocks on the island. As the island lit up with sun, I stripped my soaked clothing and laid it out along with my lighter.

I wanted to talk to someone, to anyone. I wanted a friend, a dog, a squirrel. I wished he had left me on some shore, not an island. I could've walked then, interacted with the place and its creatures.

The sun rose out of a pocket of clouds and struggled into a sky growing more and more blue. I swam out as it warmed, intending to cross the lake to the far shore, but about a quarter of the way I realized it would be too far. I swam on my back all the way to the island again, taking my time, until the lake bottom rose abruptly and I waded back to the rocks. Guppies picked at the hairs on my legs, so I stopped and stood still, talking to them.

On the shore, I slept, awoke, retrieved my sun-dried clothing, flicked the lighter a few times. Nothing. Not a single spark came from it. It didn't matter: I checked the pocket of my shorts to find my weed bag gone.

I scoured the island on hands and knees, searched under every pine needle and every rock. Climbed several trees to inspect the crooks of their limbs, walked the shore. That sweet little sandwich baggy that made everything tolerable was nowhere to be found.

I cursed and cursed and cursed, kicked things, threw rocks, calmed, searched again, found nothing, cursed further, and finally climbed up to the top of the cliff and napped once more in the warmth of the bare rock.

I woke at sunset. The mother loon called, crossing the water beneath me, her young ones behind her. Which one cares for the young, the mother or the father? I'm sure my father could tell me. *Oh, yeah, kiddo, you see the loons' nesting habits....* I heard her song, *the song, the song, kiddo,* closed my eyes and listened to that lonely call, once more and again. My head pounded. I opened my eyes and watched her. The call lingered on the trees of the distant shore.

Then she was answered. Over the hill to the west a black speck appeared, echoing her lonely calls. They skimmed across the water toward each other like two ends of a ribbon, calling louder and louder and joyously, euphorically, and skipped to a halt near each other.

My eyes felt strange. I found I was sobbing. I dropped to my stomach and leaned over the edge to watch the loons. I lay even as the dusk faded and the stars shone and the northern lights shimmered. A wilderness of light.

The world in me opened. Some of the pain and the hatred, the shame and the loneliness, was turned loose into the air. As it scattered to the wind, I felt myself buoyed up, somehow larger than before, somehow more alive.

In the night, memories flooded back. I remembered Leanna, Silas. *Hey Kaz....* I remembered my sojourns in the wilderness with Eliza. *You know, Kaz....* My grandmother pointing to ghosts. As I remembered they came to me, vivid and real as hallucinations. *When the Revolution comes....* A vision of my mother, hair cut to shoulder length, floated before me: not Leanna—someone I barely knew, someone I didn't know at all. Silas came before my eyes, pants rolled, as quiet as a heron fishing the river. They seemed more real here, in my visions, than they had ever been in my life, but maybe that was because they were gone now—except Grandma, all of them gone.

The Man, Kaz, the Beast of our own making.... My father's visions, his plans, his schemes, had taken them from me. And now he was trying to sever me from myself, so I would be his to control. His—and Ephraim's.

The morning wind dropped pine needles on my half-finished shelter. I climbed up the rock and looked over the water: red clouds gathering in the west. I gazed up at the sun, defying all the lectures I'd received in grade school about burning my retinas. When I looked back down, Eliza was standing before me.

She pointed behind me to the cliff. "So do it. Jump."

"I don't want to."

"*I don't want to, I don't want to.* Stop being a freakin' chicken."

"I'm tired, starving, and my head hurts. I'm going back to sleep. Don't talk to me anymore."

"Excuses, excuses. You've got an honest-to-God imaginary friend trying to show you something in that water and you're up here complaining about a headache. Sometimes I don't get you."

I spit over the edge and counted to five before it hit the water.

She was right, I had to do it. It would set me free.

I would jump.

I stripped down, laying my clothes under a bush on the hillside.

I would jump.

She watched me do this in silence. I stood tall, the wind licking my chest. I looked out past the edge of the cliff. The rush of fear seized me. My heart shook its cage; the strength of my legs was barely sufficient to hold me now.

Eliza sat down on the rocks and waited. Clouds scurried around the sky and the sun went in and out of them. My mind went down into the waters without my body, into the blackness of its depths, absent of light. What secret world was down there? Why should I be so afraid of the jump?

Before I could make up my mind to do it, I sprinted. My feet pummeled the wet rock, the cliff edge neared. Eliza gave a shout.

Three feet from it I felt the tug: the overwhelming strength of something moving me from beyond. But I knew it was not God that pulled me forward. I didn't know what, but it wasn't God.

I tried to pull back, I stumbled, the brink came. My legs gave out, but the momentum didn't.

My knee hit the last bit of rock as I tumbled head first into the void. My face scraped a scrub pine on my way down, my arms flailed as I plummeted toward those rocks lying underneath the water's surface.

It takes only a few seconds to drop fifty feet. It felt like a century. I knew I would hit them and die. I spun, trying to get my feet down.

Half-bent and head-first, I hit the water. My knuckles scraped a rock. My body straightened and down I plunged, forcing my hands out in front of me. The cold weight of the water surrounded me. I kicked and waved my arms. My fingers hit something that felt like a fleshy belly. I opened my eyes but it was too dim to see anything. I pushed off of it and turned myself upright.

I felt a tug again and I was drawn forward like a fish on a line. I was in the pitch black. My hands reached out into the ether.

I was being pushed, swept in a current of rushing water, strong as a river at flood. Objects large and small were rushing past me, bumping me and pushing me along with them.

Slowly, a surreal light gathered and I began to see. Bodies. Bodies bobbing, sinking, riding the current. Regnus, shoeless and haggard, a rope around his ankle. Jeremiah with the hollow of his mouth gaping. Leanna in a pioneer dress, hair floating over her face as if in a Gothic vision. My grandfather's navy coat sinking. The chest from the attic, open, the diaries washing away. Silas, eyes open, staring unnaturally. The hefty backside of Roald in overalls.

Arrowheads flitted around me cutting at my face, morphing into schools of fish.

I kicked upward, ran into something above me, pushed off of it, found my face next to Micah's. His eyes were closed, he lay on his back with his hands in prayer position, and he had a look of saintly peace. A fish hovered next to his head, a silver guardian.

All of my world was drowning; all that I loved died before my eyes. A whirlpool tugged at me, spun me one-hundred and eighty degrees. I found myself clutching the hem of my grandma's flower-print shirt. She moved her hand and brushed my forehead tenderly, but when her face turned to me it was bluish and a spout of water came from her lips. I held her shirt and tried to take her with me.

Kicking, I escaped the current and began to rise. We were a few feet from the surface, the light was ordinary now, piercing the water in columns and sinking among the fishes, the arrowheads, the shoes and spiders and fishhooks that floated around us. Then a silhouette crossed the light and I saw above me my father's huge form, his fulgurate hair like an aura around his head, his arms reaching down toward me. He pushed me back under; I looked up and he was shaking his head. *It's your fate, Kaz, this is what you were put on earth for, Kaz, it's bigger than you or me, it's the culmination of the prophecies, Kaz, Kaz, KAZ! KAZIMIR JONAH GODWIN!*

My lungs seized up. I released my grasp on Grandma's shirt and squeezed my father's enormous hands until they cracked. I kicked and kicked, rose from the water. A pebble in reverse, I crashed through the weight of water into the weight of air, and heaved myself onto the rocks.

I lay on the shore all day and did not move. Eliza sat by me but she never spoke a word. Clouds passed away over the horizon. The stars came out. The moon stared full through its arc in the sky. Eliza vanished. I lay awake all night.

In the morning I watched him drop the canoe into the water at the far shore of the lake. Watched him as he came around the edge of the cliff. I clenched and unclenched my fists. He waved at me and scraped the canoe between two rocks, lodging it there. He got out and waded onto shore.

I stood and approached him as he did this. He turned and looked me over, nodding approvingly.

"You are a man now." A tear leaked out of his eye. Before I could jump back he ensnared me in an embrace. The smell of whiskey permeated his every pore. "Oh my son, I am so sorry to see you like this. Don't be angry. I am so sorry I left you, but I had to. I had to," he told me, the sound of it resonating in his chest. "You understand that now, I know you do."

I shrugged.

Letting go of me, he leaned over the canoe and pulled out an entire package of Snickers bars. "I got them for you, Kazimir. I knew you'd be hungry."

We paddled and he asked me what I'd seen.

"I don't want to talk about it," I told him, but he pressed me.

"I know it's hard to put it into words, Kaz, but some time, Ephraim and I gotta know. We gotta know if you're the prophet or not."

"And if I'm not? What then?"

He shook his head. "You had a vision there—I know it. Your vision will reveal your fate and will guide you, and I can help you along the way."

"Help me? For years you've left me to rot in the middle of nowhere so you could go get drunk and do your shit all over the country."

He looked away.

We paddled and portaged to his campsite in silence, gathered his things in silence. He cooked some fish and I ate them, all in silence. Then we paddled through the rest of the daylight back to the parking lot where the Whale was parked.

It was well past dark. Finally, after he got into the driver's seat and put the keys in the ignition, he turned toward me. "I left because I needed change and only Ephraim could help me. Now I have learned to be a healer, a soul-guide."

"No mere warrior running drugs for the Revolution?"

"I am both a healer *and* a warrior now." He reached into the backseat and pulled out his guitar. "It's through this. I can help you, Kaz. I play my songs," he explained, "and I can heal things. You're having visions—you tell me them and I'll play my songs and then the Creator will reveal to us the truth we need."

"You going to climb up some cliff naked, too?"

"I do what I am told, and thus the powers come through me." He picked at his guitar. "I need to hear your vision, just as I revealed to you what the Creator had given me—"

"Some. *Some* of what you say the Creator has given you. Only some. Enough to keep me in the dark, keep me guessing."

"True, only some, for a visionary needs time. The call to Truth frightens; the weight of its meaning overwhelms. I know how you feel, Kaz. You are sensing it now, as you've become an adult. You are sensing something is wrong with reality."

"Maybe."

"I've had that feeling, and I've had the visions. Visions meant for a society. Kept to yourself, they will turn you mad. If you share them with me, I can help bear the weight. And they in turn will illuminate our society's role in the world."

To my embarrassment, my eyes flooded with tears. "So you come back after all these years to get this important vision from me. Not because you want to spend your days on the family land like you always said was so important when I was a kid, or because you miss me or Grandma? Not any of that? Just—you wanted to hear what my vision was so you can make sense of your cult?"

"Your vision is the most important thing in your existence. Take it seriously. It's more profound than any science, any technology, can deduce."

I closed my eyes and leaned back. "What could all the stupid shit I saw tell you?"

He leaned forward. "Son, I will tell you what I saw years ago when I sat on that same cliff, and you will understand everything." He sighed ecstatically, fingered the strings of the guitar, looked dreamy as he took a breath and began.

"From that cliff I looked out over the earth, the clouds veiling and unveiling the whole of the human miasma, and I saw it all burning—the whole earth—the black of the smoke masking the clouds themselves and spiraling and roiling and turning into a dragon as it surrounded me—a dragon with eight grasping arms and a thousand eyes. I fell to the side to escape the fury of those arms, cowering like a little child, until one bore down on me. I looked the Beast in the eye, and in its eye I saw a reflection of light, and the light surrounded me. I was bathed in light, it washed over me like a flood and swept me in its current higher and higher and higher, and then a golden rain showered down on me, and I was that rain, and I plummeted to earth. I found myself lying on that very cliff where I had started.

"I looked up into the sky filled with the dark clouds of a world burning and the light shone like a spear and stabbed me between the eyes, and shot out of every pore of my being. It was then that I realized that from me the light would become a son, and the son would come against the world and its terror, the world man had created. A Revolution would come, unfolding like an earthquake, raising a new mountain chain, and the light of my son would bring this to be. He rode on a horse and the people followed. He rode with sword and torch, and the light of his own vision emanated from him. And he brought them into a new world, free of the horrors wrought by man."

He sat back beaming, looking me over tenderly, proudly. I gaped at him.

"*That's* your fucking vision? That your son is the goddamn Messiah? All this time you were raising me to be Jesus?"

He snapped back, an injured light in his eyes, "The argot of Christianity is a little thin, Kazimir. You may be revolutionary, a prophet, a leader of all people into a new time. I have seen it. I saw him astride a—"

"Yeah, yeah, you already explained all that 'me on a horse' crap."

He looked at me like he was trying to make me disintegrate. "I had a vision, the very end of the world, the savior, how can I make you understand the relevance of—"

"I cannot fucking believe this. Dad, you were on peyote. People see all sorts of shit when they're hallucinating and running around the woods with their friends. You hallucinated. Then you spent twenty years of your life on what you hallucinated. People take peyote and watch *The Wizard of Oz* and think they find the meaning of life, too."

He pointed his finger at me. "First off, kiddo, don't raise your voice at me, I'm your father—"

"Oh, oh okay, Dad, sure Dad, great Dad, whatever you say *Dad*. Or am I supposed to call you *Aeneas* because I'm a man now?"

He slammed open his door, leapt out of the Whale, went and sat at the base of the thick birch. In the glare of the headlights, he picked on his guitar. I walked the other way, putting space between us. After a good while, the music stopped and I could hear him rise. "I know what hallucinations are, Kazimir, I lived through the sixties and seventies; hell, I *was* the sixties and seventies. I know what a hallucination is. What I saw was no hallucination. And what you have seen is not hallucination."

"What, then?"

"A vision, a prophecy."

"What the hell is the difference?"

He walked toward me. "The difference? Kaz, the difference is—"

"Is what?"

He glared. "Don't cut me off again. You're still my son, even if you're a man." We faced each other in a silent tug-of-war. "The difference, as I was saying, the difference, is in the word, as it always is.

The root of 'hallucination' is the Latin '*hallucinare*' which is a mask, or make-up, cosmetics. A mask on the face of reality. Our lives in this world are hallucinations. Everything people see and believe in the modern American world is a hallucination, from their tract homes, to their marketing jobs, to their Pink Floyd-*Wizard of Oz* game. Those people use drugs to escape, to go further into an illusion, and that's all they see. More hallucination. Drugs can be a creator of greater illusion, while on the other hand they can set you free. Recreation has no place in the sacred. I deal because some people will see through the mask—"

"Get to the point."

He tried to drown me with his stare. I took in his hulking form out of the side of my vision, his ripped shirt, ripped jeans with little dragonflies sewn to flares of his pants. "A vision, unlike a hallucination, looks past—looks *through*—the makeup and the pageantry, and stares face to face with reality. That is what I saw. That's what you see."

"You saw me riding around on a stupid horse with a sword? That's reality? That's a vision of a time to come? You based your *whole life* on that? *My* whole life?"

He braced his hand against the birch tree. "Tell me what you heard, what you saw."

"Okay, okay, Dad, you wanna know what I saw and heard those three days you left me on a rock in the middle of a lake, with no food and no water, against my will? You want to know the big truth I saw, that will lead the human race through the Revolution?"

He stared at me.

"My big satori, Dad, was that you are an absolute idiot. You're a fucking delusional freak. You're a freak and so is Ephraim. You want me to die so that you can resurrect me with your god-powers, and then you've got your stupid-ass messiah. But I'm not dying for you! All your survival crap, all your meditations, all your seeing through cards—it was a bunch of bullshit. Ephraim was using you to get to me. He manipulates your head and sends you around doing his bidding."

"Ephraim is nothing like that," he said.

"You stagger around the country dealing drugs and buying sofas, and having 'prophetic visions,' which are really his instructions for you. All the time he keeps his watchful eyes on me. All the time trying to manipulate me into being this Christ by twisting my thoughts with his arrowheads. You don't think I know? I do."

"You're not making sense. What you're talking about here is not a vision. Trust me."

"Trust you? Your whole life you've been telling me about this so-called 'Revolution.' Have you really looked at this country? People are at home, watching TV, phoning into sex lines. They're not revolting against anything soon. Our whole country is flaccid, entertained into impotence, and the Beast?" I walked past him, smelling the beer on his breath. "You know who the Beast is? It's you. The Beast is you. Ephraim is using you to be the Beast. Your role is to deliver me to his hands so he can sacrifice me. YOU JERK, YOU WHACK-JOB LU-NATIC."

I turned and ran into the woods.

"Kaz, get back here!" I heard his steps on the banks of the river.

Branches whipped my face, thorns clipped my hands. I dragged myself up by small bushes and branches. When I could go no farther I lay silent and listened. Nothing. The world spun. A buzzing worked its way into my skull, soft voices mumbled. I had no marijuana to ease the chaos into stillness.

I would never go back, I thought. I needed to go away, just go away and never see him again.

I watched from the woods as he went about with a flashlight. I listened as he called for me. He faded from sight and sound and I went deeper into the woods. An owl hooted. "What are you going to do now?" Eliza asked.

Sometime in the night I stumbled onto a paved road. I hid as a few cars and trucks rattled by. When the morning came, I stood at the shoulder and put my thumb out. I hitched back down to Du-luth, then made my way down Highway 61, taking rides with a construction worker, a casino card dealer. I took meals when offered, but mostly I sat in the passenger sides of cars and stared out the window. "Is it nonsense?" I asked Eliza in a restroom near Winona. "All this stuff? Where is my head?"

"Sounds like nonsense to me," she said from the stall next to me.

Eliza was right, I knew that: prophecy, vision, even my rage at my father was nonsense too. Maybe I'd been a little crazy. Now I just wanted to get home, forget the canoe trip I'd planned, spend the last weeks of summer with Grandma, and go off to college to begin a new life.

I made my way back to New Eden in a week on the grace of strangers. The dark early-morning air was warm and a robin sang in the willow tree as I hurried up to our house. The screen door didn't budge, so I got the spare key from under the garden gnome and went in through the back. Dust scampered over everything; Grandma hadn't been much for keeping house lately. I wondered if she was lonely, and I began to feel guilty for leaving her, and for how withdrawn I had been this year.

"Grandma?" I called softly, not wanting to wake her if she was sleeping. The door to her room was cracked, and I peeked in. The bed was made. No one was there.

Outside, the waning moon reflected on the pond even as the sun began to rise. The willow shook. I closed my eyes and listened for crickets. Where could Grandma be, first thing in the morning like this? I could not imagine what had taken her away. A dull hum filled the air. I looked out and saw a headlight float along the road, make a turn at the gas station, and continue past our place. I felt a rush of anxiety, the bottom dropping out of my stomach as if something terrible was about to happen.

I called Micah's but no one answered, so I left a message on their new answering machine.

Maybe I'm crazy, I thought. Maybe that's all it is. Always feeling that heavy weight of doom—it's some illusion, some hallucination. She's out at an early mass. That's it. I lay down and passed out on my bed.

I woke mid-afternoon and spent the next two hours cleaning and grooming myself. In the kitchen, hearty meals invented themselves as I pulled seemingly unassociated objects out of the fridge. I made coffee, and sat at the table feeling very normal. Still no Grandma.

I took a walk around the property, and then down to the river. I sank my feet in the water. On the gravel bar was the indentation left by Silas's canoe. My father had it now, but no matter. I'd spend some days working for Roald and buy one of my own. And the first thing I would do with it was to take Grandma for a paddle.

I heard Grandma's car roll into the driveway in the early evening and I rose and walked up the bank to see her. My bare feet sank into the wet grass. The screen door had been left open and I could see the hall light on inside. The steps creaked and I closed the screen door loudly so that Grandma could hear me come in.

"Grandma?" I called out.

No answer.

"Grandma, I'm home."

I heard someone move in her room and I made my way down the hall.

The door opened and out stepped Cousin Jethro. He had a suitcase in his hand.

"Kazimir?"

"Jethro—where's Grandma?"

"We were wondering when you'd come back. Your grandma's in the hospital. I was just getting some of her stuff."

"Is she okay?"

"Well—not really."

CHAPTER FIFTEEN

THE HOSPITAL SAT LIKE A CONCRETE VULTURE among a morbid streak of custard shops and fast food restaurants. Jethro parked at a Burger King and got himself a couple fat burgers and some shakes before heading into the oncology ward.

"It's all over her body," Jethro told me as we rode the elevator. "Guess she's had it a good while, but never went in because she didn't have any insurance."

"How long has she been here?"

"A few days. One of her bridge buddies came by and found her unconscious in the bathroom downstairs, called the ambulance. She's been in here since."

I still didn't believe it. This couldn't be real, I thought. Jethro dripped ketchup on the floor as we twisted down the labyrinthine halls. Lights fluoresced, machines beeped, and the bleached stench of death pervaded the entire place.

We were brought to her room by the nurse and left alone. Grandma slept underneath the blue sheets. Her cheeks were sunken; dark circles bulged under her eyes. She had lost weight—maybe thirty pounds. How? When? I hadn't been paying attention.

"Grandma?" I tentatively touched her hand, her cheek. She stirred. She opened her eyes twice. The second time, they focused.

"Kazimir," she said, slurred, syllables dragging. "What the hell am I still here for? Tell this joker to take me home."

"I'll take you home, Grandma," I said, and she nodded with her eyes closed.

"We've got to get her home," I said. "She'll die here."

Jethro took a slurp of his shake as we walked into the hall. "She's on morphine, Kaz, she doesn't know what she's saying. Roald wants her here 'cause she needs to get the treatment and stuff."

"Like what? Is she on chemotherapy?"

He shrugged. "No, they said it's too late for that. Pain killers. Anyway, who's going to take care of her if she's at home?"

"I can."

"Look at you—you're dirty as hell, and you stink. How're you gonna take care of her if you can't take care of yourself?"

"I showered this morning."

"Well, you need to do it again."

"Grandma wants to go home, I say she goes home."

"What you say doesn't mean a thing, Kaz. Uncle Roald has to decide."

"Call him, then."

"He'll be here tomorrow. You can talk to him then. We got to take off now, I work tomorrow."

"No, I'm staying here."

"You can't sleep here. They won't let you."

"I'll figure something out."

He sucked up the remainder of his shake. "Suit yourself."

I went back into the room. Grandma mumbled in her sleep and I tried to lean against the wall and get some rest myself, but I couldn't get my eyes to close.

The dim fluorescence from above the sink bathed her thin face, its bushy brows and its wrinkles, in a flickering light. I turned it off. A nurse peeked through doorway and told me visiting hours would end at eight.

I couldn't think. There must be a way to get her out of here, if I could just think.

I went out the doors of the unit at eight o'clock, found a pay phone, and called Micah.

He sounded tired when he picked up. "Kaz? Where've you been?"

"Micah, we can talk later, can you come over here? I'm at the hospital. Med-Surg room two-twelve."

"Are you sick?"

"It's my grandma, not me. Just come get me. And don't let anyone see you come."

I hung up and walked down the hall as if I were leaving, turned a corner, and inched back along the wall so no one inside the doors could see me through the little glass windows. When the coast was clear, I slipped back through the doors and walked down the hall like I knew what I was doing. I figured I would tell them I had forgotten my jacket if someone saw me. But in my mind I projected dampening energies and trusted that they would hold the nurses and orderlies in suspended animation while I entered the room.

It worked. I slipped in unannounced and went to Grandma's bedside and listened to her breathing. They would find me here if I made myself obvious, I thought, so I looked through the closets and found an extra blanket. I went back and slid myself underneath her bed. Lucky I was skinny—it was a tight fit underneath all the railings, levers, and brakes. I listened to her breathing and pressed my hands up against the bottom of the mattress. I started to get claustrophobic and focused on my breathing until my heart steadied. Then I adjusted my blanket, placed my hands back on the mattress, and closed my eyes.

Funny thing. At that very moment, I had a sudden image of a red balloon trussed to Grandma's wrist. It broke loose, floated through the ceiling. I flew out after it, following it through clouds and back to the earth. I saw the willow, the rotted-out trailer, the old barn growing larger as we descended, until we came to rest in her little garden.

She turned her head. "What the hell are you waiting for?"

I was confused. "What?"

She shook her head. "Get me the hell out of this hospital."

An hour passed and I heard footsteps enter the room and looked to see a pair of Pony sneakers.

"Kaz, where are you?" It was Micah's voice. He closed the door behind himself.

"I'm down here," I whispered.

He bent over and looked at me and shook his head. "What's going on?"

"Grandma has cancer. She's going to die and Roald and the doctor won't let her go home."

He sat down on the floor and searched his pockets for his pipe like an asthmatic in need of his inhaler. I saw he'd chopped his hair into a Mohawk and had dyed it orange. I shook my head in disbelief.

"What the hell's with your hair?"

"It's for the band." He grinned and lit his pipe. "Don't you think they'll let her go if they feel it's safe?"

"What does *safe* freakin' matter? She's dying. Every day counts."

"You're not suggesting we smuggle her out of here, are you? That's probably not a good idea." His orange hair quivered a little, as if contemplating the consequences of this course of action.

"No, I know that, but I can't really think of what to do. I figured you could help."

He thought a little. "Roald's her nearest relation so he makes the decisions?"

"I guess."

"Does Silas or your dad know about Grandma?"

"No, I don't think so. Neither of them has a phone."

"Why don't we bring Silas and Leanna down here. They'll help get Grandma out of the hospital and back home."

"I haven't talked to Leanna since I was a kid."

"No time like the present. I've got my car. We can leave now, poke around until we find him, and have him back here by supper tomorrow. Then he just signs her out because he's her son and that has to give him more authority than Roald. He'd do it, wouldn't he?"

I tried to think of a reason it wouldn't work, but I couldn't. "I guess you're right. If nothing else we should tell him what's going on. Plus, Grandma will be happy to see him."

In the dead of night we crested a small hill a few hours past Eau Claire. I tried to make conversation to stay awake. "How's the punk rockin' for Christ thing?"

"Good, good man, I think we got something. We're selling albums pretty well. You'd think we were George Strait with power chords in certain towns down south."

"That right? What are you guys called? Jezebel's Nemesis?"

"No, that's my old band. We're the Revelators."

"I like that better."

"Me too."

More silence ensued. All that had been heard was the hum of the engine for most of the four hours we'd been in the car. I didn't even know why he'd volunteered to come. I checked my rear view mirror. One headlight; the same motorcycle was behind me that had been there since we got on the interstate. We were the only two cars on the road.

Was he an enemy? Was he connected with my father? Near midnight I exited, pulled off on a side road and cut the engine.

"What are we doing?" Micah asked.

"Just taking a break."

I waited to see if the motorcycle had followed. Nothing. I turned the car back on and headed off.

"Nice break."

The sun had been up for a couple hours on a surprisingly cold August day when Micah spotted a particle board with the word "Gas" spray painted across it. It was the first indication of commerce within seventy miles, and showed all the signs of neglect one would expect. Even the gravel parking lot had seen better days; we dodged chunks of blacktop that floated atop a sea of dust like burned chicken in a bowl of soup. We slipped through them and parked next to the building where a couple of dreadlocked hackey-sackers milled about. "Friends of the family?" Micah asked.

I shrugged, too tired to respond. We made our way into the store.

In the dim interior, rickety metal shelves held dusty packaged foods with outdated labels. Postcards in a rack near the door had the faded, grainy look of nineteen-seventies nature photography. A man in a camouflage cap and aviator glasses strode down the aisle nearest us with a container of night crawlers and twelve of Miller Light, depositing himself in a line of locals that terminated at the counter. An old man bent over the counter, ringing up items on the antique register at the speed of a migrating tree and conjuring prices from thin air.

"What do we need here?" Micah asked.

"Directions to Silas's. He gets his mail here."

He nodded and pointed to a plastic tray of donuts. "Maybe a few of those too, eh?" I looked over at the Long Johns being used as a landing pad for an air force of flies. "Breakfast?"

"Yeah, get me one of those and a coffee and get yourself something too. I'll be in line."

The cash register rang. "Fourteen seventy-seven," the old guy told a barefoot lady in a peasant dress.

"What about the motor oil? Did you ring that up?" the lady asked. She tugged at the braids in her long brown hair.

"All right, hold on, hold on," he said and started ringing everything up again.

"It's all right, I'm easy," she said.

He looked over his spectacles at her. "I know you're *easy* darlin', the question is are you *good*?"

Everyone in line snickered but the guy in the camo hat. "Come on, Junior, move it along, I got fish to catch," he swore under his breath.

I watched the woman with the motor oil take her change. She looked attractive from behind: her braids fell over her shoulders and her peasant dress hung down to a pair of tanned ankles. They made me nervous. She turned from the counter, brushing her hair back as she did, giving me the conciliatory smile of a pretty woman used to men staring.

Micah shook his head. "This is gonna take forever," he said and tapped camo-boy on the shoulder. "Hey bud, are you local? We're looking for our uncle."

Camo-boy took in the orange Mohawk in all its glory and snickered. "Why don't you ask some of them hackey-sackers outside?"

"He gets his mail here, so we thought you might know him," said

Micah.

The man looked him over again. "What's his name?"

"Silas Godwin."

The man jerked his thumb toward the pretty lady, who stopped in the doorway and turned slowly around to face us.

"Who are you?" she asked, looking me up and down.

"I'm Kazimir, his nephew."

"Kaz? Don't you remember me?"

Good Lord. It was Leanna.

The place where they lived consisted of a ramshackle front house—the landlord's—two cars lying in the back fields, several sheds, a chicken shack, a few hardy goats, and a couple of moping dogs. But a large garden grew riotous with corn stalks and brightly fruiting bushes, and vines heavy with vegetative abundance threatened to collapse the sagging deer-fence. Leanna pointed us to where smoke poured out of the metal chimney of a cabin made of earth and wood.

"We live back there." She handed us the bags of groceries. "I'll let you guys alone a little while," she said, letting herself into the garden.

"Kazimir?" Silas laughed under his breath. He was older now; long gray and brown hair hung down around the bald patch on the top of his head. He scratched at a thin, pepper-colored beard. A dirty vintage flannel ran down to oil-stained jeans that looked as if he had walked the excess hem off.

"Hey Silas, been a long time."

He looked over at Micah. "Friend?"

"This is Micah."

We helped him put away items into a chipped, painted armoire that took up half the kitchen, then sat down at the table. Silas got us all glasses of rust-water straight from the rust-tap.

There were so many things I wanted to ask him, so many things he could tell me. Twelve years had passed and I'd hardly seen him. Just some letters, a few brief visits. "Any woman in your life?" he asked.

I shook my head and smiled. "Not really. I can't talk to women."

He laughed. "I never could neither."

"How's life here?" I asked.

"We do all right. Summer's great, there's lots of vegetables. A little late starting this year, though. Then we go to Arizona in the late fall and ride out the winter there."

"Sounds nice," said Micah. "Rumor has it you can pick oranges right off the trees in Arizona."

"It's a desert."

"Right, right."

Silas inspected his shoes. "We got a little community we go stay with in the desert. Nice people."

"Silas—Grandma—" I didn't know how to say it. "She's got cancer, Silas, she's gonna die real soon and you should come down there with us. I was thinking you should come down to be with her. Grandma's in the hospital and Roald wants her to stay there, and I just want her to come home and to be home when she dies and I want her to have you there...." I started to choke on the words. My eyes watered, my voice about to crack. Force it down, I thought. No crying, I said, but no matter what I said to them, the tears had a mind of their own. My shoulders broke into stiff sobs, like the shoulders of a statue breaking free from rock that encases it. I felt Micah's hand on my shoulder and brushed it off, tried to wipe away my tears. Then I couldn't stop myself from crying more. Nothing else in the whole world made a sound but my emasculate tears. I could feel the others watch me.

I tried to compose myself again, but when I looked up I saw Leanna sitting there, too. She must have come in to watch my manhood slipping down my face and onto the rough-hewn table. Seeing her made me break down again. And after my last drop of self-respect had dripped out, she handed me a Kleenex, which I used at first; but the snotty mess on my face quickly overwhelmed its daintiness and I reverted to my forearm to finish the job.

"I gotta lie down," I said as I gave my nose a final wipe. I couldn't keep my eyes open anymore. Leanna directed me over to their couch and put an afghan over me.

"What do you know about that cult? And his dad?" I heard Micah whisper as I woke up. The sun had faded and the kitchen light was on where they were talking. From where I was lying, I could see Silas and Micah but not Leanna.

"Well, you know about our crazy ancestors? Did Kaz ever tell you? They were always having visions, you know, God leading them to do this or that. I guess Aeneas and Ephraim think that the first one, Regnus is his name, was actually a Mormon who'd run away from Missouri. Because a Mormon guy called the Hidden Prophet is supposed to have found this scroll of secrets just south of our family land. So they put together that it was him. And that our family line is prophetic."

"And they sell prodigious quantities of illegal drugs to finance some utopian kingdom that will rise on the ashes of civilization," added Leanna.

"Yeah," said Silas, "yeah, they do."

"And they think Kazimir might be the second coming of Christ?" asked Micah.

"Not quite. The return of the Hidden Prophet or something. At least Aeneas hoped so. It was batty, living in that house. I don't know why I stuck with him as long as I did," said Leanna.

"If we went and found Ephraim—would he know where Aeneas is?"

"Ephraim?" said Leanna. "The opium addict posing as some kind of magic healer? He couldn't find his ass from his elbow. I doubt if Aeneas can either. He was already sliding down a slippery slope even when I was with him."

Everyone was silent for a moment. I stood and stretched and was about to go in there, when they started again.

"What about Kaz, how's he doing with that stuff?" asked Leanna. "He doesn't seem—stable."

"He's trying, I think, really trying to hold himself together—" Micah's thoughts faded off into silence.

I went in then; they all turned and looked at me. "Hey," I contributed, and made for the door.

"Can I join you?" asked Micah.

"Free country."

We walked over to the fence of the goat pasture. He lit a joint and we shared it as we walked the perimeter of the field in silence. I didn't have the stuff in my head to make sense of everything. I needed space.

"How you doing?" he asked.

"Great. Never been better."

"Pretty intense in there before."

"Yeah—lots of skeleton in the Kazimir closet."

He extinguished his joint on the ground. "You hear us talking?"

"Some."

"They said we can sleep here tonight. Tomorrow Silas will come back down with us."

"Good, maybe we can get Grandma out then. Get her back home."

Coyotes yipped in the distance. A goat lifted its head in concentration, and then went back to grazing.

"Don't you need to get back to saving souls with your bass?"

"This is where I need to be right now. I'm the only thing you got."

"A beacon of orange Mohawk in a sea of insanity?"

"Something like that. Besides, it's more interesting."

A flash of light caught my eye in the field.

"You all right, Kaz? What is it?"

I blinked again. Nothing. "I don't know."

When we went back in, Leanna and Silas had made some spaghetti and a big salad. We ate, made small talk about their little house in the big woods, college, and Micah's hair, skirting around the fringes of my meltdown. I was still tired, so we said goodnight early. Micah and I pulled our sleeping bags from his station wagon and laid them out in the field.

The stars danced in contra over our heads. It was during the Perseids, and meteors leapt merrily hither and thither across the geometric patterns of the stars. I kept thinking about Leanna. I had not seen her since the incident: thirteen years and still I felt betrayed. But I knew I had to forgive her. What did I know of how life was for her when she was with my father? Hell, my father made me crazy. And what did I know of love? She had left my father for Silas, and had been with him ever since. She loved him and he loved her and they had a happy life together. Happy, far away from me … forgetting about me … and now she was coming back with us, her and Silas, and how would that be? Awkward, that's how. Relationships were stupid. Civilization is the Beast.

A light flashed on the horizon. The headlight of a motorcycle faded off far away. Somebody was following me.

Birds twittered away on the rails of the goat fence; Leanna, inside it, was feeding the goats scraps of food. I slipped out of my sleeping bag and walked over to her.

"Mornin' Kaz. How'd you sleep?" she said, feeding an apple core to one of the goats. "I like to feed them by hand sometimes. Want to try it?" She held a bucket of food scraps toward me.

I reached in and grabbed a few more apple cores and offered them to the goat. I watched him chew and another goat pushed into him and nudged my hand. I fed him a scrap too, then rubbed his horns as he masticated.

"Silas still run his trap lines?" I asked.

"Yeah, we pretty much grow, collect, or hunt all our own food up here," she told me.

"How 'bout down in Arizona?"

"The same. Our friends run a small farm out there. We stay in a yurt and help 'em out with their animals. It's the Godwin way, as Micah put it."

"So you're a Godwin?"

"You mean are we married? No. We never married officially, just have been together since—" she stopped short.

"Since the fight?"

"Since then." She fed small potatoes to the goats. "How are Roald and Jethro taking all this with Grandma?"

"With military rigueur. They want her in the hospital for all the tests and stuff. She'll probably die there if we don't get home. I don't want her to die there. That's not right."

"I see what you mean," she said, bending to scratch the goat's neck. "Your dad gonna be there?"

"We kind of got into a fight."

"Is that right?"

"Just—just a lot of bullshit he was always doing with me. The cult and the visions and all the prophecy."

"I know. I remember."

We were quiet a moment.

"I don't know if I should come with you guys," she said. "It's been a long time."

"It'd be okay if you come," I offered.

"I don't know if I could handle seeing Aeneas—if he were to come back. You know he threatened to kill Silas if he ever saw him again."

"Funny, I told my dad the same thing."

She laughed. "Really?"

"I think Grandma's illness will make all the threats a wash."

"Or you just all kill each other. Makes more of a horror movie than a wash," she said. "If Silas goes out I think they could come to terms as brothers, but I don't know how I could help anything. She never liked me anyways, you know? Then I tore her family apart." She looked up at the sky. "I was thinking I could just head out to Arizona myself, have Silas come out after all this is over."

"I think I used to blame you when I was a kid. I didn't realize how much in love you and Silas were. I didn't know you'd be together the rest of your lives. But I don't think Grandma blames you all that much. She understood, and tried to get me to forgive you too."

She looked over my face as if searching for the little boy I'd been. "Well, Kaz, that means a lot to me. That helps. I just don't know, though. I don't know if I could handle it myself—"

She stood back up, the bucket bereft of victuals. "I gotta get back.

I've got some things to do in town this afternoon."

We left the goats and walked back to the cabin, her peasant dress swaying through the tall grass. I woke Micah up and Leanna made us all scrambled eggs. It was vaguely like old times.

Silas came out to the van with his hair combed over the balding patches, wearing his Sunday-best jeans and a clean flannel and carrying a small duffel bag. As we drove, we listened to talk radio, flea market news, and a fishing report on the local lakes. Silas whittled a twig into the shape of an old man's face, flicking the scraps out the window. He showed it to me, grinning like a child.

"Pretty neat, huh?"

I smiled and glanced into the rear view mirror. Micah was studying his Bible. No motorcycle followed.

Chapter Sixteen

Micah dropped me and Silas off at our place. We took Grandma's station wagon into town. The hospital had not changed locations, which made it easier to find.

"If we can, let's get her out right away, so she can sleep in her own bed tonight," I told him.

"All right," he said and wiped his perpetually runny nose. I let him go in before me and I waited in the car a little while, watching the entrance to the hospital parking lot. Nobody had followed. All day I hadn't seen the motorcycle.

Grandma was delighted to see Silas, half the time because it was the return of one of her prodigal sons, and half the time because she thought he was my grandfather. She would call him Herbert and he would just blush, not willing to correct her. She also thought I was the nurse, and kept asking me to get her a cup of water, until I had filled up a half-dozen Dixie cups and placed them at her bedside.

"There's an ear in the cup!" Grandma screamed as the nurse entered the room, picking up each Dixie and dumping its contents onto her gown and then tossing the cup on the ground.

Silas was trying to settle her. "That isn't an ear, Mom, that's just water. You're having a memory. Remember? I cut Aeneas's ear off, when I was a kid."

"Aeneas! Where is he? He's gotten into the damn freezer again and eaten all the apple pies!" She looked about wildly, and then fixated on tugging at her IV.

"Aeneas isn't here, Mom, you're just hallucinating," he tried to tell her, and looked at us for help.

I grabbed Grandma's hand and held it in both of mine until she'd settled a bit, while the nurse wrapped the IV site in gauze to disguise it.

"Do you want me to give her some medicine to settle her?" the nurse asked.

"We can handle it now," Silas told her.

"We'd rather not sedate her, anyway," I added. "We can hold her hands." The nurse gave me a grateful smile and vanished. Grandma was half-asleep anyway, breathing heavily and punctuating the incessant medical beeping with groans and indecipherable mumbles.

Silas reached over and gathered the spittle from her mouth with his fingers, then wiped it on his pants. I got her another Dixie of water and moistened her mouth.

"She's all hopped up on the morphine, Silas, that's why she's acting like this. We've gotta get her home. Get her to her garden, the places that keep her sane, the places that make it worth it for her to live."

"She's probably got a lot of pain and needs the morphine though. It's no good for her to just be in a lot of pain."

"You can talk to the doctor and maybe he can get us some morphine for home, something like that."

"Are you sure that's a good idea? How are we supposed to take care of her?"

"We'll just do it. I'm sure we can figure it out."

He looked doubtful.

"You can call the doctor because you have at least as much control or more than Roald does. Get the doctor to set it up. We'll sign her out tonight and she can sleep at home."

He sat trying to think it through. I had forgotten that he always did things so slowly. I paced the room. "Look at this place—no windows, no green stuff. No birds, no willow trees, no rivers. It's a dead place. How is something supposed to live in a dead place? We've gotta get her out of here."

He listened like stone listens, elbows on his thin legs, hands over his mouth. I let him sit as I paced.

A knock brought the nurse back in. "Is she doing better now?" she asked. Neither of us responded. She went about charting things on her clipboard. The trail of perfume in her wake induced a minor allergic reaction in my throat. Silas sniffled again, wiped his nose with his forearm, then spoke. "I want to talk to the doctor, Miss Nurse. We're gonna sign her out of here."

"You take her out of here, and she's going to die quick," she said, clearly agitated.

"She's not gonna live through this. We gotta think about how she's gonna die. She's got a right to die the way she'd want."

The nurse tried to convince us of the benefits of dying in the hospital until I started chiming in, too. In the end, she gave us the number to Grandma's doctor. Silas called and told the doctor that we wanted to take Grandma home.

"Uh huh, uh huh, okay, uh huh," he said for upwards of five minutes, and hung up the phone.

"What did he say?" I asked.

"He said we can't take her out of here."

"That's bullshit, Silas, you're her son; you get to decide. Call him back and tell him what you want to do."

"I'm just not good at stuff like that."

"Don't you want her to go home? Don't you want her to be at peace in her garden, in her home, where our family has been for centuries? If you were her, wouldn't you want to be there?"

He looked down, and then his hand went to the phone and he dialed again.

"We're taking her home," he said and hung up. He sighed and looked at me like a squirrel about to be hit by a truck.

"Let's go sign her out."

We conducted ourselves through the legalese, helped the nurse dress her and take off all of the IVs and tape, got Grandma situated on a wheelchair, and pushed her to the car.

When we got her home and in bed she gave us a big delirious smile and passed out against her flower print pillows. The weather was unseasonably cold; not even the crickets were out, and Silas went around and the lit the pilot lights in the heaters while I threw an extra blanket on her bed.

"Will she be warm enough?" I asked.

"I think so."

"You can sleep in my room," I told him. "I'm gonna sleep in the tipi. I've just always liked it out there better."

"I'll probably just sleep in the yard, under the willow."

"Like you used to?"

"Yeah, like I used to."

In the morning, I went to the house to check on Grandma. I walked past Silas's sleeping bag, splayed open like an empty pea pod. He was nowhere in sight, and the dark sky looked like it might spew all over us any minute. I gathered up his stuff and brought it in with me. I set it on the couch and went to check Grandma.

I knocked on the door softly, and when I slipped in she was sitting up in bed, staring at the painting on the wall.

"Morning, Grandma."

She looked at me with a blank expression.

"How're you doing this morning?" I asked.

"How'd I get here?"

"Silas and I checked you out of the hospital."

She looked out the window.

"I thought you'd want to be home. I thought you'd want to go into your garden and sleep in your own bed."

"Thank you, Kaz." Then she added, "My stomach hurts." I dug through a moldy bathroom cabinet until I found gas medicine.

"My head hurts," she said, and I emptied the Tylenol from the same cabinet. Silas tried to feed her eggs but she wouldn't eat them. We scavenged the cupboards for food she could eat but she hadn't been grocery shopping much. I found canned applesauce and peaches, which seemed to do the trick.

By mid-morning, the rain began to patter down the window and Grandma fell back asleep to its tintinnabulations.

"Morphine in her system's running out," said Silas as we walked around the property.

"Yeah. And I didn't think about food. We should go into town and get some groceries soon.

We looked over the garden: ripe tomatoes should be useful, eggplants could be cooked soft; the abundant peppers probably wouldn't help her, but we picked them anyway. Beans stretched yellowing vines heavy with pods up their catches; raspberry bushes lined the fence but only a few desiccated fruits held to the canes. Some small carrots came up prettily. Weeds were catching up with the vegetables, though, and slugs and other pests had done good damage to some of the tomatoes.

"This is going to be hard, Kaz. I talked to the pharmacy, and they said they wouldn't have her pain meds until Monday. A doctor's going to come over and bring them." He sighed and looked up to the rain coming down on us. Drops dripped from his mustache. "Alcohol's a potent pain reliever."

"Marijuana too—I got some. That should be good for it. Is she getting morphine then?"

"I don't think so. They don't let that out of the hospital."

We started making our way back to the house. Silas fiddled with the vegetables in his hands. "If she's in so much pain that we got to keep her delirious on drugs, what good is living any longer?" We stopped at the steps. "There's no point in keeping her alive just to keep her alive."

"We can't just take her off the medicines though, it'd be hell dying like that."

"I wouldn't want her to die like that," he said.

What he was suggesting suddenly hit. "I'll have to give that some thought," I told him and went inside.

Grandma stared at the ceiling as we fed her more applesauce.

"How'd I get here?"

I explained again why we brought her home.

"Thank you," she said. "I want to go outside." We helped her out, one on each arm, down the steps barefoot and in her nightgown.

"Onto the grass," she said. She swayed sideways and Silas supported her, and together we led her onto the lawn, then down below the old willow.

Robins sang inside the willow, its branches cascading down and shading the area below. She put her hand on the trunk and rubbed it. "Remember you used to sleep here, Silas," she said. "I could never get you inside." She turned to me "When did you come home?"

"I just got home a few days ago, Grandma, remember? I saw you in the hospital."

She nodded and looked out over the land. She pointed to the garden, and we started to help her to it.

"When did I get so old?" she asked. "I was feeling just fine, a little sick, Kaz left, then—I don't know."

"You got cancer in you, Grandma,"

"Oh," she said, standing up straight. "Damn."

When we reached the driveway, her feet hurt from the gravel. Silas started in to get her some shoes.

"To hell with it," she called after him, "just help me to the porch and get me some whiskey." She stopped again, closing her eyes. "Wait a second, Kazimir, let go of me."

I did as I was told and took a step back. She stood with closed eyes. I could hear it, too: a quiet sonorous call in a high pitch.

"You hear that, Grandma?"

She opened her eyes and snapped, "I can't hear it over your babbling." We listened, quiet again. Silas slipped onto the porch, setting down the whiskey and cards. The singing was gone.

Silas had poured us each a jigger of whiskey over ice and we dealt cards for rummy. Grandma was in good spirits, no pain. But her hand shook too much to pour herself another glass.

"You told Aeneas yet?" she asked.

"I don't know where he is, Grandma, not since—we had a fight."

"Oh yes," she said, laying down a set of threes and discarding her last card, "I forgot about that."

After a time she grew quiet. We set our hands down and just sat for a while. "I didn't know about your fight," she said finally. "Aeneas has a way of doing that to people. My poor son." We sat a while longer.

"Time to go to bed," she said.

We got her into bed, gave her a shot of whiskey and turned off the lights.

The phone woke me up as I napped on the couch.

"What the hell do you think you're doing?"

"Roald?"

"I'm at the hospital and they said you checked her out yesterday."

"I didn't—Silas did. We took her home."

"How did Silas get into all this?"

"Went up and told him about everything. He wanted her home, too."

"Against what the doctor said?"

"We took her home because she asked to come home."

"Dammit, Kazimir, go to hell." He hung up.

I went back to my bedroom, removed a pile of clothes I had left on a chair months ago, and replaced it with myself. I rubbed my eyes and did what had to pass for thinking. She would die, and there would be nothing, I thought. Nothing but dust on these old things. Where would the house go then? The old gravestones? The river would be dammed and the trees bleed down and the sky become emphysemic with black smoke. The whole world would drown and even the dusty trunks in the attic wouldn't matter.

CHAPTER SEVENTEEN

DAYLIGHT DYED THE CLOUDS IN BATIK, DRESSED THE WILLOW in its Sunday best, and glanced off the chimes Grandma had hung by the porch door. The prisms in the windows spun rainbows about the porch swing Silas was sitting on.

He grinned at me as I plopped down next to him and watched him work. After a few minutes he looked up and grinned again, then held out his hand. In it were tiny figurines, maybe two inches high and of varying girth. Grandma was there in a long dress bending down over a tiny flower, a basket in one hand. Silas and Leanna holding hands; Silas alone, a bindlestiff drooping over one shoulder. I paddled a tiny canoe, left arm and right leg extended in action. My father sat cross-legged, his guitar in his lap, Roald was in a military uniform, and Jethro had both hands to his mouth as if he were eating a burger.

"These are great. When did you do these?"

"Just last night. Found some nice willow sticks."

"You spend a lot of time whittling, don't you?"

"I got a lot of time. Don't really work—just odd jobs if we need money for dental or something." He shrugged. "Not much required of us on this earth except to live and die. I hunt a little, we grow some vegetables. Take care of the land in exchange for rent and everything."

I picked up the little figurine of myself and held it in my palm. "Maybe sometime you and I can take a canoe trip together. After all this is over."

"I'd like that. Or we could go skiing, too."

I gave that one back to him and picked up the one of him and Leanna. "You two together. Why aren't you hunting or something?"

He blushed again. "What I like to do best."

"You miss her?"

He looked around. "Yeah, we haven't been much apart since that fight." He was clearly uneasy and wiped his big crooked nose again. "I considered making one of your dad beating the crap out of me. Action shot." He grinned.

I grinned back.

Grandma's eyebrows furrowed in concentration as she stared at the ceiling. A thin ray of sunshine made a square of light at her feet. We fed her toast and showed her the miniatures and she gave us a half smile and a nod.

"You get any pain-killers when you brought me home?" she asked.

"No, they said they couldn't get us them till Monday. Today's Sunday. It's a small hospital; they don't have an outpatient pharmacy."

She didn't respond.

"You in a lot of pain?" asked Silas.

She gave him a half nod again. "Get me some whiskey or something."

We went into kitchen, and got down the last of the whiskey and poured her a glass. "Is this really gonna do the trick?" I asked Silas.

"Better than anything they got in the hospital, to tell you the truth. They just don't use it because it's addictive."

"And morphine isn't?"

I called Micah and asked him to bring some of our essentials over.

Silas went out to get some more whiskey, and in the meantime, Grandma woke up moaning. Twenty minutes later, Micah showed up with a backpack of necessities.

"Sorry it took me so long," he said, reaching into his pack. "Here." He held out a bag of weed.

"Let's go give it to her."

"I don't think so," he said handing me the lighter and pipe, "It's just a little too weird for me—giving ganja to Grandma. I'll just wait in here and fix myself a sandwich."

I hesitated. It hadn't occurred to me how awkward this might be. I hid the pipe in my pocket.

She was still staring at the ceiling when I came in. I held up a glass of water for her to drink.

"How's the pain?"

She didn't say anything.

"Yesterday you seemed all right … it just got really bad all of a sudden?"

She didn't respond.

"Silas went out to get more whiskey. That helped, didn't it?"

She gave me a slight nod.

"Micah came over. He's gonna stay a few days, and he brought this." I held up the bag of marijuana.

She glanced at it. "Reefer?"

"Yeah, the old wacky weed. He's got a friend who uses it and he thought—"

"Don't Eddie Haskell me, Kaz."

"Okay, it's his. But he thinks it might help with the pain. I was wondering if you want to try smoking it." I held out the glass pipe for her to examine.

"I don't know how."

"I'll help you," I said. I rested the pipe on the quilt and squeezed her hand. Outside was the overcast sky, a bird flitting by the window.

I separated the weed, pulling out the seeds, and when it was clean, I set up the pipe for her.

"Hold it to your mouth like this," I showed her. "You have to cover the carb—the little hole—with your finger, like that." The steady call of the wind chimes filtered in through the windows.

I handed it to her and flicked the lighter. The flame lit up her bloodshot eyes. The smell of spilled whiskey emanated from her nightgown.

"Inhale now. When it feels hot, take your finger off the little hole and suck a little more, not too much or—"

She coughed up two lungs' worth of smoke. I helped her drink some water.

"I don't feel anything except my lungs hurting."

"You got to hold it in longer. Take a few small hits."

"What's a hit?"

"A smoke. An inhale."

She shook her head. "I'm too old for this."

I held it for her this time. I let her only take small amounts and had her hold it in each time for as long as she could. We did this until the pipe was cashed.

I put the pipe and the weed in my sweatshirt pocket, and held her hand.

"How do you feel now?"

"Like I'm floating."

I laughed.

"Your grandpa, before the war," she said and paused, trying to collect her thoughts. "One night we went to a jazz club in Chicago, and there were some reefer addicts outside. Herbert knew one guy, and he offered us some. We tried it, but I didn't feel anything."

"But now you do?"

"Now I do," she said and closed her eyes. I waited for her to fall asleep, then slipped out, clicking the door closed.

Out on the porch, rain came down off the gutters, wove mandalas into the gravel. Micah ruminated on a sandwich. We pulled out the pipe to kill our own pain. The drops would go into the Kickapoo, and the Kickapoo into the Wisconsin, and the Wisconsin into the Mississippi. Water into sky, and then what? It simply returned to Earth, endlessly.

The station wagon pulled into the driveway. We helped Silas carry the groceries in and put them away, then pulled most of them out again to snack. Silas went in to check on Grandma.

When he came back, Micah was pulling out his pipe for another hit. "Kazimir here got her stoned. You want any?"

He shook his head. "You got her stoned?" He tried to repress a smile. "Your dad and I used to have some fields back in the woods."

I nodded. "That's where we get it. Micah still harvests and sells to his friends at Bible school. None of it's ready now, of course."

Silas put his hands in his pockets and looked at the rain. "I suppose it could do her good. And it's cheaper than whiskey."

Grandma woke later in pain. "Take me outside," she said. We lifted her up all together and carried her out like a casket. We carried her down the steps and at their base set her to her feet. "I had a dream that the rain would fall on me and I would be cured." We steadied her as she lifted her head up toward the sky and opened her mouth to let the rain wash in. Then she closed it. "I'm cold," she told us, and we brought her back to bed with a glass of whiskey.

Another hour of playing cards and listening to radio passed, and we could hear her moaning through the static-laced radio.

I went back into her room. "You all right, Grandma?"

"What does is look like?"

"What is it that hurts?"

"My stomach." She sucked in a long breath. "Get me some more of the wacky weed."

I called out for Dr. Feelgood. Micah showed up with his physician's satchel and started to pack her a pipe.

Silas watered down some whiskey for her. Once the whiskey was down her gullet, Micah inflated her lungs with the weed. I took a hit and Micah took one, then we helped her take another. The room was beginning to look like a speakeasy. The smoke alarm went off. Silas took the batteries out, then stood in the corner with his arms folded. Grandma finished off the last of it and Micah was just stashing it into his backpack when the creak of the door announced Roald's arrival to the scene.

"It smells like goddamn Woodstock in here! What the hell do you think you're doing?"

"Administering medication," said Micah.

Roald waved his hand like it was a windshield wiper. "Nice haircut."

"Thanks, I like yours too," Micah said.

Roald glared at me. "You're giving her reefer? You take her out of the hospital and bring her here so you can smoke marijuana? What do you think this is, one of your father's goddamn hippy circus parties? You're gonna kill her."

"I wanted to get out of the hospital, Roald, it's better here," Grandma said with her eyes closed.

Silas stood up straight. "Let's let her sleep. We can talk about it outside."

We gathered our paraphernalia and went out to the porch. The boards creaked with Roald's pacing, and everything was damp from the rain coming through the screens.

"Tomorrow I am calling an ambulance, and they're taking her back to the hospital where she can get some real help."

"You can call an ambulance, but she's not going anywhere. She's really weak, Roald. She can barely stay awake," I said.

"Of course she can't stay awake. You've got her smoking the marijuana, you idiot."

"When she's not smoking she's in so much pain she can barely talk."

"That's why I'm taking her back to the hospital!"

"There's nothing they can do but lessen the pain, the doctor said so himself. And they dope her up on morphine and she doesn't make sense. At least when we give her pot and whiskey we can understand her."

"She was talking nonsense."

"No, she was reasonably cogent. You just didn't agree with what she said."

"You little waste of a kid—all hopped up on marijuana—what the hell would you know?"

"He's been hopped up on the marijuana for five or six years now, and mostly makes sense," interrupted Micah.

"I didn't ask you, freak boy."

"I didn't need your permission."

They glared at each other; Roald cracked his knuckles and turned the color of Micah's hair.

"Micah, you're not helping." I said.

"Roald," Silas said, "you were in the war."

Roald looked at him like he was a talking mouse.

"When you got shot," Silas touched his own cheek, "and the bullet went through, and your teeth were all mangled and you were bleeding all over, did you think you were gonna die?"

Roald grunted.

"You thought you were gonna die, and where'd you want to be to die? Did you want to die in Korea? Or did you wish you were back home in Sparta? How many of your friends did you hear say they wished they were home as they died?"

"I would have given anything to be in an American hospital, getting decent care, not getting alcohol poured on my wounds to save me until I could get 'coptered out. That's what it looks like here—field medicine. You're digging crap out of the cupboards in hopes of it helping, when she's got a hospital she can go to."

"You were saved though," I said. "Nothing's going to save Grandma at this point. I just want to make her happy when she dies."

Roald sat on the porch swing and started to rock. "There's still a chance. She can still talk, they can still save her," he said, folding his arms. "Unlike you three, I gotta get some work done, harvest's coming up; but I'm sending Jethro over here tomorrow with an ambulance to make sure she goes back to the hospital." He stood. "You patsies lose hope so easily. You've gotta give her a chance."

"We're giving her a chance to die decently, a chance she might not get if she goes back in the hospital."

"Jethro's coming tomorrow, and he's bringing an ambulance," he said and walked off the porch out into the rain. We watched him drive off.

"What's Jethro's fat butt going to do?" inquired Micah.

"Nothing," I said. "He tries to take her, we'll just carry her around, and he can chase us until he drops of a clogged artery."

"Lucky he's bringing his own ambulance," said Silas, chuckling.

Silas stayed in the house to take care of Grandma. In the tipi, Micah went right to sleep but I stayed up thinking, staring, listening to the owls. There was a hole in the tipi and it dripped water onto my forehead. An image flashed in my mind: a headlight of a motorcycle, a man riding across the plains in the dark.

A thud in her room took us from the table. We found her on the floor next to her chair. She looked at us in disbelief.

"I don't know what happened, officer, one moment we were getting out of the car…"

"That's all right, ma'am," I told her, and helped her up. Silas smirked at me, but she complained of back pain. We gave her another glass of whiskey and a pot cookie Micah had whipped up, and sat by her bedside to finish our breakfast. Grandma wasn't making any noise but wasn't sleeping either, just staring into the distance.

"How are you feeling, Mrs. Godwin?" Micah asked. She didn't reply, only shook her head.

"Do you know what year it is?"

She looked at us as if we might tell her. "Well, let's see." She seemed to think a while. "1939?"

"How about the president?" Silas asked.

"Well, that would be FDR then," she said. "I just don't get it. I was over there, and now I'm here," she added, and started to go into a panic.

Silas tried to talk to her and settle her down. Micah got some more cookies and we fed them to her. It took a while for her to fade into sleep, lightly murmuring about the Communists.

The day was misty and rainy when we finally stepped outside.

"Wanna fish some?" Silas asked.

It was good to be that close to the river again. Its sound had lulled me to sleep in the tipi, but I hadn't actually seen it in days. Silas and Micah fished, but I just put my pole aside after a while and stepped into the river barefoot. The bottom squished up between my toes and the rain plopped on my head. It was beautiful to be there with my feet buried in the silt of sandstone, the rock of which these hills and pastures were formed. Summer's detritus floated past me: the tiny needles of pines, the leaves of oaks and maples, the hollowed exoskeletons of insects.

I closed my eyes and listened to the susurrus of the river. As soon as I did that, I felt dizzy, as if the whole world were coming to an end, splitting apart onto shards, and casting me off into empty space. There was no end to illogic in this world. *Logic is just a word for the kind of things mankind is engineered to understand,* said a voice in my head. *It's derivative and thus is confined by the parameters of what it studies.*

I looked at Micah and Silas across the river from me. "Did you guys hear someone talking?"

"Just you," called Micah.

I waited for myself to speak to myself further, but apparently I was done.

By noon they had caught a few fish and decided to go cook them for lunch and check on Grandma. Jethro was already there. He sat on the couch munching on some potato chips and reading the paper.

"Afternoon fellas," he said, chips slipping from his mouth. "I called the ambulance right before you guys got back from your vacation at the river. Somebody should be watching her the whole time."

"We weren't gone more than an hour," Silas said.

"It don't matter, they'd be doing it in the hospital."

"The hell they would," I said. "Each nurse has got like ten thousand patients."

"You take a look at her?" asked Silas. "She's not long for this world. She isn't thinking right even when she's not on drugs." He told Jethro about her fall.

"All the more reason for her to be in the hospital."

"All the more reason for her to be here. She's about to die," I said.

I went into the kitchen and saw the phone book open to the only ambulance service listed. As Silas and Jethro debated, I got hold of them and cancelled the ambulance. Then I ripped out the page and stuck it in my pocket. When I came in they were still debating.

"I just cancelled your ambulance Jethro, false alarm," I said.

He glared at me. "I don't know what the hell you guys think you're doing. She's gonna die."

"She's going to die anyway, she might as well do it at home."

"I'm waiting right here," Jethro said. "Roald's coming this evening and he's not gonna be happy."

"What's new."

It was another hour before the pain really began.

It started with her crying out. Silas and I rushed to see what was wrong. She arched her back and was holding her head, then relaxed a little and began to wrench on her hair as if it were stuck to her head and she was trying to get it out. She cried out some more and we kept asking her what was wrong, but she wouldn't respond.

The sheets were tangled around her, and I tried to straighten them as Micah mashed a couple brownies in water and poured it down her throat.

"We've got to get her to a hospital," shouted Jethro from the door.

"Shut up, Jethro," I said as I petted Grandma's damp hair.

"Shut yer own fat mouth," he mumbled and left. I could hear him in the kitchen looking around for the phone book.

"Where the hell is that ambulance page, Kazimir?" he bellowed.

"I'm cold," Grandma whispered to me.

"I'll get you a blanket," I told her and was met by Jethro's body as I tried to go into the hall.

"Where the hell is that ambulance page?" he shouted, his potato chip spittle landing on my face.

"She's cold and I'm getting her another blanket. Get out of my way."

He stared at me as I squeezed past him to the hall closet.

"She's not going to the hospital, I already told you. Get it through your fat skull," I spat back at him as I pulled the blankets out. "We'll take care of it, and everything would be fine if Roald hadn't cancelled the pain medication this morning. We could be giving her some right now."

"She *needs* to go to the *hospital*."

"*You* need to help us or go home."

"Kazimir, you better get in here!" Micah called.

I went back in to find Grandma projecting vomit onto various objects and people all about the room. She leaned herself sideways and got the rest of it over the side of the bed; but as she did, she began to slip off. I grabbed her. Micah helped get her legs up and soon we had her on the mattress again.

"You're gonna be okay, Grandma, you're gonna be okay," I whispered and stroked her hair. The whole room smelled like vomit now, and I realized that it was all over her hair, and then I realized that we were both lying in a pool of it.

"She puked up those brownies. We're gonna have to smoke her up," Micah said, going to get his backpack.

"Silas or Jethro or somebody get some new sheets, and some pajamas for her," I said.

We poured some more whiskey down her throat. Micah rejuvenated the supply of THC in her circulatory system. Pretty soon she was in an uncomfortable sleep, moaning and whispering gibberish.

We surrounded her and lifted her out of bed and onto the floor and then changed the sheets. Micah wiped up the vomit that had splattered the room.

With the sheets changed and new blankets on, I put the old ones in the washer. I noticed a big brown mess lower down on the sheets as well. We hadn't even realized she was having diarrhea.

I came back in to the room, and looked around at the other three on their knees trying to clean the mess up.

"She had diarrhea, too," I said. "We're going to have to wash her, change her nightgown, get her something for the diarrhea."

"They could be doing all this for her at the hospital."

"Yeah, well, we're her damn family, we're the ones supposed to be taking care of her. We can't let her die in one of those places when her soul wants to come to rest here."

"Dying's a messy business," said Silas.

"Who's gonna wash her?" asked Jethro standing up and panting from the exertion. "Because I don't have the stomach for it."

"I'll do it if I have to," I said.

"I'll help," said Silas.

"I've never had the experience of cleaning up an old woman's diarrhea before," added Micah.

Jethro sat on the porch and had a whiskey while we filled the bathtub, undressed her sleeping body, and carried her down the hall to the waiting bathtub.

Rashes had developed on the insides of her thighs; vomit, red spots and poo were all over the place. Twice we drained the water just to get the guck out and refilled. She woke up periodically and gave us wide eyed stares, before passing into stupor. I massaged her fancy flower-scented shampoo into her hair. "Tha's good," she whispered.

"You like that, Grandma?" I worked it in as best I could. Micah and Silas sponged her down, and then splashed water to rinse her off.

"How're you gonna get that out of her hair?" asked Micah.

"I don't know," I said. We had her head down on the far side of the tub and didn't want to turn her. Silas went out and came back with her watering can. We filled it and rinsed the shampoo from her hair. I started to condition it.

"Why are you doing that?" Micah asked.

"So it'll feel clean and nice for her."

When she was conditioned and rinsed, we drained the water and dried her, then put her new nightgown on and carried her back into bed.

She was awake by then, but not saying anything, still in a daze.

I found a brush and tried to comb her hair, which was a knotty mess. She groaned.

"No," she said.

"What am I doing wrong?"

"You have to—you have to start from the bottom. Little by little, work up."

I started over, doing it the way she had told me, working out the knots and snarls. Her hair was still long, though a little coarse, and I had to be gentle so as not to get it caught in the brush.

"My mother," she paused to catch her breath, "my mother used to do this when I was a girl, I was sad and it was floating away."

"Tell me about your mother."

"Just a balloon, and the cat, Greasy," she said, fading into sleep.

The sun peeked through the clouds as I finished her hair. I put another blanket on her and opened the window to let the room air out, and then I left her to sleep.

Silas and Micah were in the yard walking around and Jethro was still on the porch.

"Roald called. He can come tomorrow," Jethro said as I passed him. "I changed my mind, Kaz, I think you're right; she's gonna die soon. I think you should call the doctor, though."

"He was supposed to come out. Roald cancelled him."

"That's because he thought she was gonna be in the hospital. She's not."

"I know she's not. Call him back and ask if he can come out this evening for us."

"I can't. Someone took the page from the phone book."

"Doctors aren't ambulances. It's doctor Lungborg, go look it up."

I joined the other two under the willow. Micah had just finished rolling another joint and lit it. He offered it to Silas.

"I guess I'll take a whirl." He took a small puff. "Still good stuff coming up here," he commented. The sun was once again obscured by clouds.

After a few joints I decided to broach the subject of Grandma. "Her soul told me it wants to be here when she dies," I said. "But if she keeps getting worse this is gonna be dirty and messy to keep this up."

"I don't think she has much longer," Silas said, his eyes already bloodshot.

"No," said Micah.

"She's gonna keep having more and more pain," said Silas. "Leanna's sister died of cancer. She said that she got worse and worse, just agony." He sucked in another drag. "I don't want Mom to go through that."

"Jethro's calling the doctor," I told him. "Maybe she should go back on morphine. She's beginning to make less and less sense, even without it. Maybe it will help more with the pain."

"We can't just keep her on it forever," Silas said looking down at the river in the distance. "We gotta talk to her if we can, see if she wants to go before it gets to rough."

Micah sized him up. "Are you suggesting what I think you're suggesting?"

Silas looked away.

"He's saying it might be best to help her go," I said.

"She won't think so," said Micah. "She's Catholic. She can't tell you she wants to go. She would damn herself to perdition. And besides, you can't just kill her, that's a sin."

"I don't think it's gonna damn anybody to help ease some suffering," Silas said. "But if we're gonna help her like that, we got to have Roald, Jethro, everyone on board so there's no trouble."

It had begun to drizzle again by the time we finished the joint and went in to check on her. In the closed-in hall something smelled like vomit, and I realized it was me; I hadn't changed my clothes.

"Doctor's coming out, he'll be here about five," said Jethro.

"Thanks, Jethro," I told him.

"I gotta go," he said, "I have work tomorrow."

"You're not going steal her off to the hospital now?" I asked.

"I looked in on you when you were combing her hair, and I just checked her now. She's sleeping. I could smell the perfume or whatever you had put in her hair. I think maybe you're right, that's better. You still need help here. You need the doctor and some meds and stuff. But if you're willing to do all that dirty work and stuff—it's better."

"Thanks."

"Anyway, Kaz, you're doing good I think. Maybe there is nothing more they can do in the hospital. I think you guys can handle her if the pain gets worse. I'll try to talk Roald down a little."

"Thanks."

"I'm sorry for snapping at you before, you know, I just thought—"

"Jethro, just go—it's okay."

Micah and I were playing cards and Silas was fishing when the doctor came in. As far as I knew, Grandma had never gone to the hospital before this or seen a doctor for anything in her life. I explained that to him, and he said that was probably why the cancer had gotten as bad as it did before they found it. He woke Grandma, talked to her, and phoned in some medication orders. Silas came in and we all talked to the doctor; he told us how to wash her and what to look for and how to turn her. He prescribed medicines for the diarrhea, the vomit, and the pain, but said we'd have to wait on the morphine. He said he could assign us a nurse, and one could come out here within a day or two to help us. She could administer some of the stronger drugs if Grandma needed them.

"How long does she have?" Silas asked.

"Not long, unless there's some kind of miracle. It could be as much as a week or two, or as little as a few days."

We snacked on crackers and cheese. Grandma was awake on and off but wouldn't respond much to us. We gave her the pain pill, then smoked her up and gave her another swig of the good stuff for good measure. More diarrhea.

Later, some of her bridge friends came by, having inquired at the hospital and being sent here. They'd brought casseroles for everybody. Grandma greeted them as best she could but was far too tired to hold a conversation. They left after reiterating to Silas about sixteen times that we could call them if we needed anything.

At ten-thirty I heard her call out and went in from the porch where Micah and I had been watching the thunderstorm.

"The diarrhea medicine the doctor gave her didn't help none," Silas said. He had been sitting by her bedside when she woke. I got some towels from the closet.

"We're running out of sheets," I told him, giving him the last clean set. "I forgot to put the others on the line."

We cleaned her up and gave her more pain pills and sleeping pills and diarrhea pills. We gave her pot and whiskey and tried to get some bread down her. She writhed like a worm on a hook, had tremors, was too cold, too hot. She screamed out and I screamed with her like we were two wounded wolves. Micah opened her pain pills and made me take several. I swallowed them with a glass of water, and in twenty minutes I lost all sense of time.

Rain poured down, thunder, distant lightning flickered through the window. She threw up the diarrhea pills and the pain pills went out the other end. Micah brushed her teeth. I put water down her. Thunder outside. Silas holding her hand. I felt dizzy and there was a sound in my head like a distant radio. The lights in the house twitched, then died. "Power's out," Silas said when he came back in the room. I hadn't noticed he'd left. She called out for Herbert. She called for Aeneas, for her mother, Abe Lincoln, the sheriff. She talked to the wall and the wall spoke back. I was sick to my stomach.

We had her smoke pot until the room looked like a sauna. We gave her more pills, more water. She kept a little down, settled into sweaty inebriated panting, started to get up, collapsed half-off the sweat-soaked bed, and began a fitful sleep.

When I came out into the hall, the clock read two-thirty. Micah was on the couch, smoking another bowl. The room spun like a merry-go-round. The whole house was a coffin.

"You want some?" Micah asked.

I shook my head.

"That's a first."

"I'm gonna go outside for a little."

"It's pouring."

"I know."

I stepped out into the storm. Lightning lit up the willow tree in the front yard and I could see my breath. A small lake formed in the driveway, preparing for the next ice age. I could smell the night crawlers. I counted the seconds. The rain hit the gravel so hard that I couldn't hear the river. She was dying, and all I cared about was getting away from her right now. I wish it were me, I thought. I wished it were me instead of her. She liked living. I would go for her. It wouldn't even be a loss; only two people in the whole world would be affected. None of it works that way. Where are the miracles? This damn earth, this damn life. Thunder shook. Seven seconds. I was already drenched.

The light was also out in the old barn. I flipped the switch a few times just for good luck. Rats scuttled about in the rafters. I inched around carefully; there was so much to trip over. I ran my hand over a half-done sofa. Dust was an inch thick. *I'm here,* something said to me. A chill ran down my spine.

"Hello?"

Somewhere rain dripped, maybe in the rafters. I was too creeped out to go forward, so I made tried to make my way back but started getting lost in the darkness. I tripped on something and landed in a chair. I half-expected to find a skeleton in it. I didn't.

Lightning came through the cracks in the boards long enough for me to see where I was. I wound my way back to the door. Why can't I cry? I wondered. Why am I so numb? Grandma was dying and I couldn't even shed a tear. She was everything to me, and I felt nothing.

Outside it was no more illuminated. Eight seconds—the storm was moving away, but the rain continued to pour.

I went around back of the barn to the garden, took my shoes off. I wanted to feel something, anything; I wanted to be a part of the world. Take me, I thought, make the worms grow from my skull. I didn't want to be part of this heavy, miserable world where people like Grandma writhed in pain and assholes like me lived. We were stuck, all of us. Trapped. Caught. Fate, weird fate.

I took the rest of my clothes off and threw them into a pile by the barn. I waded calf-deep through the garden mud. I just wanted to be alone, just alone, just get some quiet, feel the air move about me, feel the mud of her old garden. Bury myself in it.

A light came up the road: a single headlight. It glanced off the pines that lined the farm field.

I thrust my hands into the mud about where she used to grow the peas and clenched a big chunk of dirt in each fist and raised them above my head. Lightning lit the air, the sludge in my fists; worms wriggled free, the incarnadine mud ran down my forearms onto my chest. The mud in my hands warmed and seemed to throb. The headlight slowed as it came to our driveway, turned; it slashed the tree, the house, and then settled on me.

The engine stopped. The single light remained on. I lowered my hands and squinted through the rain and the light but could see nothing.

Then the light cut. I tried to get my feet out of the mud. Fear streaked through me. *Run.* My feet were stuck. I yanked a leg free, but slipped and fell backward into the mud.

Lightning came. Thunder grumbled. Eight seconds.

Run, Kaz! It was Eliza's voice. I tried to stand and slipped again. My right foot stuck in the mud like a stick. I grabbed underneath my knee and yanked. Slowly the earth let go, but I was still sitting, would still have to stand, couldn't run away.

Kazimir? A different voice, a narrow beam of light pinning me against the night. *Kaz, is that you?*

"Who are you? What do you want with me?" I screamed.

The flashlight turned on the user, illuminating his long grizzled beard, the scars on his forehead shadowing his eyes. My father.

What he said next was garbled by the rain.

"WHAT?" I yelled.

He put his hands to his mouth. "WHAT THE HELL ARE YOU DOING?"

CHAPTER EIGHTEEN

"Dad, wait!" I slogged behind like the Swamp Thing, the rain pouring between us. Lightning struck again, illuminating him as he limped toward the house, up the steps. I freed myself from the mud and sprinted after him, panting at the screen door.

The red glow of Micah's pipe greeted us on the porch.

"What the hell?" my dad asked again, and turned his flashlight onto Micah, who was holding his breath.

"Hey Aeneas, how's life?" Micah wheezed. A puff of smoke obscured his face in the flashlight.

"What're you doing sitting in the dark?"

"Having a smoke."

"DAD!" I yelled, a little too loud. He was right in front of me.

He turned. The flashlight bored a hole in my chest.

Rain dripped off my chin and onto the toe that plays the part of the piggy who had roast beef. "Dad, you can't go inside."

"Why not?"

"There's something I need to say—before you go, something you got to understand."

He waited. "Go ahead, spit it out."

"Grandma—she's sick, really. Vomiting and I think she's gonna die, just gibberish, cats and Herbert and the sheriff just coming out of her. She asked for you."

"I didn't mean spit literally. What are you trying to say?"

"Ephraim's people we thought, but didn't know how, and plus you were gonna kill him."

He looked at Micah.

"Aeneas, Mrs. Godwin has cancer. It's terminal. It's metastasized and has spread all over. Kaz got her out of the hospital so she could die here. She's in a lot of pain, diarrhea, vomiting, a little out of her mind. We went and got Silas. He's in there now."

"Yeah," I said.

"Kaz had some pain pills—he was freaking out. Now he can't talk anymore."

Aeneas flashed the light on Micah. "And you? Is that weed?"

"Bad Ax County's finest."

Dad creaked his weight onto the porch rocker and turned off the flashlight.

"You knew," I said.

"I felt the change in the pulse. The time is at hand for me to use all that I have learned. You need to help me get her to the sacred lake."

I didn't know what that meant but I didn't have the grip on my head either to ask or to get annoyed. I tried to lean back against the wall but missed and fell to the floor.

"You okay?" Micah asked.

"Yeah, just lying down," I said and leaned against the wall.

"I don't want to see him right now," Aeneas said. "The time isn't right. It'll change the balances and I'm already walking a tightrope."

"What are you talking about?" asked Micah.

"I came home to save her. I know how. But I didn't expect Silas here, he alters the forces."

"Do you have some miracle you're going to work or something?" said Micah. Lightning flashed.

"You got into my mind," I interjected. "You told me you were coming home—in my head. But it was something else. You found a different way."

"He's likely to spew gibberish all night—maybe I shouldn't have given him the pain killers."

Thunder. Six seconds. The storm kept moving away and then coming back, moving away and coming back. It wasn't fair.

"I'll go tell Silas you're here," Jonah offered. "I'll tell him to clear out, maybe go upstairs or something, so you can see your mom for a while."

"Just as long as I don't see him."

"Your mom is his Grandma too, not just his," I said and knew it didn't come out right. "You know what I mean," I added to clarify.

I could see nothing in the thick darkness. The rhythmic creak of the porch swing could be heard under the rain.

"He's forgiven. I don't want to see him anyway." The rain just pelted the porch and the wind shook the windows. "I came to save my mother and that's what I'm doing. I didn't come here to see him again. I understand he wants to see Mom and try to make amends for tearing the family apart. But I don't want to see him. Just make sure I don't see him."

At that moment the front door added its creak to that of the swing. The porch added its creak as a foot stepped onto it. "What're you guys doing?" Silas asked. The door clicked shut.

Only the rain answered. The swing stopped in mid-rock. After a several very long moments I heard something move across the card table, and the light of Micah's pipe illuminated his face for an instant. Darkness again, the exhaled smoke, the sweet smell.

"You guys just puffing on reefer?" asked Silas.

"Yeah," I said from the floor.

"I was looking for Mom's flashlights. The only candle I could find was the one in the bathroom." He waited for one of us to respond, then went on, "Maybe you could light that for us, Micah?"

"Sure," Micah said, still holding the smoke in his lungs.

"She's moaning a lot," he said. "I think she's feeling pretty bad. Heart beat is pretty fast too. I don't see how she's sleeping."

"Pain meds aren't at work," I said, happy it made sense. "The marijuana is the best."

"You're an addict," Micah said. I began to catch on that we were trying to play as if my father wasn't here. Maybe Silas would just go back inside and my father would be fine. He hadn't seen him yet, technically.

"Silas," started Micah, "what are you gonna do if Aeneas comes home while Grandma is dying?"

"She doesn't have more than a day or two left I imagine. He's not going to be able to see her before she dies."

"Let's say he did. What then?"

"I guess I'd just talk to him or something."

I thought he'd end his thoughts right there, then we'd follow him inside and tell him Aeneas was here. I don't know what compelled Silas to choose that particular moment for the longest speech of his life.

"I can't imagine he can still be angry at me, though. I know what he said when I last saw him, but I don't think he meant it. Mom's dying, and it's time we put aside other things. He's got some weird ideas, I know, but so does Kaz, and you Micah, and me, all of us. I miss him, you know? My whole life and I only told Leanna, now I'm telling you guys. He was my brother, I love him, and I messed up bad, but I can't regret it. If he doesn't—"

The lights flickered on. I shielded my eyes. The lights went out. The lights flickered again. The lights stayed on. I squinted. *Brown bear, brown bear, what do you see?* Silas had his arms folded over his chest. My eyes focused. Micah let out a puff of smoke. Silas looked down at him, then squinted at me. "Where are your clothes?" he asked. Micah looked over at Aeneas. Aeneas stared at Silas. Silas asked me a question with his eyebrows. I looked at Aeneas' feet. Aeneas looked at me. Silas looked at Aeneas.

"Hey," said Silas.

There was a pause, then Dad gave him a slight bend of the head. "Hey."

"Been a while," said Silas.

"Twelve years."

"Lot of water under the bridge," Silas said.

"Still water under that bridge."

"It's why there's gotta be a bridge at all, I guess," Silas responded.

"You guys could write for Simon and Garfunkel," Micah said and snorted in laughter.

Aeneas looked at me. Silas looked at me. I looked at Micah. Smoke came out of his nose.

"You damn pothead," I yelled.

"I'm sorry, I'm sorry, I couldn't help it," he said, composing himself.

Dad stood and walked to the front door of the porch and fingered the latch. Rain pelted the window by his face.

"Mom's dying," Silas said. "We would've got ahold of you. We didn't know how. I didn't mean to leave you out while she was dying."

"Micah explained it already," Aeneas muttered.

We sat and waited.

"I'd like to talk, Aeneas." Silas's voice cracked. "I guess you heard what I said, then. We're here, now. We've seen each other, now."

"I didn't come here to have any part with you."

"I'd like to talk, brother."

I slid myself up the wall, leaving a streak of mud. "Need go to shower," I whispered.

"Me, too. At least go check on Grandma or something," said Micah.

We both went inside, closing the door behind us.

"What happened to you?" asked Micah, getting a good look at me for the first time.

"Just wanted fresh air," I told him.

"And your clothes?"

"Leave me alone." I said brushed past him to go down the hall.

"Hey, sorry about wise-cracking," he said.

"Just leave me alone, go smoke some more pot or something." I grabbed a towel from the hall closet, went into the bathroom and locked the door behind me.

I turned the shower on, waited for it to get hot, and stepped in. Mud poured off me until the drain was clogged, and water began to fill the tub.

My brain ran around my head. My father, Silas, the drugs, Grandma, Micah. I could barely keep everything straight. Out on the porch my father and Silas were talking, I assumed, or killing each other. I was going to kill my father. Why was I going to kill him? Was I serious when I said it before? What about now?

As much as I hated him, I couldn't kill him. As much as I hated him, I loved him also. I had seen that he was involved in something awful. And wasn't I, too? What about my hideous vision in the lake, what about the voices?

I turned and let the water pour down my back, tilted my head to let it run down my face. I looked for soap and found none, just some gooey slime where the last bar had sat. I rubbed my hand on it until the slime foamed and then ground the foamy slime into my toes.

And had he followed me? The headlight that I had seen—was it really the single headlight on the Whale? It couldn't be—I would've noticed.

Silas. Silas, and where was Leanna? I hope she wasn't going to come down. Silas had said he didn't want Grandma to suffer. But what were we to do? Wasn't that living, suffering? Now in her death, how do we ease her into it? And how do we make sure that's what she wants?

Suddenly I was gripped again by the desire to die. How was I supposed to continue after this, anyway? To go to college when my Grandma was dead? When I kept hearing what was maybe the voice of God tell me what to do?

I turned the shower off and let the water drip from my body. I closed my eyes and leaned my head against the wall. The uneasy feeling that it would disappear surged through me; the wall held. Now my feet felt like they were floating, and my legs weak. I began to spin in the blackness under my eyelids.

My legs buckled and I collapsed in a heap in the bathtub. Water dripped out of the faucet. I adjusted my body so my head was underneath the drip.

A cry of pain woke me. I didn't know how long I had slept. I gathered myself up from the tub and slung a towel around me and staggered down the hall.

I opened the door to Grandma's room. Her reading light was on. Outside water dripped from the eaves; the rain had ceased.

My father was seated on the far side of the bed, Silas on the near, leaning over Grandma.

"Where's Micah?" I asked.

"Went to the tipi to get some sleep," Aeneas said. He took a pull from a whiskey bottle, the black label barely visible in the dim light.

"I thought we were out of whiskey."

"Aeneas had a case of it in the van," Silas answered.

"She needs more than whiskey and pot," my dad said, taking another pull. "I brought something better."

"What?"

My dad put the cap back on the bottle and bent down, pulling out a large hookah from beside the bed. "Opium. It'll help her until I get her to the lake."

"She's been in pretty bad shape for the past hour or so," Silas said. "We didn't know where you'd gone to."

"I took a nap," I said.

"Get some clothes on," my dad said, giving me a stare. "We'll take care of her for now."

After dressing, I checked inside my nightstand for the Mason jar of those arrowheads. It was gone. My father—he'd come home to steal the evidence of what he'd done.

I got to thinking about Aeneas and Silas. I wondered what they'd said to each other that they could now sit in the same room together after twelve years. Perhaps it was just the circumstances. Perhaps it was just out of respect for Grandma. I returned to the room to help them.

The sun came up and lit the mist and the clouds an eerie red that looked like blood in hot water. I woke Grandma up to see it and we opened the window to get some fresh air. She couldn't sit up enough, so my dad and I boosted her. My fingers traced her ribs. She closed her eyes and let out a little air between her lips. We set her back down. I went outside.

East over the pines the sun lingered amidst the boughs. The light was diffuse, and the red fog began to fade. On the western edge of the sky, small gray clouds charged underneath the mass of black. The sky did not look like it was going to let go of the clouds; another storm was coming.

I saw Micah coming up from the river and looked at my watch. Six-fifteen.

"How is she?" he asked.

I shook my head slightly. "Not good."

"Are Silas and your dad in there together?"

"Yeah, we've been taking care of her all night. Dad brought opium."

"Wouldn't mind some myself. Get any sleep?"

"I fell asleep in the shower for a few hours."

"Sounds nice."

"You know, you don't have to be here. I appreciate it, but, you know, you don't have to do this."

"This is where God wants me to be."

We collected my sopping clothing from where I'd flung it alongside the barn, and then we went back to the house.

Silas was sitting with his head down on the kitchen table. "Your dad's casting magic spells over her," he grumbled.

I peeked into the room to see what he meant, and indeed, my dad was walking around her bed whispering something I couldn't understand. I went back to Silas and sat down. "What did you guys talk about last night?"

"Just said we could get along for Mom's sake."

"What's this lake he mentioned earlier?"

"He told me it's in a sacred mountain range in the Rockies with good acoustics."

"Good acoustics? What's he gonna do, rent an ambulance to drive to Montana and put on a concert?"

"I don't think she's got more than a day or two in her," he sighed. "I want to just focus on letting her die peacefully. I hate to say that, but it's the only thing to do."

"Why's he so interested in her now? After never being here? After all these years?"

"Because she's dying, Kazimir, what do you expect?"

"But how did he know she was dying? He just showed up, after our fight and everything. He *knew* somehow."

"Maybe he's got some kind of gift, like he's always claimed."

Micah came in and started some coffee dripping. "It's drizzling again," he informed us. Silas looked up from his view of the table and glanced out the window, then put his head back down.

"So I think it's weird," I said, "that he'd suddenly find such an interest in her."

Micah slid a cup of coffee in front of each of us and sat down.

I continued, "I say we talk to him about it right now."

"It's not important right now."

"It's pretty important to me," I said.

"We gotta talk, this morning, about what we should do before it's too late. The rest can wait."

"What can wait?" asked my father as he leaned in the doorway.

"Silas says we need to talk about what to do about Grandma," Micah informed him.

I sipped my coffee and stared at my father. He found my gaze and stared long enough to visualize eating my heart out of my chest, then looked at the others. All in all we enjoyed a pleasant silence.

"Why don't we?" Aeneas said. "Now's a good time, we're all here."

"We should ask her what she wants us to do," said Silas.

"What are you thinking?" asked my father, looking at his back.

Silas put his head down again. "She's only gonna get worse. I don't want her to go through that."

"So you're saying we should help her—go?" my dad said.

"Yeah, I guess. If she wants it."

"I don't know if she'll want that," Micah said, "she's a Catholic. Plus it's illegal to assist someone like that."

"Illegal don't matter in this family, Micah, better understand it," said my father.

"But we can ask her, still, when she's reasonably together," I said.

"I'm not against what you're saying Silas, I just think we should know for sure. If we can't know for sure, we shouldn't do it."

"How do you propose you help her die, Silas?" asked my dad.

"I was thinking maybe overdose her on the morphine when we got it, or the opium now that we have that."

"You gotta do the morphine—people will wonder how a seventy-year-old woman got opium," said Micah.

"Then the morphine. Just something painless," said Silas, "even if it's filling a bathtub up and slitting her wrists—just something painless."

"I'm not doing that," I said.

The clock in the living room struck seven.

"None if it's gonna be necessary," Aeneas said.

"How's that?" asked Silas.

"I was granted the ability to heal people's energies."

"Wow," I commented, delighted.

"Through my guitar," he explained. "I channel the power through my guitar."

"Wish you had thought of using them before."

"I didn't know before. The universe led me to know of her pain when it was the right time to know of her pain; now I'm here to take her to the Crystal Mountains."

"If you've got those healing powers," I said, "why don't you just put your hands on her now and heal her?"

"I have been, and it's been helping with her pain," he said, "but I don't have the energy to save her completely; that's why I need to go to the power source. It's the only place that will save her."

"If the universe wanted her saved, why'd it give her cancer?" asked Micah.

"The universe only puts before us what we are capable of accomplishing. I don't pretend to know why."

"Aeneas, you know I don't believe in any of that magic stuff. I never did," said Silas.

"It's not magic, Silas," he said, "it's how the universe is." He knocked on the doorway. "You think the world is only composed of matter, but there is a *real* beyond your senses. A *mythic* real."

"I've seen some healing in church," said Micah. "I've seen people get healed from all sorts of things, broken arms, whooping cough—that was an interesting one."

"Maybe it's possible," I said, "but she's going to die real soon. I don't even think she can make it to Montana."

"And she's dying right now, Aeneas. This is our mom we're talking about. We brought her home so she can have the last moments of her life here."

"If I get her there, she'll have a long time still to spend here. And if she was going to die on the way, the universe wouldn't have called me to do it."

"This is crazy," said Silas.

"*It's not crazy,*" said Aeneas.

"We've got to wake her up and ask her what she wants from you guys before you do anything," said Micah.

"Maybe we need to talk to Roald and Jethro, too," I suggested.

"They don't have any say in the matter," Aeneas said.

"All the same," I said, "they should know."

"We'll let her come down from the opium, and before we give her more, when she's more conscious, we'll ask her what she wants us to do," Silas said. "How does that sound?"

Silas looked around for support. No one said anything but there was a general air of agreement. Aeneas stood and went back down the hallway. The door to Grandma's room closed behind him.

I got up and went outside. Micah followed me.

I climbed into the willow and swung my legs from a branch. Rain dripped on my head.

"My dad, Ephraim, they've been sending me signals."

"What?"

"They've been sending me messages—through these things that look like Indian arrowheads, spearheads and fish hooks. I don't even know what for, but I have a feeling that it's too late for me. Whatever they're going to have me do they can just say the word and I'll do it. I've been trying to fight them for years now, Micah, I've been trying to get ahold of my own brain again, but it's hard."

I looked at him to try to see what he was thinking. "You've gotta believe me. Those damn arrowheads have rearranged my thinking. But if I get free, I'll be okay."

"Kazimir, do you know how crazy—*really* crazy that sounds?"

"It's not crazy, Micah, it's true. Look—" I hopped down. "I had a whole jar of them. And then my dad took me on the vision quest and he admitted it and we got into a big fight. Now I come back, and my whole jar is gone. He took them while I was hitchhiking."

"Yeah. When were you hitchhiking?"

"Just before this. He left me up there. I came back and he had stolen the evidence. Then Grandma's sick and he's not here." I looked for his reaction. "They send me the voices because I'm some sort of special prophet."

He shook his head. "Why would they leave you here to be raised by your grandma if you're so important? And what nefarious plot do they have? Are they trying to take over the world, are they going to steal arms from the Russians and explode a nuclear bomb in New York City, and you're some secret agent?" He smirked. That annoyed me. It dawned on me that he could be with them—he was always so friendly to Aeneas.

"Well, I'll admit, I don't know. I'm trying to figure that out. That's going to have to wait until after Grandma dies. Until then I got to play it cool."

"Kaz—your dad's part of a weird group of hippies who run drugs and live in the backwaters of Montana. He wants to take Grandma to a sacred mountain valley to heal her of cancer with its salutary acoustic qualities. They don't sound so violent or duplicitous, just wacky."

"You never know. Someday I'll figure it out."

"They smoke a lot of opium and probably have orgies in oak groves. The stuff you're saying—it's like the bad trip you had when we ran those drugs."

I jumped down and started running back to the house. "Maybe, but maybe *not*. Maybe you should go worry about your own family for a while."

"You need real help, Kaz. I'm telling you because you're my best friend. I'm being honest—you really need to see a shrink."

"My grandma's dying, Micah. I don't have time to see shrinks." I slammed the screen door.

Rain drummed on the windows. Silas leaned over and switched on the bed light. It shone on the circle of missing hair on my father's skull as he bent in prayer on the other side of her bed. Grandma blinked, then blinked again, then closed her eyes.

"Mom," Silas said, bending over and holding her hand, "Mom, can you hear me?"

She gave a slight nod.

"Grandma, we want to know what you want us to do," I said. "We want to know if you want to go back in the hospital, or if you want more drugs, or if you think—if you think we should give you enough drugs so that, so that you'll never feel any more pain."

We waited. She panted faintly, started to stay something, choked on the words and then lifted her hand and waved us all to come closer. Micah got up from the chair in the corner and approached. My father and I leaned over her. Silas knelt next to her. The smell of vomit filled the small quadrilateral made by our heads.

"What the hell are you talking about?" she hissed.

"We wanted to know—" Silas said, looking for the words, "if you want to keep fighting right till the end. Or if you want us to give you enough drugs—to put you down."

She lifted her head up. "I'm not a damn dog, Silas, you don't put me down," she said and rested her head again.

"Mom," Aeneas said, "I've got a place to take you. God gave me a vision of how to heal you. If you let me take you in the van, you'll be all better."

She smiled at that, and closed her eyes again.

"We have enough opium," I said, "that we could make it painless. We could just give you the drugs until you fade away."

"We thought we should ask," said Micah, "because I knew you were religious, and that you might not agree with it."

She breathed for a few minutes. I rested my head on her stomach. Silas and Aeneas each had a hand.

"Give me," she finally said, "give me a day. I want to live another day."

She faded into mumbling and sleep. We couldn't get her to wake up anymore.

"So, I'm going to need all your help getting her into the Whale," Dad said out on the porch.

"What do you mean?" asked Silas.

"I mean get her stuff together so we can go as fast as possible."

"She wants to die here," said Silas, "in a day."

He looked at us. "Don't do this now, Silas. You said on the porch you'd help me."

"Dad, you heard her. She wants to be here. She said one more day. We're all here. We can call Roald and Jethro and everyone can see her one last time. We can take her out and let her be in the garden. Then we can help her … fade away. It's what she wants."

"You're putting words in her mouth. All she said was, 'One more day.' She still wants to live and I can make that happen."

"No miracle's going to save her," said Silas.

"I can save her; God sent me here to do it."

"She's gotta stay here, Dad, that's it. I don't want her to die in the Whale in some desolate stretch of South Dakota. She wants to be here when she dies, her soul told me."

"You clearly weren't speaking the same language as her soul."

"Oh, but *you* speak God's language?"

We stared at each other.

"I said I'd help you if that's what she wanted," said Silas, "but she doesn't want that. She just wants to be here. I'm not gonna help you take her to Montana."

"Thanks, brother."

"I'm not either," I said.

Micah didn't say anything.

Finally my father looked up in the air and sighed. "If that's the way you want it."

Storms continued as we sat around in the living room reading or pacing or drinking whiskey, anything to avoid talking to each other. Aeneas got his guitar from the van and went upstairs. The music came down through the cracks like a spilled water glass.

We had contacted the church the day before, and now Father Zbigniev and others came to see her. I spoke with him afterward, but he didn't have much to say to a sinner like me. I flipped cards at Micah as he read his Christian rock music magazine, then I tried to guess the suits like old times. Still didn't work. Silas whittled on a stick, making what appeared to be a tribute to Grandma's face out of willow.

"You guys sleeping in the tipi tonight?" he asked.

I nodded. The thought of Grandma weighed on my mind. I went and looked in on her. There were old ladies by her bedside. One read the police blotter from the local newspaper. Grandma lay in the shine of the reading light, her eyes closed. I shut the door softly.

Tomorrow would be her last day on earth. The last day I would know her. I felt nothing. Nothing. No pain, no sorrow, no remorse; just numbness. *Be still,* a voice whispered beyond the rain. I could feel Ephraim's presence. I could feel the cold weight of his eyes. "What do you want of me?" I asked him. There was no response. If she died in the house would she haunt it like the others? She wasn't even a Godwin, had just moved here to raise her boys in the ancestral home of her husband. Her whole life was a sacrifice for us.

Outside the rain tapped the rhythm of a death march, and the sun of our world was snuffed out.

By eight-thirty the house was vacant of visitors. Roald called and said he and Jethro would be by tomorrow. The four of us gathered once more to dose Grandma up with opium, Aeneas taking a puff for every one she took. Soon she was asleep in a quiet haze and my father fell back into the chair in the corner.

"I can just keep giving her this stuff until morning," he told us, staring at the darkened ceiling. "She'll be out all night."

"Then tomorrow—" I said.

"Yeah, then tomorrow," he answered and put his hands to his mouth. We stood around shifting our weight to different legs and looking at him. He picked up his guitar and fingered a few notes. "Just leave me here. I'm gonna play for her," he said. "I'll do what I can with my music here."

None of us moved. He started to play and he took us all with him. Every note flowed from his fingers as if he had dipped them in an invisible stream. He hit a diminished chord and chills ran up my spine. I closed my eyes and leaned against the yellow wallpaper of her room. My head spun and then seemed to lift straight from my body.

When I opened my eyes, Silas and Micah had left. The room was dark and the stream of notes continued to pour off him. It was religious music he played. It had always been a religion to him—to play his guitar. And he sat in the dark corner and played for Grandma now straight from his soul. A twinge of regret ran across my stomach like a rat. How can I hate him? I wondered, and I thought I should talk to him. But I didn't want to break his opium dream of music. So I left.

We slept in the tipi again. The rain came down steadily. Drown her. Drown you. I passed from uneasy thoughts to uneasy dreams. The hole in the tipi was never fixed; its drips formed a small pool by my face. I listened to it for hours and hours. Tomorrow we would drug my grandmother to death. Tomorrow I would be a murderer. We all would. Would Jesus still love us, I wondered. But it was facetious, and filled with the despair of all black ramblings. I knew better now. He had never loved us.

When the morning came, I got up before either Silas or Micah and paced along the river. My breath was a mist in the wind and the pines shook rain from themselves like dogs in a bath. I was half-drenched from the fog in the air and I made my way back by instinct alone, over the grass, up the creak of the porch, and into the silent house. Silas was snoring on the couch.

I looked in the fridge and found some English muffins and had them with butter. As I sat at the table, a dark chord echoed from the direction of Grandma's room. My father must have played all night, I thought, all night for his mother. He gave his all to her this last night of her journey on earth. And for a moment I loved him again.

The sound of the guitar echoed faintly once more. I walked up the hall, traced my fingers on the wall underneath the pictures of our family. I stopped by the photo that we had taken when I was a child, the picture of us on the porch. I examined each of the faces: younger, happier, but not really careless. Even the little child I was had a wistful look, as if knowing any happiness he had would end too soon.

I carried on, came to the door and turned the cold knob. The door creaked open and I stuck my head in.

A cool wind blew in from the open window and struck me on the face. The bed light illuminated her pillow, and it took me a second to see the impression that her head had left. The room was vacant.

"Grandma?" I called out. Nothing.

"Aeneas? Dad?"

Nothing.

Nobody. I ran up the stairs and swung open the door to his room. He was gone.

CHAPTER NINETEEN

I had dragged them out of bed to the kitchen table. I had made coffee and seated myself opposite them. Four bloodshot eyes under drooping lids stared at me. My bones ached. We were already at the ends of our ropes, and now this. This one more thing... only one more thing I could ever do for Grandma... I shook my head abruptly, as if to fling off sleep's cobwebs. "I'll find him," I said. "Silas, you told me you've been out to Montana once with my dad?"

He rubbed his hands over his face. "That was a long time ago, Kaz, and I've never been out to the commune."

"What about the so-called sacred mountains? 'Crystal' whatever?"

"I could get you to the Indian reservation they lived by or the bar he took me to. That's all."

Then it hit me. "I know where it is—kind of. My father took me to Montana once. Had me sit on a hillside and wait for him. A bear came and I hid in a tree until he got back. He said he had gone to a healer's ritual in the mountains. He said someday he would take me there—when I was of age."

"You can buy cigarettes and vote, I think you're of age now," Micah opined without a smile.

"What's the point, now?" said Silas. "She's already near dying and we'll never find them on that information. Montana's a big place."

"When I was lying under her bed that night in the hospital, trying to heal her, I promised her soul I would bring her home, and I will."

The other two stared at me.

I looked at Micah. "We can use your car. We'll all go."

"Leanna's coming down tomorrow morning," Silas said. "I think I'll wait for her, then follow you out."

"Okay." I looked at Micah. "Let's go," I said, almost half question.

He nodded.

The wind shook the car all the way to the interstate in Iowa. Still unseasonably cold; rain splatted down at random. Some hard-rocking Christian band blared from Micah's tape deck. The music was punctuated by the sound of his pipe lighting up for a puff every half hour or so. That's the way he liked to do it when he was on a drive, just a puff or two at a time for a steady high.

After six hours, we stopped and switched places.

I shut off the music, slipped low into my seat, and tried to sleep. We were well into the nether regions of the United States: Nebraska. It was pitch black, neither a star nor moon in the sky. I rolled down the window one time in the night. The sting of manure, dust, and pesticide that passed for air was flung into the car. It smelled a lot like home.

I shut my eyes and opened them again. I would never sleep. I would never again sleep. Grandma was gone, on my watch, and my father had taken her.

A bumper crop of storm clouds grew so far off on the flat horizon that it took us three hours to hit them. Rolling the window down to let the rain in, I felt a presence in the backseat. I checked the visor mirror: Eliza. Making faces at me.

"If you ask me we should just cut Nebraska right out of the map, staple Colorado to Iowa. It would make traveling in this country so much nicer. I mean, a few hours of this is fine, even nice, but Nebraska is huge, eh?" Micah said. I didn't respond.

In an hour he pulled over at a rest stop. I stretched my legs under the cover of some large oaks as Micah went in the bathroom.

"So, what, aren't you speaking to me?"

I turned around. Eliza grinned her elvish grin.

"C'mon, cut me a break. I can't talk to you around other people."

"What? Am I not good enough for your buddy?"

"Don't give me that. You know how it is with people and hallucinations."

"Is that what I am to you? Just a hallucination?"

"No, no, I don't mean it like that. You're so much more than a hallucination. It's just, well … I don't know. This is crazy. I think I'm going nuts."

"Nuts? Look at those freaks playing at their little rat-wheel jobs and their rat-wheel ideas, and their rat-wheel world. That's nuts. It's all made up. It's all illusion, you nincompoop."

Maybe she was right; she always seemed to be right. I assumed she knew more of the world and truth, she being in some way magical, fantastical or whatever.

"What're you looking at over there?" asked Micah.

"Nothing."

I drove, and Micah laid back and started to doze. "I get it," she said from the back seat. "Your little pal over there. You're afraid he'll hear you. Embarrassed by my company, are you? Well, I'll just say things and you respond with a nod or a shake. Okay?"

I nodded.

"So what's been keeping you from talking to me all these months? You got a new girl? It's okay if you do. It's not like our relationship can go anywhere—me being immaterial and all. You like them big college words?"

I nodded, admiring her vocabulary. She leaned forward and draped her arms around my neck. "I remember Montana from when we were kids. I loved it there—the b'ar and everything—you remember?"

"Yeah, I do," I said forgetting to nod.

Micah sat up. "What?" He stretched. "What did you say?"

"Nothing, nothing at all." I focused on driving until she disappeared again.

In Ogallala, we sat down for dinner, biding our time till the rain slackened.

"What are we going to do if we find them?" Micah asked through a mouthful of mashed potatoes.

"Just convince him to bring her home. If she's—passed away—just bring her home to be buried in the family plot."

"And if by some miracle he's really healed her?"

"I guess we'll all go for a hike then," I said.

"Yeah."

We drove in a light drizzle all the way up to Scott's Bluff. Too cheap for a hotel, we looked for a back road where we could pull off. If there was one thing Scott's Bluff had, it was back roads, so we didn't look long. We found a cozy little spot near the national monument. My head was spinning and the little drummers in my temples beat their djembes in a fury, completely out of sync with each other. I decided to take a walk by myself.

"Need a little exercise," I told Micah.

Eliza was hanging from a branch in a tree.

"What's happening to me, Eliza?" I asked her. "What's going on? Why am I seeing you now?"

"I don't know nothing, remember, I'm an illusion, a hallucination. How could you trust what your delusion says?"

"I don't know, maybe Micah's right and I need to see a shrink. What do you think?"

She laughed. "Awe shucks, you're gonna trust me with determining whether you're sane or not? That's a bit odd, but for you I'll do it. I'll keep an eye on you from now on."

"Thanks."

"But what do you want to be considered sane by all them for? So you can function in their little rat-race world? So you can see reality the way they want you to see it? You take their pills and poof, I disappear in a cloud of logic and chemicals. That's all. Once you get control, the visions disappear because *you're* in charge of what you're gonna see. But what's so untrue about me, huh? I'm here—here for you at least. And that's just as real as anything else. Maybe me and you are the only things that are actually real. Maybe the rest of it is make-believe."

"Gee, thanks. Advice like that is sure gonna help me keep things straight."

She giggled and disappeared.

It was about an hour before dawn. Our headlights spit into the black as the rain continued to run into us. I drove. Micah ripped strips of beef jerky thick enough to make a purse from. His Mohawk banked to one side like a sailboat in a strong wind.

"Am I going crazy?" I asked.

Micah had to chew deliberately for several moments before creating room to move his tongue around the mouthful of jerky. "I don't know anything about that stuff."

"I think maybe I am."

"You're fiddling a different tune than when you were having visions of your Grandma's soul being led home, and telling us Ephraim was running radio interference on your soul."

"I don't know." I clutched my head. "I don't know what I believe."

"Well, how about if I play devil's advocate. Maybe there's religious experience and then there's mental disorders, but they're not the same. One just looks like the other. Mental illness is the work of the devil, and true religious experience, that of the Lord," he said.

"What does it matter which is which—if there's no way to tell the difference? All the Jesus freaks and their 'saving,' they're a bunch of arrogant bastards. Same with my dad and Ephraim and their entire hippy Judeo-pagan shit. 'Saving' is just a code word for making everyone like you."

"When have I ever been arrogant, you jerk?" He glared at me. I'd never seen that look on his face.

"I didn't mean you."

"What you said is not fair. Isn't it arrogant to think *anything* you know can fix *anyone's* problems? It's human nature, Kazimir, it's not the problem of any religion. You could say it's arrogant to diagnose people as 'insane' and give them medications just because they don't believe that the world is only made of matter and energy. Anybody who doesn't fit into the little box of 'normal' is schizo, or nutball. *Jesus* asks us to seek truth and act in truth regardless of what's considered normal, safe, or sane. And churches, and individuals, act as Christians only as far as they do that. It's the same with shrinks, it's the same with secularists—you just do the best you can and stick to you what you know is true. But if you forget that none of us knows anything at all, then you're stepping into God's shoes."

"I'm sorry," I said, "I'm sorry. I shouldn't have said that."

"Just forget about it, I forgive you. I'll chalk it up to your schizophrenia."

The radio was all local. I turned it up so I didn't put my foot in my mouth again. Flooding in Missouri, Kansas, Iowa. Strange to have floods in August. People out there sandbagging, rowing their boats to the grocery stores. The Feds were sending disaster relief, helicopters and such. And more rain expected. Maybe this was it. Armageddon. No Russians. Just floods and plagues and pestilence. An image of a valley flashed before my eyes, dead bodies stuck in the branches of a downed tree over a flooding river. One foot bare, deformed and blue.

Were these to be my visions?

By the time we got to Staab, the wind was pushing the car like a piece of paper, and the rain was coming on sideways.

The only real building in the town was a bar/restaurant in the shape of a large yurt. We parked in a garden of rust where neon beer lights reflected on old trucks that sprouted from puddles. Dim-lit and dusty inside, the place had all the ambience of a knife in the back. Several drunken Blackfeet slept at the bar and a big-boned fella with a ponytail and black Aerosmith shirt shot a solitary game of pool in between pulls off a bottle of hard liquor. If you replaced the Blackfoot Indians with drunken Norsemen, shunned Amish, and Winnebago, the whole scene could have taken place in western Wisconsin. So all in all I felt right at home.

We ordered food from the bartendress, a once attractive Indian lady with her life of bar work rubbed into her skin and hanging over her jeans. Micah ordered shots of whiskey. She asked us for our I.D.s, gave them the cursory glance used in lawless places, and handed them back. We clinked glasses and drank them down. I fought back the urge to gag as a whiskey-induced grassfire spread down my esophagus. The Indian lady slugged one herself, then puffed on a cigarette while she looked me over. She tapped her cigarette on the ashtray embossed with a grizzly bear. "I've seen you before."

"Recently?"

She puffed on that one. "Maybe."

"Try adding a hundred pounds, twenty years, and a bad attitude."

She made a sound somewhere in between a laugh and the mating call of a jackal. This woke the sleeping Blackfoot at the bar, who looked over his shoulder at us. "That's it!" she crowed. "That homeless bastard's your dad ain't he? Ha!"

I leaned forward. "He's been here then? Recently?"

She shrugged. "Name's Anus, right?"

"Aeneas," Micah corrected her.

"Same shit. He used to come in here and drink and play us songs on his guitar. Someone said he stays with those hippies in the mountains."

"How would we get out there?" I asked.

She ignored the question. "People say they're dangerous."

"What makes them dangerous?"

She pulled out a can of chewing tobacco and packed it like a professional rodeo clown. "I wouldn't mess with them. People have disappeared. They got whole arsenals back there. Even us Injuns leave them alone. Nobody hunts, nobody takes their bikes or their four wheelers back there."

She masticated the testicle-sized bulge of tobacco in her mouth and spit on the floor. We waited.

"We're not trying to settle here, lady, we're just looking for my father," I said.

"Nobody knows where them hippies are at exactly, just northwest of here is all." She started picking up the shot glasses. "They might be already gone. Not many people stay up here for winter."

"You know of any sacred lake they might do their stuff at? He mentioned it."

She spit again. "You whities think this country is Disneyland. There's dozens of little lakes back there. Every one of them is sacred."

"Point taken," Micah said.

We paid ten bucks for a room, which wasn't much more than a chicken coop with a cot and a nightstand. But it was better than another night in the car. We flipped for the bed. Micah won.

"She handed us our metaphysical asses back there," said Micah. He shaved his non-existent facial hair in the crusty mirror. I lay on my sleeping bag. *There's nothing to quiet us,* said faint voices in my ear. *There's no drug to stop us, no ear plug to silence us.* Whispers over a static radio.

"So," Micah changed the subject, "where do you think Silas is by now?"

"Back home."

"You don't think he's coming out here?"

"Why would he? There's nothing he can do here."

The rain poured on the tin roof and made it hard to hear anything, so our conversation stalled. Micah finished shaving and turned off the light. Soon he was asleep. Through the rain I thought I made out the sound of footsteps, of someone's body pressed against the side of the shack. I could be hallucinating, I thought lucidly. A voice whispered through the clapboard siding but I couldn't make out what it was saying.

"Get the hell out of here or I'll kill you," I hissed at it . Car lights flashed through the window. I made out Eliza's shape at the foot of my sleeping bag. She laughed and tried to play footsie with me and disappeared. A low buzz continued in my ear.

"Eliza?" I whispered. "Eliza. I'm never going to find Grandma. I don't even know where to begin. I'm going nuts. I—"

My voice broke. She wasn't there. I stood and looked through the cracks in the wall out into the dark rain.

A louder, more insistent version of last night's buzzing greeted me as I woke. It didn't feel like waking, as my eyes never seemed to adjust to the light of day. Thunder rumbled far away. I stared at the wall. Micah got out of bed. We bought ponchos at a gas station and headed out to I didn't know where. In truth my whole head wasn't right; I felt like I had a hard case of labyrinthitis. Left here, right there, slogging up old logging roads in Micah's station wagon. The only sounds were the bright patter of rain on the hood and the ascending pitch of rpm as we climbed farther into the foothills.

"Where now?" Micah asked.

"I don't know—this way." I pointed north.

"You're just guessing."

"Yeah."

I felt dazed, which I figured must be the effect of getting closer to the origin of the buzz. The turning of the car made me sick to my stomach. I felt the burn of last night's whiskey in my throat. At one point we came upon a spruce spreading its limbs over a hillside campsite. "Stop," I said. I got out and rain poured over me. Eliza smiled from a large boulder by the spruce. I felt a rush of love for her. I sat by her and closed my eyes. Micah was there, pointing at the sky, "Didn't you see?" Smoke, smoke in the sky. "You okay, Kaz?" Then donning backpacks, descending along the creek, wet bear grass, columbine, the darkened canopy of old-growth pines. Smoke creeping through the woods. It was quieter, the canopy deflected rain, the old-growth was webbed in lichen, the sun was blotted out. We wore our backpacks and our ponchos and followed a dirt road along the stream, deep under the trees, abandoning the car, abandoning sense, ridiculous.

The trees strangled words as they rose. Occasional slight movements of the bushes, the stirrings of birds or small mammals, were the only sounds. All was quiet, primal. Until we turned a corner. It took me a second to register what I saw. A cluster of beat-up trucks and, in the middle of them, the Whale, its old yellow Wisconsin plate dripping rain into the ruts of its tires.

Chapter Twenty

I peeked in the window. Familiar blankets and pillows were piled in the rear, a few books lay about, and a beaded necklace hung from the rear view mirror. It made me shiver.

"Did you look on the passenger seat?" asked Micah.

I walked around front. On the split vinyl was a framed picture of me and my father. I must have been four or five at the time it was taken. He stood with his arm around me, grinning under his long beard. I stared ahead, unsmiling.

Through the rain-streaked glass Eliza stared at me. She shook her head and disappeared.

The other trucks seemed innocuous. They were all parked up against a row of large boulders carved with elaborate Celtic knots, which looked like tattooed bellies on fat Irishmen. Behind the boulders a wide trail four feet at its genesis opened into the dark interior of the valley. Tire tracks of four-wheelers crisscrossed the route.

"This must be it then," I said.

"Looks pretty murky," Micah said. "Should we just—go?"

"What else is there to do?"

Behind the boulders, the path descended, narrowed, and continued west along a small river, where a fog was resting. The sound of the river drowned out all else. My poncho was so wet by now that it had begun to soak into my skin. I watched small trout hide amid the colored rocks and wished for my fishing pole.

Then fog cleared, revealing a chunk of foliage moving into the path and pointing a rifle at us.

"What do you think you're doing here?" it said.

"I'm looking for my dad," I said. "Aeneas Godwin."

I heard something move behind me. I spun around just in time to watch a rifle butt slam into my temple.

Kaleidoscope trees, a struggle went on beside me, and Micah crumpled on top of me shouting in pain. A man stood over me. He aimed the rifle at my stomach. I heard them mumble to each other. Then he fired. I cried out in pain, and clutched my stomach. He fired again, and Micah cried out. Everything looked like a Picasso. Now two men stood over me. Everything looked like a Pollock. I felt the needle in my stomach and pulled it out, let it fall to the mud. Everything faded to black.

Little men sledgehammered concrete over my forehead. I imagined steel toothpicks to hold my eyelids open and I stared up into the blurry mess that might be the world. A warm dampness filled my nostrils, my left arm ached as I rolled off it, and a disturbing urge to stick a rake down my esophagus and scratch out my insides emanated from some point in my interior. After a moment I was charmed to discover the epicenter was my stomach. I moaned.

I was on a fur rug and so was somebody else, but I couldn't see whom. Beneath the fur, I gripped the pliant skin of a moose or bear or some other endangered charismatic macrofauna.

My vision was taking its good sweet time coming into focus. A fire crackled, convected heat on my bare feet. Whoever was there sniffled. I rolled over to look: a pale angelic blur hovered just off the ground.

I looked at the ceiling. It seemed a rather odd ceiling. Heavy, white, striated with dark lines that looked like branches.

"Where am I?" I said, my words coming out slurred.

"You're under a large aspen system growing in one of the last remnants of wilderness in continental America."

I looked up again. The striations must be roots.

I heard him light a match and the smell of cherry tobacco mingled with the fire's smoke. "There's water and some soup."

I sat up and immediately toppled over. My stomach was too weak to support me. I closed my eyes until the spinning stopped and then took another look at the angelic blur, which turned out it to be a man.

His torso was bare, he was wearing loose cotton pants, and there was the possibility of his having a long white beard. That or it had snowed on his chin recently. Either seemed plausible at this point.

"Where am I?" I asked, hoping this time his answer would be a little more helpful.

"Sometimes I call it Nephelokokkygia."

"Bet that goes over well in the press."

"No, there's never any press with us."

I sat up, again, with a grunt. "Where's that water?"

He handed the cup to me, but my hand was too shaky to hold it, so instead I set it down and stared at it in hopes that my vision would come into focus. I breathed. I tried all the breathing exercises my father had taught me in rapid succession. The cup split in two, went around my head, then started coming back together. Then my focus began to come. The cup was pottery, handmade, like it had been thrown in a fire and baked in the ash. I leaned over and lapped up some water from it. The little men that were breaking bricks on my forehead remained hard at work. I decided to ignore them and use my newly established faculties of sight to take a look around.

The place did indeed seem to be underneath a tree, or trees. Roots exposed themselves and then slipped back into the grayish mass of the concrete ceiling. The high fire burned in a fireplace made of large river stones; a metal teapot sat on the stones in front of it. The fur rug that spread from it was indeed bear, I assumed of the local *Ursus horriblis* variety, and the edges of it were lined with large phlegmatic pillows. On one of them, to my left, sat the man as erect and cross-legged as a yoga action figure. An excessively long gray-white shock of hair spurred out every which-way from his head like flood waters issuing from a broken dam. His eyebrows erupted from his forehead like spears in a drunken phalanx as they contemplated mu above his wide, doey eyes. He discharged the distinct impression that he had once been struck by lightning and half the voltage was yet to leave his body.

His body was lean, muscular, and half-hidden by the extraordinary beard that wound from his chin to his navel. All in all it was a figure that seemed purposely cultivated to convey both divine wisdom and avuncular familiarity. It annoyed me.

"You're Ephraim," I said. "You looked different when I saw you last. But you sound the same as in my head."

He nodded. "Many years ago, Kazimir."

"Am I supposed to be impressed that you remember me?" I asked.

"Do you feel the need to be impressed?"

"Answering my question with a question—very sophisticated. Is that the way of the wise, guru Ephraim: to say something is true simply if I believe it to be? Is the spiritual world composed of opinion? Is there no true fact? Two plus two can equal seven if we believe it hard enough?"

"That may be the most sarcastic flurry of metaphysical questioning ever posed to me. You're clearly your father's son."

"The arrowheads. You tell me things."

"The arrowheads?"

"Don't play dumb."

"You're awful full of piss and vinegar for someone lying on the floor of a secret cave beneath an aspen grove in the middle of nowhere."

He had me there. "Ever since I went to see you in that circus tent, dad wanted me to do all this breathing, this meditation. He thought I was going to be some great savior. He thought I was some special hidden prophet. Stories, survival trips, visions quests."

"Your father's a unique man. He had high hopes for you."

"He wasn't much of a father." I propped myself up against some pillows and tried the soup, now lukewarm. It smacked of potato and onion. I decided to forego the spoon and just suck it down from the edge of the bowl. I wiped my hand on my forearm, then picked my teeth and wiped it on the bear. He wouldn't mind. "What is this elven funland you have out here, Ephraim, and what is it for? Why have you been spying on me all these years? Where is Aeneas? Where did he take my grandmother? Why did your goons knock the crap out of

Micah and me? And for that matter where is Micah?"

He laughed. "Elven funland—that's clever—more of the famous Godwin wit."

"You owe me some answers."

"You sound like a bad action flick. I *owe* you nothing—but I can *give* you some answers. Where do you want me to start?"

"Your choice."

"You met the guards. We have had people come here randomly in the past, and nearly cause this place to be discovered. We deal harshly with anybody who comes out here as a form of self-protection."

"Not very guru-like—smacking people with rifles and shooting them full of tranquilizer."

"We are not satyagraha, Kazimir. We attempt to come to accord with the ways of nature—to strike balance. Nature is sometimes harsh and cruel. Animals protect themselves, animals eat each other. Nature is ambivalent toward such things. None of this is done out of 'violence': it has not *violated* the balances of nature."

"Sounds just like my father."

"He's a good student. This is a community I run here. We began it so that peaceful people could avoid the Vietnam war. We ask for nothing but to be left alone, to make our own things, to practice our meditations and rituals that bring us closer to God. We've been here many years now, and have several other communities as well. I travel between them guiding my people. Your father has been one of us."

"And you sell drugs to make money for this?"

"I'll assume your father told you that. It's true. We grow all sorts of things here. Including what we use ourselves. 'Drugs,' put properly into their place among ritual and religion, have a powerful effect on humans. They are no longer a veil, but a conduit for What Is. We have experienced a kind of reality here, Kazimir, which few would believe. This is a powerful place, and our inquiries into the spiritual world have had amazing results. Some would say miraculous."

"My father always said that. I never saw any of your miracles. I know about your plans for the coming of a New Age, the apocalypse, your plans to destroy the Beast you call civilization. I know what you've been doing. And I'm part of it. You send me some electric signals. You've fucked up my brain."

"You don't make much sense, do you? We don't have any electricity. Anything that removes us from direct relationship with What Is has an aspect of evil. Civilization's very paradigm is to remove us from What Is, to set us off and separate us from our natural unity with all. And thus, the further you move into that world, the further you move from What Is. Technology usurps miracle. I don't spy on you with radios or cameras. Again—I'm not sure where you're getting these ideas. I'm not sure you have full control of your own head."

"Bullshit. I've touched the arrowheads you use to spy on me. I've found them buried in the earth, around my house, in my school stuff."

I dug in my pocket for an arrowhead but couldn't find any. I tried to stare him down instead. He didn't look worried.

"We use sacred artifacts for certain healing effects. We use them to ward off evil spirits on occasion. We don't use them to spy on anyone. If you've found arrowheads around where you live, my guess is Aeneas put them there to protect your house from evil spirits or disease. We have them all over our place here, and I know that Aeneas studied them as well."

"Protect us from disease? Your little electric waves gave Grandma cancer."

"What did I just explain to you? I don't use technology."

"You use it to spy on me, you and my father. You've been using them ever since my father left me with Grandma. I can hear the buzz of their signals, and I could hear them more and more as I came closer to here."

"Why would we have a need to spy on you?"

"Because I am a prophet. I am some kind of second coming of Jesus."

He laughed. I couldn't believe he laughed.

"Aeneas thought you'd have the power like he does, like your ancestors had. I hoped you might have the Sight. You're no Jesus. That's ridiculous."

"But my father told me so. He told me about his vision of me when he took me on a survival quest."

"Your father is a healer, a prophet. But he is a man between worlds. Sometimes he doesn't know what's real either—just like you."

I lay back on the pillow, bewildered, unable to make sense of this information. "Where's my father now?"

"He's here, doing the proper rituals to heal your grandmother."

"So she's still alive?"

"Very near death. He had to take her to the medicine lake to heal her."

"He can't heal my grandmother. She's about to die of cancer. He stole her from her bed against her will and drove her out here for nothing."

"This is a place of miracles. Cancer is a true weapon of the Beast—one of its most insidious. Nearly all the things of the Beast have a hand in causing it. Your father's and the lake's powers may not work, but they just may. You may need to prepare yourself for a miracle."

"Where's Micah?"

"Your friend? He's safe. I wanted to talk to you, not him."

I tried to stand but stumbled back onto the rug. "I came here to bring my Grandma back so she can be at home when she dies. I'm sure you know where they are," I said.

"Of course I know where they are, but that's irrelevant, because you're not going out there. First of all, we're getting a storm soon. Second, your presence is bound to destroy the subtle energetic fields he needs to perform what he has been called to do. Third, there'll be no need to. It's quite possible he'll be back here soon, with her healed."

"If not?"

"If not there's nothing you can do at this point anyway. This is enough talk." He reached down and took up his hookah, setting it before me, and nodded. "It's time."

I declined. He insisted.

"No one comes here without it, and no one leaves. This is how it has to be done."

"I don't need it. I'm messed up as it is."

He held it out and I knew I had no choice. He lit it and I inhaled the sweet smoke, letting it out in a crystal puff.

I sat back and closed my eyes. When I began to feel spiders crawling on my arms, I opened my eyes to pick the spiders off. Strange ecstasy filled the room. The smoke looped into dragons, sometimes scattered by the vibrations of rattles. He led me to the door and down a black hall. My head drifted away, taking with it all thoughts of what I had come for. We wound through an enigmatic puzzle of streets and alleys of dirt and root. Hands reached out and brushed me. My eyes jumped out and smacked the ceiling. Turtles crawled in a line over my feet and on their backs were images of my life. It went on. I tried to get out but couldn't see where I was in the smoke. I tried to regain my head as the night set on, as I walked, as everything spun and morphed. How long would I be like this? How long would I walk in the dark?

"You don't look so good."

It was Eliza's voice. I stumbled around, looking for her.

"Where are you, Eliza?"

"I should be asking you that."

"What—what's that supposed to mean?"

"You look pretty lost."

"Where are you? I'm coming over to you."

She called out in a jay's song and I followed through the halls, and there I saw her, leaning against the root of a tree. I lay down beside her and she brushed my hair, held my head in her lap. She loved me. I closed my eyes and the world slowed its spin, wobbled, then settled into stasis. I opened my eyes and looked at her in the thin light. She rested her head against the trunk of the tree, her eyes closed. She was always most beautiful in the shadows of night.

"What is happening to me?" I asked.

"Too many poppy seeds on the proverbial bagel."

My head was in her lap. "What is my head really resting on? I mean, I think you're here, but you're not. What am I resting on—a tree root? A rock?"

"I wish you were real," she said.

"How am I not real?"

"I wish we could be together."

"I don't know what the parameters are for inter-metaphysical relationships."

"I don't think there are any. But you'll leave me. I know. I'm just here to protect you for now, while you need it."

"I have to get to Grandma."

"You want me to go find her for you?"

"Can you do that?"

She performed an exaggerated sigh. "All in a day's work."

We lay a long time like that, her calming my head, and things drew to a pause, to sanity. The world around me rested like an ocean at low tide. Everything was normal.

I heard footsteps in the dark.

"Are you back, Eliza?" I asked.

"Who are you talking to?"

It was Ephraim. He turned on a flashlight, which hurt my eyes.

"Someone in my head."

"I lost you. You were supposed to follow me, Kazimir."

Off in the distance I heard the jay call. I rose up shakily. He held my arm. "Follow the leader," he said.

Finally we came to a door. Light shone from beneath it. I heard him press a latch and a world of light opened before us. On the carpet next to a fire lay Micah.

"Micah," I said as I staggered in.

"He's all right," Ephraim told me. "He's taken his turn at the pipe and should be out until morning." He led me to the couch and set me down. I looked at the window. Snowflakes pressed up against it, transmogrified into human faces, and moaned at me.

"It's snowing," I said.

"As I told you, there's a huge storm hitting us."

"Grandma."

"Aeneas will be back tomorrow, with your Grandma. He knows what he's doing in the snow. You can sleep on the rug there, next to your friend. Just sleep it off. Tomorrow will be more of the same until Aeneas comes back. He can take control of you when he returns."

I turned to him. "We're prisoners?"

"You're no prisoner. There's food in the kitchen. You're welcome to stay here, in this house, for your own safety. It's best for your own health if you don't know too much about this place. Same with your friend." He made his way to the door. "Good night." He evanesced into the darkness.

I staggered over to Micah and put my head to his chest. He was still breathing. I lay down on the rug next to him.

Bats leapt off the mantel toward my mouth. I kept my lips closed as they darted around me. I was angry and sad, delirious, unsure, full of fear. Ephraim was telling the truth. I could feel it in my gut. All the relics, the voices, it didn't add up. What I'd seen had some other significance—or maybe none. My world was being turned on end; I had fallen off the map of the known world into the steaming mists where there be dragons. When I got back nothing would ever be the same. Grandma, dead or dying. My father's idiocy, my own delusions revealed to me by Ephraim. He was right. He verified what Micah—and I, secretly—had feared: this wasn't prophecy. It was the beginning of a mental disorder.

A finger tapped on the window. A black figure appeared there, enshrouded in snow. I rose and went to it. Eliza. I opened the window a crack; wet snowflakes came in to warm up from the cold. They landed on my hand and melted there.

Eliza backed off against a tree, and through the window I could see her beckon to me. I slid it open farther, and worked my body through till I was standing outside. Inside, Micah lay sprawled on the floor, mumbling, in the holds of his drugged sleep. I slid the window shut.

"You got here just in time," she told me.

I shivered in my sweatshirt as the soggy flakes bombarded me. "How so?"

"I found your father. We have to go, now, before the snow settles."

"Why?"

"Grandma's not gonna make it."

"Let me get Micah."

"No. We have to leave him. Just let's go."

I had nothing but a little Maglite in my pocket. I did not have the sense to stop, to consider what I was about to do. I had reached the brink of sanity.

Chapter Twenty-One

My eyes and ears came untethered from their chemical leashes. The world quickened in spirit and light, swirled and spun like a current, whispered in occult languages. I answered in logos occult to me.

It was guesswork mostly, making our way around berry patches that were receding into the earth in their un-birth, around old-growth trees limned in moss, around faint edges of snow. Twice I crossed dry creek beds. A third creek ran, thin as old man's blood, down rocks gray and red within the smear of mud and fallen leaf. I bent to drink from it.

I had nothing to guide me but the stream. Up I went, crossing pathways cut into the mountainside by moose, deer, and sheep. Logic played no part, and my atrophied tracking skills were of no help. As I went higher and higher into the mountains, as the dawn began to crack and the snow continued to fall steadily, I found human tracks in the snow, heavy and uneven. How I had found his trail I had no idea. By the look they were already old, several days or more, and were now being worked over by a fresh blanket of snow.

The sun lit the sky, and the world around stunned me with its rawness. Black and white and angular were the snow and rocks. Whispers of gray grass showed through the powder at times, and matted, woody plants crawled over the gravel between boulders. I thought I had been in wilderness before, but it had been but soft, gentle wilderness. Not this calloused harshness, not this looming power. I worried about bears, the last stragglers before hibernation looking for a final meal.

It seemed something stalked me. Several times I spun to see what was there. It would be wind, or stunted trees, or creatures small and furtive. Once leaves erupted from trees, folded themselves into birds and swooped. I sprawled on the ground and waited them out. I crawled through the snow a long time after that, afraid they would attack again. Once up, I fell, my face in the snow, and slipped into dark dreams in which I stumbled along, cold and shivering.

Snow crystals gathered like monks to prayer; the whole world shimmered with their fractal glyphs in front of my eyes. Wards that would protect me from demons, I was veiled in them. A dimmed sun glowed through the clouds like phosphorescence on the deeps of an abyss.

After a time I rose from the ground, cut and sore and soaking wet. All sound fell into a black hole. I brushed off my blanket of snow, shivered, and looked around. Still beside the creek, I took a drink, scooping water into my hands, reanimating the blood that had dried on my lip. I forgot for a moment what I was doing and thought I might just lie down again. I looked down the mountainside where clouds obscured the valleys.

I dropped and took another drink in the creek. The cold laid bare the nerves of my hands and tongue and brought me back to this world. I remembered where I was and where I was going; I looked around and could no longer find any human prints save my own. I sighed and continued up the mountain.

Mist cleared ahead, and beside a distant boulder I could make out a round gray figure in the creek. I clapped my hands. No response. A waterfall braided down a ridge in the distance. I continued toward it. The blur moved behind the boulder, out of sight.

I struggled, picking my way through the rock-strewn basin. I called twice more, but even I could not hear my own echoes under the rush of the waterfall. I moved to cross the snowy scree field, but the pebbles shifted beneath my feet, forcing me to scamper up along larger rocks. As I drew near and the blur came from behind the boulder, my vision focused. It was only Eliza.

"Where've you been?" I asked.

"No time for questions, just follow me." She went behind the rock for a moment. I wondered what she was doing. A second later, a mountain goat emerged.

"I didn't know you could do that," I said, genuinely astonished. "I don't think I can keep up, Eliza; you're gonna lose me."

Her head bent in search of food. I called to her; the head raised, alert, two curved horns shooting back from its white cap. She paid me no more interest and continued to graze as I crept toward her. She didn't run or hide, only kept her ear attuned to my movements. I moved within a body's distance and crouched down to watch. I looked at her knife-slit eyes. I reached out my arm to cover half the distance between us, and left it suspended there. In her own time she looked up, ruminating on some small tuft of wet grass, and studied me further. Then she took several steps toward me, and bending her neck rubbed her cool horns against my hand like a cat would if cats had horns.

"Friendly, eh?"

I looked up. There was Eliza, on top of the boulder.

"You could have told me. You've been watching me all this time?"

"Yep, making a general idiot of yourself."

"I thought you were the goat."

"I guess I could've been. You're really losing it, you know that? I don't pretend to know what's going through your mind every second."

"Well, why the hell not? You're my imaginary friend."

"Doesn't mean I can read your mind."

"That's nuts."

"Nuts? I'm the only one keeping you sane. What are you going to do when you get back and get those medications Micah's talking about? I'll disappear if you take them, and then you'll go nuts for sure."

"You might be right."

"I'm getting out before that happens. There's no way you're locking me into your head for the rest of your life. I'm finding a new home."

"Can you do that?"

"I can do anything I want really." She sighed. "Which way are you going?"

I pointed toward the waterfall. "I figured I'd head that way," I told her. "There has to be a lake of some kind up there."

"What are you going to do when you get there?"

"Find my dad, what else?"

"You ready for that?"

"When will I ever be ready for it? I just gotta do it, before it's too late."

She laughed and seemed to fade a little. I rubbed the goat under the chin. After a time it moved away, then began to head toward the waterfall.

"I love you, Kazimir," Eliza whispered.

"I know."

She laughed, made a wild leap and disappeared into the goat's anus. It shuddered, turned its head to look at me, and began to climb again.

I followed her prints, clawing my way up the steep cliffside as the waterfall thundered down. I muscled my way over the rise, catching my breath every few minutes to deal with the altitude, the exertion. The goat disappeared over the ledge, and I followed. Near the top the slope lessened, and I walked my way up until I crossed a lip and could see what lay in front of me.

A high glacial lake spread the entirety of a basin ringed with the peaks of mountains on three sides. The snowfall had paused momentarily, but wind was whipping the fallen snow into billowing clouds in the moonlight. On the far side of the lake, battered by wind and snow, was a wicki-up. In it would be my grandma. And my father.

Through the blur of snow that again came down, through the tides of snow that blew from the ground, I could see the little goat make her way steadily across the field and begin another ascent.

Snowflakes dissolved as they hit the surface of the water, and I walked along its edge toward the shelter. Where is she going? I wondered, and I wished I could follow her.

An empty fire ring lay before the hut. I dipped my hand through the layer of snow and found small coals void of life. A cover of hide worked as the door of the hut. I went to it, kicking an empty liquor bottle hidden in the snow. I took a deep breath, then slid the hide away. The interior was pitch black.

"Dad?"

No response. I felt in my pocket for my miniature Maglite.

The dim finger of light ran over a pile of refuse and mess akin to the dumpster at a rodeo. Whiskey bottles littered the floor, and the light passed through their translucence to dried skins, piles of pine needles, a broken lantern, a battered rifle, and finally to a sleeping bag knitted over with duct tape and kept to the ground by the mass of a human figure it held in its belly like a python. The light followed the bulge up to a flannel shirt, a beard, and the face of my father, hollowed and sunken, ghostly in the light. A few weak strands of hair ran over his face; others skirted his shoulders.

"Dad?"

His eyes opened but didn't look toward me. A hand came out of the sleeping bag and scratched his chest.

"What do you want?" he asked.

"It's Kaz, your son."

"I know who you are."

"Where's Grandma? What did you do with her?"

"She's right here," he said, though I couldn't make her out. "How did you get here?"

"I don't know." Snow sliced through the cracks in the hut and pelted me in the face. "Is she okay?"

He didn't say anything for a long while. I figured he'd passed out, and I crawled through the junk to enter the tomb. I felt books under my knees, more bottles, clothing—a pair of jeans and a pair of leather boots devoid of shoelaces. I crawled up till I felt his feet beneath the cloth, and there I waited for him to be conscious.

"I'm going nuts, Dad. I'm seeing things—like you. You were right all those years when you thought I was a prophet. Visions—just like our ancestors."

"You're not a prophet."

I didn't know how to answer. "I want to be sane."

"Sanity—the anesthesia we take as the Beast devours us."

I paused and waited, expecting the usual tirade. Nothing came.

"Where is she?" I asked. "We can get still get her back so she can die at home like she wanted."

"That's not going to happen."

Outside the wind howled. Snow blew in through the doorway and onto my back.

I waited, but he did not answer. Here, something said. I did not recognize the voice. Something moved my hand to a spot on the floor and I found a thing hard and cold beneath a fur blanket. I pulled back the blanket and felt again. At first I didn't recognize the shape; my hands were too numb to feel. It was waxy, cold, yet still bendable like putty; the ends of it were torn off into five parts. Then it occurred to me what it was and I let go and quickly covered it up.

"Grandma," I whispered.

"She's dead," he said.

"Why did you do this? Why did you take her up here?"

He didn't answer. I searched for my Maglite but couldn't find it in the mess on the floor. I crawled toward him, over the lump beneath the blankets that was my grandmother's cadaver, and reached my hands out until I felt his beard. I yanked. His head jerked toward me and I hit him as hard as I could with my other hand. I screamed. I hit him again. I could feel his ear as I smashed my hand into the side of his head.

He didn't resist. I hit him in the nose, and felt it crunch beneath my fist; again across the forehead, felt my wrist turn as I hit bone. He didn't resist. I screamed and stood, staggered over something and kicked him, then again, then again. He didn't resist.

I kicked him one last time and staggered over his leg and fell to the ground. I rolled off of him, off the furs, and onto the cold ground, where I rested.

I panted in the dark. I was warm now, even sweating. The silence was punctuated by my breathing and my father's sniffles.

We lay there a long time then. I was numb. I couldn't feel. I realized I hadn't hit him because I was angry. I had hit him because it was appropriate. I hit him because I should be angry, because I should want to hit him for what he had done to my Grandma. But I felt nothing: sorrow, anger, fear, pain. I felt nothing and I hated myself for it, hated the whole world for making me emotionless. I had hit him because I hated myself for feeling nothing.

"I thought I could help her," he whimpered.

I didn't answer.

"I carried her up here on my back," he continued. "I did all the rituals I've learned. I poured my soul-force into her." His voice faded into the wind. "She died."

I waited a long while. "When?"

"This morning."

Eliza had been wrong. "Why didn't you take her down then?"

He didn't answer.

My leg touched something and it squeaked. I reached beneath piles of clothing to find my father's guitar. I plucked one steel string, and then brushed my freezing fingers across them all. The sound was stolen by the wind.

"How come you never taught me to play guitar, Dad?" I asked. "You loved this thing. You taught me all this crap I didn't need to know, and that you hardly knew yourself. How to make a shelter, how to breathe some spiritual way, how to read through cards. Then you just ditched me. You just left me and Grandma and hardly ever came back. Why? Why did you just leave me and her? You never came back, you never taught me to play guitar, the one damn thing you loved— the one thing that was really you."

"There's no leaving Ephraim."

A shiver went down my spine. "You never forgave Silas. You never forgave Leanna. You ran away from all that, and ran away from me. All you've done since I was seven is mess up my life. I spent so much of my childhood thinking I was supposed to be some special prophet, and then I get to my teens and I find out I'm just another dick with no social skills and a warped brain. Spirit quests and card tricks, years of loneliness," I hissed at him, "and now this. I try doing one decent thing in my life. I try to let Grandma die happily and you steal that from me."

I was done then. I had said what I wanted. I didn't expect him to answer. I said it just to say it. I heard him sniffle again.

"They'll lock me up," he said, and adjusted himself in his sleeping bag. "I either go to an insane asylum or I die here. I don't want to be in chains.

"I'm sorry," he said, "I'm sorry for being a freak. I can't control my head. I'm sorry for forcing you to live in the world like this—like I have. Ephraim's was the only place that gave some value to the way I saw things. I had so much hope for you—for you to be like the Godwins of old.

"The silver scrolls of Regnus Godwin, they are hidden on our land—I saw it in a vision. He had been a Mormon, an exiled prophet. We have the power in the family," he said. He sniffled. I heard him wipe his nose. It must have been bleeding.

"I didn't believe well enough," he continued. "I didn't have real faith—that's why I failed with Grandma. I had to be here, Kaz. Once you're part of Ephraim's society, you are always a part of it. And my visions—I couldn't be a father. I couldn't have been what you needed me to be. I wanted you to have a chance to be normal too, so I left you with Grandma. Because I'm not normal. I couldn't do it. I'm sorry for putting you up on that rock. I'm sorry for everything. I'm sorry. I'm so sorry."

I lay there and closed my eyes. I lay there and tried to forgive him for being who he was.

"I had a vision, Dad, on that vision quest. A world drowning. Everyone I loved swept away."

He started crying.

"You said you had the power to help me, dad. Well, I need the help. I see stuff. I hear Ephraim in my head. I don't know what's going on."

"I don't know anything, Kaz, nobody does. Not me, not Ephraim, not you. And we never will."

"Maybe all the stuff you believed meant something. Maybe the visions, the voices do. We're prophets, aren't we? A long line of prophets."

I hear him shudder. His crying settled. After a time , he moved through the dark.

"Come here, if you want," he said.

A lighter switched on, illuminating his face. He had his opium with him.

"I thought you only did that for your visions."

"All my visions have been a lie."

"I don't want any more," I said. "I don't want any more drugs at all. Not even pot. I just want to be normal—whatever that means in this world."

He smoked his opium, and for a while things were quiet. I shivered and tried to get as much of myself as I could under the blanket.

"There's no place for Sight in our world. It's only a disease now."

Then he began to writhe. He was tortured by ghosts. I could not see them, but I could feel them slip by me, could feel their hands outstretched for his throat as the wind blew and the snow fell. After a time, he mumbled and slurred, and then once again he writhed. I waited for light; I shivered through the cold. I waited for the day.

I stepped outside to find the snow had stopped falling. Fierce winds spit over the mountain, blurring a vague moon shaded by clouds.

I took an empty bottle and filled it in the lake. Ice had built in shards around the shore. My numb feet stumbled over the footing, but I drank as I walked back to the hut, and the cold water restored my cogency briefly. Renegade snow blew in with me as I entered. My father slept in the corner, wind-beaten, grizzled, comatose under the sleeping bag. I crawled in and pulled the guitar out. I began to strum and after a while he opened his eyes.

I handed him the guitar. His hands came out, shaking, and he started to pick, slow and pretty. I closed my eyes and sounds from childhood came back, the smell of campfires. Angels and dreams, games of bow-and-arrow in the cornfields and forests, passed over me like waves. I sighed and sank into the music, and after a time it slowed, stopped. He reached into the musical void and pulled out a series of harmonics.

I looked up, and he rubbed his fingers.

"Too cold," he said.

"How come you never taught me to play, Dad?"

He looked as if he would answer, then stopped.

A long silence ensued.

"You're aren't cold?" he asked.

I shook my head.

"Always were a tough son-of-a-bitch. I taught you that at least."

"You did." We shared more silence. "We need to get out of here when daylight comes. We need to bring Grandma with us. Bury her in the graveyard of our ancestors. You and me. Then we'll get help for both of us. Get us some psychologists."

"Trade one religion for another. You think any of it's gonna help? There's nothing they can do. They just make you fit inside the common paradigm or set you out on the street—or put you in a strait-jacket."

"I don't know. I don't know about any of that. I don't know what's right. I don't even know what's real, Dad."

"It's all bullshit." He rolled his eyes, then laid his head back.

"Dad?" I said. My hands began to shake, I leaned forward and touched his forehead. His hand stroked Grandma's hair.

"I just want her back again. I just want to do it all over," he whispered. He faded into sleep.

I looked around the hut, the mess of all that he had brought. There beneath a blanket, tucked into a mummy bag, was the body of my grandmother. *Touch her*, something said in my head.

I crawled over, hesitated, then pulled back the blanket to reveal her face.

It was cold, blue, her brow in frozen furrows. She had died in pain.

I checked her pulse. Nothing. I reached over and lifted back a cold eye lid, flipped it open like a window shutter. A single eye stared at me. Gray hair swayed over her forehead. On some lonely mountain she had never heard of, away from everything she ever loved. This is how she died, a death as meaningless as any other. A death just as good, I guessed.

"Goodbye," I whispered. I leaned down and kissed her on the forehead. "I'm so sorry I couldn't be a good son, Grandma. I'm so sorry you had to do this. I wish it was me. I wish I could trade."

On the shore of the lake, I found a quartz pebble, smooth and flat, and skipped it across the water onto the edge of a waiting glacial field. "Hello?" I called out, and the sound seemed to ring from the mountain peaks.

When he woke, I would ask him to play me his guitar. I wanted to hear it in this place he loved. Have him play a funeral dirge for Grandma, smooth the creases from her brow and let her rest. We would get her back down somehow. We would bury her at home. I found more of the circular crystals and skipped them. I would say to anyone who asked that she wanted to die here, so they didn't harass my father. I'd make up to him; he'd make up to Silas.

Crystals gathered like sea turtles as they skipped onto the far shore. We could get help, both of us. We could say the "I'm sorrys" and the "I forgive yous." We could work on being some kind of family. I picked up a red pebble and rubbed the pad of my thumb across its wet surface. A white line of quartz coursed through it like a vein and glimmered like a firefly. I bent my arm and flung it. It skipped once, twice, sank beneath the surface.

A shot rang out in the air.

It had come from the hut. I spun and sprinted. I pulled back the flap, and in the dim light I took it all in; guitar, Grandma, clothing. There was my father resting in his sleeping bag. Everything as it was. Then he made a sound. I squinted. His arms were on top of his bag. The rifle was in his hands. It pointed at his head.

"Dad!" I crawled toward him.

"Oh, God," he said.

Light flitted between the cracks in the hut. A dark mass of blood pooled on his chest.

"What did you do, oh God, Dad, what did you do?"

I grabbed a pair of jeans, a T-shirt. I grabbed everything I could. The blood poured out of the side of his head, down his temple, into his beard.

"Kaz, just let me die."

"No." I started trying to lift him. "I'm getting you out of here."

"I got a right to die."

"I'll get you to Ephraim. He can help you. You hit the side of your face I think."

"It's enough. You'll never get me out of here."

He was right. I didn't have the faintest idea how to get him down. I let go.

"Get me the opium, give me some."

I did as he asked.

"I brought it for Mom." He took some more opium. "Get me outside. I want to see the mountains one last time."

I dragged him by the armpits over Grandma's body and rested him against the fire pit. The sun shone down on him and he squinted. Blood glistened all over his hair, his face; it was smeared all over his sleeping bag, all over me.

"Water."

I went and did as he asked. Then he was cold. I took the blanket off Grandma and laid it over him.

"Come sit by me now, just sit by me."

I scooted over. He reached out for my hand and I took his. A tiny moth circled in a sunbeam, then came to rest in the center of his forehead.

"It's time now, Kaz."

"For what?"

"Pick up my rifle."

I stood up. "Dad, I can't do that."

"I don't want to hurt anymore."

"I can't do that."

"I got a right to die."

"And go to hell?"

"Who knows?"

I paced about, stalled for time. But the end of time had come for him—I knew it. I went and dragged through the stuff in the hut, found the last half bottle of whiskey and gave it to him. I sat next to him, helped him finish it.

"Okay," he said, after it was dry. "Promise me you'll take us home. Bury us with the rest of our family."

I stood and straddled him, took the rifle and held the barrel toward him. He clutched it in his shaky hands and guided it deliberately into his mouth.

"I can't do this, Dad." My voice cracked.

"Do i fo' e."

"What?"

"Do i fo' e."

"What?" I took the gun out of his mouth.

"Do it for me."

Sweat ran down my back in a cold trickle; the trees shook in the wind. Every hair in his beard trembled, life hung in his brown eyes, the tiny red veins on his nose quickened with the course of blood.

Then his hand moved to mine, holding it, holding it like he did when I was a child. Cold and firm, and for all the things he was and did, I forgave him.

His fingers wrapped around mine, curled around the trigger. My hand shook and he steadied it in his strength. Then, with his strange love, he began to squeeze.

I pulled my hand away.

"NO!"

I don't even remember the sound of the shot. His head jerked back. His feet ripped through the bottom of the sleeping bag, bare toes exposed to the cold. He went slack.

I was alone.

CHAPTER
TWENTY-TWO

THE LAST OF THE OPIUM ENTERED MY LUNGS. I staggered into the hut and lay next to Grandma. Outside the sun was headed toward the western sky, never to come back up. I entered the night, let myself go to the freeze that blew through all things, the cold flow that animates the dead and the living. I was too numb to mourn, the stream in me frozen.

As the sky tortured the earth, I lay in his hut, surrounded by his smell, the old jeans, the empty bottles. Wind blew through it all, playing notes on the guitar and storming to the ends of the earth. I surrendered to what angel or demon would have me, would take me from a world I no longer knew how to live in.

"You should leave." Eliza was beside me. "Get up." I didn't respond. "You'll die here, you understand?"

Fingers that ran through my hair, the burly hugs of my father, the smooth cartilage of the ear where Silas had cut him once. *You know, Kaz, you know, Kaz, you know, Kaz....*

I had the odd feeling that my eyeballs had fallen out, and I crawled about the room looking for them. I shook the guitar and heard them rattle inside, shook them free like a lost pick, held a chord and strummed with the eyeballs, the wind picking up the notes like dandelion seeds. I opened my eyes and I was staring out from the palms of my hands. Across from me a ghost stared back.

"Who the hell are you?" I yelled.

A handlebar mustache showed underneath frost like shredded wheat. His feet were bare, raw and blue-yellow toenails on bloated toes as if he had drowned in a river. He only pointed outside.

Then he was gone. I looked out. The wind blew under a quarter moon. The cuts on the ghost's feet left tracks of blood.

What do you do when the dead beckon?

I made my way into the darkness.

I too would head westward. It was time. Eighteen years of pointlessness. My hands felt around for the rifle; it must be near my father's body. No bullet left in it. I scoured the hut. I couldn't find a light. I couldn't find the bullets.

Then my fingers touched the bone handle of my father's knife. I pulled it out and ran the blade along my cheek, touched my cheek to see if it had cut. My hands were too numb to tell but I held them to the sliver of moonlight and saw my palm darkened. I unrobed myself and put it to my stomach, just below my navel. I cut a shallow smile. I was cold, it would be painless. I would go deeper, through the skin, the fat, through the tensed plate of muscle. I could do this and end it all, release myself from the weight of things. This was what God wanted of me. This was what God wanted of us all: to die. The only thing we could be sure of.

A chasm opened before me: I wanted to leap. My soul would come out, as if hooked; it would be flung out my mouth as I pierced my stomach; it would be free of the weight.

I was afraid. I let go of the knife. I became weak; I fell over and lay my head on my father's stomach. I hyperventilated with sorrow. I became panicked, jumped up and tripped over my father, who groaned a ghostly breath. I ran to the edge of lake.

"Come back to the hut," Eliza called from the doorway.

"Get out Eliza, get out!"

"You freaking moron, there's nothing chasing us!"

"Go to hell," I told her.

She laughed. "We're already there."

At the far edge of the lake, the glacier's terminus loomed, darker than all other shadow by degrees. The moon was gone and snow fell again, hard as needles. Then lights began, baubles that shifted over the darkness but illuminated nothing. There at the edge of the lake

I found the bloody tracks the ghost had left. I waded into the water, and the black beast that stalked my soul dissolved into the air. It couldn't reach me in the sacred water—my father had been right. I was safe here. My legs froze up to my knees, and I fell forward. So this was hell? Poetic justice. A kid from Wisconsin goes to hell to find it frozen over.

"Kazimir, I'm serious, come back to the hut, wait out the night."

Chest-deep into the water, I felt the world swim around me. Now everything was distant: her voice, the glacier, my skin burning in cold. A good way to die. I could float away with the lights.

Stars danced above me, then faded out.

"…alive!…"

Something hooked my skin; I could feel the weight of the water as I was dragged. The black face of the mountain drowned the stars. There was gravel on my neck, the sound of wading. Gravel on my back, my own weight bearing down again on the earth. I was caught. I had been reeled to shore.

A light flickered and darted, was extinguished and renewed. The sound of water trickled in, animals mumbling, radios lilting in languages I could not understand. The sounds became organized and I thought to stand, but my body wasn't taking orders. The light returned in my eyes.

"Kaz!" A rooster pecked my numb cheek. The cheek was floating disembodied above me. It was connected to the rest of me in some way I couldn't put my finger on. I willed it back onto my face.

"Kaz!" The rooster slapped me squarely on my newly assembled cheek.

"Ow!"

The rooster crowed and then the light flashed on it. My eyes adjusted to the face. Micah.

"That damn Mohawk," I said, half-laughed, and closed my eyes.

"Kaz, listen to me." A hand slapped me again. "Don't sleep, don't fall asleep, never fall asleep."

I looked into his eyes.

"Kaz, don't close your eyes again, keep them open, promise me, promise me that."

We stared at each other.

"I never asked you for anything until now, Kaz. You're my best friend, you're my best friend, don't close your eyes. Don't close your eyes. That's all I ask."

"Okay."

A shadow moved behind him.

"Alive," it hissed, and my ability to comprehend began to dissolve.

"Stay with me, Kaz!" Micah slapped me again. Then he sang. I had never heard him sing. He had a nice voice, somehow comforting, like the sound of a boat being rowed. The moon was now out, and the snow shimmered under the panoply of night. I turned my head. My father's face flashed before me. The shadow I saw earlier ducked into the hut, re-emerged to where my father lay. It dropped things into a pile. Micah's orisons slipped into my ears and coursed through my body, warming me. My hands tingled. Stars were spit out of the shadow's hands. Stars and more stars, like a waterfall of fireflies. Then the stars stopped; a red glow levitated, hovered by the shadow's face and then burst into flame. He dropped it into the pile of things from the hut, ducked his head and blew.

A fireball exploded into a campfire. Silas was the shadow in the moonlight, Silas in the firelight. Micah grabbed me and dragged my body to the fire. Put a coat on me, helped me get my pants on. I put my hands out to warm; sweat formed on my palms as the fire blazed. Micah handed me a thermos of water, opened it, and poured me a cup. Put the thermos in my armpit. I sipped the hot tea under my own power.

"Just another survival camp. Remember that?" called Micah from over by the hut. He was tearing it apart; so was Silas. They were tossing it onto the fire. "Remember that, Kaz? Remember when we ate the gopher? Me and your dad? Talk to me, Kaz, talk to me."

"Yeah."

"Yeah what?"

"Of course, I remember. I remember."

"Remember when I met you, Kaz? The schoolyard? Remember Sammy the guinea pig?"

"Sammy was nice."

"How bout Skeeter? Do you remember Skeeter?" asked Silas. He threw some dry skins onto the fire.

I thought about that. "I never met him, he died."

"Good, good memory, Kaz," Silas said. "Trick question."

They had brought wool mittens, gloves, a sweater; I put them on. My legs throbbed, my whole body began to tingle, to sting, then was warm. My feet felt the earth. I breathed. I began to sweat; I stood to move away from the fire. I sipped some tea and became aware of stomach pain. I realized I had a gaping wound strung across my abdomen. I felt oddly normal. Oddly at ease, almost pensive; I sipped and noticed Silas and Micah staring at me.

"You okay?"

"Fine," I said, "I guess. Considering." I looked around. "We need to get Grandma home."

"We need to get you and your father out of here, too."

"We'll build travois," said Silas. "We have skins, wood. It's how I used to take deer back. We'll go tonight. We'll get one for your dad, and one for you and Mom."

"I don't need one, I'm fine."

They stared at me.

"We just pulled you out of the freaking lake!" Micah said. "You shouldn't be standing up, much less getting ready to walk five miles through the mountains."

"I'm fine."

We didn't argue anymore. They went about preparing the sleds. I finished my tea in a gulp. "I'll help you."

We left a scattered remnant of the sacred hut with its sacred trappings by the sacred lake. Sacred skins that had once been sacred blankets we stretched across sacred poles. Silas worked on the bottoms to make them function as sleds, then I gently slid Grandma's corpse onto one, covered in the mummy sleeping bag. It took all three of us to drag my father's body onto the other.

We tied rope to the front of each travois. I settled into the one carrying my grandmother like a bull pulling a plow. Silas gave me a flashlight and duct-taped it to my head. He and Micah took up the yoke of my father's body together. Our flashlights bobbed and wove in the semi-dark of the moon; our breath shimmered in the light. Then we were off across the high plateau.

Within ten minutes I had to remove my sweater under the heat of the exertion. Micah and Silas struggled worse; my father's weight bore down on the snow and caught on every rock and minor crevasse.

We reached the lip where the waterfall tossed itself into oblivion. I began to edge my way down the rocks I had climbed earlier with Eliza the goat. Large boulders stood in the way of the travois. I pulled it by hand. I slipped, skidded down a ways before catching myself. Snow filled my cuffs and shoes. Grandma's travois stayed stuck on the rock. I looked up to see Micah and Silas looking over the lip.

"That's not gonna work," called out Silas.

I climbed back to the travois and the other two helped me pull it back to the lip.

"There's no way we're gonna be able to get Aeneas down that," said Silas between breaths.

"What do we do?" I asked when I could speak. We looked over the ledge at the water flowing down.

"We'll tie them on to the travois," said Micah, "then hop on and ride them down the hill like sleds."

We had no better ideas. Micah went back and got more rope from the now defunct sacred hut as Silas and I tugged the travois a distance to a gentler incline.

"Sometime you gotta tell me what happened up here," he said as we panted. "Not right now."

"How did you find me?"

"Leanna remembered being out here. Tracked your car through the mud. Found it and followed your foot path to Ephraim's place. I was worried because of the storm. I convinced him to let me and Micah go out and find you. We tracked you after that."

Micah was back and we did as said, Silas on one travois-sled and Micah on the other. I was to follow behind. I gave each a push and they started down the slope where the snow covered the scree more uniformly, far away from the water and the larger boulders.

They zigzagged down the slope and I began to post-hole my way down after them. A strong wind was blowing up the mountain, which made it terrible going; I put my head down against it, and put my sweater back on. I watched them cross in figure eights as they went, and soon I was far behind them. My fingers were cold. I felt weak again, the sudden flush of superhuman strength sapped. My grandmother's sled receded into an ever-smaller speck below.

I found a small boulder to rest on. Crystals of snow cast themselves into my face, and I closed my eyelids to get my eyeballs out of their way. Maybe I would just take a small rest, I thought, just gather my strength for the last push down the hill.

The sound of a snuffle came from my side. I looked and saw Eliza the goat standing there. She rubbed her horns on my leg.

"Horny?" she asked.

Small delegations of light came from the sky where the moon splintered the clouds. It was warmer here. Less snow.

"Wanna ride?" she asked. "Might as well take advantage of your four-legged friend."

"Thank you," I told her and hopped onto her back. We began to descend.

"Kaz, I've been thinking. It's not gonna work between us. Not after all this. You need some help, the kind an imaginary friend can't give you. It's time to say good bye. I want you to make me go."

"But what will I do without you? What will you do without me?"

"I don't know what you'll do. I don't know how my life will work without you either. But I kind of like this goat thing—get to spend my time outdoors in the real world. Maybe you could just imagine me into this goat, and come visit me from time to time. I do love you, Kaz. I love you so much that I know that I'm no good for you. Leave me here."

"I won't. No. Things have been fine—well, up on the mountain I guess they weren't. That was terrible." I held her horns. "But maybe that's over now. Look, I got to get through all this, all this stuff going on inside me, this stuff about my father, my grandma, Ephraim and his people. I gotta face it and I can't do it without you."

"You did it before. I disappeared and it was fine. You can do it again."

"I have no one to help me. I can't do it."

"You have Micah, Silas, maybe Leanna. You have a whole life ahead of you."

"I need you."

She materialized at my side, though I was still on the goat. The night's shadows made the planes of her face unrecognizable, foreign. I reached for her arm, but she stepped away. "I got you through some tough stuff. You gotta do the rest. Goodbye Kaz. I'll miss you."

All the things Eliza and I had been through came flooding back to me. Everyone went away from me. "You are gone, then," I said, closing my eyes. "I disappear you."

I rode on the goat all the way into the valley. The trees stole the voice of the wind. Their branches had taken the brunt of the snow storm, and she trod on pine needles. Some trees showed signs of old burns. Tiny drifts of snow accreted at the base of firs.

My light had dimmed to just a small yellow flicker, but I could see Micah and Silas in the moon-latticed shadows of the forest. They watched me approach. I had the sudden feeling that I looked like the king of asses.

"That's different," said Micah.

Under the trees the wind was dampened and the stream could be heard trickling through the forest. I got down off the goat. She went and picked at some tufts of grass that held their heads above the snow.

The snow was thinner here than it had been above, so the pulling was even harder. We had to stop every few minutes to rest. Eliza came along, stopping graze or pee without much regard for our movements but always steadily behind us.

Through the pines we saw a flicker of lights, and we snaked toward them along the edge of the stream. The moon had nearly set below the mountains when a small lake became visible. As we drew near, Micah tapped me on the arm and pointed toward the trees. Ringing the large trunks were circular decks, and in the crooks of the trees were dark tree houses. Water dripped down from their canopies.

We came to a circular clearing beside the lake where stones dusted with snow were arranged into elaborate Celtic knots. A large clay sculpture of abstract design stood at the very center, and off to the left of the clearing a large timber hall and a few small outbuildings huddled. None of these had lights in it, but beside the lake, set off from the others, was a stately cabin made of river stone. Its chimney spiraled like a helix, and from it a column of smoke continued the upward spiral until disappearing into a veil of mist. The hearth fire's glow was visible through the windows.

We hauled the bodies to the large fir-plank door of the cabin and set them to rest. I collapsed to the ground, as did Micah and Silas, and we lay a long while in the thin snow, letting our breathing slow its steamy puffs. After a time I shivered, rolled over, and put on my sweater again.

"Let's go in," said Silas finally.

He guided us through the door and into a dark kitchen. A solid, rough-hewn table half as long as a bowling lane dominated the room. Baskets, pots, and pans hung from the walls, and several braids of garlic bulbs draped the large windows that looked onto the lake. The stone fireplace bulged out of the interior wall, and a dim light emanated from its coals. Silas made his way toward a brighter glow that paved the wood floor in front of a closed door. He swung it open and beckoned us in.

CHAPTER TWENTY-THREE

Leanna sat in a rocking chair with her back to us, snoring lightly. On a pillow, sitting in perpetual lotus, was Ephraim. He stared at the fire, his back perfectly erect. As we walked into the room he turned his head slowly.

"You're back."

"Yes," said Micah.

Leanna's head lifted; she turned and saw us. "Oh, Silas!" She shot up and clung to him; he kissed her hair repeatedly.

Ephraim stood and met us. "Aeneas? Your grandmother?"

"They're dead," I told him.

He seemed at a loss for words. "How?"

"Lack of oxygen to the brain, just like everyone," said Micah.

"All his hocus-pocus didn't work," I told him. "She died before I got there."

"But Aeneas?"

"Shot himself."

He looked away. Silas and Leanna broke apart from each other as she turned toward me.

"We brought their bodies," Micah told him, "so they can be buried back home."

"You carried them all the way down here?" asked Ephraim.

I nodded.

"Where are they?"

I brought him out to where we had laid them to rest. The others followed behind. Ephraim loomed over the bodies, shirtless in the cold, then squatted down and placed his ear on my grandmother's lips. He reached out and fingered my father's pale face.

"He's not dead," he told us.

"What?" we all asked at once.

"He's not dead. He's speaking to me this very moment." He stood up and touched his necklace. "Bring him to the fire." I looked at Micah and he at me, and we did as Ephraim had commanded.

Silas held the door as we pulled my father on the travois through cabin and laid him out on the rug.

We were all sent out to get more firewood, and then we stoked the fire until the flames shot out of the chimney. All the while Ephraim sat very still on his pillow, first smoking his hookah, then bending at the waist and whispering into my father's one remaining ear. He told us to keep fueling the fire and then he had us put my father closer to the flames. We rolled him over several times until he was face up with his left side against the stones. The right side of his face was mangled, a mass of dried blood acting as a net to catch collapsing bones. Flames licked at his beard and eyebrows, singing them.

"He is very near gone; I'm not sure if I can save him," Ephraim told us.

"I'm not sure either," muttered Micah.

"It'll take all that I have to do it, if I can," he told us, then closed his eyes and began mumbling prayers. We watched him for a time; then he sat up again, opened his eyes and concentrated on the fire, and finally turned to address us again. "It may take all night. Stack as much firewood as you can next to me here, and then leave this room. Sleep in the kitchen if you think you do not believe in such things. Disbelief weakens a prayer; the farther from me the better."

Then he turned back to my father and began to whisper again.

We did as he asked. We took blankets from the living room and laid them out on the stone floor of the kitchen, on the far side of its minimal fire. Micah and Silas were instantly asleep; Leanna lay in Silas's arms. I added logs to the fire. I was wide awake.

"How are you, Kazimir?" whispered Leanna.

I saw the green of her eyes in the glow of the firelight. She was on her side, spooned by Silas, his arm draped around her waist.

"I don't know."

The fire crackled, sending a few sparks into her hair. She patted her head.

"That must have been hard—up there."

"Yeah," I said, "it was."

"Aren't you tired?"

"I can't sleep real well lately," I told her. "When did you guys get here?"

"Yesterday."

"Have you ever been here?"

"Yes," she said, "we came when you were very little. When I was with Aeneas." She sighed. "Your dad believed so strongly in Ephraim's work."

"More than he cared for you—is that why you left him?"

She hesitated. "Yes, that had something to do with it." She rubbed her eyes. "Silas and I were just meant to be, I think."

"I didn't see it when I was a kid. I do now."

"Do you have a girlfriend or anything?"

"No. I'm not so good with people."

"I'm sorry, Kaz, I'm sorry you had to go through all that stuff with us."

"I'm sorry too—I'm sorry I never forgave you before."

"Maybe when we get back, and all this is over, we can see you more. I always wondered what you've been doing with yourself."

"A lot of drugs," I told her. She laughed. "I've got to stop. I'm going nuts."

"Your father would say it's spiritual revelations."

"I wonder what Ephraim would say?"

"Do you think Ephraim can really save your dad?"

"No. But he can try. I don't care."

"I understand." She smiled at me. I nodded at her and turned away.

Much later, the fire had dimmed; everyone else slept. The living room door opened, and a figure moved slowly through the room and out through the fir door. After a moment, I slid from between the others and followed it.

Outside, Ephraim knelt by my grandmother. He stroked her hair in the starlight.

"This poor, precious child of creation," he said to me. "This beautiful creature. I wish he hadn't brought her here."

"But I thought it was 'the will of God.' At least according to you people."

"How are any of us to know the will of God?"

I was confused and a little irritated. "Doesn't God communicate with you through visions and prophecy? Didn't he do the same to my father? Aren't I some kind of 'hidden prophet?'"

"Even our 'knowing' that something is of God does not guarantee it is. I don't believe God is absent from this world. Yet that doesn't mean we can fully understand what God communicates with us any more than we can know the sum of all numbers," he said. "There are mysteries we will never understand. I have never claimed to be a prophet. Prophecy was your father's fascination."

"But what about the Beast of civilization? What about planting the seed for a better tomorrow after the crash of the Beast? I've never understood how my dad and you could believe these things. I don't mean to be an ass—I just don't get it."

"Don't you think it's accurate sometimes? The Beast? But these are just metaphors, or something like them—mythology. We cannot know what is going on in this world. All math, science, religion, myth, prophecy ultimately mean nothing. We are powerless, tiny little creatures of little meaning. The best of us try to continually refine what we understand good to be, and do it. Most of us do little more than what is required to live."

I sighed. "But Ephraim, if you don't have any special powers, how're you going to save my dad?"

"I have no power, Kazimir. I have little understanding. Stranger things can happen than a near-dead man rising. I'm human, so if I want such things to happen I have to do what I think results in them, based on experience, intelligence, and intuition." He stopped and smiled at me. I yawned.

"What time is it?" I asked.

He shrugged. "We don't have clocks here."

"The end of his life, like the rest of his life, was a mess. I don't know why you want to save him. When I was up there—I had visions. What I saw up there, after my father died—his legacy is not a new world order; it is the work of the Beast."

"Then what you saw is not prophecy." He shook his head and put his hands to his mouth. "It is not prophecy."

"I don't think that's fair of you. I don't say what you want me to say so suddenly I'm not a prophet."

"It was your father who believed in you, not me. Years ago—that card I had you read—you were wrong."

I didn't know what to say.

"I gave your father things to do with you to help ease his mind. Religion is the only thing that kept him sane. Without it, he would have been a murderer, or worse."

"You tell me this now, after years of spying on me, years of ruining my life."

"Spying on you?"

"The arrowheads."

He shook his head. "I told you, you're wrong. You think we've been plotting some tremendous takeover of the world, starting with you? There's nothing here but our crops, our tree houses, some marijuana plants, some opium. Nothing, you understand?"

I didn't know whether to believe him or not.

He stood, reached over and put a hand on my shoulder. "Do you know what separates a madman from a religious fanatic?"

"What?"

"The fanatic can still tie his shoes in the morning."

I looked down at his bare feet. "If he has shoes to tie."

He laughed and smiled at me. "You want to do something for me, Kazimir? Your grandmother's spirit, I sense, is interrupting my ritual. Could you sit here and talk with her?"

I shrugged. "Sure. I have nothing else to do."

He went back in. I sat down next to my grandmother's body and sighed. "Hello," I said.

No response.

And I began to talk. I talked to her about dreams. I talked to her about her card-counting, about her garden, about the cold front that caught us all on the mountain. I talked and talked as if some spell had been put over me.

I told her how much I loved her.

How she kept me together. How she had been there in her quiet way. How I appreciated her giving me the freedom to roam the woods, to make my mistakes. How I would keep her plants up, keep her house together. How I would get help, how I would go to college and be a decent person.

Then I began to cry. Cry and cry and cry, tears everywhere. I didn't care if anyone saw me. I didn't care if the whole world saw me. I cried and cried and laid my head on her stomach.

Eventually I was nudged in the back by a goat.

"Where did you go to?" I asked. She just butted me again. I turned and rubbed her horns, then scratched her ear, and she tilted her head in delight. When I grew tired and put my hand down, she licked my face.

A current ran through the air. I shivered. Something was here. It felt almost like the creature that stalked me in my dreams, but its presence was benign; my fear was absent. Warmth lay over me like a kiss, like an apology, and then disappeared.

Eliza stopped licking me and bleated, then wandered away into the forest. I was overcome by sleep.

Birds woke me. Somewhere in the far distant east, the sun was preparing to hit the horizon. I sat up and looked out. Mist spread over the water. A thin whisper of smoke was all that came from the chimney. I was cold; I got up from my grandmother and returned inside.

The kitchen smelled of body odor. The dim light of the fire quickened the rooms. My family slept in a pile of blankets.

I slipped into the living room. Ephraim remained there, his hand on my father's chest, eyes closed. A crease had formed between his eyes.

I sat, or tried to sit, in lotus next to them. I close my eyes and prayed the prayer my Grandma had prayed for me. *Lord, I believe; help me in my unbelief.*

My father's shirt and beard were crusted in blood, littered with dirt and small stones. His hairs nearest the fire had been singed, and the scar that ran the length of his lip was exposed.

But his cheeks were clean. His jawbone intact, his cheeks clean and flushed with color. It didn't seem odd at first; it was the way I had known him. But slowly it dawned on me.

"Dad?"

I reached out, touched the cheek that he had shot a hole into a day earlier. A small round scar remained, the size of a cigarette burn.

"Dad?"

I touched his mouth, brushed away the leftovers of his mustache and pushed back his lip. There were his teeth—intact. I reached in and felt about the cold cavern. There was no hole. The back of his head—no wound.

Ephraim's hand went to my shoulder.

"Dad?"

I bent down and put my ear to his chest. I listened for the dull thud of life, the awkward footstep of his heartbeat. The fire crackled; the world was muffled by his shirt on my ear. The fire crackled, but there was no thump. There was no life in him.

"He wouldn't come back," said Ephraim, after letting me rise again. "He returned, and hovered above us. But he had done as God commanded, and was allowed to enter the Eternal. He decided to leave this earth."

"I don't blame him," I said.

Ephraim winced. "Our time here is very short, Kazimir. There's no point in making it even shorter. The world is a good place."

"I don't know about that. It seems there's no fighting all the terribleness of this world. There's no winning."

He looked at me with sadness, then turned back to my father. "I am sorry to see him go. He was my oldest friend, a man of vision. I am sorry too for your grandmother. I am sure you'll be at a loss without her."

"She's in a better place," I said.

He nodded and stood. "I need to talk to you now."

"Okay."

"I have need to protect our land. We're in a unique position; this is the first time we've had visitors such as you. I can't let you all go the way you came."

"What do you plan to do with us, then?"

He considered this. "Silas and Micah will be given sleeping pills to knock them out a long time. You and Leanna will be blindfolded and smoke opium and we will help you get your cars to the road. When you feel better, you can be on your way."

"With Grandma and Dad?"

"Of course. I'm going to tell you something here, Kazimir, about how we found this place. It has to do with your father."

"I've always liked stories."

"We were hippies. Even before your father was in the band—I can't remember exactly how I first met him—we knew many of the same people, had grand talks late into the night. I saw in how he approached his music that he had revelatory inclinations. We'd take longer and longer hikes together, he playing music, I leading us in the occult practices of wisdom I had been trained in. In the late sixties, word came down that the USGS needed people to work in remote places mapping some of the last uncharted areas of the country. We both wanted to be out in the woods and needed the cash, so we took the jobs. After a year, we were sent up to Montana, where we discovered this land. In the Crystal Mountains we took peyote, he played his guitar, and we had a shared vision of a village here, subsistence farming. Drug sales for income. It was to be the straw that broke the Beast's back, and the phoenix that would rise from the ashes of a nuclear holocaust. A new order. We altered the maps."

He waited to see if I understood. I didn't.

"This place is not on any modern map. It did not go down in the annals of the country's political or geographic consciousness or its scientific lore."

"*Terra incognita?*" I suggested.

"Not even that, Kazimir. There's not even a blank spot on the map for this place. You look on a map, and the two miles before and after it are seamless. Then you walk it and it is twenty miles long, not four. We don't exist. People can't come here because there is no here. The government can't tax us because it could never find us. And we have other places like this across the west—a shadow nation. Only your father and I know the connections, where they all are. They are kept in our heads. He was our messenger, our Gabriel."

"I came out here once," I told him. "We went all over the west. He never took me to those villages, but I think we camped near them."

"I know," he said. "In some ways your very life endangers the lives of all my people. We are a shadow nation, and you can see in the dark."

We stared at each other.

"When you found us a few days ago, I took you beneath the power tree. I tried to figure out whether to trust you or not. Given your information about us and your rebellion against your father, I tried to decide what to do with you. I decided to wait for Aeneas."

I was beginning to feel uncomfortable.

He looked at my father's body. "He's gone now, so I must decide myself." He sighed. "You are free to go," he told me. "This freedom is a gift from your father's spirit. Without your connection to him, I would have to make other plans. But remember us. We want peace, but peace cannot be kept without certain strength. Remember that."

"What are you saying?"

"I said what I said. You're a big boy; you can figure out the rest." He turned and left the room. I sat down by my father's body. The embers of the fire flickered in the dark.

Micah awoke in the car next to me. His Mohawk bobbed as he looked around.

"Where are we?"

"Welcome back to the land of the living," I said.

He saw a road sign. "Minnesota—sad place to wake up, eh?"

I looked out the window at the late-summer fields. A silo thrust out from the ground in the distance. "Could be worse."

He pressed his fingers between his eyebrows. "You looked like death incarnate," he said.

I thought about that. "Not so far from the truth."

After a while he spoke again. "What happened up in the mountains? Before we found you?"

I told him everything that I could remember: drifting up the mountain, the goat, Eliza appearing, my father's hut. I told him about Ephraim and his prayers, the healing of my father's body, the refusal of my father's spirit to return.

"I'll tell you," he said, "when we found you, floating in that lake, we thought you were dead. You barely had a pulse, and we set you next to that fire, and ten minutes later you were helping us out of there. I don't know how you did it—just a scab on your stomach. It's a miracle," he said, shaking his head. "Do you believe in Ephraim and his people? Do you think there's something … powerful … about them?"

"You saw my father's body when we were on the mountain—the bullet holes. Well, the holes are gone."

We buried Grandma and my father on the small hill in the cornfield behind her place. On a day in early September, we laid them to rest amid the battered limestone batholiths that marked the bones of my ancestors. Roald and Jethro came, the Polish priest, Silas, Leanna, Micah and his parents, a few of Grandma's bridge friends. That was all. No one came from Ephraim's group.

The Polish priest said prayers over Grandma, but not my father. Silas, Jethro and I took shovels and buried them ourselves. My shovel clinked a rock and I stooped to pick it up. It was an arrowhead. I laid it on top of my father's casket, and rested a moment.

"*Deus vult*," I said for him.

Then I threw another shovelful of dirt over him.

A few days later I woke to find the Whale sitting in the driveway. I took it to college.

Silas and Leanna moved into Grandma's place in October. They visited me often, helped me find a psychiatrist, helped me find my way through the Byzantine world of psychiatric medications. They are my family now. It feels right.

CHAPTER TWENTY-FOUR

Years flow by so quickly.

I got my medications and my degree. I sold furniture with the other philosophy majors. I tried to cross South America, but got homesick and returned home. I wasn't a traveler. Not in that sense.

I read. I went back to grad school and taught undergraduate classes in philosophy. It was foolish but fated.

One day I was at my desk—shoved into what was formerly a closet in White Hall—when there was a knock at the door. Without waiting for me to answer, in she walked.

I didn't believe it was a real person.

My gaze followed the chlorophyll on her toes and ankles up the line of her white cotton dress to her freckled face saying, "Hey there Mr. Professor-fella. Name's Liza. Dr. Janus says you're a mess, and that I should come here and get you organized."

My tongue curled itself into a knot and my mouth went dry even before I said a word. "I once know you," I told her, fumbling with my papers. "I mean I don't really once know you, but *I know you*. I mean, I know I've felt like I once met you really well before—once when I knew you."

She smiled and crinkled her nose. "Is that a come on? It didn't entirely sound like one but I think it was. You're going to have to do better than that if you want to go out with me."

"I don't want that. I mean, that's not what I meant. I mean, I didn't mean that want to marry." At that point I just shut up.

She gave a raise of her eyebrows and laughed. "You sure have a way with words."

"Ever been to Montana?" I managed to ask.

"As a matter of fact, I am from Montana."

I married her, to make a long story short. I had to; she wouldn't leave me alone after that. I don't know how any of this came about. I don't know how a guy like me gets a girl that miraculous. I don't know how I managed to manifest my imaginary friend into a real-world person. It sounds like lunacy. But it's what happened. That's just how this world is sometimes.

Micah and I still keep in touch. The punk craze died off after a few years and he shaved the Mohawk, went to seminary of his own free will. He does mission work in Chile. I visited him there some years ago, back when I still had a full head of hair. The south of Chile is as cold as it is here, with mountains like a wolf's teeth. He never wants to leave. He writes me a long letter every month. I reply every month.

I have a daughter. A beautiful, precious eight-year-old, whom I obsessively dress in overalls.

I spent this past week in a cabin up in Door County. It's the longest I've been away from either Liza or my daughter since she was born. Skied cross-country through the emptiness. I split wood and watched the snow come down. I let my medications dissolve in my bloodstream and I wrote in memory of the dead.

Yesterday, Liza and our daughter skied in to stay with me over Winter break. In three days, Silas and Leanna will come to spend Christmas day with us. We'll ski and snowshoe, follow the tracks of little winter mammals, read books by the fire, drink hot chocolate. Remember only the things worth remembering. Tell my daughter stories of my father. Tell her stories of my grandma.

I have never heard another thing from Ephraim or his group. A part of me, the part long removed from the events of that fall—the part of me that lives on the other side of my chemical wall—likes to believe it never happened. If Silas and Leanna weren't here to remind me, I think I'd have written it off as hallucination a long time ago. Vision, prophecy, madness: what are any of these things to the world as we know it?

This morning I woke in the dark, and the snow fell light on the blue-gray world. I split wood, and my sweat rose in vines and stems of steam. The weight of the ax over my head felt balanced and powerful; the cold air stung my lungs like I breathed fire.

I tramped through the snow carrying the logs and started a fire in the hearth. I sipped coffee as I watched my daughter sleep, the quilt surrounding her, its squares quaking with her; and I lay down beside her, touching her hair.

I closed my eyes and felt the pull of a deep river, all the world drowning; and when I opened them again, I was stunned by the light.

Delicate as the touch of a child's fingers the whole world is woven. Living is not a passing through it, but a being caught in it, a being borne upon its stream. Subtle, lighter than my daughter's hair, is all the good we take for granted, every benign connection—fiber, chemical, atom—that holds the world together.

It is this world, creation, that has always kept me sane. It is this world that frees us, not some distant God. If *I Am* is, then *I Am* is here.

This is my revelation.

The evil my father thought was consuming the world is the anomaly, not the norm; every neutral act of the natural world is an act of God, an act of love. Our burden is so light that any weight seems great. All the dark world rushing by: yet we are held afloat. Goodness holds us, the light bears us.

This is my revolution.

My daughter stirs, sits up, yawns. She sees I am writing and she finds a tattered picture book to occupy her. Liza sleeps, her head tucked under the pillows. I put down my pen, go to my daughter and stroke her hair. Her hair is the color of my father's. She touches my hand, looks up, and smiles the smile of her great-grandmother.

The world goes on, as God wills it. *Deus vult.*

In the blurry hours of this day we will ski to a lake, find the ice shanty I put there. We will ski, crunching on snow, over the lairs of dormant fireflies, over all that is life waiting to quicken in the light. We'll catch perch and sunfish under the layers of ice, unhook them and let them go. I'll hold her hand and she mine. Oh my dear, dear God, my dear, dear Life, this is all, this is all. We do not need to be set free from any thing; we do not need to be released by any deity. We need no revolution of guns and times and beasts. We are not imprisoned. We have always been free, all of us.

ACKNOWLEDGEMENTS

Thanks to Katie Quarles, Dana Rooks, Casey Strom, and Kathleen Weber for assistance with proofreading and editing, and to Nick Millanes, Brad Neu, Anna Kats, and Alex Barangan for providing feedback on an early draft. Thanks to Anna West for providing the LOC number, to Heather McDougal for help with PhotoShop, and to Lisa Grillos for the final cover design.